D0483906

DIANA PALMER

A HUSBAND FOR
✤CHRISTMAS✤

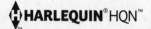
HARLEQUIN® HQN™

ISBN-13: 978-0-373-77918-5

A Husband for Christmas

Copyright © 2014 by Harlequin Books S.A.

The publisher acknowledges the copyright holders
of the individual works as follows:

Snow Kisses
Copyright © 1983 by Diana Palmer

Lionhearted
Copyright © 2002 by Diana Palmer

Recycling programs
for this product may
not exist in your area.

This edition published by arrangement with Harlequin Books S.A.

For questions and comments about the quality of this book, please contact us at
CustomerService@Harlequin.com.

® and TM are trademarks of Harlequin Enterprises Limited or its corporate
affiliates. Trademarks indicated with ® are registered in the United States Patent
and Trademark Office, the Canadian Intellectual Property Office and in other
countries.

Printed in U.S.A.

HARLEQUIN®
™ www.Harlequin.com

CONTENTS

SNOW KISSES 7

LIONHEARTED 217

SNOW KISSES

To the state of Montana,
whose greatest natural resource is her people.

✢ 1 ✢

The road was little more than a pair of ruts making lazy brown paths through the lush spring grass of southern Montana, and Hank was handling the truck like a tank on maneuvers. But Abby gritted her teeth and didn't say a word. Hank, in his fifty-plus years, had forgotten more about ranch work than she'd ever learn. And she wasn't about to put him in a bad temper by asking him to slow down.

She stared out over the smooth rolling hills where Cade's white-faced Herefords grazed on new spring grass. Montana. Big Sky country. Rolling grasslands that seemed to go on forever under a canopy of blue sky. And amid the grass, delicate yellow-and-blue wildflowers that Abby had gathered as a girl. Here, she could forget New York and the nightmare of the past two weeks. She could heal her wounds and hide away from the world.

She smiled faintly, a smile that didn't quite reach her pale brown eyes, and she clenched her hands around the beige purse in the lap of her shapeless dress. She didn't feel like a successful fashion model when she was on the McLaren ranch. She felt like the young girl who'd grown up in this part of rural southern Montana, on the ranch that had been absorbed by Cade's growing empire after her father's death three years earlier.

At least Melly was still there. Abby's younger sister had an enviable job as Cade's private secretary. It meant that she could be near her fiancé, Cade's ranch foreman, while she supported herself. Cade had never approved of Jesse Shane's decision to allow his eldest daughter to go to New York, and he had made no secret of it. Now Abby couldn't help wishing she'd listened. Her brief taste of fame hadn't been worth the cost.

She felt bitter. It was impossible to go back, to relive those innocent days of her youth when Cade McLaren had been the sun and moon. But she mourned for the teenager she'd been that long-ago night when he'd carried her to bed. It was a memory she'd treasured, but now it was a part of the nightmare she'd brought home from New York. She wondered with a mind numbed by pain if she'd ever be able to let any man touch her again.

She sighed, gripping the purse tighter as Hank took one rise a little fast and caused the pickup to lurch to one side. She clutched the edge of the seat as the vehicle all but rocked onto its side.

"Sorry about that," Hank muttered, bending over the steering wheel with his thin face set into rigid lines. "Damned trucks—give me a horse any day."

She laughed softly—once she would have thrown back her head and given out a roar of hearty laughter. She might have been a willowy ghost of the girl who left Painted Ridge at eighteen, come back to haunt old familiar surroundings. This poised, sophisticated woman of twenty-two was as out of place in the battered pickup as Cade would be in a tuxedo at the Met.

"I guess you've all got your hands full," Abby remarked as they approached the sprawling ranch house.

"Damned straight," Hank said without preamble as he slowed at a gate. "Storm warnings out and calving in full swing."

"Snow?" she gasped, looking around at the lush greenery. But it was April, after all, and snow was still very possible in Montana. Worse—probable.

But Hank was already out of the truck, leaving the engine idling while he opened the gate.

"Drive the truck through!" he called for what seemed the tenth time in as many minutes, and Abby obediently climbed behind the wheel and put the truck in gear.

She couldn't help smiling when she remembered her childhood. Ranch children learned to drive early, out of necessity. She'd been driving a truck since her eleventh birthday, and many was the time she'd done it for Cade while he opened the endless gates that enclosed the thousands of acres he ranched.

She drove through the gate and slid back into her seat while Hank secured it and ambled back to the truck. He'd been part of Cade's outfit as long as she could remember, and there was no more experienced cowboy on the place.

"New York," Hank scoffed, giving her a disapproving glance. He chewed on the wad of tobacco in his cheek and gave a gruff snort. "Should have stayed home where you belonged. Been married by now, with a passel of younguns."

She shuddered at the thought, and her eyes clouded. "Is Cade at the ranch?" she asked, searching for something to say.

"Up in the Piper, hunting strays," he told her. "Figured he'd better find those damned cows before the snow hits. As it is, we'll have to fan out and bring them into the barn. We lost over a hundred calves in the snow last spring."

Her pale eyes clouded at the thought of those tiny calves freezing to death. Cade had come home one winter night, carrying a little white-faced Hereford across his saddle, and Abby had helped him get it into the barn to warm it. He'd been tired and snappy and badly in need of a shave. Abby had fetched him a cup of coffee, and they'd stayed hours in the barn until the calf was thawed and on the mend. Cade was so much a part of her life, despite their quarrels. He was the only person she'd ever felt truly at home with.

"Are you listening?" Hank grumbled. "Honest to God, Abby!"

"Sorry, Hank," she apologized quickly as the elderly man glared at her. "What did you say?"

"I asked you if you wanted to stow your gear at the house or go on down to the homestead."

The "house" was Cade's—the main ranch house. The "homestead" had been her father's and was now Melly's. Soon, it would belong to Melly and her new husband.

"Where's Melly?"

"At the house."

"Then just drop me off there, please, Hank," she said with a pacifying smile.

He grunted and gunned the engine. A minute later, she was outside under the spreading branches of the budding trees and Hank was roaring away in a cloud of dust. Just like old times, she thought with a laugh. Hank impatient, dumping her at the nearest opportunity, while he rushed on to his chores.

Of course, it was nearing roundup, and that always made him irritable. It was late April now—by June, the ranch would be alive and teeming with activity as new calves were branded and separated and the men worked twenty-four-hour days and wondered why they had ever wanted to be cowboys.

She turned toward the house with a sigh. It was just as well that Cade wasn't home, she told herself. Seeing him now was going to be an ordeal. All she wanted was her sister.

She knocked at the door hesitantly, and seconds later, it was thrown open by a smaller girl with short golden hair and sea-green eyes.

"Abby!" the younger girl burst out, tears appearing in her eyes. She threw open the door and held out her arms.

Abby ran straight into them and held on for dear life, oblivious to the suitcase falling onto the cleanly swept front porch. She clutched her sister and cried like a lost child. She was home. She was safe.

2

"I was so glad when you decided to come." Melly sighed over coffee while she and Abby sat in the sprawling living room. It had changed quite a bit since Cade's mother died. The delicate antiques and pastel curtains had given way to leather-covered couches and chairs, handsome coffee tables and a luxurious, thick-piled gray rug. Now it looked like Cade—big and untamed and unchangeable.

"Sorry," Abby murmured when she realized she hadn't responded. "I had my mind on this room. It's changed."

Melly looked concerned. "A lot of things have. Cade included."

"Cade never changes," came the quiet reply. The taller girl got to her feet with her coffee cup in hand and wandered to the mantel to stare at a portrait of Donavan McLaren that overwhelmed the room.

Cade was a younger version of the tall, imposing man in the painting, except that Donavan had white hair and a mustache and a permanent scowl. Cade's hair was still black and thick over a broad forehead and deep-set dark eyes. He was taller than his late father, all muscle. He was darkly tanned and he rarely smiled, but he could be funny in a dry sort of way. He was thirty-six now, fourteen years Abby's senior, although he seemed twice that judging by the way he treated her. Cade was always the patronizing adult to Abby's wayward child. Except for that one magic night when he'd been every woman's dream—when he'd shown her a taste of intimacy that had colored her life ever since, and had rejected her with such tenderness that she'd never been ashamed of offering herself to him.

Offering herself… She shuddered delicately, lifting the coffee to her lips. As if that would ever be possible again, now.

"How is Cade?" Abby asked.

"How is Cade usually in the spring?" came the amused reply.

"Oh, I can think of several adjectives. Would horrible be too mild?" Abby asked as she turned.

"Yes." Melly sighed. "We've been shorthanded. Randy broke his leg and won't be any use at all for five more weeks, and Hob quit."

"Hob?" Abby's pale brown eyes widened. "But he's been here forever!"

"He said that was just how he felt after Cade threw the saddle at him." The younger woman shook her head. "Cade's been restless. Even more so than usual."

"Woman trouble?" Abby asked, and then hated herself for the question. She had no right to pry into Cade's love life, no real desire to know if he were seeing someone.

Melly blinked. "Cade? My God, I'd faint if he brought a woman here."

That did come as a surprise. Although Abby had visited Melly several times since she'd moved to New York, she had seen Cade only on rare occasions. She'd always assumed that he was going out on dates while she was on Painted Ridge.

"I thought he kept them on computer, just so that he could keep track of them." Abby laughed.

"Are we talking about the same man?"

"Well, he's always out every time I come to visit," Abby remarked. "It's been almost a year since I've seen him." She sat back down on the sofa next to her sister and drained her coffee cup.

Melly shot her a keen glance, but she didn't reply. "How long are you going to stay?" she asked. "I never could pin you down on the phone."

"A couple of weeks, if you can put up with me...."

"Don't be silly," Melly chided. She frowned, reaching out to touch her sister's thin hand. "Abby, make it a month. At least a month. Don't go back until you feel ready. Promise me!"

Abby's eyes closed under a tormented frown. She caught her breath. "I wonder if I'll ever be ready," she whispered roughly.

The smaller hand that was clasping hers tightened. "That's defeatist talk. And not like you at all. You're a Shane. We wrote the book on persevering!"

"Well, I'm writing the last chapter," Abby ground out. She stood up, moving to the window.

"It's been two weeks since it happened," Melly reminded her.

"Yes," Abby said, sighing wearily. "And I'm not quite as raw as I was, but it's hard trying to cope...." She glanced at her sister. "I'm just glad I had the excuse of helping you plan the wedding to come for a visit. What did Cade say when you asked if it was all right?"

Melly looked thoughtful. "He brightened like a copper penny," she said with a faint smile. "Especially when I mentioned that you might be here for a couple of weeks or more. It struck me at the time, because he's been just the very devil to get along with lately."

Abby pursed her lips thoughtfully. "He probably has the idea that I've lost my job and came back in disgrace. Is that it?"

"Shame on you," her sister replied. "He'd never gloat over something like that."

"That's what you think. He's always hated the idea of my modeling."

Melly's thin brows rose. "Well, no matter what his opinion of your career, he was glad to hear you'd be around for a while. In fact, he was in such a good mood, all the men got nervous. I told you that Hob had just quit. Too bad he didn't wait an extra day. Cade's bucking for sainthood since I announced your arrival."

If only it were true, Abby thought wistfully. But she knew better, even if Melly didn't. She was almost certain that Cade avoided her on purpose. Maybe it was just her sister's way of smoothing things over, to prevent a wild argument between Cade and Abby. It wouldn't be the first time she'd played peacemaker.

She glanced sharply into her sister's green eyes. "Melly, you didn't tell Cade the truth?" she asked anxiously.

Melly looked uncomfortable. "Not exactly," she confided. "I just said there was a man…that you'd had a bad experience."

Abby sighed. "Well, that's true enough. At least I'll be down at the homestead with you. He shouldn't even get suspicious about why I'm here. God knows, it's always been an uphill fight to keep peace when Cade and I are in the same room together, hasn't it?"

Melly shifted suddenly and Abby stared at her curiously.

"I'm afraid you won't be staying at the homestead," Melly said apologetically. "You see, my house is being painted. Cade's having the old place renovated as a wedding present."

Abby felt a wave of pure tension stretch her slender body. "We'll be staying…here?"

"Yes."

"Then why didn't you tell me when I asked to come?" Abby burst out.

"Because I knew you wouldn't come," Melly replied.

"Will Cade be away?" she asked.

"Are you kidding? In the spring, with roundup barely a month away?"

"Then I'll go somewhere else!" Abby burst out.

"No." Melly held her fast. "Abby, the longer you run away the harder it's going to be for you. Here, on the ranch, you can adjust again. You're going to have to adjust—or bury yourself. You do realize that? You can't possibly go on like this. Look at you!" she exclaimed, indicating the shapeless dress. "You don't even look like a model, Abby, you look like a housekeeper!"

"And that's a fine thing to say about me," came a deep but feminine voice from the doorway.

Both girls turned at once. Calla Livingston had her hands on her ample hips, and she was wearing a scowl sour enough to curdle milk. She was somewhere near sixty, but she could still outrun most of the cowboys, and few of them crossed her. She took her irritation out on the food, which was a shame because she was the best cook in the territory.

"And what do I look like, pray tell—the barn?" Calla continued, ruffled.

Melly bit her lip to keep from smiling. Dressed in a homemade shift of pink and green, her straggly gray hair pulled into a half bun, her garter-supported hose hanging precariously just above her knees, Calla was nobody's idea of haute couture. But only an idiot would have told her that, and Melly had good sense.

"You look just fine, Calla," Melly soothed. "I meant—" she searched for the right words "—that this isn't Abby's usual look."

Calla burst out laughing, her merry eyes going from one girl to the other. "Never could tell when I was serious and when I wasn't, could you, darlin'?" she asked Melly. "I was only teasing. Come here, Abby, and give us a hug. It's been months since I've seen you, remember!"

Abby ran into her widespread arms and breathed in the scent of flour and vanilla that always clung to Calla.

"Stay home this time, you hear?" Calla chided, brushing away a tear as she let go of the young woman. "Tearing off and coming back with city ways—this is the best you've looked to me since you were eighteen and hellbent on modeling!"

"But, Calla…" Melly interrupted.

"Never you mind." Calla threw her a sharp glance. "Call her dowdy again, and it'll be no berry cobbler for you tonight!"

Melly opened her mouth and quickly closed it again with a wicked grin. "I think she looks…mature," Melly agreed. "Very…unique. Unusual. Rustically charming."

Calla threw up her hands. "What I put up with, Lord knows! As if that hard-eyed cowboy I work for isn't enough on my plate…. Well, if I don't rush, there'll be no peace when he comes in and doesn't find his meal waiting. Even if he doesn't come in until ten o'clock." She went away muttering irritably to herself.

Melly sat down heavily on the couch with an exaggerated sigh. "Oh, saved! If I'd realized that she was out there, I'd have sung the praises of your new wardrobe."

"Still hooked on her berry cobbler, I notice?" Abby smiled, and for just an instant, a little of her old, vibrantly happy personality peeked out.

"Please tell him," Melly pleaded.

"And give him a stick to beat me with?" Abby asked with a dry laugh. "He's been down on me ever since I coaxed Dad into letting me go to New York. Every time I see him, all I hear is how stupid I was. Now he's got the best reason in the world to say it all again, and add an 'I told you so.' But he's not getting the chance, Melly. Not from me!'

"You're wrong about Cade," Melly argued. "You always have been. He doesn't hate you, Abby. He never did."

"Would you mind telling him that?" came the cool reply. "I don't think he knows."

"Then why was he so anxious for you to come home?" Melly demanded. She folded her arms across her knees and leaned forward. "He even had Hank bring up your own furniture from the homestead, just so you'd feel more at home. Does that sound like a man who's hating you?"

"Then why does he avoid me like the plague?" Abby asked curtly. She searched momentarily for a way to change the subject. "I sure would like to freshen up before we eat," she hinted.

"Then come on up. You've got the room next to mine, so we can talk until all hours."

"I'll like that," Abby murmured with a smile. Impulsively, she put her arm around Melly's shoulders as they went up the staircase. "Maybe we can have a pillow fight, for old time's sake."

"Calla's room is across the hall," Melly informed her.

Abby sighed. "Oh, well, we can always reminisce about the pillow fights we used to have," she amended, and Melly grinned.

It was just after dark, and Melly was helping Calla set the table in the dining room when the front door slammed open and hard, angry footsteps sounded on the bare wood floor of the hall.

Abby, standing at the fireplace where Calla had built a small fire, turned just as Cade froze in the doorway.

It didn't seem like a year since she'd seen him. The hard, deeply tanned face under that wide-brimmed hat was as familiar as her own. But he'd aged, even she could see that. His firm, chiseled mouth was compressed, his brow marked with deep lines as if he'd made a habit of scowling. His cheeks were leaner, his square jaw firmer and his dark, fiery eyes were as uncompromising as she remembered them.

He was dusted with snow, his shepherd's coat flecked with it, his worn boots wet with it as were the batwing chaps strapped around his broad, heavy-muscled thighs. He was holding a cigarette in one lean, dark hand, and the look he was giving Abby would have backed down a puma.

"What the hell happened to you?" he asked curtly, indicating the shapeless brown suede dress she was wearing.

"Look who's talking," she returned. "Weren't you wearing that same pair of chaps when I left for New York?"

"Cattlemen are going bust all over, honey," he returned, and a hint of amusement kindled in his eyes.

"Sure," she scoffed. "But most of them don't run eight thousand head of cattle on three ranches in two states, now do they? And have oil leases and mining contracts...."

"I didn't say I was going bust," he corrected. He leaned insolently against the doorjamb and tilted his head back. "Steal that dress off a fat lady?"

She felt uncomfortable, shifting from one foot to the other. "It's the latest style," she lied, hoping he wouldn't know the difference.

"I don't see how you women keep up with the latest styles," he said. "It all looks like odds and ends to me."

"Is it snowing already?" she asked, changing the subject.

He took his hat off and shook it. "Looks like. I hope

Calla's loading a table for the men, too. The nighthawks are going to have their hands full with those two-year-old heifers."

Abby couldn't help smiling. Those were the first-time mothers, and they took a lot of looking after. One old cowhand—Hob, the one who'd resigned—always said he'd rather mend fence than babysit new mamas.

"Who got stuck this year?" she asked.

"Hank and Jeb," he replied.

"No wonder Hank was so ruffled," she murmured.

A corner of Cade's disciplined mouth turned up as he studied her. "You don't know the half of it. He begged me to let him nurse the older cows."

"I can guess how far he got," she said.

He didn't laugh. "How long are you here for?"

"I haven't decided yet," she said, feeling nervous. "It depends."

"I thought spring was your busiest time, miss model," he said, his eyes narrowing suspiciously. "When Melly told me you were coming, it surprised me."

"I'm, uh, taking a break," she supplied.

"Are you?" He shouldered away from the doorjamb. "Stay through roundup and I'll fly you back to New York myself."

He turned, and her eyes followed his broad-shouldered form as he walked into the hall and yelled for Calla.

"I hope you've got enough to feed the hands, too!" he called, his deep voice carrying through the house. "Jeb's nighthawking with Hank!"

Jeb was the bunkhouse cook—some of the cowboys had homes on the ranch where they lived with their families, but there was a modern bunkhouse with a separate kitchen for the rest.

"Well, I'll bet the boys are on their knees giving thanks for that!" Calla called back. "It'll be a change for them, having decent food for one night!"

Cade chuckled deep in his throat as he climbed the stairs. Abby couldn't help but watch him, remembering old times when she'd worshipped that broad back, that powerful body, with a schoolgirl's innocent heart. How different her life might have been if Cade hadn't refused her impulsive offer that long-ago night. Tears formed in her eyes and she turned away. Wishing wouldn't make it so. But it was good to be back on Painted Ridge, all the same. She'd manage to keep out of Cade's way, and perhaps Melly was right. Perhaps being home again would help her scars to heal.

✣ 3 ✣

Abby might have planned to avoid him, but Cade seemed to have other ideas. She noticed his quiet, steady gaze over the dinner table and almost jumped when he spoke.

"How would you like to see the new calves?" he asked suddenly.

She lifted her eyes from her plate and stared at him, lost for an answer. "Isn't it still snowing?" she asked helplessly.

"Sure," he agreed. "But the trucks have chains. And the calving sheds are just south of here," he reminded her.

Being alone with him was going to unnerve her—she

knew it already—but she loved the sight of those woolly little creatures, so new to the world. And she liked being with Cade. She felt safe with him, protected. Despite the lingering apprehension, she wanted to go with him.

"Well?" he persisted.

She shrugged. "I would kind of like to see the calves," she admitted with a tiny smile. She dropped her eyes back to her plate, blissfully unaware of the look Cade exchanged with Melly.

"We'll have dessert when we get back," Cade informed Calla, pushing back his chair.

Minutes later, riding along in the pickup and being bounced wildly in its warm interior, snow fluttering against the windshield, it was almost like old times.

"Warm enough, honey?" Cade asked.

"Like toast." She wrapped the leather jacket he had loaned her even closer, loving its warmth. Cade was still wearing his shepherd's coat, looking so masculine he'd have wowed them even at a convention of male models.

"Not much farther now," he murmured, turning the truck off onto the farm road that led to the calving pens, where two cowboys in yellow slickers could be seen riding around the enclosures, heads bent against the wind.

"Poor devils," she remarked, watching.

"The men or the heifers?" he asked.

"Both. All. It's rough out there." She balanced her

hand against the cold dashboard as he stopped the truck and cut the engine at the side of the long shed. Cade was the perfect rancher, but his driving left a lot to be desired.

"Now I know how it feels to ride inside a concrete mixer," she moaned.

"Don't start that again," Cade grumbled as he threw open the door. "You can always walk back," he added with a dark glance.

"Did you ever race in the Grand Prix when you were younger, Cade?" she asked with a bright, if somewhat false, smile.

"And sarcasm won't do the trick, either," he warned. He led the way through the snow, and she followed in his huge footprints, liking the bite of the cold wind and the crunch of the snow, the freshness of the air. It was so deliciously different from the city. Her eyes looked out over the acres toward the distant mountains, searching for the familiar snow-covered peaks that she could have seen clearly in sunny daylight. God's country, she thought reverently. How had she ever been able to exist away from it?

"Stop daydreaming and catch up," Cade was growling. "I could lose you out here."

"In a little old spring snowstorm like this?" She laughed. "I could fight my way through blizzards, snowshoe myself to Canada, ski over to the Rockies..."

"...lie like hell, too," he said, amusement gleaming in the dark eyes that caught hers as they entered the lighted interior. "Come on."

She followed him into the airy enclosure, wrapping her arms tight. "Still no heat, I see." She sighed.

"Can't afford the luxury, honey," he remarked, waving at a cowboy farther down the aisle.

"Is that why it's so drafty in here? You poor thing, you," she chided.

"I would be, if I didn't keep the air circulating in here," he agreed. "Don't you remember how many calves we used to lose to respiratory ailments before the veterinarians advised us to put in that exhaust fan to keep stale air out of these sheds? Those airborne diseases were bankrupting the operation. Now we disinfect the stalls and maintain a rigid vaccination program, and we've cut our losses in half."

"Excuse me," she apologized. "I'm only an ignorant city dweller."

He turned in the aisle and looked down at her quietly. "Come home," he said curtly. "Where you belong."

Her heart pounded at the intensity of the brief gaze he gave her before turning back to his cow boss.

Charlie Smith stood up, grinning at Cade. "Hi, boss, get tired of television and hungry for some real relaxation? Jed sure would love to have somebody take his place—"

"Just visiting, Charlie," Cade interrupted. "I brought Abby down to see the newcomers."

"Good to see you again, Miss Abby," Charlie said respectfully, tipping his hat. "We've got a good crop in here, all right. Have a look."

Abby peeked into the nearest stall, her face lighting up as she stared down at one of the "black baldies," a cross between a Hereford and a Black Angus, black all over with a little white face.

"Jed brought that one in an hour ago. Damn...uh, doggone mama just dropped it and walked away from it." Charlie sneered.

"That's not his mama, huh?" Abby murmured, noticing the tender licking it was getting from the cow in the stall with it.

"No, ma'am," Charlie agreed. "We sprayed him with a deodorizing compound to keep her from getting suspicious. Poor thing lost her own calf."

Abby felt a surge of pity for the cow and calf. It was just a normal episode in ranch life, but she had a hard time trying to separate business from emotion.

Cade moved close behind her, apparently oblivious to the sudden, instinctive stiffening of her slender body, the catch of her breath. Please, she thought silently, please don't let him touch me!

But he didn't attempt to. He leaned against the stall and rammed his hands in his pockets, watching the cow and calf over her shoulder. "How many have we lost so far?" Cade asked the cow boss.

"Ten. And it looks like a long night."

"They're all long." Cade sighed. He pushed his hat back over his forehead, and Abby, glancing up, noticed how weary he looked.

"I'd better check on my own charge down the aisle here," Charlie said, and went off with a wave of his hand as the ominous bleating of the heifer filled the shed.

"Prime beef," Cade murmured, chuckling at Abby's indignant expression.

She moved away from him with studied carelessness and smiled. "Heartless wretch," she teased. "Could you really eat him?"

"Couldn't you, smothered in onions...?"

"Oh, stop!" she wailed. "You cannibal...!"

"How does it feel to be back?" he asked, walking back the way they came in.

"Nice," she admitted. She tucked her cold hands into the pockets of her jacket. "I'd forgotten how big this country is, how unspoiled and underpopulated. It's a wonderful change from a crowded, polluted city, although I do love New York," she added, trying to convince him she meant it.

"New York," he reminded her, "is a dangerous place."

She stiffened again, turning to study his face, but she couldn't read anything in that bland expression. Cade let nothing show—unless he wanted it to. He'd had years of practice at camouflaging his emotions.

"Most cities are," she agreed. "The country can be dangerous, too."

"It depends on your definition of danger," he returned. He looked down at her with glittering eyes. "You're safe as long as I'm alive. Nothing and no one will hurt you on this ranch."

Tears suddenly misted her eyes, burning like fire. She swallowed and looked away. "Do I look as if I need protection?" She tried to laugh.

"Not especially," he said coolly. "But you seemed threatened for an instant. I just wanted to make the point. I'll protect you from mountain lions and falling buildings, Abby," he added with a hint of a smile.

"But who'll protect me from you, you cannibal?" she asked with a pointed stare, her old sense of humor returning to save her from the embarrassment of tears.

"You're just as safe with me as you want to be," he replied.

She looked into his eyes, and for an instant they were

four years in the past, when a young girl stood poised at the edge of a swimming pool and offered her heart and her body to a man she worshipped.

Without another word, she turned around and started back out into the snow.

✤ 4 ✤

As she walked toward the truck, huddled against the wind, her mind suddenly went backward in time. And for an instant, it was summer, and she was swimming alone in the pool at Cade's house one night when her father was in the hospital.

She'd been eighteen, a girl on the verge of becoming a woman. Her father, far too ill during that period of her life to give her much counsel, hadn't noticed that she was beginning to dress in a way that caught a lot of male attention. But Cade had, and he'd had a talk with her. She'd marched off in a huff, hating his big-brother attitude, and had defiantly gone for a swim that night in his own pool. There was no one around, so she had quickly stripped off her clothes and dived in. That was against the rules, but Abby was good at breaking them. Especially when they were made by Cade McLaren. She wanted him to look at her the way other men did. She wanted more than a condescending lecture from him, but she was too young and far too naive to put her growing infatuation into words.

She'd been in the pool barely five minutes when she'd heard the truck pull up at the back of the house. Before she had time to do any more than scramble out of the pool and pull on her jeans, she heard Cade come around the corner.

She was totally unprepared for what happened next. She turned and Cade's dark eyes dropped to her high, bare breasts with a wild, reckless look in them that made her breath catch in her throat. He just stood there, frozen, staring at her, and she didn't make a move to cover herself or turn away. She let him look his fill, feeling her heart trying to tear out of her chest when he finally began to move toward her.

His shirt was open that night, because he'd just come in from the corral, and the mat of thick black hair over the bronzed muscles of his chest was damp with sweat. He stopped a foot in front of her and looked down, and she knew that all the unspoken hunger she'd begun to feel for him was plain in her wide, pale brown eyes.

Without a word, he bent and lifted her. Very, very gently, he brought her body to his and drew her taut breasts against his chest, letting her feel the rough hair against her soft, sensitive skin in a caress that made her moan and cling to him, while her eyes looked straight into his and saw the flash of triumph in them.

He turned and carried her into the house, up the stairs and into his own bedroom, and laid her down on the bed. And then he sat there, with one hand on the bed beside her to support his weight, and looked at her again, letting his dark eyes feast on the soft, pink bareness of her body. She wasn't even aware of being wet, of her body soaking the coverlet. All she saw, all she knew, was Cade's hard, dark face and his eyes.

Finally, he moved and his fingers traced a pattern from her shoulder down over her collarbone. She held her breath as they kept going down, and she felt the slow, sweet tracing of them on the curve of her breasts— exploring, tantalizing with the light pressure—until they reached the burgeoning peak and caught it lightly between them.

She gasped, arching at the unexpected surge of pleasure, and his eyes looked straight down into hers.

"Hush," he whispered then. "You know I won't hurt you."

"Yes," she whispered back, as if the walls could hear them, her eyes wide with unexpected pleasure. "I...I want you...to touch me."

"I know." He bent, one hand still cupping her, and she lifted her arms hesitantly until they were around his neck. He looked into her eyes as his warm, hard mouth brushed hers, so that he could see the reaction in them. "Open your mouth for me, Abby," he breathed, moving his hand to tip up her chin, "just a little more...."

She obeyed him mindlessly and felt the delicious probing of his tongue between her lips, working its way slowly, sensuously, into her mouth. She gasped, moaning, and he eased down so that she could feel his bare chest against her breasts. She lifted herself, clinging, and for one long, unbearably sweet moment she felt his warmth and weight and the fierce adult passion of a man's kiss.

She thought she imagined a tremor in his hard arms before he suddenly released her, but when he sat up again he was as calm outwardly as if he'd been for a quiet walk. His eyes went down to her breasts and drank in the sight of them one last time before his big hand caught the coverlet and tossed it carelessly over her bareness.

"You wanted to know," he said gently, holding her hand tightly in his as if to soften the rejection, "and I've shown you. But this is as far as it goes. I care too much to seduce you just for an hour of pleasure."

She swallowed, studying his hard face, her body still tingling from the touch of his fingers, her mouth warm from the long, hungry kiss they'd shared. "Should I be ashamed, Cade?" she asked.

He brushed the damp hair away from her face. "Of what?" he asked tenderly. "Of wanting to know how it felt to be touched and kissed by a man?"

She drew in a deep, slow breath. "Not…by a man," she corrected. "By you."

The impact of that nervous confession was evident on his face. He hesitated, as if he wanted desperately to say something but thought better of it. His jaw tautened.

"Abby," he said, choosing the words carefully, "you're eighteen years old. You've got a lot of growing up to do, a lot of the world to see, before you tie yourself to one man. To any man." He toyed with the coverlet at her throat. "It's natural, at your age, to be curious about sex. But despite the modern viewpoint, there are still men left who'll want a virgin when they marry." His eyes met hers levelly. "Be one. Save that precious gift for the man you marry. Don't give it away to satisfy your curiosity."

"Will you?" she asked involuntarily.

"Will I what, honey?" he asked.

"Want a virgin?"

He looked strange at that moment. Thoughtful. Hungry. Irritated. "The biggest problem in my life," he said after a minute, with a flash of humor, "is that I want one right now." He bent then and kissed her briefly, roughly, before he stood up.

"Cade…?" she began, her hand going to the coverlet, the offer in her young eyes.

"No," he said firmly, loosening her fingers from the material. "Not yet."

"Yet?" she whispered.

He traced her mouth with a lazy, absent finger. "Make me the same offer again in about three or four years," he murmured with a faint smile, "and I'll drag you into a bed and make love to you until you pass out. Now get dressed. And don't try this again, Abby," he warned firmly. "It's the wrong time for us. Don't force me to be cruel to you. It's something I'd have hell living with."

Her head whirling with unbridled hope, she watched him walk to the door with her whole heart in her misty eyes.

"Cade?" she called softly.

He'd turned with one hand on the doorknob, an eyebrow raised.

"I'll hold you to that…in three or four years," she promised.

He smiled back at her, so tenderly that she almost

climbed out of the bed and threw herself at his feet. "Good night, honey," he chuckled, walking out the door.

Neither of them had ever mentioned it, or referred to it, in all the time since then. Shortly afterward she had left the ranch; she'd seen Cade only a few times in the intervening years. It was odd that she should remember the incident now, when her promise was impossible to keep. She'd never be able to offer herself to Cade now.

She opened the door of the truck and got in.

Cade was quiet on the way back to the house, but that wasn't unusual. He never had liked to talk and drive at the same time. He seemed to mull over problems in the silence, ranch problems that were never far away. In winter it was snow and getting enough feed to the livestock. In spring it was roundup and planting. In summer it was haying and fixing fence and water. Water was an eternal problem—there was either not enough or too much. In May and June, when the snow melted on the mountains and ran into streams and rivers, there would be enough water for agriculture—but there would also be flooding to contend with. After roundup, the cattle had to be moved to high summer pastures. In fall they had to be brought back down. The breeding program was an ongoing project, and there were always the problems of sick cattle and equipment breakdowns and the logistics of feeding, culling, selling and buying cattle. Cade had ranch managers, like Melly's husband-to-be, but he owned three ranches, and ultimately he was the one responsible to the board of directors and to the stockholders, as well. Because it was a corporation now, not just one man's holdings, and Cade was at the helm.

Her eyes sought his face, loving it as she'd loved it for four, long, empty years. Cade, the eternal bachelor. She wondered if he'd ever marry, or want children of his own to inherit Painted Ridge and the other properties he had stock in. She'd thought once, at eighteen, that he might marry her one day. But he'd made a point of avoiding her after that devastating encounter. And in desperation, she had settled for the adventure and challenge of modeling.

It had been the ultimate adventure at eighteen. Glamour, wealth, society—and for the first year or so it had almost satisfied her. She remembered coming home that first Christmas, bubbling with enthusiasm for her work. Cade had listened politely and then had left. And he'd been conspicuously absent for the rest of the time she was at Painted Ridge. She'd often wondered why he'd deliberately avoided her. But she'd been ecstatic over the glitter of New York and her increasing successes. Or she had been at first…

Cade seemed to sense her intense appraisal. His head

suddenly turned and he caught her eyes as he pulled up to the house and parked at the back steps. Abby felt a shock of pure sensation go through her like fire. It had been a long time since she'd looked into those dark, glittering eyes at point-blank range. It did the most wonderful things to her pulse, her senses.

"You've been away longer this time," he said without preamble. He leaned back against his door and lit a cigarette. "A year."

"Not from the ranch," she countered. "You weren't here last summer or at Christmas when I was."

He laughed shortly, the cigarette sending up curls of smoke. "What was the use?" he asked coolly. "I got sick of hearing about New York and all the beautiful people."

She sat erect, her chin thrusting forward. "Are we going to have that argument all over again?"

"No, I'm through arguing," he said curtly. "You made up your mind four years ago that you couldn't find what you wanted from life anyplace except New York. I left you to it, Abby. I know a lost cause when I see one."

"What was there for me here?" she demanded, thinking back to a time when he wouldn't come near her.

But his face went cold at the words. It seemed actually to pale, and he turned his eyes out the window to look at the falling snow. "Nothing, I guess," he said. "Open country, clean air, basic values and only few people.

Amazing, isn't it, that we have the fourth largest state in the country, but it's forty-sixth in population. And I like it that way," he added, pinning her with his eyes. "I couldn't live in a place where I didn't have enough room to walk without being bumped into."

She knew that already. Cade, with his long, elegant stride and love of open country, might as well die as be transplanted to New York. This was Big Sky country, and he was a Big Sky man. He'd never feel at home in the Big Apple. A hundred years ago, however, he would have fit right in with the old frontier ways. She remembered going to the old Custer battlefield with him, where the Battle of the Little Bighorn was fought, and watching his eyes sweep the rolling hills. He sat a horse the same way, his eyes always on the horizon. One of his ancestors had been a full-blooded Sioux, and had died at Little Bighorn. He belonged to this country, as surely as the early settlers and miners and cattlemen had belonged to it.

Abby had wanted to belong to it, too—to Cade. But he'd let her get on that bus to New York when she was eighteen, although he'd had one hell of a fight with her father about it the night before she left. Jesse Shane had never shared the discussion with her. She only knew about it because she'd heard their angry voices in the living room and her name on Cade's lips.

"You never wanted me to go to New York," she murmured as she withdrew from the pain of memory. "You expected me to fall flat on my face, didn't you?"

"I hoped like hell that you would," he said bluntly, and his eyes blazed. "But you made it, didn't you? Although, looking at you now, I could almost believe you hadn't. My God, Calla has better taste in clothes."

She avoided his eyes, puzzled by the earlier statement. "I'm very tastefully dressed for a woman on a ranch," she threw back, nervous that he might guess why she was wearing loose clothing, why she couldn't bear anything revealing right now.

"Is that a dig at me?" he asked. "I know ranch life isn't glamorous, honey. It's damned hard work, and not many women would choose it over a glittering career. You don't have to tell me that."

How little he knew, she thought miserably. She'd chuck modeling and New York and the thought of being internationally famous if he asked her to marry him. She would have given up anything to live with him and love him. But he didn't know, and he never would. Her pride wouldn't let her tell him. He'd rejected her once, that magic night years before, even though he'd done it tenderly. She couldn't risk having him do it again. It would be too devastating.

Her eyes dropped to her suede boots. The boots would

be ruined. She'd forgotten to spray them with protective coating, and she'd need to buy a new pair. Odd that she should think about that when she was alone with Cade. It was so precious to be alone with him, even for a few minutes. If only she could tell him what had happened, tell him the truth. But how could she admit that she'd come back to be healed?

"Hey."

She looked up and found him watching her closely. He reached out and caught a lock of her long hair and tugged it gently.

"What's wrong?" he asked quietly.

She felt the prick of tears and blinked to dispel them. It was so much harder when he was tender. It reminded her forcibly of the last time she'd heard his voice so velvety and deep. And suddenly she found herself wondering how she would react if he tried to hold her, touch her, now.

"Nothing's wrong," she said shortly. "I was just thinking."

His face hardened and he let go of her hair. "Thinking about New York?" he demanded. "What the hell are you doing here in April, anyway? I thought summer was your only slack time."

"I came to see Melly, of course," she shot back, her

face hot and red. "To help her get ready for the wedding!"

"Then you'll be staying for a month," he said matter-of-factly, daring her to protest. How could she when she'd stated the lie so convincingly?

She swallowed. "Well…"

"I understood you were designing her a dress?" he continued.

"Yes," she agreed, remembering the sketches she'd already done. Over the past few years she had discovered that she enjoyed designing clothes much more than modeling them.

"My God, you're quiet," he observed, his eyes narrowing against the smoke of his cigarette. "You used to come home gushing like a volcano, full of life and happiness. Now you seem…sedate. Very, very different. What's the matter, honey, is the glitter wearing off, or are you just tired of going around half-naked for men to look at?"

She gasped at the unexpectedness of the attack and drew in a sharp breath. "Cade Alexander McLaren, I do not go around half-naked!"

"Don't you?" he demanded. He had that old familiar look on his face, the one that meant he was set for a fight. "I was up in New York one day last month on business and I went to one of your fashion shows. You were wearing a see-through blouse with nothing under it. Nothing!" His face hardened. "My God, I almost went up there and dragged you off that runway. It was all I could do to turn around and walk out of the building. Your father would have rolled over in his grave!"

"My father was proud of me," she returned, hurting from the remark. "And unless you missed it, most of the people who go to those shows are women!"

"There were men there," he came back. He crushed out the cigarette. "Do you take off your clothes for men in private, too, Abby?"

She lifted her hand to hit him, but he caught the wrist and jerked. She found herself looking straight into his narrowed eyes at an alarming distance. But worse, she felt the full force of his strength in that steely grip, and she felt panic rise in her throat.

"Let me go, Cade," she said suddenly, her voice ghostly, her eyes widening with fear. "Oh, please, let me go!"

He scowled, freeing her all at once. She drew back against her door like a cornered cat, actually trembling with reaction. Well, now she knew, didn't she? she thought miserably. She'd wondered how she'd react to Cade's strength, and now she truly knew.

"Remember me?" he asked angrily. "We've known each other most of our lives. I was defending myself,

Abby. I wasn't going to hit you. What the hell's the matter with you? Has some man been knocking you around?" His face became frankly dangerous. "Answer me," he said harshly. "Has one of your boyfriends been rough with you? By God, if he has…!"

"No, it's not that," she said quickly, drawing in a steadying breath. Her eyes closed on a wave of remorse. "I'm just tired, Cade. Tired. Burned out. Too many long hours and too many go-sees that didn't work out, too many demanding photographers, too many retakes of commercials, too many fittings, too many temperamental designers…." She slumped back against the door and opened her eyes, weary eyes, to look at him. "I'm tired." It was a lie, but then, how could she possibly tell him the truth?

"You came home to rest, is that what you're telling me?" he asked softly.

"Is it all right?" she asked, her eyes searching his. "A whole month, and I don't want to interfere with your life…."

"That's a joke," he scoffed. His eyes went over the shapeless dress. "You don't know what a joke it is." He turned abruptly to open the door. "Let's go in. It's freezing out here. We can sit around inside for the rest of the night and watch your sister and Jerry climb all over each other."

He sounded utterly disgusted, and she laughed involuntarily. "They're engaged," she reminded him.

"Then why don't they get married and make out in their own house?" he growled.

"They're trying," she said.

He gave her a hard glare before he opened his door and went around to open hers. "The wedding can't be soon enough to suit me," he said. "The only place I haven't caught them at it is in a closet."

"They're in love." She stepped down from the running board, landing in the soft, cold snow. "My gosh, you're old-fashioned, Cade."

"Don't tell me you hadn't noticed that before?" he asked as they walked toward the house through the driving snow. It tickled Abby's face, melting cold and wet over her delicate features.

"It's hard to miss," she agreed. She glanced up at him, walking so tall and straight beside her. He moved with easy grace, long strides that marked him an outdoorsman. It would take wide-open country like Montana to hold him. "But people in love are notoriously hard to separate."

"What would you know about love?" he asked, shooting a glance down at her. "Have you ever felt it?"

She laughed with brittle humor. "Most people have a crush or two in a lifetime."

"You had one on me once, as I remember," he said quietly. He was staring straight ahead, or he'd have seen the shock that widened Abby's pale brown eyes.

"I'm surprised you even noticed," she muttered. "In between raising cattle and fighting off girls at square dances."

"I noticed." The words didn't mean a lot, but the way he said them did. There was a world of meaning in the curt, harsh sound of them.

She drew in a slow breath and wrapped her arms around her chest, averting her gaze from him. Would she ever forget that night? Despite the recent experience that had soured physical relationships for her, she felt an explosion of pleasure at the memory of Cade's warm, rough mouth on her own, his hands touching her so gently....

They were at the back door. He opened it and let her into the warm, dry kitchen ahead of him. Calla had apparently stepped out for a minute, because it was deserted.

"Abby," he called.

She turned at the entrance to the dining room and looked back at him. He'd pulled off his hat, and his dark hair glittered damply black in the light.

His eyes slid down her body, taking in the ill-fitting clothing, and went back up to her flushed face and wide, soft eyes. The tension was suddenly between them, the old tension that she'd felt that night at the swimming pool when he'd seen her as no other man ever had. She could feel the shock of his gaze, the wild beat of her own heart in the silence that throbbed with unexpected promise.

"Are you happy in New York?" he asked.

She faltered, trying to get words past her tight throat. She had been—or she'd convinced herself that she had been—until the incident that had made her run home for shelter, for comfort. But always she'd missed Painted Ridge…and Cade.

"Of course I am," she lied. "Why?"

His tall frame shifted impatiently, as if he'd wanted an answer she hadn't given him. He made a strange gesture with one hand. "I just wondered, that's all. I saw your face on a magazine cover the other day," he added, studying her. "One of the better ones. That means something, I gather?"

"Yes," she agreed with a wan smile. "It's quite a coup to have a cover on that kind of magazine. My agency was thrilled about it."

His eyes wandered over her face, searching eyes that grew dark with some emotion she couldn't name. "You're beautiful, all right," he said quietly. "You always were. Not just physically, either. You reminded me of sunlight on a morning meadow. All silky and bright and sweet to look at. Whatever happened to that little girl?"

She felt an ache deep inside, a hunger that nothing had ever filled. Her eyes touched every hard line of his face, lines she would have loved to smooth away. She withered away from you, she wanted to tell him. Part of her died when she left Painted Ridge.

But of course she couldn't say that. "She grew up, Cade," she said instead.

He shook his head and smiled—a strange, soft smile that puzzled her. "No, not quite. I carry her around in my memory and every once in a while, I take her out and look at her."

"She was dreadfully naive," she murmured, trying not to let him see how his statement had touched her.

He moved slowly toward her, stopping just in front of her. He towered over her, powerful and big and faintly threatening, and she fought down the fear of his strength that had already surfaced once that night.

She looked up, intrigued by the smell of leather and wind that clung to him. "I'd forgotten how tall you are," she said involuntarily.

"I've forgotten nothing about you, Abby," he said curtly. "Including the fact that once you couldn't get close enough to me. But now you back away the minute I come near you."

So he had noticed. She dropped her eyes to the front of his shepherd's coat. "Do I?"

"You shied away from me in the calving shed tonight. Do you think I didn't notice? Then in the truck…" He drew in a deep breath. "My God, I'd never hurt you. Don't you know that?"

Her eyes traced the stitching on the coat and she noticed a tiny smudge near one of the buttons, as if ashes from his cigarette had fallen on it. Silly things to be aware of when she could feel the heat of his big body, and she remembered as if it were yesterday how sweet it was to be held against him.

"I know," she said after a minute. She forced her eyes up to his. "I…have some problems I'm trying to work out."

"A man?" he asked curtly.

She nodded. "In a way."

His face hardened, and his hands came up as if he would have liked to grip her with them. But he abruptly jammed them into his pockets. "Want to tell me about it?"

Her head went slowly from side to side. "Not yet. I have to find myself, Cade. I have to work it out in my own way."

"Does it have something to do with your career?" he asked.

"Yes, it does. I have to decide whether or not I want to go on with it," she confessed.

He seemed to brighten. His face changed, relaxed, making him look strangely young. "Thinking of quitting?"

"Why not?" she asked, grinning. "Need an extra cowhand? I close gates good—you ask Hank if I don't."

He smiled back, his dark eyes sparkling with humor. "I'll do that."

She sighed. "You'll be ready to run me off by the time that month's up," she said with a short laugh. "Anyway, I've got a lot of thinking to do."

He searched her quiet face. "Maybe I can help you make up your mind," he murmured. One hand caught her chin and turned it up, while his eyes searched hers curiously. "Melly said there was a man. A bad experience. What happened, honey, a love affair gone sour?"

She flinched, moving backward to release herself from the disturbing pressure of his fingers. She hadn't fled New York only to wind up back in Cade McLaren's hip pocket again; letting him get too close would be suicide in more ways than one. His strength unnerved her, but there was more to it than that. She reacted to him in ways that she'd never reacted to any other man. Every man she'd dated or been with socially had been for her a poor imitation of this one, and she was only now realizing how large he loomed in her memory. For years she'd pushed that night at the swimming pool to the back of her mind, afraid to take it out and look at it. And to-night, going back in time had stirred something deep inside her, had momentarily banished the bad memories to make way for remembered sensations and longings.

She stared up into Cade's dark eyes and saw her whole world. He was as big as this country, and nothing she ever found in New York was going to replace him. But there was no way she was going to let him know it. He'd pushed her away ever since that long-ago night. It was as if he couldn't bear having her close to him, in any way. Even now, when she backed away, he wasn't following. He could still let her go without flinching, without re-gret, even in this small way.

"A man," she agreed, and let it go at that, not looking at him. "What do you think I did in New York, stare out windows longing to be back here?" That was the truth, little did he know it. The glitter had long ago worn off her life there, leaving it barren and lonely.

"Not me, honey," he said. "I know all too well how dull this place is to you. You've done everything but shout it from the roof." He glared at her. "Did the man come too close, Abby? Did he want to settle down, and you couldn't face the thought of that?"

She stared at him blankly. "Is that shocking?" she

asked, adding fuel to the fire. "I told you, Cade, I like my life the way it is. I like having money to spend and things to see and places to go. I went to Jamaica to do a layout last month, and in September I'm going to Greece for another one. That's exciting. It's great fun."

He stared at her with cold eyes, believing the lie. "Yes, I can see that," he growled.

He pulled a cigarette from his pocket and lit it while his eyes ran quietly over every line of her face. "Then where does your boyfriend come in?"

She swallowed and turned away. "He wasn't…a boyfriend, and it's a long story."

"I'll find time to listen."

She shifted restlessly and turned. "Not tonight, if you don't mind. I'd like to say hello to Jerry."

He drew in an angry breath, and for just an instant she thought he was going to insist. But he reached past her and opened the door.

She went ahead of him, relieved that he'd swallowed her explanation. Boyfriend! Oh, God, what a horrible joke that was, but she'd rather have died than tell him the truth. Anyway, what would it matter? Let him think she was just getting over a love affair. What did it matter?

5

Melly was curled up on the sofa next to the tall, blond man who was going to be her husband. They both jumped when Cade deliberately slammed the door behind Abby and himself.

"Oh, hi, boss." Jerry Ridgely grinned, looking over the sofa back with dancing blue eyes. "Hi, Abby, welcome home!"

"Thanks, Jerry," she said, grinning back. She'd known him almost as long as Melly had. One of the advantages of growing up in country like this was that you knew most everybody from childhood onward. It gave peo-

ple a sense of security to know that some things stayed
constant.

"Staying for the wedding?" he asked, and Melly
smiled at her sister.

"I wouldn't miss it for the world," she promised.
"Which reminds me, Melly," she added, sticking her
hands in her pockets, "I've roughed out some sketches
for your wedding dress. They're in my suitcase."

"I'd love to see them," Melly said, enthusiastic. "You're
sure you don't mind making it for me?"

"Don't be silly, of course I don't mind. Sometimes I
wonder why I got into modeling when I love designing
so much." Abby sighed. *Modeling.* The word reminded
her of New York, which brought back other memories,
and she turned away, her eyes clouding.

Melly got to her feet quickly. "Let's go see if Calla has
the berry cobbler dished out," she said, catching Abby's
arm. "Can you men live without us?"

"Cade can." Jerry laughed, glancing toward the taci-
turn rancher. "But I'll have trouble, sweetheart, so hurry,
will you?"

"Sure," Melly agreed, in a tone that was meant for
the foreman alone. She winked and tugged Abby along
with her, closing the door behind them.

"Have you and Cade been at it again?" she asked Abby

as soon as the door was closed behind them. "He looks like a thundercloud, and you're flushed."

"He's persistent as all get-out," Abby groaned. "He nearly backed me into a corner in the kitchen just now. He's not going to worm it out of me, Melly. I can't talk to him about it, I can't!"

Melly sighed and hugged her sister. "Oh, Abby, I hoped you might be able to, once the two of you were alone."

"Talk to Cade?" She laughed. "My God, all I have time to do is defend myself. He's even worse than I re-membered. Why does he hate my career so much?"

"You really don't know, do you?" Melly murmured.

Abby ignored that, wrapping her arms tight around herself. "We got into it in the truck, and I tried to hit him, and when he grabbed my wrist…." She shivered. "He's so strong…."

"He's also Cade," Melly reminded her. "He'd never hurt you, not the longest day he lived."

Abby tried to smile. "I want a miracle, I guess. I want Cade to touch me and make the fear all go away."

"That could still happen," Melly said softly. "But you have to give it time. And telling Cade the truth would be a heck of a start. For God's sake, Abby, it wasn't your fault…!"

"So everyone tells me." She sighed. "Let's go help

Calla. I just want to get my mind on something else right now. It will all work out somehow, I suppose. Someday."

She carried that thought all through the long evening, watching Cade sit in his big chair and smoke cigarette after cigarette while he went over paperwork with Jerry and drank two neat whiskeys after the delicious dessert Calla put before them. Cade was so good to look at. He always had been, and the four years since he'd kissed her for the first time hadn't changed him very much on the surface. He was still overpoweringly masculine. Strong and capable and as tough as well-worn leather.

She watched the way his hands held the sheets of paper in their firm grip. They were tanned and sprinkled with dark hair. He didn't wear jewelry of any kind; the watch strapped around his wrist had a thick leather band and a dial that did everything except predict the future. He went in for utility, not style. But he managed to look like a fashion plate for all that, even in worn jeans and a faded shirt. He had a big, powerful body, and it was all steely muscle. Cade was just plain man, and he stood out anywhere.

He looked up once and caught her gaze, and she felt just a touch of the old magic. But she looked away and only the fear was left.

Later, Melly went into the bedroom with Abby. They

sat on the old bed that had been Abby's from girlhood and went over the wedding dress pattern.

"It's just magnificent," Melly breathed. "But it will take forever for you to make it...."

"A week, in my spare time." Abby grinned. "Do you really like it?"

"I love it!" She traced the design with a caressing finger. "It's the best design I've ever seen. You ought to sell it."

"Sell your wedding gown?" Abby exclaimed. "Do I look like I have a cash register for a heart?"

"Don't be silly. You know very well what I mean. It's good, Abby. It's really good. You're wasted showing other people's designs."

"Thank you for thinking so," Abby said with a smile.

"I'm not the only one, either. Did Jessica Dane ever get in touch with you?" Melly asked. "She absolutely raved over that dress you made me last summer."

"The boutique owner?" Abby asked. "No. Actually, I was kind of hoping she might. I do love designing, Melly. I feel as if modeling is burning me up. I stay tired all the time, and I have no social life at all. The money's nice," she added quietly. "But money isn't worth much in the long run if you aren't happy. And I'm not."

"Will you mind if I tell you that I never thought you would be?" her sister asked softly. She smiled. "You pretended it was what you wanted, but I saw right through you."

Abby stared at her ringless hands. "I hope nobody else did," she said.

"He's thirty-six now," Melly reminded her. "Inevitably, he'll marry sooner or later."

Abby laughed bitterly. "Will he? He hasn't exactly been in a flaming hurry to commit himself to anybody. You know what he used to say about marriage? That it was a noose only a fool stuck his head into."

"He's a lonely man, Abby," came the surprising reply. "I know better than anybody—I work for him. I see him every day. He works himself into the ground, but there are still evenings when he sits on the porch by himself and just stares off into the horizon."

That hurt. Abby turned her face away to keep Melly from seeing how much. "He could have any woman he wanted," she said, forcing herself not to let her voice show the emotion she was feeling. "He used to stay out with some woman or other every day I was here."

"So he let you think," Melly murmured. "He runs three ranches—a corporation the size of a small city—and in his spare time he sleeps. When does he have the time to be a playboy? I'll grant you, he's got the money to be one, even if he weren't so good-looking. But he's a puritan in his outlook. It even makes him uncomfortable when Jerry kisses me in front of him."

"Just like Donavan," she agreed, remembering Cade's father. "Remember the night you were kissing Danny Johnson on our front porch and Donavan rode by with Cade? Whew! I didn't think Danny would ever come back again after that lecture."

"Neither did I. Donavan had an overdeveloped sense of propriety. No wonder Cade's got so many inhibitions. Of course, being brought up in a small place like Cheyenne Lodge…"

"Only you could call Montana a small place," Abby teased.

"This little teeny corner of it, I meant," came the irrepressible reply. "I'll bet you get culture shock every time you come here from New York," she added.

"No," Abby denied. Her eyes began to glow softly. "It's like homecoming every time. I never realize how much I miss it until I come back."

"And stand at the window, hoping for a glimpse of Cade," Melly said quietly, nodding when Abby flushed. "Oh, yes, I've caught you at it. You watch him with such love in your eyes, Abby. As if the sight of him would sustain you through any nightmare."

Abby turned away. "Stop that. I'll wear my heart out on him, and you know it. No," she said firmly when

Melly started to speak. "No more. Melly, you do love Jerry, don't you?" she added, concern replacing the brief flare-up of irritation.

"Unbearably," Melly confessed. "We fought like animals the first few weeks I worked here, when I came home from business college. But then, one day he threw me down in the hay and fell on me," she added with a grin. "And we kissed like two starving lovers. He asked me to marry him on the spot and I said yes without even thinking. We've had our disagreements, but there's no one I'll ever love as much."

Abby thought about being pushed down and fallen on, and she trembled with reaction. She felt herself stiffen, and Melly noticed.

"Sorry," she said quickly, touching Abby's arm. "I didn't think about how it might sound to you."

"It's just the thought of being helpless," she said in a suppressed tone. Her eyes came up. "Melly, men are so strong...you don't realize how strong until you try to get away and can't!"

"Don't think about it," Melly said softly. "Come on, we've got to decide on the trimmings for this dress. Calla has a bag full of material samples she got from the fabric shop. We'll look through them, and she'll go into town and get what you need tomorrow, okay?"

"Okay." Abby hugged her warmly. "I love you," she said in a rare outburst of emotion.

"I love you, too," Melly returned, smiling as she drew away. "Now, here, this is what I liked especially…" She pulled out a swatch of material and the girls drifted into a discussion of fabrics that lasted until bedtime.

Abby spent the next few days reacquainting herself with the ranch. She was careful to keep out of the way of the men—and Cade—but she trudged through the barns looking at calves and sat on the bales of hay in the loft and remembered back to her childhood on her family's ranch. It was part of Painted Ridge now, having been bought by Cade at Jesse Shane's death. It would have gone on the auction block otherwise, because neither Melly nor Abby had any desire to try to run it. Ranching was a full-time headache, best left to experts.

When the snow melted and the weather turned springlike again, Abby wandered through the gates up to a grassy hill where a small stand of pines stood guard, and settled herself under one of the towering giants. It was good to breathe clean air, to sit and soak in the cool, green peace and untouched beauty of this land.

Where else were there still places like this, where you could look and see nothing but rolling grassy hills that stretched to the horizon—with tall, ragged mountains on the other side and the river that cut like a wide ribbon through it all? Cade had liked to fish in that river in the old days, when Donavan was still alive to assume some of the burden of their business. Abby went with him occasionally, watching him land big bass and crappie, rainbow trout and channel catfish.

The nice thing about Cade, she thought dreamily, was that he had such a love for the land and its protection. He was constantly investigating new ways of improving his own range, working closely with the Soil Conservation Service to protect the natural resources of his state.

Her eyes turned toward the gate as she heard a horse's hooves, and she found Cade riding up the ridge toward her on his big black gelding. He sat a horse so beautifully, reminding her of a Western movie hero. He was all muscle and grace, and she respected him more than any man she'd ever known.

He reined in when he reached her and swung one long leg around the pommel, a smoking cigarette in his lean, dark hands as he watched her from under the wide brim of his gray Stetson.

"Slumming, miss model?" he teased with a faint smile.

"This is the place for it," she said, leaning back against the tree to smile up at him. Her long, pale hair caught the breeze and curved around her flushed cheeks. "Isn't it peaceful here?" she asked. "No wonder the Indians fought so very hard to keep it."

His eyes darkened, narrowed. "A man does fight to keep the things he wants most," he said enigmatically, studying her. "Why do you wear those damned baggy things?" he demanded, nodding toward her bulky shirt and loose jeans.

She shrugged, avoiding that piercing gaze. "They're comfortable," she said inadequately.

"They look like hell. I'd rather see you in transparent blouses," he added coldly.

Her eyebrows arched. "You lecherous old thing," she accused.

He chuckled softly, deeply, a sound she hadn't heard in a long time. It made him seem younger. "Only with you, honey," he said softly. "I'm the soul of chivalry around most women."

Her eyes searched his. "You could have any woman you want these days," she murmured absently.

"Then isn't it a hell of a shame that I have such a fussy appetite?" he asked. He took a draw from the cigarette and studied her quietly. "I'm a busy man."

"You look it," she agreed, studying the dusty jeans that encased his hard, powerful legs, and his scuffed brown boots and sweat-stained denim shirt. There was a black mat of hair under that shirt, and a muscular chest that she remembered desperately wanting to touch.

"It's spring," he reminded her. "Cattle to doctor, calves

to separate and brand and herds to move up to summer pasture as soon as we finish roundup. Hay to plant, machinery to repair and replace, temporary hands to hire for roundup, supplies to get in… If it isn't one damned thing, it's another."

"And you love every minute of it," she accused. "You'd die anywhere else."

"Amen." He finished the cigarette and tossed it down. "Crush that out for me, will you, honey?"

"It's not dry enough for it to cause a grass fire," she reminded him, but she got up and did it all the same.

"Back in the old days, Indians and white men would stop fighting to battle grass fires together," he told her with a grin. "They're still hard to stop, even today."

She looked up at him, tracing his shadowed face with eyes that ached for what might have been. "You look so at home in the saddle," she remarked.

"I grew up in it." He reached down an arm. "Step on my boot and come up here. I'll give you a ride home."

"It's a good thing you don't ride a horse the way you drive," she observed.

"That's not a good way to get reacquainted," he said shortly.

"It's only the truth. Donavan wouldn't even get in a truck with you," she reminded him. "Although I have to admit that you're a pretty good driver on the highway."

"Thanks for nothing. Are you coming or not?"

She wanted and dreaded the closeness. He was so very strong. What if she panicked again, what if he demanded an answer to her sudden nervousness?

"Abby," he said suddenly, his voice as full of authority as if he were tossing orders at his cowboys. "Come on."

She reacted to that automatically and took his hand, tingling as it slid up her arm to hold her. She stepped deftly onto the toe of his boot in the stirrup and swung up in front of him.

He drew her back against him with a steely arm, and she felt the powerful muscles of his chest at her shoulder blades.

"Comfortable?" he asked shortly.

"I'm fine," she replied in a voice that was unusually high-pitched.

He eased the horse into a canter. "You'll be more comfortable if you'll relax, little one," he murmured. "I'm no threat."

That was what he thought, she told herself, reacting wildly to the feel of his body against her back. He smelled of leather and cow and tobacco, and his breath sighed over her head, into her loosened hair.

If only she could relax instead of sitting like a fire poker in his light embrace. But he made her nervous, just as he always had; he made her feel vulnerable and soft and hungry. Despite the bad experience in New York, he appealed to her senses in ways that unnerved her.

He chuckled softly and she stiffened more. "What's so funny?" she muttered above the sound of the horse's hooves striking hard ground.

"You are. Should I be flattered that you're afraid to let me hold you on a horse? My God, I didn't realize I was so devastating at close range. Or," he added musingly, "is it that I smell like a man who's been working with cattle?"

Laughter bubbled up inside her. It had been years since she and Cade had spent any time alone, and she'd forgotten his dry sense of humor.

"Sorry." She sighed. "I've been away longer than I realized."

His big arm tightened for an instant and relaxed, and she let him hold her without a struggle. His strength was less intimidating now than it had been the last time, as if the nightmare experience were truly fading away in the scope and bigness of this country where she had grown up. She felt safe. Safer than she'd felt in years.

"Four years," he murmured behind her head. "Except for a few days here and there, when you could tear yourself away from New York."

She went taut with indignation. "Are you going to start that again?"

"I never stopped it. You just stopped listening." His arm contracted impatiently for an instant, and his warm breath was on her ear. "When are you going to grow up, Abby? Glitter isn't enough for a lifetime. In the end, it's not going to satisfy you as a woman!"

"What is?" she asked curtly. "Living with some man and raising children?"

He seemed to freeze, as if she'd thrown cold water in his face, and she was sorry she'd said that. She hadn't meant it—she was just getting back at him.

"It's more than enough for women out here," he said shortly.

She stared across at the horizon, loving the familiar contours of the land, the shape of the tall trees, the blueness of the sky. "Your grandmother had ten children, didn't she, Cade?" she asked, remembering the photos in the McLaren family album.

"Yes." He laughed shortly. "There wasn't much choice in those days, honey. Women didn't have a lot of control over their bodies, like they do now."

"And it took big families to run ranches and farms," she agreed. She leaned back against him, feeling his muscles ripple with the motion of the horse. Her eyes closed as she drank in the sensation of being close.

"It was more than that," he remarked as they approached the house. "People in love want children."

She laughed aloud at that. "I can't imagine you in love," she said. "It's completely out of character. What was it you always said about never letting a woman put a ring through your nose?"

He didn't laugh. If anything, he seemed to grow cold. "You don't know me at all, Abby. You never have."

"Who could get close enough?" she asked coolly. "You've got a wall ten feet thick around yourself, just like Donavan had. It must be a McLaren trait."

"When people come close, they can hurt," he said shortly. "I've had my fill of being cut to the quick."

"I can't imagine anyone brave enough to try that," she told him.

"Can't you?" He sounded goaded, and the arm that was holding her tautened.

She got a glimpse of his face as he leaned down to open the gate between them and the house, and its hardness unsettled her. He looked hurt somehow, and she couldn't understand why.

"Cade?" she murmured before he straightened again.

His eyes looked straight into hers, and she trembled at the intensity of the glare, its suppressed violence.

"One day, you'll push too hard," he said quietly. "I'm not made of stone, despite the fact that you seem to believe I am. I let you get away with murder when you were younger. But you're not a child anymore, Abby, and the kid gloves are off. Do you understand me?"

How could she help it? Her heart shuddered with mingled fear and excitement. Involuntarily, her eyes went to his hard mouth and she remembered vividly the touch and taste and expertness of it.

"Don't worry, Cade, I won't seduce you," she promised, trying to sound as if she were teasing him in a sophisticated way.

He caught her chin and forced her eyes back up to his, and she jumped at the ferocity in his dark gaze. "I could have had you that night at the swimming pool, Abigail Jennifer Shane," he reminded her with merciless bluntness. "We're both four years older, but don't think you're immune to me. If you start playing games, you could goad me into doing something we'd both regret."

She tried to breathe normally and failed miserably. She forced her eyes down to the harsh rise and fall of his chest, and then closed them.

"Just because I had a huge crush on you once, don't get conceited and think I'm still stupid enough to moon over you, Cade," she bit off.

As if the words set him off, his eyes flashed and all at once he had her across the saddle, over his knees, with her head imprisoned in the crook of his arm.

She struggled, frightened by his strength as she'd been

afraid from the beginning that she would be. "No," she whispered, pushing frantically at his chest.

"Let's see how conceited I am, Abby," he ground out, bending his head to hers.

One glance into those blazing eyes was enough to tell her that he wasn't teasing. She groaned helplessly as his hard mouth crushed down onto hers in cold, angry possession.

It might have been so different if he'd been careful, if he hadn't given in to his temper. But she was too frightened to think rationally. It was New York all over again, and a man's strength was holding her helpless while a merciless mouth ground against her own. Through the fear, she thought she felt Cade tremble, but she couldn't be sure. Her mind was focused only on the hard pressure of his mouth, the painful tightening of his arms. Suddenly she began to fight. She hit him with her fists, anywhere she could, and when the shock of it made him lift his head, she screamed.

An indescribable expression washed over his features, and he seemed to go pale.

Abby hung back against his arm, her pale brown eyes full of terror, her lips bloodless as she stared up at him, her breasts rising and falling with her strangled breaths.

"My God, what's happened to you?" he asked in a shocked undertone.

She swallowed nervously, her lips trembling with reaction, her body frozen in its arch. "Please...don't handle me...roughly," she pleaded, her voice strange and high.

His eyes narrowed, glittering. His face went rock-hard as he searched her features. "What made you come here, Abby?" he demanded. "What drove you out of the city?"

Her eyes closed and she shuddered. "I told you, I was tired," she choked out. "Tired!"

He said something terrible under his breath and straightened, moving her away from him with a smooth motion. "It's all right," he said when her eyes flew open at the movement. "I'm only going to let you sit up."

She avoided his piercing scrutiny, sitting quickly erect with her back to him.

He spurred the horse toward the house. "If you can't bear to be touched, there has to be a reason," he said shortly. "You've been hurt some way, or frightened. I asked you if you'd been knocked around by a man, and you denied it. But you lied to me, didn't you, Abby?"

Her jaw set firmly. "All this fuss because you kissed me against my will and I fought you!" she burst out. "Are you so conceited that you think I can't wait to fall into your arms, Cade?"

He didn't say a word. He rode right up to the front steps and abruptly set her down on the ground.

She stood by the horse for a long moment before she looked up. "Thanks for the ride," she ventured.

He'd lit a cigarette and was smoking it quietly, his face grim as he looked down at her. "You're going to tell me what happened sooner or later."

"Nothing happened," she lied, raising her voice.

"I didn't wind up with three ranches and a corporation because I was an idiot," he informed her. "You didn't come rushing down here a month early just to help Melly get ready for her wedding. And it damned sure wasn't because you were dying for the sight of me."

He was hitting too close to the truth. She turned away. "Believe what you like, Great White Rancher."

"Abby!"

She whirled, eyes blazing, as gloriously beautiful in anger as a sunburst, with her pale hair making a frame for her delicate face and wide brown eyes. "What?"

His eyes went over her reverently, from toes to head, while the cigarette smoked away in his tanned fingers. "Don't fight me."

It was like having the breath knocked out of her. She looked up at him and felt the anger drain away. He was so gorgeously masculine, so handsome. Her eyes softened helplessly.

"Then don't hurt me," she said quietly.

He laughed mirthlessly. "That works both ways."

"Pull the other one," she muttered. "I'd have to use dynamite. You're hard, Cade."

"This is hard country. I don't have time for the limp-wristed courtesies you city women swear by in men."

"Sophistication doesn't make a man peculiar," she returned. "I like a polished man."

His dark eyes glittered. "Not always," he replied. "There was a time when I could look at you and make you blush."

"That old crush?" she said. "I thought the sun rose and set on you, all right. But you made a career of pushing me away, didn't you?"

"You were eighteen, damn it!" he shot at her. "Eighteen, to my thirty-two! I felt like a damned fool when I left you that night. I should never have touched you!"

The one beautiful memory in her life, and he was sorry it had happened. If she'd ever wondered how he really felt inside his shell, she knew now.

She lowered her eyes and turned away. She walked to the house without another word, without a backward glance. As she went up the steps, she imagined she heard him swear, but when she looked back, he was riding away.

Abby brooded about the confrontation for the rest of the day, and at the supper table it was patently obvious to

Melly and Jerry that something was wrong. Even Calla, walking back and forth to serve up the delicious beef the ranch was famous for, with the accompanying dishes, commented that the weather sure had gotten cold quick.

Cade finished his meal before the rest of them and lit a cigarette over his second cup of coffee.

"I've got those reports printed out whenever you want them, Cade," Melly ventured.

He nodded. "I'll look them over now. Jerry, come on in when you finish," he added, rising. "We'll have to make a decision pretty quick about those cows we're going to sell off. Jake White wants a few dozen head for embryo transplants."

"Wants them cheap, too." Jerry laughed. "I reckon he thinks our culls will be the very thing to carry his purebred Angus."

Melly grinned at them, aware of Abby sitting rigidly at her side. "Oh, the advances in cattle breeding. Herefords throwing Angus calves, without even the joys of natural conception."

Cade gave her a hard glare and walked out of the room.

"Shame on you," Jerry muttered as he started to join the boss. "Embarrassing him that way."

"I'm just helping him lose some of his inhibitions, darling," Melly whispered back, blowing him a kiss before he winked and left the room.

"He'll get even," Abby said solemnly, picking at her food. "He always does."

"You could help him with those inhibitions, too," her sister said, tongue in cheek.

"Not me, sis," came the instant reply. She glared toward the doorway. "He can keep his hang-ups for all I care."

Melly stared at her hard. "Why don't you and Cade start kissing and stop fighting?"

"Ask him," she grumbled, getting up. "It's one and the same thing with Cade, if you want to know. I've got a frightful headache, Melly. Say good-night to the others for me, will you?" And she rushed upstairs without another word before Melly could ask the questions that were forming on her lips.

Abby hadn't had a nightmare since she arrived at the ranch, but after the confrontation with Cade, it was almost inevitable that it would recur. And sure enough, it did.

She woke up in the early hours of the morning, screaming. Even as the sounds were dying away, her door burst open and Cade came storming into her room, flashing on the overhead light, with Melly at his heels.

✤ 6 ✤

Abby sat there in the plain cotton gown that concealed every inch of her body, her hair wild, her eyes raining tears down her pale cheeks, and gaped at them on the tail of terror.

Cade was in his pajama trousers and nothing else. They rode low on his lean hips, and the sheer masculinity of his big body with its generous black curling hair and bronzed muscle was enough to frighten her even more.

"How about making some coffee?" Cade asked Melly, although his tone made it an order, not a request.

"But…" Melly began, nervously looking from her sister to her employer.

"You heard me."

Melly hesitated for just an instant before she left them alone, her footsteps dying away down the hall.

Cade put his hands on his hips and stared down at Abby. With his hair tousled and his face hard, he looked as threatening as any storm.

"Get up and put on a robe," he said after a minute, turning away, "while I get dressed."

"You don't have to," she managed weakly.

He half turned, his eyes glittering. "Don't I?" he growled. "You're looking at me as if I were a rapist."

Her face blanched and he nodded. "That's how you feel, too, isn't it, baby? Put on a robe and come into the living room. And stop looking at me like that. I'm not going to touch you. But you're going to tell me the truth, one way or the other."

He left her sitting there, his back as stiff as a poker.

Melly brought the coffee in just as Abby came out of her room, wrapped to the throat in a heavy navy terry-cloth robe.

Cade was dressed, barely, in jeans and an open-throated blue shirt that he hadn't tucked in. He was barefoot, sitting forward in an armchair, worrying his hair with his hands. He looked up as Abby came in.

"Sit down," he said quietly. "Melly, thank you for the coffee. Good night."

"Cade..." Melly began.

"Good night," he repeated.

The younger woman sighed as she looked over at Abby, her whole expression one of regret and apology.

"It's all right," Abby said gently. "You and I both know that Cade would never hurt me."

Cade looked faintly shocked by the words, but he busied himself with lighting a cigarette while Melly said good-night and left them alone.

"Fix me a cup, will you, honey?" he asked.

Abby automatically poured cream in it and handed it to him.

He took it, cup and saucer balanced on his big palm, and smiled at her. "You remembered, didn't you?"

She flushed. Yes, she had, just the way he liked it. She remembered almost everything she'd learned over the years—that he didn't take sugar, that he hated rhubarb, that he loved a thick steak and cottage potatoes to go with it, that he could go for forty-eight hours without sleep but not one hour without a cigarette....

"Tit for tat?" he murmured, and reached out to put two sugars and cream in the second cup and hand it to her, smiling when she raised astonished eyes to his.

She took it, sitting back on the sofa to study the

creamy liquid, turning the cup nervously back and forth in its saucer.

"Little things," she murmured, finally lifting her eyes to his. "Isn't it amazing how we remember them after so many years?"

"I remember a lot about you," he said quietly, studying her. "Especially," he added on a rueful sigh, "how you look without clothes."

She flushed, dropping her eyes. "It was a long time ago."

"Four years," he agreed. "But it doesn't seem that long to me." He took a gulp of his coffee, ignoring the fact that it was hot enough to blister a normal throat, stubbed out his cigarette and leaned back in his chair. "Tell me what happened, Abby."

She felt the cup tremble in her hand and only just righted it in time. "I can't, Cade."

He took another sip of coffee and leaned forward suddenly, resting his hands on his knees. "Look up. That's right, look at me. Do you remember when you ran over your father's dog with my old jeep?"

She swallowed and nodded.

"You couldn't face him, but you came running to me bawling your heart out, and I held you while you cried." He shifted his hands, studying her drawn face. "When

Vennie Walden called you a tomboy and said you looked like a stick with bumps, you came crying to me then."

She nodded again, managing a smile for him. "I always cried on you, didn't I?"

"Always. Why not now?" He reached out a big hand and waited, patiently, until she could put her own, hesitantly, into it and feel its warmth and strength. "From now on, it's going to be just like this. I won't touch you unless you want me to. Now tell me what happened. Did you find out he was married?"

"He?" she asked, studying him blankly.

"The man you had an affair with," he said quietly. "The one you wake up screaming over in the middle of the night."

She swallowed down the urge to get up and run. How in the world was she going to be able to tell him the truth. How?

"Come on, Abby, tell me," he coaxed with a faint smile. "I'm not going to sit in judgment on you."

"You've got it wrong, Cade," she said after a minute. "It...wasn't an affair."

His heavy brows came together. He searched her face. "No? I understood Melly to say there was a man...."

"There was." Her eyes opened and closed, and the pain of admission was in them suddenly. She tried to speak, and her mouth trembled on the words.

He was beginning to sense something. His face seemed to darken, his eyes glittered. His hand, on hers, tightened promptingly. "Abby, tell me!" he ground out, his patience exhausted.

Her eyes closed, because she couldn't bear to see what would be in his when she told him. "I was assaulted, Cade."

The silence seemed to go on forever. Forever! The hand around her own stilled, and withdrew. Somewhere a clock was ticking with comical loudness; she could hear it above the tortured pounding of her own heart....

At first, she wondered if he'd heard her. Until she looked up and saw his lean hands, tough from years of ranch work, contract slowly around the cup until it shattered and coffee went in a half-dozen directions onto the deep gray pile carpet.

Her eyes shot up to his face, reading the aching compassion and murderous rage that passed across it in wild succession.

"Who?" he asked, the word dangerously soft.

"I don't know," she said quietly.

"Surely to God there was a suspect!" he burst out, oblivious to the shards of pottery and the coffee that was staining his jeans, the carpet.

"Not yet," she told him. "Cade, the carpet...look, you've cut your hand!" she exclaimed, seeing blood.

"Oh, to hell with that," he growled. He glanced at his hand and tugged a handkerchief from his jeans pocket to wind haphazardly around it. "What do you mean, not yet?"

"Just what I said. It's a big city." She got up, kneeling beside him. "Let me see. Come on, let me see!" she grumbled, forcing him to give her the big warm hand. She unwrapped the handkerchief gently; there was a shallow cut on the ball of his thumb. "We'd better put something on it."

"Is that why you backed away from me earlier?" he asked, his eyes on her bent head. "Why you were afraid when I was rough with you earlier, outside?"

Her eyes clouded. "Yes."

He started to touch her hair and froze, withdrawing his hand before it could make contact. He laid it back on the arm of the chair with a wistful sigh. "What can I say, Abby?" he asked gently. "What in hell can I say?"

Her fingers let go of his hand and she got to her feet. "There's some antiseptic in the guest bathroom, isn't there?" she asked.

"I suppose so." He got up and followed her down the hall, sitting uncomfortably on the little vanity bench, which swayed precariously while she rifled through the medicine cabinet for antiseptic and a bandage.

He sat quietly while she dressed the cut, but his eyes watched her intently.

"Please don't watch me like that," she asked tightly.

His eyes fell to his hand. "It's an old habit." His chiseled mouth made a half smile when she looked down at him, startled. "You didn't know that, I suppose." The smile faded. "Can you talk about it?"

She studied him quietly and lowered her eyes. "I was coming home from an assignment, at night. It was a nice night, just a little nippy, and I had a coat on over my dress. I only lived a few blocks away, so I walked." She laughed bitterly. "The streets were deserted, and before I realized it, a man started following me. I ran, and he caught up with me and dragged me into an alley." She shuddered at the memory. "I tried so hard to get away, but he was big and terribly strong...." Her eyes closed. "He pushed me down and started kissing me, touching me... I screamed then, just as loud as I could, and there were three men coming out of a nearby bar who heard me. They came running and he took off." She drew in a steadying breath, oblivious to Cade's white, strained face. "Thank God they heard me. People talk about cities being cold and heartless places, but it didn't happen that way for me. The people at the emergency room told me I'd been damned lucky."

"Was there someone to take care of you?" he asked as if it mattered, really mattered.

"Yes. There was a Rape Crisis Center. All women," she said with a faint smile, recalling the gentle treatment, the care she'd received. "They sent me over there, despite the fact that I hadn't been raped. It's still a mentally scarring thing, to be handled that way, mauled. Thinking about the way it might have been… But I felt dirty, you know. Soiled. I still think about it constantly…."

His face hardened as he watched her quietly. "If I'd made love to you that night, kept you here with me, none of this would ever have happened."

"Did you want to, really?" she wondered softly.

He drew in a long, steady breath. "I wanted to," he admitted after a minute, and his eyes darkened. He got to his feet, towering over her. "But it would have been a slap in the face to your father. He trusted me to look after you. And God knows, it would have been a mistake, a bad one." He studied her intently. "I'd never touched a virgin until that night."

She felt a surge of pride at that confession, and it showed in her eyes.

"I've never touched one since, either," he added with a quiet smile.

"Learned your lesson, huh?" she murmured with a feeble attempt at humor.

He nodded. "Can you sleep now?"

The thought of the dark room was disquieting, but she erased the nervousness from her eyes. "Yes. I think so."

"You can sleep with me if you want to," he said quietly, and she knew exactly what he meant—that he'd die before he'd touch her, unless she wanted it.

Hesitantly, her hand went out to touch his arm, a light touch that was quickly removed. "Thank you," she said softly. "But I'll be all right now."

His eyes searched hers for a long moment. "You trust me, don't you?" he asked gently.

"Yes," she said simply. "More than anyone else in the world, Cade, if it means anything."

"Yes," he bit off, "it means something."

"The carpet!" she exclaimed suddenly. "Oh, Cade, I'll bet the carpet's ruined...."

"I'll buy a new one. Go to bed."

"Thank you," she said as he turned to go out into the hall. "I...I... Melly said I should have told you about it, but I didn't...I wasn't sure...."

"You didn't think that I'd blame you?" he asked softly.

She stared down at the carpeted floor, embarrassed now that he knew.

"Stop it, for God's sake," he said bluntly. "So you got mauled. You've had a terrible experience, and I'm sorry as hell, but it doesn't change who you are!"

Her lips trembled. "I feel unclean," she whispered, shaken. "As if I'd been robbed of something I had the right to give to a man I chose. He touched me in ways no man ever did, not even you…"

He drew in a ragged breath. "Yes, you were robbed, but not of your chastity. Even if he'd raped you, you'd still have that."

She stared up at him numbly. "What?"

He lit a cigarette with unsteady fingers. "Oh, hell, I'm putting this badly." He blew out a cloud of smoke and stared down at her with narrowed eyes. "Abby, how long ago did it happen?"

"Week before last," she confessed.

"Okay, and you're still raw, that makes sense. But you'll get over it. And it will be different, with a man you care about."

Her lips pouted. "It wasn't any different this afternoon. You scared me to death."

His face paled, but he didn't look away. "My fault. I've been without a woman for a while, and the feel of you went to my head. I was rougher than I ever meant to be. But you've got to help yourself a little by not dwelling on what happened to you."

"How can I help it? It makes me sick just remembering…!" she burst out.

"Put it in perspective, honey," he said curtly, jamming

his bandaged hand in his pocket as if he were afraid he might try to touch her with it. "Has it occurred to you that by letting the experience warp your mind, you're giving that piece of scum who attacked you more rights over you than you'd give a husband?"

She stared at him, stunned.

He took another long draw from the cigarette. "You're giving him the right to dominate your life, by dwelling on what happened, by blowing up what he did to you and letting it lock you up emotionally and physically."

"I...hadn't thought of it like that."

"Suppose you start."

She wrapped her arms around her trembling body. "You can't know how it is for a woman," she murmured. "Against a man's strength..."

"I can remember a time in your life when you very much liked being helpless against mine," he said under his breath.

"That was different. I knew you'd never hurt me."

"You knew that this afternoon, but you fought me like a wildcat."

She flushed. "You hurt me!"

His jaw tightened. "Do you think because I have to be hard with my men that I'm that hard inside? You get under my skin like no other woman ever has. You de-

liberately needle me and then take offense when I defend myself. It's always been that way."

"I never thought you could be hurt," she murmured,
avoiding his piercing gaze. "Least of all by me."

"Why talk about it?" he asked wearily. "It's all water
under the bridge now."

"Thanks for the therapy session," she said softly and
smiled, because she meant it.

He smiled back. "Did it help?"

She nodded. Her eyes searched his. "Cade, I'm sorry
I screamed this afternoon."

He reached down and smoothed a lock of hair from
her face. "I didn't know. Now I do. Give it time—you'll
be fine. I'll help."

"Thanks for letting me come."

He looked strange for a minute. "When Melly said
you wanted to get here early for the wedding, so you
could spend some time on the ranch, I didn't know the
real reason. I thought…" He dropped his hand with a
gruff laugh. "You can still sleep with me, if you want. I
wouldn't touch you."

Her soft eyes searched his, and he looked back as if it
were beyond his power to remove his eyes from hers.
"Calla and Melly would be shocked to the back teeth,"
she whispered, trying to joke about it and failing. It

would have been heaven to lie in his arms all night. "But thank you for the offer."

He shrugged. "It wasn't for purely selfless reasons," he said, winking at her. "Bed's damned cold in early spring," he chuckled.

She hit him softly. "Beast!"

"Think you can sleep now?"

She nodded. "I feel a little different about it. Maybe I just need time to put things into perspective, after all."

"If you'd like something to occupy your mind, I'll take you out to see the rest of the calves in the morning."

"Oh, boy," she said enthusiastically. "But what if it snows again?" she asked. "It was awfully cloudy this afternoon and cold as blazes and the radio says—"

"When has snow ever stopped me?" he asked, chuckling. "Night, honey." He turned and strode off toward the stairs.

When has anything ever stopped you? she asked herself silently.

Except once…she'd never realized until now that he'd really wanted her that night. He'd been so cool and calm on the surface that she'd halfway convinced herself he had only been satisfying her curiosity to keep her from experimenting with younger, more hot-blooded males. But now she began to wonder. She was still wondering when she fell into a deep, satisfying sleep.

7

Cade had offered to take Abby back to see the calves, but by morning the snow had covered Painted Ridge and he was out with his men trying to bring in the half-frozen calves and their new mothers. According to Hank, Cade was cursing a blue streak from one end of the ranch to the other.

"Wants his other gloves," Hank growled at Calla when he paused in the hall, the familiar wad of tobacco tucked into his cheek. "Ruined a pair trying to unhook one of them damned cows from the barbed wire."

"He goes through gloves like some men go through

food," Calla grumbled, shooting an irritated glance at Hank for interrupting her in the middle of lunch preparation. "Only got one pair left as it is. You best remember to tell him that!"

"Can't tell him a damned thing," Hank muttered, waiting uncomfortably in the hall. His wide-brimmed hat was spotted with melted snow, and his heavy cloth coat was equally damp. "He hit the ground cussing this morning and he ain't stopped yet. I just follow orders, I don't give 'em!" he shouted after Calla.

"Is it bad out there?" Melly called from the den, where she was busily operating Cade's computer.

"Bad enough," Hank replied. "Hope your fingers are rested, Miss Melly, 'cause you're sure going to do some typing when we get a tally on these new calves!"

"As usual." Melly laughed. "Don't worry about it, Hank, I get paid good."

"If we got paid what we was worth, Cade would go in the hole, I guess," the thin cowboy said to no one in particular. He glanced at Abby, who was standing there quietly in her jeans and a blue turtleneck sweater. "I hear you're going to stay with us till Miss Melly's wedding. How're you settling in?"

She smiled. "Just fine. It feels like old times."

"Far cry from the city," he observed.

She nodded. "Less traffic," she said with a hint of her old humor.

Hank looked disgusted. "Give me a horse any day," he muttered, "and open country to ride him in. If God wanted the world covered in concrete, he'd have made human beings with tires!"

It was the cowboy's favorite theme, and Abby was looking for a way to escape before he had time to get started when Calla came thumping back down the hall with a worn pair of gloves in her hand.

"Here," she said shortly, slapping them into Hank's outstretched hand. "And make sure he doesn't get holes in them. That's all there is."

"What am I, a nursemaid?" he spat out. "My gosh, Calla, all I do is babysit cows these days. If Cade gave a hang about my feelings, he'd give me some decent work."

"Maybe he'll set you to digging post holes," the older woman suggested with malicious glee. "I'll tell him what you said."

"You do," he threatened, "and I'll tell him what you did with that cherry cake he had his heart set on the other night."

She sucked in a furious breath. "You wouldn't dare!"

He grinned, something rare for Hank. "You tell him I like digging post holes, and I'll do it or bust. Bye, Abby,

Melly," he called over his shoulder as he stomped out the door.

"What did you do with Cade's cherry cake?" Abby asked with a sideways stare.

Calla cleared her throat and walked back toward the kitchen. "I gave it to Jeb. Cade's not the only one who's partial to my cherry cake."

Abby smothered a chuckle as she wandered into the den. With its bare wood floors, Indian rugs and wood furniture, it was a far cry from the luxury of the living room.

Melly looked up as Abby came toward the desk where the computer and printer were set up. "I didn't want to desert you last night," she said apologetically. "Did you tell him?"

"I had to," Abby admitted, perching herself on the edge of the chair beside Melly's. "You know Cade when he sets his mind on something. But it wasn't as bad as I thought it would be. He didn't even say 'I told you so.'"

"I didn't expect him to. You underestimate him sometimes, I think." Melly looked smug. "There's a brown spot on the carpet in the living room."

Abby looked guilty. "I was afraid of that, but he wouldn't hear of my cleaning it up." She sighed. "He was holding the coffee cup when I told him. He…crushed it."

Melly closed her eyes for an instant. "I noticed his

hand was bandaged this morning," she murmured. "I wondered why…"

"He said some things that made me think," Abby recalled, smiling faintly. "He may not be a psychologist, but he's got a lot of common sense about things. He said I was giving the man who attacked me a hold over me, by dwelling on it. I'd never considered it in that light, but I think he has a point."

Melly smiled at her gently. "Maybe he ought to open an office," she said impishly.

Abby grinned back. "Maybe he ought." She studied her sister closely for a minute as her head bent over the computer keyboard while she typed in a code and glanced up at the screen. The abbreviations were Greek to Abby, but they seemed to make sense to Melly.

"What are you doing?"

"Herd records. We're getting ready to cull cattle, you know. Any cows that don't come up to par are going to be sold off, especially if they aren't producing enough calves or if the ones they're producing aren't good enough or if they're old…."

"Slavery," Abby burst out. "Horrible!"

Melly laughed merrily. "Yes, Cade was telling me what you thought about veal smothered in onions."

"That's really horrible," she muttered. "Poor little

thing, all cold and half-frozen and its mama turned her back on it, and Cade talks about eating it...."

"Life goes on, darling," Melly reminded her, "and a cattle ranch is no place for sentiment. I can't just see you owning one—you'd make pets of all the cattle and become a vegetarian."

"Hmm," Abby said, frowning thoughtfully, "I wonder if Cade's ever thought of that?"

"I don't know," came the amused reply, "but if I were you, I'd wait until way after roundup to ask him!"

Abby laughed. "You may have a point."

Melly murmured something, but her mind went quickly back to the computer and her work. Abby, curious, asked questions and Melly told her about the computer network between Cade's ranches, and the capacity of the computer for storing information about the cattle. There was even a videocassette setup so that Cade could sell cattle to people who had never been to the ranch to see them—they could buy from the tape. He could buy the same way, by watching film of a bull he was interested in, for example. It was a far cry from the old days of ranching when ranchers kept written records and went crazy trying to keep up with thousands of head of cattle. Abby was fascinated by the computer and the rapidity of its operation. But after a few minutes the phone started ringing and didn't stop, and Abby wandered off to watch the snow.

"Isn't Cade going to come in and eat?" Melly asked as Calla set a platter of ham and bread and condiments on the table, along with a plate of homemade French fries.

"Nope." The older woman sighed. "Said to pack him a sandwich and a thermos of coffee and he'd run up to the house to get it." She nodded toward a sack and a thermos on the buffet.

"Is he coming right up?" Abby asked.

"Any minute."

"I'll carry it out," Abby volunteered, and grabbed it up, hurrying toward the front door. She only paused long enough to tug on galoshes and her thick cloth coat, and rushed out onto the porch as she heard a pickup skid up to the house and stop.

Cade was sitting in the cab when she crunched her way through the blowing snow to the truck. He threw open the passenger door.

"Thanks, honey," he said, taking the sack and thermos from her and placing them on the seat beside him. "Get in out of the snow."

She started to close the truck door, but he shook his head. "In here," he corrected. "With me."

Something about the way he said it made her pulse

pound, and she shook herself mentally. She was reading things into his deep voice, that was all.

"Hank said you were turning the air blue. Is this new snow your fault?" Abby asked him with humor in her pale brown eyes.

He returned the smile and there was a light in his eyes she hadn't noticed before. "I reckon," he murmured, watching the color come and go in her flushed face. "Feel better this morning?"

"Yes, thank you," she said softly.

He reached out a big hand and held it, palm up.

She hesitated for an instant before she reached out her own cold, slender hand and put it gingerly into his. The hard fingers closed softly around it and squeezed.

"This is how it's going to be from now on," he said, his voice deep and quiet, the two of them isolated in the cold cab while feathery snow fell onto the windshield, the hood, the landscape. "I'll ask, I won't take."

She looked into his eyes and felt, for a second, the old magic of electricity between them. "That goes against the grain, I'll bet," she said.

"I'm used to taking," he replied. "But I can get used to asking, I suppose. How about you?"

She looked down at his big hand swallowing hers, liking the warmth and strength of it even while something in the back of her mind rebelled at that strength. "I don't know," she said honestly.

"What frightens you most?" he asked.

"Your strength," she said, without taking time to think, and her eyes came up to his.

He nodded, and not by a flicker of an eyelash did he betray any emotion beyond curiosity. "And if I let you make all the moves?" he asked quietly. "If I let you come close or touch or hold, instead of moving in on you?"

The thought fascinated her. That showed in her unblinking gaze, in the slight tilt of her head.

"Therapy, Cade?" she asked in a soft, steady tone.

"Whatever name you want to call it." He opened his hand so that she could leave hers there or remove it, as she wished. It was more than a gesture—it was a statement.

She smiled slowly. "Such power might go to my head," she said with a tentative laugh. "Suppose I decided to have my way with you?" she added, finding that she could treat the matter lightly for the moment.

He cocked an eyebrow and looked stern. "Don't start getting any ideas about me. I'm not easy. None of you wild city girls are going to come out here and lure me into any haystacks."

She let her fingers curl into his and hold them. "It's a long shot," she said after a minute.

"My grandfather won this ranch in a poker game in Cheyenne," he remarked. "I guess it's in my blood to take long shots."

"Won't it interfere with your private life?" she added, hoping her question wouldn't sound as if she were fishing.

He studied her closely for a minute before he replied. "I thought you knew that I don't have affairs."

She almost jumped at the quiet intensity of his eyes. "I...never really thought about it," she lied.

"I've had women," he said, "but nothing permanent, nothing lasting. There's no private life for you to interfere with."

She was suddenly fiercely glad of that, although she didn't know how to tell him. "It's not going to be very easy," she confessed shyly. "I've never been forward, even before this happened."

"I know," he murmured, smiling down at her. "I could sit here and look at you all day," he said after a minute, "but it wouldn't get the work done," he added ruefully.

"I could come and help you," she volunteered, wondering at her sudden reluctance to leave him.

"It's too cold, honey," he said. His eyes wandered over her soft, flushed face. "Feel like kissing me?"

Her heart jumped. She felt a new kind of excitement

at the thought of it. "I thought you weren't easy," she challenged as she slid hesitantly toward him.

Surprise registered in his eyes, but only for a second. "Well, only with some girls," he corrected, smiling wickedly. "Come on, hurry up, I've got calves to deliver."

"Young Dr. McLaren," she murmured, looking up at him from close range, seeing new lines in his face, fatigue in his dark eyes. There were a few silver hairs over his temples and she touched them with unsteady fingers. "You're going gray, Cade."

"I got those because of you, when you were in your early teens," he reminded her. "Hanging off saddles trying to do trick riding, falling into the rapids out of a rickety canoe, flying over fences trying to ride Donavan's broncs...my God, you were a handful!"

"Well, Melly and I didn't have a mama," she reminded him, "and Dad was in poor health from the time we got in grammar school on. If it hadn't been for you and Calla and the cowboys, I guess Melly and I wouldn't have made it."

"Stop that," he growled. "And don't make me out to be an old man. I'm just fourteen years older than you, and I never did feel like a relative."

She put her fingers against his warm lips and felt their involuntary pursing with a tingle of satisfaction. "I didn't mean it that way." She looked into his dark eyes with a thrill of pure pleasure. "Can I really kiss you?"

His chest seemed to rise and fall with unusual rapidity; his nostrils flared under heavy breaths. "Do you want to?"

"I...I want to." She reached around his neck to pull his dark head down to hers, letting her fingers savor the thick coolness of his hair. Her eyes fell to his hard lips and she noticed that they didn't part when hers touched them, as if he were keeping himself on a tight rein to prevent the kiss from becoming intimate.

She liked the warmth of his mouth under hers, and she liked the faint rasp of his cheek where her nose rubbed against it as she pressed harder against his lips. His breath was even harder now but he wasn't moving a muscle. With a quiet, trusting sigh she eased away from him and looked up.

His face was rigid, his eyes blazing back at her. "Okay?" she asked uncertainly, needing reassurance.

A faint smile softened his expression. "Okay."

She frowned slightly, studying his set lips. "You kept your mouth closed, though," she said absently.

"I don't think we need to go that far that fast, baby," he said quietly.

He moved away from her, his hand going to the ignition to start the truck and let it idle. "It's like learning to walk. You have to do it one step at a time."

"That was a nice step," she told him with a smile.

"I thought so myself." He raised his chin and his eyes were all arrogance. "Are you going to need an engraved invitation every time from now on?"

"I guess I could sneak up on your blind side," she confessed with a grin. "Or drag you off into dark corners. Maybe if I watch Melly and Jerry I'll get some new ideas. She said he pushed her into a hay stall and fell on her."

He burst out laughing, and she found that she could laugh, too—a far cry from her first reaction when Melly had confessed it.

"That sounds like Jerry," he said after a minute. His eyes searched hers. "It's what I'd have done, once."

The smile faded, and she felt a deep sadness for what might have been if she hadn't been so crazy to go to New York and break into modeling.

"In a hay stall?" she teased halfheartedly.

"Anywhere. As long as it was with you, and I could feel you...all of you...under my body."

She turned away from the hunger in his eyes with a tiny little sound, and he hit the steering wheel with his hand and stared blindly out the windshield, cursing under his breath.

"I'm sorry," he ground out. "That was a damned stupid thing to say…!"

"Don't handle me with kid gloves," she said, looking back at him. "Melly was right, and so were you. I can't run away from the memory of the attack, and I can't run away from life. I'm going to have to learn to deal with… relationships, physical relationships." Her eyes met his bravely. "Help me."

"I've already told you that I will."

She studied the worn mat on the floorboard. "And don't get angry when I react…predictably."

"Like just now?" he asked, and managed a smile.

She nodded, smiling back. "Like just now." Her eyes searched his, looking for reassurance. "It frightens me, still, the…the weight of a man's body," she whispered shakily, and only realized much later that she'd confessed that to no one else.

"In that case," he said gently, "I'll have to let you push me down in the hay, won't I?"

Tears misted in her eyes. "Oh, Cade…"

"Will you get out of my truck?" he asked pleasantly, preventing her, probably intentionally, from showing any gratitude. "I think I did mention about a half hour ago that I was in a flaming hurry."

"Some hurry," she scoffed. "If you were really in a

hurry," she added, nodding toward the snow, "you'd walk."

"That's an idea. But I left my snowshoes in the attic. Out! Go let Melly show you how to work the computer. You do realize that somebody's going to have to do her job while she's on her honeymoon?"

"Me? But, Cade, I don't know anything about computers...."

"What a great time for you to learn," he advised. He searched her flushed face, seeing a new purpose in it, a slackening of the fear, and he nodded. "Don't rush off to New York after the wedding. Stay with me."

"I'd like to stay with you," she said in a soft, gentle tone as she looked into his dark eyes.

He held her gaze for a long, warm moment before he averted his eyes to the gearshift. "Now I'm going," he said firmly. "Either you skedaddle or you come with me."

"I'd like to come with you," she said with a sigh, "but I'd just get in the way, wouldn't I?"

"Sure," he said with a flash of white teeth. Then his eyes narrowed. "Do you want to come, really? Because I'm going to let you, and to hell with getting in the way, if you say yes."

She took a deep, slow breath, and shrugged. "Better

not, I suppose," she said regretfully. "Melly's wedding dress…I have to get started."

"Okay. How about fabric?"

"Calla bought it for me. It's just a matter of deciding what to use," she told him. "Don't get sick, okay?"

He lifted an eyebrow. "Why? Afraid you'd have to nurse me?"

"I'd stay up all night for weeks if you needed me. Don't be silly," she chided, reaching for the door handle.

"Tell Calla not to keep supper, honey, it's going to be another long night."

She nodded as she held the door ajar. "Want me to bring your supper down to you?"

He smiled. "On your snowshoes? Better not, it's damned cold out here. I'll have a bite later. See you."

"See you."

She closed the door and watched him drive away with wistful eyes. She already regretted not going with him, but she didn't wait around to wonder why.

That night, she and Melly chose the fabric from the yards and yards of it that Calla had tucked away in the cedar chest.

"Isn't it strange that I'm getting married first?" Melly asked as they studied the pattern. "I always thought it would be you."

"Me and who?" Abby laughed.

"Cade, of course."

Abby caught her breath. "He never felt that way."

"Oh, you poor blind thing," Melly said softly. "He used to watch you like a man watching a rainbow. Sometimes his hands would tremble when he was helping you onto a horse or opening a door for you, and you never even noticed, did you?"

Abby's pale brown eyes widened helplessly. "Cade?"

"Cade." Melly sat back in her chair and sighed. "He was head over heels about you when you left here. He roared around for two weeks after you were gone, making the men nervous, driving the rest of us up walls. He'd sit by the fire at night and just stare straight ahead. I've never seen a man grieve like that over a woman. And you didn't even know."

Abby's eyes closed in pain. If she'd known that, career or no career, she would have come running back to Montana on her bare feet if she'd had to. "I didn't have any idea. If I'd known that, I never would have left here. Never!" she burst out.

Melly caught her breath at the passion that flared up in her sister's eyes. "You loved him?"

"Deathlessly." Her eyes closed, then opened again, misty with tears. "I'll die loving him."

"Abby!"

She took a steadying breath and slumped. "Four years.

Four long years, and a nightmare at the end of it. And if I'd stayed here... Why didn't he tell me?"

"I suppose he thought he was doing the best thing for you," Melly said gently. "You were so excited about a career in modeling."

"I thought at the time that it would be better to moon over Cade at a distance instead of going to seed while I waited in vain for him to notice me again," Abby said miserably.

"Again?"

Darn Melly's quick mind. "Just never you mind. Let's go over this pattern."

"He still cares about you," Melly murmured.

"In a different way, though."

"That could change," came the soft reply, "if you want it to."

"If only Cade didn't have such a soft spot for stray things," Abby said, her eyes wistful. "I never know what he really feels—I never have. He was sorry for me when I was a kid and, in a way, he still is. I don't want a man who pities me, Melly."

"How do you know that Cade does? You're a lovely woman."

"A woman with a very big problem," Abby reminded her, "and Cade goes out of his way to help people, you know that. We go back a long way and he's fond of me.

How can I be sure that what he feels isn't just compassion, Melly?"

"Give it time and find out."

"That," she said with a sigh, "is sage advice. By the way, you're going to have to teach me how to do your job, because he's already maneuvered me into replacing you while you're on your honeymoon."

"Oh, he has, has he?" Melly pursed her lips and her eyes laughed. "That isn't something he'd do if he really felt sorry for you!" she assured her sister.

"Now cut that out! Here, tell me if you like the dress better with a long train or a short one...."

And for the rest of the night, they concentrated on the wedding gown.

8

In the days that followed, Abby learned more about the logistics of roundup on Painted Ridge than she wanted to. The whole ranch suddenly revolved around preparations for it. There were supplies to get in, men to hire and add to the weekly payroll. And at the head of it all was Cade, mapping out strategy, tossing out orders as he organized everything from the butane for the torches they used to heat the branding irons to ear tags. At the same time, he was involved with roundup on the other two ranches he had interests in, and in between were cattle auctions, board meetings and a rushed trip to New

York to discuss his corporation's plans to buy a feedlot in Oklahoma.

Abby couldn't help thinking how sexy Cade looked in his pale gray suit with matching boots and Stetson when he came downstairs with his suitcase in his hand.

"Well, I guess I'm ready," he grumbled, heading toward the front door. Hank was waiting impatiently outside in the truck.

"You really need something snazzier than a pickup truck to ride to the airport in," Abby remarked with a smile. "You look very sophisticated."

He glanced at her, his eyes clearly approving her jeans and pale T-shirt. "I'd rather be wearing what you've got on."

"You'd sure look funny in it," she murmured wickedly.

He chuckled softly. "I guess I would. Oh, damn, I hate these dress-up things, and I hate to ride around the country on airplanes with other people at the controls."

"If you fly like you drive——" she began.

"Cut that out," he said darkly. He checked his watch. "Stay off the horses until I get back, too. I told Hank to make sure you do."

Her eyes flashed, and she drew herself up to her full height, lifting her shoulders proudly. "I'm not a child."

His gaze went pointedly to the high, firm thrust of

her breasts and he smiled faintly. "No, ma'am, you sure aren't."

"Cade Alexander McLaren!" she gasped.

He chuckled at her red face. "Well, you can't blame a man for noticing things, honey."

"Hank's leaning on the horn," she murmured, glancing nervously toward the door.

"Let him lean on it. Or stand on it. Hank was born in a hurry." He studied her for a long moment. "I'll let you kiss me goodbye if you ask me nice."

She colored even more. "Why do I always have to do all the kissing?" she asked.

"Because you might not like the way I do it," he said.

"Are you sure?" Her heart pounded wildly and she felt her breath coming hard and fast when she saw the expression that washed over his dark face. He dropped the suitcase with a hard thud and strode right for her.

Before she even had time to decide whether to run or duck, he had her by the waist. He lifted her completely off the floor so that she was on a level with his glittering dark eyes, and she noticed that he was breathing as raggedly as she was.

"Let's see, Abby," he said quietly, and tilted his head.

His mouth bit softly at hers in brief, rough kisses that made her blood run hot. Her hands tangled in his dark hair as she tried to hold his mouth over hers, hungry to feel the full pressure of it. Her body felt taut as a cord and she opened her lips to the coaxing play of his. It seemed to be just what he was waiting for, because he took possession then, and she felt his tongue go into her mouth in an intimacy they'd shared only once before.

She caught a sharp breath, but she didn't protest. Not even when he eased her sensuously down and held her close against his taut body. He forced her mouth open farther, tasting it with growing hunger, increasing the pressure until she moaned with sudden pleasure.

One big hand released her and slid up her side to her breast. It hesitated for an instant, and then it engulfed her, his thumb coaxing a helpless response even through two layers of fabric. She moaned again.

He lifted his mouth, breathing roughly, and studied her rapt face. "Look, Abby," he whispered, glancing down to the darkness of his hand where her body was frankly showing its response to his touch. "See how you react to me...."

"Don't," she whispered achingly, pushing his hand away even as she leaned her head against his vest while she caught her breath. Her heartbeat was still rapid, and she felt flushed with embarrassment.

His forehead nuzzled against her soft blond hair. "Don't be shy with me," he said quietly. "I know you wouldn't let another man touch you like this. I don't think less of you for it."

Tears welled in her eyes. He was the most tender man she'd ever known; he had a way of making the most traumatic things seem easy, uncomplicated.

"It shocked me a little," she whispered unsteadily.

"I like the way you kiss me when you're shocked," he mused with a faint smile when he lifted his head.

Her eyes darkened as she looked up at him, unafraid. "I tasted you," she whispered shakily.

His hands tautened like steel around her upper arms and his face seemed to harden even as she watched. "Don't say things like that to me," he said unsteadily. "You don't realize the effect it has, and I'm already late for the airport."

She looked down at his broad chest. "Sorry. Will you be gone long?"

His hands contracted and then released her. "A couple days. I can't spare them, but I don't want the man to change his mind about that feedlot. The corporation needs it."

She nodded, glancing up at his set features. "I'll do my best not to foul up your bookkeeping while you're gone."

"Melly won't let you," he replied. He took a long breath and moved back to the suitcase, swinging it up easily. "Besides, all the bookkeeping we do here is payroll, and you'll be doing cattle records, not that. Take care, honey."

"You, too," she said softly, missing him already. He would take the color away when he left. It had been that way all her adult life.

Hank was blowing the horn again, and Cade shook his head. "He's afraid the plane will leave me behind," he said amusedly. "I chewed him out this morning for forgetting to put in a supply order. He feels safer when I'm a state or two away."

"Don't they all," she murmured with a wicked grin.

He tilted the Stetson low over his eyes. "Bye. Don't kiss any other boys while I'm gone, okay?"

"What's the matter, afraid I might make comparisons?" She laughed.

"How did you know?" He winked at her and walked down the steps without looking back, yelling at Hank to stop wearing out his best horn.

Abby spent her time with Melly, learning how to use the relevant computer programs. It gave the sisters time to talk and get reacquainted, and it gave Abby something to occupy her mind.

Even when Cade returned, she hardly saw him. He was up with the dawn and out past dark, getting every-thing ready for the roundup and the massive task of moving the cattle up to summer pasture. By the end of the week, Abby could pick out a single registered bull from the herd records, print out the information required and do it without losing a single punctuation mark.

Meanwhile, Cade, in his spare time, dictated one letter after another to Melly and answered the flood of phone calls that never seemed to stop. The next week, Cade was called out from signing letters at his desk by one of the men when his prize-winning bull keeled over in the barn. He went stalking out the door with Abby at his heels. Melly and Jerry had gone out just after breakfast, and Abby was trying to keep up with Cade's machine-gun dictation and quick temper all alone.

Abby followed him outside with a typed letter in her hand as he took the reins of his black gelding from one of the men and started to swing into the saddle.

"Cade, could you sign this letter before you go?" she called. "It's about that new hay baler."

"Oh, hell, I forgot," he muttered. "Hand it here, honey."

He propped it against the saddle and slashed his name in a bold scrawl across the bottom of it. "I'll see if—"

"Mr. McLaren," one of the new cowboys interrupted, reining up beside them. "Hank said to find you and tell you that the new tractor we just bought is busted. Axle broke clean in half on us while we were planting over in the bottoms. Hank says you want we should call that feller who sold it to us and see if it's still under warranty. The other tractor's still down, you know. Billy's trying to fix it, and we loaned three out to Mr. Hastings and let Jones have one...."

"Oh, good God," Cade muttered angrily. "All right, tell Hank to check with the salesman and see how long it will take to get a replacement."

"Yes, sir," the cowboy agreed politely. "And the hardware wants to know if you'll want any more butane."

Cade looked positively hunted. "They can wait until I get through looking at my sick bull, can't they?" he asked the man. "Damn it, son, that bull cost me a quarter of a million dollars, and the insurance won't heal my heart if he dies!" He glowered at the cowboy. "Tell Jerry to take care of it."

"Uh, he's kind of busy," the young cowboy muttered, avoiding Cade's eyes.

"Doing what?" came the terse reply.

"Uh, he and Miss Melly are down at their house, her house, checking paint swatches..."

Cade's cheeks colored darkly with temper. "You get down there and tell Jerry I said he can stop that kind of thing. I pay him to run this damned ranch, not to go around checking paint swatches on my time!"

"Yes, sir, Mr. McLaren!" He saluted and rode quickly away.

Abby was watching Cade with twinkling eyes. It was something else to watch him delegate. He did it well, and his temper mostly amused the men because it was never malicious.

He turned, catching that gleam in her eyes, and cocked an eyebrow at her from under the wide-brimmed hat. "Something tickle your fancy, Miss Shane?"

"You," she admitted quietly. "I just stand in awe of you, Mr. McLaren."

He chuckled softly. "And you thought a rancher's life was all petting cattle, I suppose?"

"I grew up here," she reminded him. "But I never realized just how much work it was until I started helping Melly. How do you stand it, Cade?"

"I'm used to it." He was holding the reins in one hand, but he reached out and drew his fingers down her cheek. "I love it. The way you love the glitter of your own work, I imagine, miss model."

"I wish you wouldn't make fun of what I do," she said sadly, searching his dark eyes. "I've worked very hard to get where I am. And modeling is much more than painting on a pretty face and smiling."

He withdrew his hand and lit a cigarette. "It must seem pretty tame to you out here."

"Tame?" Her eyes widened. "Are you kidding?"

He frowned thoughtfully, and his searching eyes

caught hers. They stared at each other quietly, while the silence grew tense and electric around them, and her lips parted under a wild rush of breath.

His breath was coming hard, too. He dropped the reins as if he couldn't help himself and moved close, so that she could feel the heat of his body and the smell of the spicy cologne that clung to him. Her eyes went to his mouth and she wanted it so much that she ached with the wanting.

His steely fingers bit into her waist. "Want to kiss me, Abby Shane?" he asked roughly.

"Very much," she whispered, unembarrassed and un-intimidated as she looked into his darkening eyes. "Lift me up, please…"

She felt his hands contract, and she seemed to float within reach of that chiseled mouth. Her hands slid around his neck to the back of his head and she eased her mouth onto his, letting her lips part softly as they touched him.

His head tilted and his mouth opened under hers with a heavy sigh. He didn't insist, but she could sense his own growing hunger, and she fed it. Her lips nibbled softly at his, her tongue eased out to trace the firm line of his upper lip. And the reaction she got was startling.

All at once, she was swept against the long hard line of his body and he was kissing her, violently. His mouth demanded in a kiss so sensuous she moaned at the sensations it aroused. She felt his tongue in her mouth, against her lips. A shudder worked its way down her body and fires blazed up in her blood.

"No," she protested when he tried to lift his dark head. She trembled in his arms as she clung. "Cade, please, just once more...."

She heard the ragged breath he took before his mouth crushed back against hers, warm and rough and forceful for an instant. Then she was back on her feet again and leaning heavily against him, his lips brushing her forehead.

"What do you want from me, Abby?" he ground out.

Your love, she thought miserably. *I want you to love me as fiercely as I love you.* "I'm sorry," she muttered against his shirt front. "I like kissing you."

He was trying to get his breath back, or at least it sounded that way. "I like kissing you, too. But I'm a man, not a boy. Kissing isn't enough for me anymore."

Her fingers curled against his shirt, and she could feel the thick hair on his chest through it. She wanted to open his shirt and touch him there. Involuntarily, her fingers moved across his chest and he shuddered.

"No, baby," he said softly. He stilled her hands, and she wondered dizzily what had happened to the cigarette he'd been holding. Her eyes found it, smoking away in the dirt, where he must have flung it.

She sighed wearily, loving the comforting feel of his hands at her back. She didn't want to move away from him, but it was obvious that he wasn't going to let her get any closer.

"I forgot," she murmured.

"What?"

She drew away and grinned, although her heart was aching. "That you're wary of us wild city girls," she said, her light brown eyes sparkling in the pale frame of her hair. "You needn't worry, Cade, I'm not quite strong enough to wrestle you down in a haystack."

Her quip should have made him smile, but it didn't. He searched her face for a long time, touching every curve and line of it with his eyes. "I think we both need to remember that you're here to recuperate, Abby," he said after a minute. "This is temporary. You've got a successful career waiting for you in New York, but this is my world." He nodded toward the distant hills, dotted with red-coated, white-faced Herefords. "I don't have time for casual flings, even if I believed in them."

She drew away from him as if she'd been burned. "Excuse me for throwing myself at you...."

"Stop it." His fingers caught her upper arms and held her in front of him when she would have moved away. "A few kisses aren't going to hurt either of us. I just want you to understand the limits. You're very vulnerable right now, Abby. You could easily make a decision that you'd regret for the rest of your life."

He was speaking in riddles, and she stared up at him with wounded eyes, because it sounded as if he were gently rejecting her. Well, she should be used to it, shouldn't she? And if he could be adult about it, so could she. Damn her breaking heart, she'd never let him see it!

Keep it light, girl, she told herself, keep your pride, at least. She managed a bright smile. "Sensible Cade," she murmured. "Don't worry, I promise not to rip your clothes off."

He tried to smother a chuckle and failed. "That would be one for the books, in several ways." He touched her lips with a lazy finger. "Abby, I've never undressed in front of a woman."

She could feel her own surprise coloring her cheeks. "Never?" she burst out.

"Look who's shocked," he mused. "Have you ever stripped for a man?"

"For you, once," she reminded him, avoiding his suddenly explosive gaze. "It was an accident, of course, I had no idea you were anywhere near the ranch that night."

"I know that." A rough sound broke from his throat, as if an unwanted memory was plaguing him. "I'd better go see about that bull. We'll be moving cattle into the pens today. If that call I'm expecting from California comes, take the number and call Hank on the radio. He'll find me."

"Yes, boss," she said smartly.

He looked down at her with narrowed eyes. "How did you get so short?"

"I'm wearing flat-heeled shoes," she said. "And you tower over everybody."

He grinned. "Keeps the men intimidated."

"Your temper's enough to do that." She laughed. "Don't work yourself into a stupor."

"Work keeps my mind off other things," he returned, letting his eyes run boldly up and down her body. "If it's pretty tomorrow, I'll take you on a picnic."

Her whole face brightened and she smiled so sweetly that his eyes froze on her and she couldn't seem to move away.

"Down by the river?" she asked hopefully.

"You love those damned cottonwoods and pines, don't you?" he asked.

"It's spring," she reminded him. "I love the color of the cottonwoods when they're just budding out. The softest kind of green, and the grass is just beginning to get lush…."

"Well, I need to check the fences down there," he mused.

"You work all the time," she grumbled. "You can't even go on a picnic without combining it with business!"

"The ranch isn't my business, Abby. It's my life," he said quietly.

She sighed angrily. "Don't I know it? You're married to it!"

His dark eyes narrowed. "What else have I got?" he demanded.

The question startled her. She watched him swing gracefully into the saddle. The rich leather creaked under his formidable weight as he settled himself and gripped the reins.

"Don't forget about that California call," he said. "And keep close to the house. I don't know some of these new men except by reputation."

"Cowboys are mostly polite and courteous," she reminded him.

"And some of them aren't." He stared down at her hard. "I'd kill a man who tried to hurt you while you were on my land. You keep that in mind."

He wheeled the big horse and went cantering away, leaving Abby standing in the shade of the trees, staring after him. She hadn't needed to ask if he meant that threat. She knew him too well. In the old days, when he was younger and much more hot-tempered, she'd seen him give "object lessons" to cowboys who thought they could push him. He was quick on his feet, and he knew how to handle himself in a fight. The men might grin when he blustered around in a temper over ranch problems, but they knew just the same that there was a line nobody crossed with him.

She wrapped her arms around herself and walked back into the house. It was only then that she realized how vague the memory of the attack was becoming. Being here, away from the city, had given her new perspective, healed the mental wounds. She'd be more careful in the future, but she wouldn't let that one bad experience ruin her life. Her mind kept going back to what Cade had said, about giving the would-be rapist rights over her. Trust him to know the right thing to say.

She wandered back into the den and sat down at the computer. She was glad Cade didn't have a ranch office as such, like many cattlemen did. The den was comfortable and informal, and she liked its homey atmosphere.

The sudden jangling of the phone made her jump, but she recovered quickly and reached for it.

"McLaren Ranch office," she said automatically.

"Abby Shane, please," came a pleasant female voice in reply.

"This is she."

There was a tinkling laugh. "Well, I've run you down

at last. This is Jessica Dane, Abby. Has Melly mentioned me to you?"

The boutique owner! Abby's pale brown eyes glittered with excitement. "Heavens, yes!" she returned, bubbling over. "I was afraid she'd got it wrong and you weren't really interested."

"I was, I am, but I couldn't catch you in your apartment." Jessica laughed. "Now I've got you trapped. Listen, I own a little boutique over the border from you in Sheridan, Wyoming. I'm never going to be able to compete with Saks, you understand, but I have a good mailorder business in addition to a thriving shop."

"Yes, I've heard all about your success from Melly," Abby said. "She thinks you carry the prettiest leisure clothes short of New York."

"And that's why I'm bothering you," the other woman replied. "Those dresses you designed for Melly are just what I'm looking for to add to my spring and summer line. They're simple and elegant, they wouldn't cost a fortune to make and my customers would eat them up."

"Do you mean it?" Abby burst out.

"Of course I mean it. We could work something out, if you're interested. I know you make a lot modeling—I broke out of that rat race ten years ago and risked everything to open this shop. Now I'm making just as much as I did in New York, but my feet don't hurt so much anymore," she added with laughter in her voice.

"You were a model? Then you know how it is, don't you?" she asked.

Jessica laughed. "Oh, yes, I know very well. I spent half my time trying to stay out of trouble, and I imagine it's even worse now."

"I don't just go to the parties," Abby confessed, "and I keep to myself. But then, too, I'm not in that top ten percent. Frankly, I'm sick of it all. I can't think of anything I love more than designing...."

"Then why not do some work for me?" Jessica pleaded. "At least think about it. I know we could come to an arrangement. You could come down here and look over my business, and I could show you what I have in mind."

"I'd like that," Abby said. "I have commitments lined up for the next few months, but come late September, I'm a free agent. Could I let you know then?"

"Fine! Meanwhile, give me your address in New York and I'll send you some of my catalogs." There was a smile in the woman's voice. "Maybe they'll tempt you."

"I'm already tempted." Abby sighed.

"Good. You'll be easy to convince." She laughed. "Here, take down my number and call me the minute you make up your mind." She dictated the digits while

Abby jotted them on her calendar. "By the way, Abby, are you going to be at Melly's wedding?"

"Yes. I designed her wedding dress."

"Fantastic! I'm invited, too, so we'll get a chance to meet then. We'll go off in a corner and I'll describe some of the new designs I'm looking for. How about that?"

"I can hardly wait," Abby said genuinely. "Jessica, I can't tell you how much I appreciate the offer."

"I'm the one who ought to do the thanking. You've got great potential, honey. And believe me, in the long run, you'll make as much designing for the boutique as you will trudging all over New York. And you can do it at your own pace, too."

"I hope I'm not dreaming all this. Thanks again, Jessica. I'll look forward to seeing you at the wedding."

"Me, too, honey. Have a nice day. Enjoyed it!"

"So did I!" Abby laughed. She hung up and stared at the receiver in astonishment. It was like the answer to a prayer. She could give up the long hours and the stress and do what she loved best. She could even come home to Montana!

For one insane moment, she thought about going out to find Cade, to tell him. Maybe it would show him that she wanted to give up all the glitter he thought she couldn't do without. But as soon as the thought came, she shut it out. He'd just blow up if she interrupted him.

And why should he care if she came home? He was letting her stay on his ranch to be near Melly and get herself back together. He might want her—why not?—she was an attractive woman. But wanting wasn't loving, and he was the world's most determined bachelor. Marriage wasn't in his vocabulary—he'd said as much. The ranch was his woman.

Abby sighed and pulled out the herd records she was working on. Anyway, it was nice to have a choice. She could look forward to talking to Jessica about her boutique, and it would pass the time.

The day was a long one, even after Melly came back to help her catch up with the work.

"I'm just tickled pink about Jessica's offer," Melly confided as she watched Abby seal a letter. "Are you going to do it?"

"I don't know," Abby said honestly. "I'd love to come home. But I don't know if I could bear it."

"The loneliness, you mean?"

"Being so close to Cade and so far away from him, all at once," Abby replied. Her eyes showed the wound of loving hopelessly. "I'd rather be hundreds of miles away than practically next door, Melly. If I can't have him, I'd just as soon not have to see him at all. It hurts too much."

"For someone who doesn't care, he sure kisses you a lot lately."

"He said it wouldn't hurt either one of us," she said bitterly. "But he reminded me all the same that I'm here to get over the attack, and I've got a career to go back to. You'd think he couldn't wait to get me off the place."

"Has it ever occurred to you that he might want you gone for the same reason you're going?" Melly asked quietly. "I get the idea that he doesn't think you could give up modeling."

"It's not that at all," Abby protested. "This ranch is his whole life. He's always talking about how stupid people are to get married, and that he never will. And almost in the same breath, he'll swear that he doesn't believe in affairs. I don't know what to make of him."

Melly threw up her hands. "I give up. You're as dense as he is. Okay, show me these records and I'll help you catch up. When are you supposed to get back to Jessica, by the way?"

"She's coming to the wedding, and we're going to talk. What does she look like?"

Melly grinned. "Wait and see. It'll be a revelation to you. Now, this is where we need to start taking off cattle...."

They worked steadily until supper. Melly went out with Jerry to a friend's house. Abby had just finished changing her clothes and was telling a persistent caller for the fourth time in as many hours that Cade was still out when he came slamming angrily in the door. His face was rigid, his lips compressed. He was still wearing his chaps and the brim of his wide hat was crushed in one hand.

"Well, don't just stand there, for God's sake, hang that thing up and get the liniment," he muttered, hobbling up the stairs to his room.

"What happened?" she called after him, absently hanging up on the caller before she thought.

"Cow fell on me," he growled. "Hurry up, damn it!" He went into his bedroom and slammed the door.

Abby rushed into the kitchen to get the liniment. Calla got it out of the cabinet for her.

"Bull again, huh?" old Jeb asked from the doorway as he entered the kitchen.

"He said it was a cow," Abby volunteered.

"Told him he ought to let the younger boys wrestle them things." Jeb nodded. "Yep, I told him, but he wouldn't listen. He's got more broke bones and scars than any man I ever knowed. Lot of them were from his rodeo days, but he's got more being bullheaded and doing jobs he's too brittle for."

"He never listens," Calla agreed, nodding her head. "Why, I remember one time…"

She was still going strong when Abby left the two

of them recalling other incidents of Cade's intentional deafness.

He had his shirt off when she went into the bedroom. She closed the door behind her, hesitating. The last time she'd been in this particular room was that night when he'd carried her in from the swimming pool in nothing but her damp jeans. It brought back bittersweet memories.

"Open the door if you're nervous being alone with me," he growled, rubbing his shoulder.

"Sorry," she murmured, trying not to appear too interested in his naked chest. Without his shirt, he was the sexiest thing she'd ever seen, bronzed and muscular, with a thick wedge of dark, curling hair narrowing down to his flat stomach.

She uncapped the bottle of liniment and wrinkled her nose. "My gosh, you'd better make your men sign affidavits that they won't quit if I put this stuff on you."

"Shut up and rub," he grumbled, indicating the smooth flesh of his shoulder.

She poured liniment in her palm and began to apply it. Her fingers tingled at the feel of his flesh under them. "How did a cow manage to fall on you?"

"It's a long story." He lit a cigarette while she massaged the aching limb, wincing as she went over a tender spot.

"Should you smoke?" she murmured. "We might both blow up if a spark ignites the fumes...."

He glared at her. His hair was tousled over his broad forehead, over his dark, glittering eyes and heavy brows, and he looked impossibly masculine.

"Funny girl," he mocked.

"Laughing beats crying, my papa always used to say," she reminded him.

He turned his eyes away and sighed. "I can't imagine you crying over me."

Abby blinked, wondering at how stupid God had made some men. "That works both ways. I'll bet you're just counting the days until I'm on my way back to New York."

He didn't answer her. He took a long draw from the cigarette and exhaled through pursed lips. "Nightmares fading away, honey?" he asked.

She managed a faint smile. "All but gone, in fact." She shrugged, applying more liniment. "It was so hellish at the time. But looking back, I was lucky. Really lucky. All he did was push me around a little before the bystanders chased him off. It was the idea of what could have happened that was so scary. Gosh, men are strong, Cade."

"Some men," he agreed. He glanced at her.

She looked down as he looked up, and her eyes drowned in his dark, intense stare. Her hands stilled on his arm, and time seemed to go into a standstill around them. She was remembering another night, another time, when she'd lain on this very bed in his arms and experienced her first intimacy with a man. But Cade had changed since then. The easygoing, humorous man she'd once known had been replaced by a far more mature man, a harder man. He'd never been easy to read, but now nothing showed in his expression.

He reached out without warning and caught her around the waist, pulling her down on the bed beside him.

"Cade!" she gasped, too shocked to struggle.

He rolled over on his side and one bare arm arched across her body to hold her there while he leaned on an elbow and watched the expressions cross her face. Her eyes dropped to his chest, and she wanted to touch him so desperately that she closed them to resist the impulse.

"Afraid?" he asked softly.

Her fingers touched his hard face, sensitive to the rough texture of it where he needed a shave, to the feel of his cool, thick hair against them. "I'm with you now. I'm safe."

"Not so safe," he said with a faint smile. "But protected, for what it's worth. Suppose I kiss you half to death and then I can grab a bite to eat and go back out."

"Suppose you just kiss me half to death and forget

about going back out?" she asked, tingling all over as she waited to feel that hard, warm mouth over hers.

"Because," he breathed, fitting his lips slowly, sensitively to hers, "as sure as God made little green apples, Calla's going to be knocking at that door any minute to make sure you're safe. And once I'm fed, she'll want to make sure that I'm too tired to find my way to you."

"Calla wouldn't…"

He kissed her slowly, softly. "Calla would. She's not blind. She sees the way I look at you."

Her heart was racing. "How do you look at me?" she asked.

His mouth smiled mockingly against hers. "Haven't you noticed? Hush. I seem to have waited half my life to get you in bed with me like this…."

She felt his lips nibbling at hers, nudging at them with exquisite slowness, and she relaxed, letting her fingers curl into the hair at his nape.

His tongue teased its way into her mouth and she gasped sharply at the sudden intimacy, even as she felt his body moving sensuously against hers. His mouth softened and became coaxing with expert sureness as his chest scraped abrasively, teasingly across her breasts until the tips hardened. She moaned softly and he lifted his dark head to look into her eyes, searching them quickly. "Was that fear or pleasure?" he whispered.

Her lips parted involuntarily. One slender hand moved from the back of his head down over his chest and stroked him, smoothing the curling dark hair over the warm muscles. "I'm not afraid of you," she said in a breathless whisper, searching his dark eyes.

"I could make you afraid, though, couldn't I, Abby?" he asked, as if it mattered. "You're still very vulnerable."

"You make me sound like a terrified virgin," she replied.

His warm fingers stroked the long, pale hair back from her flushed face. "I'm doing my damndest to remember that you are one," he said softly. "It's hard for a man to make love like this, Abby. To remember not to kiss too hard, not to touch too intimately…."

Her eyes betrayed the surprise she felt at what he was confessing. "Have you been deliberately holding back all this time?" she asked, searching his eyes. "Because you thought you might frighten me?"

He drew in a deep breath, and she felt his chest expand against her breasts. "I couldn't bear to hurt you," he said. His voice was like velvet, deep and dark and softly textured. "I've treated you like porcelain since you've been here. I've damned near worked myself into an early grave to keep away…and tonight, I caved in. I kept remembering how you were this morning, how you begged for my mouth…." His eyes closed, his face tautened. "Oh, God, Abby, what am I going to do about you?" he groaned.

She couldn't even speak. He looked so incredibly vulnerable, as if he were at the end of some imaginary rope. Her fingers stroked his broad shoulders, loving the very texture of his skin. She loved everything about him, every line and curve of him.

"You said this morning," she reminded him softly, "that a few kisses wouldn't hurt either one of us. Didn't you?"

His eyes opened, and they were like black fires. "And that's the whole problem, little one. I want more than a few kisses."

Her eyes fell to his chiseled mouth and she felt her body begin to tremble. "Cade...I don't mind if you touch me," she whispered.

His face moved against hers, his breath sighing out heavily at her ear. "That could be dangerous."

With a surge of fearlessness, she caught one of the hands beside her on the bed and lifted it in hers. Before her courage gave out completely, she took it to her T-shirt and eased it hesitantly over the soft curve of her breast.

She wasn't prepared for the sensations it caused. She drew in a sharp breath and bit her lip to keep from crying out.

Cade lifted his dark head and looked at her, holding her eyes while his hand pressed softly against her. His thumb moved onto the taut peak and teased it. His heart slammed wildly against her with the action, and she could see the desire that was smoldering in his eyes.

"Four years," he said in a hunted tone. "And I haven't forgotten a second of it. I remember the way you looked, the way you cried out when I touched you like this."

"Do you think I don't remember, too?" she asked under her breath. "I lived on it for years, Cade—" Her voice broke, her mouth trembled as she looked up at him.

"So did I," he breathed out shakily. He bent again and let his mouth brush warmly against her parted lips. "You were so young. You still are. Years too young, and a world away from me. Abby, are you wearing anything under this?"

She wished she were more sophisticated. She blushed, feeling her body stiffen as he slid his hand under the hem of the shirt and up to find the answer himself. He caught his breath when he touched her, really touched her, and felt the helpless response of her soft, bare flesh.

Her own hands reached up to stroke the tangled mat of hair on his chest. "I used to dream about touching you like this," she confessed, watching him. "Feeling you…"

"Oh, God!" he ground out, trembling. His free hand cupped her head and held it still while his mouth devoured hers in the static stillness of the room. She felt his other hand moving over her bareness in a long, aching caress that made her arch up and moan with exquisite pleasure.

She protested once, gently, drawing away to breathe.

"Come back here," he murmured, "I'm not through."

"I have to breathe," she whispered as he turned her mouth back to his.

"Breathe me," he murmured against her soft, eager mouth. His hands smoothed over her back, pushing up the shirt as they swept with warm abrasiveness across her soft skin.

"You told me once that you'd never let another man touch you this way. Did you mean it?" he asked roughly.

"I meant it," she whispered, her voice trembling. Her fingers were clinging at the nape of his neck, her body arching to give him freer access to it. "I've never, ever wanted a man…after you."

Breathing like a distance runner, he lifted his head and looked down at her where the shirt was pulled up. His eyes darkened with a hunger she could actually see. Against her pale golden flesh, his hands were as dark as leather.

"You can't imagine how it feels," she breathed, her eyes loving him.

"Being touched?" he asked, lifting his eyes to watch her rapt face.

She shook her head slowly. "Being with you…like this. Oh, Cade, I'd be embarrassed with my own sister, but I love it when you look at me…this way."

His breathing, already ragged, seemed to freeze inside him. His thumbs edged up, dragging softly against the rigid peaks, and she moaned sharply, looking straight into his eyes.

All at once he removed his hands and sat up, his big body shuddering with the force of his heartbeat, his eyes reckless and faintly dangerous.

"That's enough," he said roughly.

But it wasn't for Abby, and without even thinking, she followed him, kneeling just in front of him. She placed her trembling hands on his shoulders and swayed close, brushing her body softly, slowly against his hair-roughened chest, watching her own paleness disappearing into the curling hair with awe.

"Abby," he whispered shakily. His hands moved to her bare back and brought her slowly against him, prolonging the contact, easing her closer with a rhythm that made her tremble all the way to her toes.

His hands caught her hips and ground them against his, and she cried out as she felt the force of his hunger. Trembling, her arms locked around his neck as they fell sideways on the bed. He was beside her, then they shifted, and she felt his full weight evenly distributed along the length of her aching body. She could feel the abrasiveness of his wiry hair against her bareness where they touched, the scent of the liniment becoming as potent as perfume as they kissed wildly, and she wondered at the depth of her own love for him.

Feeling unusually reckless, she began to move. Her hands slid down his back to the base of his spine, and the mouth crushing hers groaned harshly. Against her body, he was warm and hard and she could feel every steely muscle in him. Even all those years ago, it had never been like this between them. The feel of him drowned her in sensation, in need and half-awakened hunger. She wanted to be closer than this, she wanted all the fabric out of the way, she wanted his eyes and his hands to touch her. She shifted restlessly, hungry as she never had been in her life, needing him…!

She touched him with hands that trembled, delighting in the feel of his smooth back muscles. Her fingers moved around to caress the thick mat of hair over his chest, and hesitantly, softly, traced the arrow of hair that ran below his belt. *I love you,* she thought silently. *I love you.…*

Cade's big body contracted as if he'd been shot, and all at once he seemed to come to his senses. He muttered a harsh curse and jerked himself away from Abby, rolling over to lie on his back. His body shuddered with frustrated need; his eyes closed, his jaw tautened. His breath came wildly. Watching him, she felt guilty that she'd let it go so far, because they'd both known all the time that Cade wasn't going over his own limits. Only she'd forgotten, and he hadn't.

Fumbling, she pulled down her shirt with shaking hands and sat up. She took a deep breath and threw her legs over the side of the bed. "Excuse me," she said in a barely audible voice, "I didn't know where the limits were."

"Well, you found out, didn't you?" he shot at her.

She got off the bed and glanced toward him. He was pale, and his face was drawn as he sat up and reached for his shirt.

"I'm sorry," she said unsteadily. "I...I know it's unpleasant for men to...well..."

"Don't turn the knife," he said. His voice was cutting. He dragged a cigarette from his pocket and lit it with unsteady hands. "Damn it, Abby, I can't handle it when you do unexpected things like that! You knocked me right off balance."

She tried to smile. "And after I promised not to try and have my way with you, too."

But he didn't smile. His face grew harder. "You're tearing me inside out," he said, standing. "If I'd thought

I could stand Calla's infernal sarcasm, I would have let her put the liniment on!"

"Next time, I'll remember that," she shot back. She whirled, her eyes simmering with anger. "You started it!" she accused childishly.

His nostrils flared. "Yes, I started it," he said under his breath. "Nothing's changed. Nothing! I touch you, and we both start trembling. It was that way when you were only eighteen, and I carried you in here, wanting you until I was just about out of my mind!" He ran an angry hand through his thick hair and glared up at her. "But I didn't take you then, and I won't take you now. There's no future in it. There never was."

"What an ego," she threw back. "My God, you're full of yourself!"

"That's what you think," he said harshly. "I went through the motions of work all day, but all I could think about was how it felt when we kissed this morning. I remembered your mouth the way a man dying of thirst remembers ice water, soft and sweet. Just how much do you think I can take?"

"Well, don't strain yourself," she said, turning away with a hot ache all the way to her toes. "I'll be gone soon enough."

"I know that," he said. His voice sounded hollow. The mattress creaked as he got to his feet. "Sex is a lousy foundation for a relationship, Abby. We're not going to build on it."

She flushed in spite of herself, but she wouldn't turn and let him see it. "Amen," she agreed. "If you want to call off the picnic tomorrow—"

"No," he said unexpectedly. "No, I don't want to call it off. It will be the last time we have together."

He said that as if it meant forever—that they'd never spend another minute alone—and she wanted to scream and cry and beg him to try and love her just a little. But she clenched her jaw and drew in a steadying breath. "Calla's going to scream about fixing a picnic with those new hands to feed."

"We'll risk it," he said shortly. "Right now, I've got to get back to the barn. That damned bull's improving a little, but I want to see what the vet has to say when he checks him for the night."

"I could pack you a sandwich and some coffee," she offered.

"I don't want anything."

She opened the door and paused. "Especially me?" She laughed shakily and ran down the stairs with tears shimmering in her eyes.

❖ 9 ❖

Calla was cursing a blue streak when Abby walked into the kitchen the next morning at six, wearing a yellow sundress with an elasticized bodice and tiny straps that tied over each shoulder.

"Having to fry bacon and chicken all at once," the housekeeper muttered darkly as she stood over the stove. "Picnics, with all I got to do!" She glared over her shoulder at Abby. "Well, don't just stand there, girl, go set the table!"

"Yes, ma'am," Abby said smartly and curtsied. The dress was one she'd designed herself, and with her loosened blond hair, she looked like something out of a fashion magazine. Calla stopped muttering long enough to give her an approving stare. "Nice," she said after a minute. "You make that yourself?"

"Sure did." She whirled around for Calla's benefit, her skirt flying against her long, smooth legs. "It's cool and comfortable and it doesn't bind. I'll make you one, if you like."

"I can just see me in something like that." The older woman sighed, indicating the dowdy housedress that covered her ample figure. Then her watery blue eyes narrowed. "You watch Cade while you're out there alone with him, you hear me? I ain't blind. I saw how you looked when you came out of his room last night. You make him keep his distance."

Abby felt her cheeks go hot. "Now, Calla…"

"Don't you 'now, Calla' me! I know Cade. He hasn't been the same since you walked through the front door, and it ain't because of the cattle." Her chin lifted. "You and I both know how he feels about weddings, Abigail," she added gently, using the younger woman's full name, as she rarely did except when she was serious. "You're my lamb, and I love him, too, but I don't want you hurt. Melly told me what happened. Don't you jump out of the frying pan into the fire. All you'll find here is heartache."

Abby smothered an urge to hug the concerned old

woman, knowing it wouldn't be welcome. "You're sure about that?" she asked softly.

"He looks at you like a starving man looks at a steak smothered with onions," Calla replied. "But once he's fed, young lady, he's just as likely to find he's lost his taste for steak. You get my meaning? Wanting ain't loving."

"I know that," she said on a wistful sigh.

"Then act accordingly. He's been sticking close to the ranch for quite a while now," Calla added gently. "A hungry man is dangerous."

"I'm a big girl," Abby reminded her. "I can look out for myself—most of the time, anyway."

"And what time you can't, I will," came the fervent promise. "Now go set the table."

"Yes, ma'am," Abby said, grinning.

She carried two place settings of everyday china into the dining room and helped put the food on the table. Cade was uncharacteristically late getting downstairs, and she was almost ready to go up and call him when he walked into the room.

He looked as if he hadn't slept a wink. His dark hair was damp from a shower, and he was wearing a tan patterned Western shirt over rust-colored denims, and polished tan boots. He looked rugged and formidable, and so solemn that he intimidated her.

"I thought you were going to fix fences," Abby remarked.

"I am," he muttered. He sat down at the head of the table and stared at her for a long moment, taking in every line of her face and body. "When you finish your breakfast, go back upstairs and get dressed. I'm not taking you on a picnic half-naked."

The sudden attack left her dumb. She gaped at him with wide, hurt eyes before she put down her napkin and got up from the table in tears. She'd worn the sundress especially for him, to please him.

"Where are you going?" Calla demanded, elbowing in with a platter of scrambled eggs.

"To put on some clothes," Abby said in a subdued tone, and didn't look back.

"Now what have you done?" Calla was demanding, but Abby didn't wait around to hear the answer. She rushed up to her room and slammed the door with tears boiling down her flushed cheeks.

She cried for what seemed hours before she dragged herself up and put on her blue jeans and a short-sleeved blue blouse. She put on a vest over that, a fringed leather one, and put her hair up in a bun. Before she went back downstairs, she scrubbed off every trace of makeup, as well.

When she walked back into the room, pale and silent, Cade barely glanced at her.

"If you'd like to call the picnic off, I can finish Melly's wedding dress instead," she said as she sipped her coffee, ignoring the eggs and sausage and fresh, hot biscuits.

"I'd like to call everything off, if you want to know," he said shortly.

"That's fine with me. I have plenty to keep me busy." She finished her coffee and, trying not to let him see how hurt she really was, smiled in his general direction and got up.

"Abby."

She stopped, keeping her back to him. "What?"

He drew in a slow breath. "Let's talk."

"I can't think what we have to talk about," she said with a careless laugh, turning to face him with fearless eyes. "I'll be leaving as soon as Melly comes back after her honeymoon, you know. But I can go right now, if you like. I've had an interesting offer from a boutique owner—"

His eyes flashed fire, and he cut her off sharply before she could tell him the rest. "And you'll be off to another landmark in your career, I suppose?" he asked with a mocking smile. "It's just as well, honey—I plan to do some traveling on my own in the next few months. There's only one job here, and Melly's got it."

"Don't worry, I don't particularly enjoy keeping records on cattle," she replied with a cool smile.

He stood up and lit a cigarette, leaving his second cup of coffee untouched on the table. "Calla's got the picnic basket packed. We might as well spend today together. It'll sure as hell be the last time we have, because starting tomorrow I'll be out with the boys constantly."

"Why don't you take Calla on a picnic?" she asked coldly. "You like her."

His nostrils flared as he stared down at her from his superior height. "I used to like you pretty well," he reminded her.

"Sure, as long as I stayed away." She moved about restlessly. "I should have stayed in New York. I didn't think I'd be welcomed here with open arms...."

"You might have been, once," he said enigmatically, "if you hadn't decided that the world of fashion meant more to you than a home and family."

She glanced up at him narrowly. "Pull the other one." She laughed. "If I'd stayed here, I would have withered away and become just another old maid dotting the landscape, and you know it. Or are you going to try and tell me that you were dying for love of me?" she added mockingly.

His dark eyes went quietly over her face. "Why would I waste time telling you something you wouldn't believe in the first place?" he asked. "If we're going, let's go. I don't have time to stand around talking."

"Oh, by all means, the ranch might fall apart!" she replied, and walked into the kitchen.

Calla glanced at her and scowled, a scowl that grew even fiercer when she saw Cade. "There's the basket," she grumbled at him.

"Thanks a hell of a lot," Cade snapped back, grabbing the picnic basket. "If you need extra help here, hire it. Or quit. But don't bother me with it. I'm slam out of patience, Calla."

And he slammed his hat over his brow and stormed out the back door ahead of Abby.

"Watch out," the housekeeper said sympathetically. "Something's eating him today."

"If he keeps that up, I'll find something that really will eat him!" Abby promised. "A wandering cannibal…" she muttered as she followed him out the door.

Cade drove them through pastures where there were little more than ruts for the truck to follow, and Abby held on to the seat for dear life, afraid to say a word. His face was grim, eyes doggedly on the ruts, and he looked as if the slightest sound would set him off.

But later, after he'd stripped off his shirt and rewired two or three strands of barbed wire in a pasture near the river, he seemed to have worked off some of his irritation.

Abby, who'd already spread out the picnic lunch under

the cottonwoods near the river, wandered through the towering break of pines and spruce to find him.

He was leaning back against the truck smoking a cigarette, his eyes on the distant mountains across the rolling grasslands. His hat was off, his gloves were still in place and he looked as much a part of the land as the tall grasses that grew there. With his shirt gone, his chest was revealed, the thick wedge of hair damp with sweat, his tanned shoulders gleaming with moisture. Abby almost closed her eyes at the sight of all that provocative masculinity so close and tempting. She wanted desperately to touch him, to run her hands over those broad shoulders and feel the texture of the thick hair that covered the bronzed muscles of his chest. But she didn't dare.

"Lunch is ready, when you are," she said quietly.

He glanced at her solemnly. "I've patched the fence," he said. His eyes went back to the mountains. "God, I love this country," he added in a tone deep and soft with reverence. "I could stand and look over it for hours and never tire of the sight."

"It wouldn't have been much different in the old days, when trappers and fur traders and explorers like William Clark came here," she remarked, going to stand beside him. The wind was tearing at the tight bun of her hair, but she pinned it back relentlessly.

"It's different," Cade said shortly, his eyes straight

ahead. "It's damned hard balancing between environmental protection and progress, Abby."

"Between mining and ranching, agriculture and industry?" she asked gently, because it was a subject that could set him off like a time bomb.

"Exactly." He glanced toward one of the grassy ridges that faced away from the mountains. There was mining a few miles beyond that ridge, on land Cade had leased for the purpose. It had been a struggle, that decision, but in the end he'd bowed to the nation's struggle for fuel independence.

"I wanted to keep the ranch exactly as it was, for my sons to inherit," he said, his voice strangely intense. His eyes searched hers for a long moment. "Do you want children, Abby?"

The question knocked her sideways. She hadn't thought much about children, except when she was around Cade. Now she looked at him and pictured him with a child on his knee, and something inside her burst into wild bloom.

"Yes," she murmured involuntarily.

His gaze dropped lower, to her slender body. "Aren't you afraid of losing your figure?" he asked carelessly, and averted his head while he finished the cigarette.

She didn't dare answer, afraid that her longing for his children would be evident in her voice. Instead, she changed the subject. "Where do you plan to get those sons to leave Painted Ridge to? Are you adopting?"

His dark eyebrows shot up. "I'll get them in the usual way. You do know how people make babies?" he added, a mocking smile shadowing his hard face.

She flushed and turned away. "You always say marriage isn't in your book, Cade. I just wondered, that's all."

"Maybe I'll be forced to change my mind eventually," he remarked, tossing his gloves in the open window of the truck as he followed her back through the trees to the river.

She knelt on one side of the red-checked tablecloth, where she'd laid out foil-covered plates of food and the jug of coffee Calla had packed in the basket.

"Are you going to taste it first?" he asked, moving to the river to slosh water over his face and chest while she dished up the food.

"I think I'll let you, after what you said to her," Abby replied. "She might have put arsenic in it."

"She didn't have time." He came back to the cloth, grabbing up one of several linen towels in the basket. He dabbed at his face and chest, and Abby watched him helplessly, hungrily, as his hands drew the cloth over the warm muscles with their furry covering.

He happened to look up, and his eyes flashed violently at her intense scrutiny.

She couldn't remember a time when she'd felt so intimidated by him or so attracted to him, all at once. She dropped her eyes back to the cloth and dished up the fried chicken, potato salad and rolls, with hands she could barely keep steady.

"Nervous of me, Abby?" he asked quietly, easing his formidable bulk down beside her, far too close, to take the plate she handed him.

"Should I be?" she countered. She poured him a cup of black coffee and automatically added cream before she handed him the foam cup. "After all, you're the one who should be worrying. I seem to make a habit of throwing myself at you," she added with bitter humor.

"And if you don't get off my ranch pretty quick, Abigail Shane, you may do it once too often," he said flatly. His eyes were dark and full of secrets as he nibbled at a piece of chicken.

"I have utter trust in your remarkable self-control, Mr. McLaren," she muttered, picking at her own food while he put his away like a last meal.

He made a strange sound, a laugh that died away too quickly, and finished his food before he spoke again. He swallowed his coffee and stretched out lazily on the ground while Abby gathered up the remnants of the picnic and put everything except the red-checkered cloth back in the hamper and set it aside.

"You'll be busy with roundup from now on, I guess," she commented after a long silence. Her eyes went to the distant grassy ridges, green and lonely, with pale blue mountains beyond them. The only trees in sight were the ones they were under, and the small thicket of pines nearby. It was like paradise, all clean air and open land and fluffy clouds drifting overhead.

"It's spring," he remarked. "Calves won't brand themselves."

"How's your shoulder?"

"I reckon I won't die," he muttered. He was smoking another cigarette, something he seemed to be doing constantly these days. He had once said it was something he did a lot when he was nervous. That almost made her laugh. He would never be nervous around her.

She drew up her jean-clad legs and rested her chin on her updrawn knees, sighing as she watched the river flow lazily by. "Remember when we came fishing up here the summer I graduated from high school?" she said. "You and me and Melly and a couple of the hands? You caught the biggest crappie I'd ever seen, and Melly got her hook caught in one of the cowboy's jeans...." She laughed, remembering the incident as if it were yesterday.

She stared at the river, lost in memory. It had been a day much like this one. Green and full of sun and laughter. Hank had been along; so had a cowboy whose name she couldn't remember—one Melly had a crush on. But Abby had somehow wandered close to Cade and stayed there while they fished in the river.

It was just a few weeks after he'd taken her to his room, and she'd been much too shy to approach him, but she'd eased as close as she could get.

"Cold?" he'd teased, glancing down at her.

And she'd blushed, looking away. "Oh, maybe a little," she'd lied. But they both knew the truth, although it didn't seem to bother him a bit.

"Jesse said you'd been thinking about going to New York," he'd mentioned.

"One of my teachers said I had the right carriage and figure and face for it," Abby had said enthusiastically, dreaming how it would be to have Cade and a career all at once.

"New York is a long way from Painted Ridge," he'd murmured, scowling at his fishing rod. "And full of disappointment."

That had pricked her temper, as if he didn't think she were pretty enough or poised enough for such a career in a big city.

"You don't think I can do it?" she'd asked with deceptive softness.

He'd laughed. "You're just a kid, Abby."

"I was eighteen last month. I'm a woman," she'd argued.

His head had turned. His dark eyes had gone over every inch of the shorts and tank top she wore, darkening at the sight of her slender, well-proportioned body.

"You're a woman, all right," he'd said, and looked up.

Her eyes had met his at point-blank range. Even now, she could remember the wild feelings that look had stirred, the hot pleasure of his eyes holding hers. Oblivious to everything around them, she'd actually moved toward him.

And Melly had said something to break the delicate spell. For the rest of the afternoon, they'd fished, and Cade's manner had relaxed a little. She'd tossed a worm at him out of pique when he caught the fish she'd been trying to land for several hours. And he'd picked her up bodily and thrown her in the river....

"You threw me in the river," she remarked suddenly, glaring at him.

His eyebrows arched. "I what?"

"That day we went fishing, the month before I left for New York," she reminded him. "You threw me in the river."

He chuckled softly. "So I did. But you started it, honey. That damned worm hit me right between the eyes."

"It was my fish you caught," she muttered. "My big crappie. I'd half hooked him and he'd gotten away three times. And you just sat there and hauled him out of circulation forever."

"I let you have half of him when Calla cooked him," he reminded her. "That should have made up for it a little."

Her full lips pouted. "I don't know about your half, but mine tasted bitter."

"Sour grapes," he said, grinning. "If you'd caught him, your half would have been twice as good as mine, wouldn't it?"

She shrugged. "Well, I guess so." Her eyes gazed over the river dreamily. "I used to love fishing. Now I don't have time for anything except work. Or didn't have, until I came back here. Funny how time seems to stop in a place like this," she added quietly. "Not another soul in sight, and you can drive for miles without seeing a ranch house or a store. It must have looked like this when the first settlers came and put down roots. The winter killed a lot of them didn't it?"

He nodded. "Montana winters are rough. I know. I lose cattle every year, and once we lost a man in a line cabin. He froze to death sitting up."

She shivered. "I remember. That was when I was just out of grammar school. When Melly and I went riding, we wouldn't go near that cabin, thinking it was haunted."

He shook his head. "Well, I've got a couple of old hands now who feel the same way. Hank's one."

"I didn't think Hank was afraid of anything."

He lifted an amused eyebrow. "Do you ever miss this, in New York?"

She searched his face, thinking how she missed him every waking moment. She looked away. "I miss it a lot. There's so much history here. So much privacy and peace." She remembered the role she had to play, almost too late. "But, of course, New York has its good points, as well. There's always a new play to see. Sometimes I go to the opera or the ballet. And there are nightclubs and little coffeehouses, and museums...."

"None of which you find around here," he said harshly. "There's not much place for sophistication in the middle of a cattle spread, is there?"

He was watching her with narrowed, calculating eyes, and a dark kind of pain washed over his face before she saw it. Deliberately he crushed out the cigarette on the ground beside him.

She turned, glancing down at him. He was lying on his back with his hands under his head, and his eyes were closed. His powerful legs were crossed, stretching the denim sensuously over their muscular contours. Her eyes took in every detail, from head to broad chest to quiet face, and she felt suddenly reckless.

She picked up a long blade of grass and moved close enough to draw it lightly over his chest.

He grabbed it. "Courting trouble, Abby?" he asked curtly.

There was a wildness in her that sprang from looking at his impassive face. He wouldn't let her close—he spent his life pushing her away. Today would be the last day she'd ever have with him to remember, and today she was going to make him feel something. Even if it was only rage.

"Oh, I just live for it, Cade," she murmured, edging closer. She bent over him before he could stop her, and pressed her lips down on his broad, warm chest.

"God!" he burst out, catching the back of her head. But his hands hesitated, as if he couldn't decide whether to push or pull.

Her nostrils tickled where the thick, curling hair brushed them and she smelled the faint traces of soap and cologne that clung to him. His chest rose and fell with ragged irregularity and she felt the powerful muscles stiffen as she drew her mouth across them, acting on pure instinct alone.

"You sweet little fool," he rasped. "Oh, God, I'm

only human, and I want you until I can hardly stand up straight…!"

He jerked her alongside him and bent over her with hands that trembled as his mouth homed in on hers.

Hungry as she'd never imagined she could be, she turned in his big arms and pressed close, half shocked to find his body blatantly aroused as it touched hers. For an instant she tried to draw away, but one lean, steely hand slid quickly to the base of her spine and gathered her hips back against his.

"You wanted it," he ground out against her mouth. "Don't start fighting me now."

Her hands were tangled in the hair over his chest, but she was still rational enough to realize just how involved he already was. "Cade, I only wanted—" she began, only to have the words crushed under his devouring mouth.

"This is what I've been trying to tell you all along," he whispered shakily, moving his lips to her throat. "I want you, Abby. I'd die to have you! And you can feel how much now, can't you? This is how it is between lovers. This is what happens to a man when he's pushed beyond his limits."

Even as he spoke, his hands were sliding under her blouse, finding bare skin at her back and a clasp that snapped apart with devastating ease.

"I haven't been with a woman for so damned long,

I'd forgotten how soft..." he murmured, sliding his fingers under her breasts to cup their tender weight. His thumbs found suddenly hard peaks, making her shudder with new pleasure.

Abby's legs moved restlessly as Cade's eased between them. He turned, and she felt the ground under her and the full weight of his big body over her. She moaned at the intimacy, unfamiliar and arousing.

Her sharp nails dug into his back and raked down to his waist, feeling the warmth and moistness of his flesh as his hands touched her in ways that should have shocked her. His mouth was hungrier than she would ever have believed possible. She opened her own mouth helplessly, eagerly, tasting him, experiencing him.

She felt his hands on the buttons of her blouse, and seconds later his chest crushed the softness of her breasts in a joining that made her cry out again.

He lifted his head and his eyes glittered frighteningly. He was trembling all over with desire, and his face was hard with it.

"Is this what you wanted to know?" he demanded unsteadily. "If you could drive me out of my mind with wanting? To see how it would be if you pushed too hard? I want you, all right. I wanted you when you were eighteen, I'd have killed for you. But when I'd made up my mind to ask you to stay with me, you got on that damned bus and you never looked at me!"

Her eyes widened with shock. "What?"

He searched her face with eyes that barely saw. "Every vacation, all I heard about was how great New York was, how well you were doing in your damned career. Until finally I made sure I was out of the house when you came to visit, because it hurt so much to hear how happy you were away from me."

"But, I wasn't..." she began.

He wasn't listening. His hands slid under her hips and forced her up against his. "Feel it, damn you," he whispered harshly. "You've done this to me since you were fifteen. But it's something I hate, Abby, and I hate you, too, for doing it to me, for teasing me. Because I know you don't give a damn for anything except your career and your city men. And nothing you say is going to convince me otherwise!"

She swallowed nervously, her mouth trembling as she realized how set his mind really was. He'd cared, and she hadn't known. Even when Melly told her, she had refused to believe. What had she done?

"Cade," she whispered, reaching a hand up to his face.

"What do you want, baby, to see how I make love? To get a taste of what you missed when you stepped onto that bus four years ago?" He jerked her closer and bent his head. "I don't mind showing you. It will be something to tell your sophisticated friends about when you get back to your own world!" He kissed her again, hurting her, as if it didn't matter anymore whether he hurt her.

She could hardly believe what she'd just heard. He'd cared, he'd really cared enough to ask her not to leave Painted Ridge. And because she'd put on a brave front and gone away laughing, he'd believed it was because she was glad to be leaving him. Of all the horrible ironies…

She went limp in his arms, tears washing her face while he treated her like something he'd bought for the night, his hands insulting, his mouth probing mercilessly into hers. It didn't matter that she loved him more than life, because if she told him now, he wouldn't believe her. He'd just said so, and he thought she was only teasing, playing games with him until she went home. Home. If only he knew that Painted Ridge would always be home—because it was where he was.

She felt cold to the bone, as though there were not a trace of warmth anywhere inside her trembling body. She felt the restless motion of his body against hers, and wondered through a fog of misery if he really meant to take her completely.

But seconds later, he lifted his head as if he'd just tasted the tears, and looked down at her. His face was haunted-looking, his eyes blazing with frustrated passion. His powerful body shuddered.

"And this is as far as it goes, honey," he said with a cold, mocking smile. "You wouldn't want to risk going back to New York with my child growing inside you, would you, Abby? That would be taking the game too far."

Her face felt tight with hurt. She could feel her body trembling under the hard pressure of his, but he'd never know it was with helpless desire, not fear. Despite everything—even his harsh treatment—she still wanted him, would always want him. Nor did the thought of a child bring any terror to her. It was the very door of heaven.

He took a deep breath and rolled away from her, lying with his eyes closed and his bare chest lifting and falling unevenly while she fumbled with catches and buttons.

She got jerkily to her feet and smoothed down her wild blond hair, trying to find the hairpins his insistent fingers had removed. She leaned against one of the sturdy trees by the riverbank until she could get her breath back and stop crying. Finally, she dragged the hem of her blouse over her red eyes to remove the hot salty tears from her cheeks.

She heard a sound behind her, over the noise of the river washing lazily between the banks, and she knew Cade was standing behind her. But she didn't turn.

"Are you all right?" he asked after a minute, and the words sounded torn from him.

She looked over her shoulder at him, and her ravaged face caused something violent to flash in his eyes.

"Don't look so worried, Cade," she said with enormous dignity. "You made your point. I'm through throwing myself at you. You've cured me for good this time." She managed a soft little laugh, although her swollen lips trembled and spoiled the effect.

He rammed his hands into his pockets and stared at her stiff back. "I'll keep out of your way until Melly gets back from the honeymoon," he said curtly. "I'll expect the same courtesy from you. What happened... almost happened here isn't going to be allowed to happen again."

She bit her lower lip to keep from crying. "Cade... what you said...were you really going to ask me to stay, when I was eighteen?" she asked in a ghost of a whisper.

He laughed bitterly. "Sure," he said. "I was going to offer you the job I finally gave Melly." He looked away so that she wouldn't see the lie in his dark eyes, or the deep pain that accompanied it.

She straightened, a surge of disappointment and hurt raging through her body. She had hoped that he'd wanted to marry her.

"Can we go back now?" she asked in a subdued tone.

"Might as well. I've got cattle to work."

"And I've got a wedding dress to finish." The sound of her words made her want to scream with anguish. There would never be a wedding for her. She walked quietly to the truck without looking at him and got in.

He loaded the basket and the cloth in the back of the truck with quick, furious motions and paused to shrug into his shirt and slam his ranch hat on his head before he got in beside her.

She felt his eyes on her, but she was staring out at the landscape.

"Abby," he said quietly, "it's better this way. You'll hate me for a while, but you'll get over it."

"I don't hate you," she said in a whisper. "You don't want commitment any more than I do, Cade, so there's nothing to regret."

His hands gripped the steering wheel until his fingers went white. "Don't make it any harder than it already is," he said under his breath. "Let's forget today ever happened, Abby."

"That suits me," she said. She stared out the window as he started the truck and gunned it back onto the road. She wasn't going to cry, she wasn't. She'd thrown her pride at his feet once too often already. He couldn't wait to be rid of her, and she was just as anxious to get away from him. The torment of loving him was too much. As far as he was concerned, she was just a city girl amusing herself by playing up to him, and nothing was going to convince him otherwise. What a horrible opinion he had of her. Only a man who thought her utterly contemptible could have treated her as he had.

She drew in a shaky breath. It had been so beautiful at first, feeling the hunger raging in him, knowing that he wanted her that much. Until he told her what he really thought, and she realized that it was only physical desire with him, after all. Why hadn't she remembered what he'd said the night before about sex being a lousy foundation for a relationship? Well, she remembered now, and she wouldn't forget again. She'd harden her heart and grit her teeth and pray that the three weeks left would go by in a rush. Cade would never get close enough to hurt her again. She was going to make sure of that.

❧ 10 ❧

Melly's wedding day was a flurry of last-minute preparation, with caterers all over the house and wedding guests arriving in droves even as Abby was helping her sister get into the wedding gown she'd designed.

"It's just heaven." Melly sighed, looking at herself in the mirror. The dress had a keyhole neckline, and it was lavishly trimmed with appliquéd Venice lace. The veil of illusion net that went with it fell from a Juliet cap down to drape over an elegant train. The sleeves were pure lace, the skirt a fantasy of satin and chiffon and more lace, and the Empire waistline featured a row of the most intricate tiny roses in contrasting oyster white. With Melly's blond hair and fair skin, it was sheer magic.

"I can't believe I actually finished it on time," Abby murmured as she made a last tuck in the hem.

"I can't believe you actually designed it," her sister replied. "Abby, it's the most gorgeous thing! Jessica will just die."

"I hope not," came the amused reply. Abby sighed, thinking about what might have been. She'd have to refuse that attractive offer now. It would only have worked if she had stayed in Montana. And, of course, that was impossible. Cade had done everything but move away to keep the distance between them. He wasn't ever at home now, finding excuse after excuse to be up with the dawn and out until bedtime. Sometimes he even camped out with the men in the line cabins, shocking Calla, who gave up on keeping his supper for him and started sending his meals up with Jeb and the boys.

"Melly, be happy," she said suddenly, breaking out of her reverie.

Melly turned, her eyes sparkling and full of love and excitement, her hands trembling with anticipation. "How could I help but be, when I'm marrying Jerry?" she asked. Her joy faded slightly though, when she looked at Abby. "Darling, what's gone wrong between you and Cade?"

"Nothing that hasn't always been wrong," she replied with a cool smile. "Don't you worry about me on your wedding day! Let's get you married, okay?"

"Are you sure you can cope with the computer and all the extra work?"

"I can cope," Abby said quietly. Impulsively, she hugged Melly. "I want years and years of happiness for you. I only wish our parents could be here, to see what a beautiful bride you make!"

"Maybe they're watching," came the soft reply. "Did you see the flowers, Abby? Wasn't it grand of Cade to let us have the wedding here? All those guests…"

"…will probably have the opportunity to take a look at the bulls he's selling while they're on the place," Abby finished with a bitter smile.

"Shame on you," Melly said gently. "You know how generous Cade is."

Abby flushed and turned away. "We see him in different ways, though. I wonder if he'll show up for the ceremony?"

"He's best man—he'll have to." Melly laughed. "Think you can walk down the aisle on his arm without tripping him?"

"I'll fight the temptation, just for you. You'll listen for the music?"

"I'll listen. See you downstairs."

Abby smiled. "See you downstairs."

She walked out into the hall, checking her own long, V-necked lavender gown for spots or wrinkles. It was sleeveless, and her hair was pinned elegantly atop her head. She carried a bouquet of cymbidium orchids, and she was shaking with nerves. This would be her first wedding, and while she was honored to be her sister's maid of honor, she would rather have been an observer. The hardest thing of all was going to be standing beside Cade at that altar.

She went down the stairs and stopped dead when she caught sight of a redheaded Amazon standing in the doorway. Ignoring the ranch wives, some of whom she knew, she made a beeline for the newcomer, knowing instinctively who she was. Cade, watching from the cleared-out living room where the ceremony would take place, scowled darkly when he saw her bypass the country women to rush to the elegantly dressed newcomer.

"You've got to be Jessica Dane," Abby said immediately.

The towering redhead grinned. "How'd you guess? It was my beaming smile, right?" She laughed, towering over Abby in her three-inch heels. Barefoot, Jessica would have been almost six feet tall. With her red hair and pale skin and big black eyes, she would have drawn eyes anywhere, even without the mink stole and vivid green silk dress she was wearing with matching shoes and bag.

"You must be Abby, then," Jessica said, extending her hand in a firm, warm handshake. "Come on out to my car for a minute, and let me show you what I brought! Have we got time?"

"A few minutes, anyway." Abby laughed. She went out with Jessica without a backward glance, unaware of the dark scowling face watching her.

"These were just some of my lines," Jessica said when they were seated in the Lincoln Continental's comfortable interior, and Abby thumbed through several catalogs, admiring the fashions.

"They're very good," she said finally.

"They could be better, if I had a house designer," Jessica said. "I'm prepared to offer you a percentage of my gross, Abby. I think you could make us both rich. Richer," she corrected, laughing. "You've got some unique designs, if Melly's wardrobe is anything to go by. I'd love to have you do a few sketches, at least, and send them to me."

Despite her haste to get back to New York, Abby was willing to do that. In fact, she and Jessica got so caught up in a discussion of the particulars, they almost missed the opening chords of the organ. It wasn't until Cade shouted from the front porch that Abby clambered out of Jessica's car and rushed up the steps, with the Amazon at her heels.

"If you can spare the time, everyone else is ready to start," Cade said under his breath as she passed him.

"And the sooner this is over, the sooner she'll be back from her honeymoon, which means I can leave," she shot back, glaring up at him.

"Lady, it won't be quick enough to suit me," he returned hotly.

She brushed past him, oblivious to Jessica's puzzled stare, and went right to the doorway of the living room, arriving just as the prelude finished.

Cade joined Jerry at the altar, the two of them such a contrast in their suits—Cade dark and elegant, Jerry blond and obviously uncomfortable. Then the wedding march sounded and Abby gripped her orchids, shooting a glance at the staircase to find Melly waiting there. As she walked between the folding chairs, she discovered that down the aisle Cade was watching every step she made, an expression in his eyes that she couldn't begin to understand.

For one wild instant, Abby pretended that this was her own wedding, that she was giving herself to Cade for all time. It was so delicious a fantasy that she stared at him the whole length of the aisle. He stared back at her, his face momentarily softening, his eyes black and glittering as she went to stand at her place beside the flowered arch of the altar. His eyes held hers for a long blazing moment, and her lips parted on a rush of breath as she felt the force of the look all the way to her toes.

Then the organ sounded again, and the spell was broken as Melly came down the aisle in the gorgeous gown, carrying orchids and wildflowers in a unique bouquet.

Melly walked to the altar and stood nervously beside Jerry. The minister, a delightful man with thick glasses and a contagiously happy expression, read the marriage service. Jerry and Melly each read the special wording that they'd prepared for themselves, and they lit one candle together from two separate candles to signify the joining of two people into one. The final words were read. Jerry kissed the bride for so long that some members of the wedding party began to giggle. And all at once it was over and they were running down the aisle together.

Abby kept out of Cade's way at the reception, sitting aside with Jessica while they discussed modeling and clothes and the future of Jessica's boutique.

Then, all too soon, Melly was dressed in her street clothes and the happy couple rushed out the door to start on their honeymoon. Abby kissed them both and wished them well, and stood by while Melly stopped at the car to toss her wedding bouquet. Calla, dressed in gray and looking unusually sedate, caught it and blushed a flaming red—especially when thin old Jeb, suited up in a rare concession to civilization, looked at her and grinned.

Abby was grateful that she hadn't caught it. That would have been the final thrust of the knife, to feel Cade's sharp eyes on her, seeing the aching hunger she couldn't have hidden from him.

Hours passed before the guests drifted away, and Abby saw Jessica off with a promise to put some sketches in the mail at her earliest opportunity. She liked Jessica very much. And perhaps there was a way for her to accept the job. If she moved to Wyoming, she'd be far enough away that she wouldn't ever have to see Cade again.

Abby changed into a cotton dress with gold patterning that complemented her pinned-up blond hair and sat down at the supper table expecting to eat alone. It was a surprise when Cade walked into the dining room, wearing a white shirt and blue blazer with dark slacks. He looked impossibly handsome, and as elegant as anything New York might produce.

"Ain't we pretty, though?" Calla murmured, eyeing him as she began to serve the food.

"We shore is," he returned, pursing his lips at her gray dress, which she hadn't changed. "I noticed the way Jeb was looking at you." His eyes narrowed. "Did you bake me another cherry cake and give it to him again?"

The older woman flushed and scowled all at once. "You hush, or I'll burn your supper. You know I gave him the cake on account of he bailed me out when I burned the supper I was cooking for those ranchers you invited here! And what are you doing back here with roundup in full swing? I thought you'd be heading for the hills the minute the words were spoke."

"I live here," he reminded her.

"Could have fooled me," she muttered, waddling out of the room.

Abby fixed her coffee and kept her eyes on her plate. She was still smarting from the ugly remark Cade had made earlier.

"Since we're not speaking, shall I ask Calla to ask you to pass me the salt?" Cade asked coolly.

She handed it over, setting it down before he could take it from her.

"Who was the redheaded Amazon you couldn't part company with?" he asked.

She didn't like the bite in his tone, but it was none of his business who Jessica was. "Another model," she lied, staring at him.

His face hardened. "A successful one, judging by that mink and the Lincoln," he remarked. He smiled bitterly. "Or is she being kept by some man?"

Abby slammed her napkin down by her plate and got

up. "Eat by yourself. I can't stand any more of your self-righteousness!"

"You can't stand ordinary people, either, can you?" he challenged. "You walked right past Essie Johnson, and you grew up with her. She wasn't good enough for your exalted company, no doubt, being a simple rancher's wife and all."

That cut to the quick. How could he think her so heartless when in fact she'd gone out of her way to find Essie at the reception and had apologized for what might have appeared to be a snub?

"Think what you like—you will, anyway," she said and walked out of the room.

During the week that followed, Cade made himself scarce. Abby spent her lonely days answering correspondence, putting records into the computer, ordering supplies and answering the phone. If she'd had any hopes that Cade might decide to ask her to stay, they were destroyed by his very indifference. He didn't seem to care whether she spoke to him or not, and while he was courteous, he wasn't the friendly, teasing man of happier times.

The Thursday night before Melly and Jerry were due back on Friday, Abby wandered out by the swimming pool, lost in memory.

Her eyes narrowed on the bare concrete—it was still

too early in the year to fill the pool, so it was empty. It seemed a hundred years ago that she'd defiantly stripped off her clothes and gone swimming in it, a lifetime since Cade had found her here half-nude. She'd been hopeful then. She'd had dreams of sharing more than a bed with him. But he'd gently pushed her away. And he hadn't let her come close again, except briefly and physically.

"Remembering, Abby?" Cade asked quietly, coming up behind her from the house.

He was wearing slacks and a burgundy knit shirt that made him look darker and more formidable than ever. His hair was damp, as if he'd showered, and he made Abby's heart race.

She glanced away from his probing gaze. "I was just getting some air, Cade," she murmured.

"The kids come home tomorrow," he remarked carelessly, although the look in his eyes was anything but careless. "I suppose you'll be leaving shortly?"

That hurt. It was as though he couldn't wait to be rid of her, and she felt the hot threat of tears. She shrugged. "I have commitments. I told you that when I first got here."

He nodded. He held a smoking cigarette in his hand, but he gave it a hard glare and tossed it to the ground and crushed it under his boot.

"You smoke too much," she observed.

He laughed shortly. "I know. I hate the damned things, but it's a habit of long standing."

Like pushing me away, she thought, but didn't speak. Her eyes scanned the starry sky and she wrapped her arms tight around the little blue dress she was wearing.

"Cold, honey?" he asked gently.

She shook her head. "Not very. Calla and Jeb have gone to a movie," she said for no reason.

"And that means that we're alone in the house, doesn't it?" he said. His eyes narrowed. "What do you want me to do about it, Abby, carry you up those stairs to my bedroom, the way I did once before?" He laughed bitterly. "Sorry, honey, I stopped giving lessons that day by the river. Maybe you can find somebody in New York to take over where I left off."

It was like being cut to pieces. "Maybe I can," she said in a taut voice. She turned. "It's late. I'd better go in."

He caught her arm hesitantly, and that puzzled her. He didn't pull her closer, but held her just at his side. "Were you hoping I might come out here?"

She had been, but she would have died rather than admit it now. "I told you before, I'm through throwing myself at your feet, Cade," she replied calmly. "Don't worry, you're perfectly safe. You can always lock your bedroom door, can't you?"

"Stop that. It's nothing to joke about."

"I wasn't joking." She tugged her arm free. "Good night, Cade."

"Talk to me, damn it!" he burst out.

"About what?" she shot back. "About my bad manners, my sickening career or my loose morals, all of which you seem to think I enjoy!"

He stiffened. "I've never accused you of having loose morals."

"Except when I come anywhere near you," she said with a bitter laugh.

"You won't try to see my side of it," he ground out. "You're just playing games, but I'm not. I'm too old for it."

"Excuse me, grandpa, I'll try not to unsettle you… Cade!"

He jerked her against him and his hands hurt where they gripped her arms. "I want you," he said under his breath. "Don't tempt me. I'm very nearly at the end of my patience as it is. I want you away from Painted Ridge before I do something I don't want to do."

Her lips trembled. "You think I'd let you?" she whispered.

His eyes met hers. "I know you would, and so do you. We go off like dynamite when we start touching each other." His hands dropped. "But it isn't enough. I want more than a feverish night of physical satisfaction. You'd give me that, and I'd give it back. But it's nothing I couldn't have from any of a dozen women," he added coldly. "And it's not going to happen—if you get out of here in time."

It was a warning that she was willing to heed. A night with Cade would make it impossible for her to live without him, and she was wise enough to realize it. She dropped her eyes.

"I'll arrange to go Saturday morning," she said.

His face hardened at her subdued tone, but he only nodded. "It's for the best. You came to me hurt, and I hope I've helped you to heal. But your world isn't mine. The longer you stay, the harder it gets...."

He didn't finish it. Instead, he lit another cigarette. "You'd better go in. It is getting cold out here."

"Arctic," she mused, glancing up at him. She gathered her poise and her pride and smiled grimly as she brushed past him and went back inside. She moved quickly, grateful that he couldn't see the tears that slid down her cheeks as she went up the stairs. They made her oblivious to the dark eyes that followed her almost worshipfully until she was out of sight.

Melly and Jerry came home looking tanned and rested from their Florida vacation and blissfully happy with each other. Abby could hardly bear their happiness, since it reminded her so graphically that she'd lost every chance of having any of her own with Cade.

"How's everything going here?" Melly asked when they were alone, Jerry having ridden up into the hills to help with roundup.

"Just fine," Abby lied, "but I've had a call from my agency and there's a possibility of a long-term contract for a bottling company. I'm terribly excited about it."

Melly's face fell. "You're going back to New York? But I thought...?"

"Now that you're home, I can leave it all in your capable hands," Abby said with a forced smile. "I've missed New York, and it will be great to get back to work."

"But the attack, the reason you came here..."

"Cade helped me over it," Abby said quietly. "I'll always be grateful to him for that. But he wants no part of me—he's made that quite clear. I'm going to do him a favor and go away."

"He loves you, you stupid idiot!" Melly burst out.

Abby flinched and tears welled up in her eyes. "No!" she said huskily. "If he feels anything, it's anger because I preferred modeling to ranch life."

"Have you talked to him, at least?"

"Sure," Abby agreed, not adding that they'd argued every second they were together. "We've both agreed that I have no place in his life, or he in mine." She turned around and walked toward the stairs. "I'm going to pack. Want to help me? I've made reservations on a plane in the morning."

"Oh, Abby, don't do it!" Melly pleaded.

But all her pleading and all her reasoning didn't sway her stubborn sister. The next morning Cade drove the two women out to the airport.

It had been a shock to find him at the wheel of the big sedan when it pulled up at the front door. He was wearing the same navy blazer and dark slacks he'd worn the other night at supper, but he had a striped blue tie over his white silk shirt. The only Western thing about him was his dressy cream Stetson and leather boots.

Her flight was being called as they walked into the terminal, and Abby hugged Melly quickly, suitcase in hand, before she boarded the plane. Tears welled up in her eyes.

"Write to me," she pleaded.

"I will," Melly promised. Her eyes narrowed. "I wish you wouldn't go."

"I have to. I have commitments." She told the lie with panache and a faint smile.

Cade didn't say a word. He stood looking down at her with eyes so dark they seemed black, a smoking cigarette in one hand, his face like flint.

Abby forced herself to look up at him. She was wearing shoes with only tiny heels, and he was taller than ever. Bigger. The most impossibly handsome man she'd ever known, and her heart ached just at the sight of him.

"Bye, Cade," she said quietly. "Thanks for letting me stay so long."

He only nodded. His chest rose and fell heavily, quickly, and his lips were set in a thin line.

"Well...I'd better go," Abby said in a high-pitched tone.

Cade threw the cigarette into one of the sand-filled ashtrays and abruptly reached for Abby, crushing her against the length of his body. The suitcase fell and she struggled helplessly for a moment, until he subdued her with nothing more than his firm hold.

She stared into his fierce eyes and stopped fighting, and they looked at each other in a tense, painful exchange that made Abby's knees feel as though they would fold under her. Her lips parted on a sobbing breath, and he bent his head.

It was like no kiss they'd ever shared. His mouth eased down over hers so softly she hardly felt it, and then it moved harder and deeper and slower and rougher until she moaned and reached up, clinging to his neck. He lifted her against him, still increasing the pressure of his arms, his mouth, until she felt as if they were burning into each other, fusing a bond nothing would ever sever. She wanted him. She wanted him! Her mouth, her body, her aching moan told him so, and she could feel the tremor of his own body as the kiss went on and on.

Finally, slowly, he eased her back down onto the floor and breath by breath took his mouth away. His arms slackened and withdrew, although his steely hands held her until she was steady again.

His eyes searched hers. "Goodbye, Abby," he said in a voice like steel.

"Goodbye, Cade," she whispered brokenly.

He brushed his fingers against her cheek, unsteady fingers that touched her as if she'd already become a beautiful illusion. "My God, how I could have loved you!" he breathed. And then, before she could believe her own ears, he turned and strode quietly away, without once looking back.

Abby stared after him, uncomprehending. "Did… did I just hear what I thought I heard?" she murmured.

"What, honey?" Melly asked gently, coming back within earshot. "I was being discreet. Gosh, what a kiss that was! And you're leaving?"

Abby sighed bitterly. Surely she'd dreamed it, or misunderstood…or had she? She took a steadying breath. "I have to go. I'll miss my flight. Melly, take care of him?"

"You could have done that yourself, if you'd told him

the truth," Melly said softly. "It's still not too late. You could catch him."

"He wouldn't listen," she said wearily. "You know how Cade is when he makes up his mind, and I've gone mad and started hearing things again. Back to the salt mines, Melly. I'm fine now, I'm just fine. Take care. I love you."

"I love you, too." She searched her sister's eyes. "He couldn't have kissed you that way without caring one hell of a lot. Think about that. Hurry now!"

Abby waved and ran for the plane. And all the way back to New York she thought and thought about that long, hard kiss and what she imagined Cade had said until she all but went crazy. Finally, in desperation, she tucked the memory in the back of her mind and closed her eyes. It was over now; he'd sent her away. Looking back was no good at all. She'd had time to recuperate and get herself back together. Now she had to put Montana and Cade behind her and start over. She could do it. After all, her career was all she had left.

❖ 11 ❖

It took several days for Abby to adjust to city life again after the wide-open country of Montana. Accustomed to staying up late at the ranch, she now had to go to bed early, watch her diet, be concerned with shadows and lines of weariness, add to her wardrobe and pack her huge handbag with the dozens of items she might need for an assignment. And every night she soaked her aching feet and smothered herself in cold cream and longed for Cade McLaren with every cell in her body.

She did Jessica's sketches in the weeks that followed and mailed them to Wyoming. Jessica phoned her shortly afterward and invited her out to see the boutique, but Abby had to put her off. She was working feverishly, and the lie she'd told Melly about the bottling company commercials had been amazingly prophetic. She was offered a television commercial for a soft drink company, which she immediately accepted. Her career was skyrocketing. And it was as empty as her life.

She didn't even bother dating other men. What was the use, when all she could do was compare them to Cade. So she worked and grieved for him, and before very long the toll of loneliness began to show on her.

All the years before, she'd had that sweet memory of him to sustain her, and the hope that someday things might change. But now there was no hope left. There was nothing to cling to, only a future that was empty and lonely. Even if she accepted Jessica's offer and went to live in Wyoming, she might be near Cade but she'd still be alone. She didn't know how she was going to bear it.

Late on Friday night, she was halfheartedly watching television when the phone rang. She couldn't imagine who it could be at that hour, and she was frowning when she picked up the receiver.

"Hello?" she murmured.

"Hello, honey," came a deep, painfully familiar voice. She sat down, paling. It had been almost four months since she'd last heard that particular voice, but she would have known it on her deathbed.

"Cade?" she whispered shakily.

"Yes." There was a pause. "How are you, Abby?"

She drew in a slow breath. Don't panic, she told herself, don't give yourself away. "I'm just fine, Cade," she said brightly.

"No date on a Friday night?" he murmured.

She drew her gold caftan closer around her, as if he could see her all the way from Montana. "I was tired," she replied. "Is everything all right? Melly...?"

"Melly's fine. She and Jerry are down at Yellowstone for the weekend."

"Oh." She gripped the receiver tightly. "Then nothing's wrong?"

"Everything's wrong," he said after a minute. "Hank's quitting."

"Hank!" She sat straight up. "Why?"

He laughed mirthlessly. "He says I'm too damned mean to stay around."

"Are you?" she asked softly. There was something strange about his voice, different. "Cade, are you all right?" she asked, and the concern seeped through.

"I'm...fine." He laughed again. "I'll be finer when I get through this bottle."

"You're drinking!" It was the only thing that could explain the way he sounded.

"Are you shocked? I'm human, Abby, although you sure as hell never thought I was, did you?" There was a thud and a muffled curse. "Damn, why does furniture have to sprout legs when you try to go around it?"

She wrapped the telephone cord around her fingers. "Cade, is someone there with you? Calla?"

"Calla's gone to a movie with Jeb. Any day now I expect to be asked to the wedding." He sighed. "Abby, before long you and I are going to be the only two single people on earth."

"Why are you drinking?" she asked, worried. "You haven't gotten hurt, have you?"

"You're a hell of a person to ask me that," he growled. "You cut the heart out of me when you got on that damned plane. Just the way you cut it out when you got on the bus four years ago. Oh, God, Abby, I miss you!" he ground out, his voice throbbing with emotion. "I miss you!"

Tears burst from her eyes and rolled down her cheeks. "I miss you, too," she whispered. Her eyes closed and she bit her lip. "Every hour of every day."

There was a long, deep sigh from the other end of the line. "We should have made love that day by the river," he said achingly. "Maybe we would have gotten each other out of our systems. I've got a picture of you by my bed, Abby. I sit here and look at it and ache all over."

Her fingers clenched until the blood went out of them. She had one of him, too, that she'd carried to New York with her four years before. It was wrinkled from being hugged against her heart.

"You're the one who told me sex was a bad foundation to build on," she reminded him wearily.

"It wasn't just sex," he said. "It's never been that. Four years ago, I couldn't risk getting you pregnant, don't you see? I couldn't take the choice away from you. To hell with how I felt, I couldn't force you to stay here, Abby."

Her breath caught in her throat. She caught the receiver with both hands and sat as still as a poker. Did he even realize what he was admitting?

"You…you thought that given the choice between you and modeling…"

"You showed me which was more important, didn't you, honey?" he asked with a bitter laugh. He sighed heavily. "You got on that bus, laughing like a freed prisoner, and you never even looked at me. I told your father I'd marry you, if you'd have me, and we fought it out half the night. He said you were too young and you wanted a chance to get away from the ranch, to be somebody. I argued with him then, but when it came down to it, I couldn't make you stay with me." His voice was faintly slurred, but just as beautiful as ever, and Abby was hurting in ways she'd never dreamed she could. "You see, I'd already realized how vulnerable you were with me. And I was just as vulnerable with you. I had to be careful not to come too close, Abby, because we could have gotten in over our heads. I figured you'd go to New York and get tired of the city and come back to me. But you didn't."

There was a world of emotion in those words. Bitterness. Hopelessness. Hurt.

"You never asked me to stay," she whispered. "You said you didn't want a commitment to any woman, a...a leash on your freedom."

He laughed. "I haven't been free since you were fifteen years old. I've never wanted anyone else. I never will."

"You let me go!" she burst out, suddenly hating him. "Damn you, you let me go! I was only eighteen, but there was nothing New York had to offer that could have torn me away from you if you'd just told me to stay! One lousy word, just one word—*stay*. And you let me go, Cade!"

There was a shocked pause on the other end of the line, a silence like darkness in a graveyard.

But she didn't notice. The words were tumbling out of her, while tears burned down her cheeks. "I loved the glamour, you said, I couldn't live without the city! And all I've done for four years is stare at this picture of you and cry my eyes out! You put me on a bus four years ago, and you put me on a plane four months ago…damn you, what do you care? You push me away, you accuse me of teasing you, you…Cade? Cade!"

But the line was dead. She slammed the receiver down and burst into tears. If he called back, she wasn't even going to answer. Let him sit and drown in his whiskey. She didn't care! She turned off the lights and went to bed in a fit of furious temper.

Several hours later, she sat straight up in bed as the doorbell rang and rang and rang. Maybe she was dreaming it. It had taken her forever to get to sleep, and she was still drowsy. She laid her head back on the pillow, but there it came again, even more insistently.

Frowning sleepily, she padded to the front door of her apartment with her gold caftan swirling around her.

"Who is it?" she grumbled.

"Who the hell do you think? Open the door, or do I have to break it down?"

"Cade?" Her heart jumped wildly and she fumbled the catch and the safety latch off and opened the door. And it was no dream.

He came into the apartment with a scowl as black as thunder on his dark face, looking sleepy and tired and worn-out. He was wearing jeans and a half-open denim shirt, and old boots and the battered brown ranch hat he wore to work cattle. His boots were dusty, his face needed a shave and he was altogether the most beautiful sight Abby had seen in her life.

"Cade!" she breathed, blinking up at him out of sleepy eyes, her tangled hair glorious in its disarray, the caftan clinging lovingly and quite revealingly to every line of her body.

"I've had half a bottle of whiskey," he said, towering over her with the locked door behind him. "And I'm not quite sober yet, despite the three cups of black coffee I had on the plane. But you said something to me that I'm sure I really heard and didn't dream, and I flew up here to let you say it again. Just to make sure."

She stared at him unblinkingly, loving every unshaven plane of his face.

"You hung up the phone and got on a plane in the middle of the night...?" she began nervously.

His eyes roamed down her body and one dark eyebrow arched curiously. "You've lost weight, Abigail," he murmured, studying her. "A lot of it, and you look like pure hell."

"Have you seen yourself in a mirror?" she countered, noticing new lines, new shadows under his dark eyes.

He shook his head. "Couldn't stand the sight of myself," he admitted. "Come on, Abby, let's hear it."

She swallowed. "It was easier when you were still in Montana," she began nervously.

"I guess it was." He took off his hat and tossed it onto a chair. His big hands framed her face and he looked down at it like a starving man. "Suppose I take you to bed, Abby?" he asked softly. "And after we've made love for three or four hours, I'll ask you again."

✤ 12 ✤

She could barely breathe when she saw what was in his eyes. It was hardly possible that she was dreaming, but it was so much like a dream come true that she felt faint.

"Look at me, Abby," he whispered.

She raised her eyes and his gaze fell to the transparent material over her firm, high breasts. He reached out and drew his knuckles down from her collarbone over one perfect breast, and he smiled at her body's helpless reaction to his touch, at the hunger he could see and feel.

"Same damned thing happens to me every time I think about you," he murmured with a soft, deep laugh.

"Four months, Abby. Four long months, and I've walked around aching every minute of every day, wanting you until I was like a wounded bear with everyone around me. Tonight I'd had all I could take, I couldn't even get properly drunk…damn you, come here!"

He lifted her in his hard arms, taking her mouth with a hungry, aching thoroughness, ignoring her sweet moan of pleasure and her clinging arms as he walked back into her bedroom and slammed the door behind them.

"I'm going to make love to you all night long," he said as he carried her straight toward the bed. "In the morning, you'll be damned lucky if you can walk at all. Then we'll talk."

"Cade, I could get pregnant!" she said in a high-pitched tone, afraid that it was only the liquor talking.

"Yes, you could," he said quietly, staring into her eyes. "And that would mean total commitment. To me. For life. Say yes or no. But if it's no, I'm going straight back to Montana, and I'll never come near you again."

She felt her body trembling in his strong embrace, and her heart yielded totally as she searched his face with a loving, possessive gaze.

"I don't know if I can survive an affair with you," she said softly. "But if that's what you want, I…I can try. I just don't understand what we'd do about a child…."

He breathed slowly, deliberately, and his eyes softened. "Melly said you were blind about me. I suppose she knew better than I did," he murmured. He laid her gently down on the bed and unbuttoned his shirt with slow, easy motions, tossing it aside. His hands went to his belt and unfastened it. His trousers followed, while Abby watched him, shocked to the bone.

"If you think it's rough on you," he muttered, glancing at her as he turned to divest himself of everything else, "remember what I told you before, Abby. I've never undressed in front of a woman."

"That's the loss of women everywhere," she whispered, awed as he turned around again. "Oh, Cade...!"

His face softened, and the red stain on his cheeks faded away. He sat down beside her, coaxing her to sit up so that he could remove the caftan. And then he just looked and looked, until she felt her heart trembling wildly, her body helplessly arching in invitation, moving restlessly under the pure sensuality of the appraisal.

"Before this goes any further," he said quietly, sliding a big, warm hand over her smooth belly, up to rest maddeningly below one taut breast, "you'd better tell me if you meant what you said on the phone."

She swallowed. "About being lonely and lost in the city?" she whispered.

He nodded. "Are you happy?"

"When I'm with you," she managed through trembling lips. "Only when I'm with you. Oh, God, you don't know…you'll never know how it was to leave you!"

His fingers trembled and he searched for his voice. "I know how it was to be left, Abby," he said slowly. "I've been walking around like half a man for four years. And until tonight, I had no idea, no idea at all what you felt."

"How could I tell you, when you kept going on about not wanting a commitment, not wanting marriage?" she asked unsteadily. "You pushed me away.…"

"I had to," he ground out. "I can't control what I feel for you, I never could. You'll never know how close I came to taking you the night I found you by the pool. When I left you I was shaking like a boy. I had to drink myself to sleep—the only other time I've been at the bottle like I have tonight." His fingers moved up to her breasts, touching them like a man touching a treasure trove. "So beautiful," he whispered. "You were then, you are now. My Abby. My own."

Abby's hands reached up and stroked his chest, tickling as they pressed into the tangle of dark hair. "I never knew," she whispered.

"Neither did I." He shuddered as her hands caressed him. "Don't do that, not yet. I go crazy when you touch me that way."

"You said we were going to make love," she reminded him softly.

"We are. When you agree to marry me," he said quietly. "I couldn't handle an affair with you, either. If I take you, you take me for life."

It was important to know the truth, not just guess at it. There had been too much misunderstanding already. "Because you need sons to inherit Painted Ridge?" she asked in a whisper.

"Because I love you, Abigail Shane," he corrected breathlessly. "Because I've loved you for so many years that loving you is a way of life for me. Because if you don't come home with me, I'll pack my bags and move in with you and make love to you until you'll marry me in self-defense, just to get some rest."

Tears welled up in her wide brown eyes as they searched his. "You love me, Cade?" she burst out.

"What a mild word for so much feeling," he managed in a voice that shook. His hands framed her face, and his eyes worshipped it. "I want to be with you all the time. I want to sit and watch you when we're together. I want to stay by your bed when you're sick and you need me. I want to hold you in my arms in bed at night, even when we don't make love. I want to give you children. Most of all, I want to live with you until I die. All the good days and bad. All the way to the grave."

She was crying helplessly at his admission, at having all her wildest dreams come true. Her fingers moved up to his hard face and lovingly traced every warm inch of it. "I couldn't look at you when I got on the bus four years ago," she said brokenly, "because if I had, I would have thrown myself at your feet and begged you to let me stay. I started loving you when I was barely fifteen, and I've loved you every day since. Hopelessly, with all my heart. Oh, God, Cade, it was never New York and modeling. It was you! I love you until I hurt all over! I'll love you all my life, all the days I live…!"

He stopped the frantic words with his mouth and eased down beside her. They kissed slowly, sweetly, rocking in each other's warm arms, savoring the newness of belonging to each other, of shared loving. Until his tongue gently penetrated her mouth. Until her lips opened to its deep searching. Until they moved, together, slowly, into a new and shattering kind of intimacy with each other.

"Teach me how, Cade," she whispered with love splintering her voice as she felt his hands touching her in new ways. "Teach me how…to show love…this way."

His mouth gentled hers. "We'll learn it together, honey," he whispered back. "Because this is like my first time, too. Tell me if I hurt you. I'd rather die than hurt you now."

But even as he spoke, his mouth was moving against her body, and she forgot that it was the first time, she forgot everything but the glory of being kissed and touched so tenderly by the only man she'd ever loved. She relaxed and moved deliberately, touched deliberately, delighting in his reactions to her fingers, her mouth. She whispered her love; her body shouted it.

Sensation piled on sensation, while she turned and arched and whispered wildly into his ear as he moved against her so slowly, with such staggering control. She could barely believe that the level of pleasure she was experiencing was bearable as it mounted and mounted and began to possess her.

Her eyes opened on a surge of mingled need and fear, and his were open, too, staring back at her.

"Don't be afraid of me," he whispered shakenly, urgently. "I love you. Trust me."

It was all she needed to push her over the edge. Her eyes closed again, and she felt his mouth gentling hers, preparing her for what was coming.

Her hands tangled in his thick, dark hair as his body slowly, tenderly, overwhelmed hers. His mouth was gentle, despite the need she could feel in him, a need he was deliberately denying for her sake. The very tenderness of his movements, his slow, soft kisses, made it so beautiful that she forgot her fear and gave herself up to the incredible intimacy of belonging to him.

If there was pain, she hardly noticed it, so involved was she in trying to get closer to him, trying to please him as he was pleasing her. She wanted nothing more than the joy of giving everything she had to give.

He cherished her as she'd never dreamed a man could cherish a woman, every second fueling the hunger and the sweetness of sharing love. She clung to him, loving him, loving him! And it was so easy. So perfect. So beautiful. Her eyes burned with tears that rolled helplessly down her cheeks into their joined mouths. A moment later she heard his voice in her ear, whispering words that only vaguely registered, whispering her name like a litany.

And from tenderness came passion—suddenly, like a summer storm billowing over them, lifting and tossing them in a vortex of urgency that blazed brighter than the lights around them.

She heard her voice break, and felt his hands controlling her wild movements firmly, guiding, teaching. Her teeth bit into his hard shoulder in an agony of pleasure, so exquisite that she cried out. And then there was no more time for the gentle beginnings, only for the wild, furious stretch toward fulfillment that sent them crashing together in frantic torment, trembling wildly, whispering urgently until there was oneness. And then peace.

Later, she curled up against him, trembling, while he

lit a cigarette and smoked it. She laughed softly, triumphantly, delightedly.

His arm drew her closer, and he chuckled softly, too. "My God, in all my wildest dreams I never imagined feeling like that."

"Neither did I," she returned. "I thought I'd died."

His chest rose and fell heavily. "I'm going to have that book framed and hung over our bed after we're married."

She blinked. "Book?"

He chuckled wickedly. "There's this book about making love that I bought a few weeks ago," he murmured. He lifted his brows at her stunned expression and laughed uproariously. "Well, hell, Abby, I told you I spent half my life working with the damned cattle? Where did you expect me to learn about sex? You women, always expecting men to know all the answers and hating us for the way we get them...."

Her face brightened with wonder. "Why, you old devil," she said. "And I thought you had a string of women a mile long!"

He kissed her nose. "You're my woman. The only one I ever wanted. I haven't been a monk, but there was never any joy for me in sleeping with women I didn't even like."

She stared up at him curiously. "You mean, you learned everything you just did to me out of a book?"

His eyebrows arched. "It was a good book," he said defensively, "kind of a primer...well, damn it, I thought that after I gave you a while to think about me and the ranch, and maybe miss me, I might come up here and try to change your mind. I was going to wait until Christmas...." He shrugged his powerful shoulders. "Then tonight, after Calla went out with Jeb, I got lonely and started drinking." He sighed. "First time I've put away that much whiskey in years." He looked down at her radiant face. "When you started ranting and raving at me, it was the sweetest music I'd ever heard. I didn't even take time to shave, I just got Hank out of bed to drive me to the airport."

"You said he was quitting!"

"When he found out I was on my way to you, he took back his resignation," Cade said, grinning. "Told me he had wondered if I planned to stay stupid all my life."

"I think we were both a little dense," she replied. Her eyes devoured him. "I love you," she whispered intensely.

"I love you," he replied, bending to kiss her softly, slowly, with tender promise. "Can you live with me on Painted Ridge and give up all you've accomplished? If not, I'll compromise, now that I know you love me."

"I could give up breathing if you'll make love to me every night," she murmured, pressing close. "I hate it here. After the first few months, all the glamour and adventure wore off. I worked like a zombie all day and dreamed all night about how it would be to sleep in your arms and carry your child in my body...."

He drew in a sharp breath. "Don't say things like that to me, I'll go crazy."

"Take me with you," she said, brushing her hand over his chest and smiling when he trembled. "Let's go together."

"In a minute." He put out the cigarette and leaned over her, his eyes solemn. "I can't expect you to sacrifice four years of hard work just to raise children. I don't want you to give up being a person just because you're my wife. We all need to feel fulfillment, a sense of purpose."

"Oh, my gosh, I didn't ever tell you about Jessica Dane!" she burst out, and explained it all, even her behavior at the reception.

He sighed angrily. "Well, I was a damned fool over that, wasn't I?" he ground out. He kissed her gently. "I'm sorry, honey."

"It's all right. You didn't know." She touched his mouth. "So you see, I could work for Jessica and never leave the house except to supervise some seamstresses once in a while. And I've always preferred designing to modeling, anyway."

"Lucky me," he said. He grinned. "If we have little girls, you can make party dresses for them, too."

She laughed. "Not for the little boys, though. I don't want my sons parading around in petticoats." She leaned forward and kissed him lazily. "My throat's sore from talking. Teach me some more things you learned in that book of yours."

He chuckled. "There's just one more little thing to talk about. I had Hank promise to make a few phone calls for me after daylight."

"Did you?" she murmured, nibbling at his lips.

"I had him invite the minister over for next Saturday."

"That's nice," she whispered. Her hands smoothed over his long, tanned body.

"Plus about fifty other people."

"Um," she murmured. Her hands moved to his hair-roughened chest and she pressed against him. "That's nice, too."

"For the wedding."

She drew away. "Next Saturday?"

"Why wait?" he asked, biting at her mouth. "I sure was hoping you'd say yes, Abby. All the way here I had nightmares about trying to line up a bride and groom at such short notice if you refused me...."

"Cade Alexander McLaren, what am I going to do with you?" she asked sharply.

"Lie down here and I'll show you," he murmured

with a laugh, easing her onto her back. "This is the best chapter of all...."

Abby smiled as she met his hungry mouth. When they got home to Painted Ridge, she had some heavy reading to do.

★ ★ ★ ★ ★

LIONHEARTED

To the FAO Schwartz gang on Peachtree Road, Atlanta,
and at the Internet Customer Service Department.
Thanks!

❧ Prologue ❧

Leo Hart felt alone in the world. The last of his bachelor brothers, Rey, had gotten married and moved out of the house almost a year ago. That left Leo, alone, with an arthritic housekeeper who came in two days a week and threatened to retire every day. If she did, Leo would be left without a biscuit to his name, or even a hope of getting another one unless he went to a restaurant every morning for breakfast. Considering his work schedule, that was impractical.

He leaned back in the swivel chair at his desk in the office he now shared with no one. He was happy for his brothers. Most of them had families now, except newly married Rey. Simon and Tira had two little boys. Cag and Tess had a boy. Corrigan and Dorie had a boy and a baby girl. When he looked back, Leo realized that women had been a missing commodity in his life of late. It was late September. Roundup was just over, and there had been so much going on at the ranch, with business, that he'd hardly had time for a night out. He was feeling it.

Even as he considered his loneliness, the phone rang.

"Why don't you come over for supper?" Rey asked when he picked up the receiver.

"Listen," Leo drawled, grinning, "you don't invite your brother over to dinner on your honeymoon."

"We got married after Christmas last year," Rey pointed out.

"Like I said, you're still on your honeymoon," came the amused reply. "Thanks. But I've got too much to do."

"Work doesn't make up for a love life."

"You'd know," Leo chuckled.

"Okay. But the invitation's open, whenever you want to accept it."

"Thanks. I mean it."

"Sure."

The line went dead. Leo put the receiver down and stretched hugely, bunching the hard muscles in his upper arms. He was the boss as much as his brothers on their five ranch properties, but he did a lot of the daily physical labor that went with cattle raising, and his tall, powerful body was evidence of it. He wondered sometimes if he didn't work that hard to keep deep-buried needs at bay. In his younger days, women had flocked around him, and he hadn't been slow to accept sensual invitations. But he was in his thirties now, and casual interludes were no longer satisfying.

He'd planned to have a quiet weekend at home, but Marilee Morgan, a close friend of Janie Brewster's, had cajoled him into taking her up to Houston for dinner and to see a ballet she had tickets for. He was partial to ballet, and Marilee explained that she couldn't drive herself because her car was in the shop. She was easy on the eyes, and she was sophisticated. Not that Leo was tempted to let himself be finagled into any sort of intimacy with her. He didn't want her carrying tales of his private life to Janie, who had an obvious and uncomfortable crush on him.

He knew that Marilee would never have asked him to take her any place in Jacobsville, Texas, because it was a small town and news of the date would inevitably get back to Janie. It might help show the girl that Leo was a free agent, but it wouldn't help his friendship with Fred Brewster to know that Leo was playing fast and loose with Janie's best friend. Some best friend, he thought privately.

But taking Marilee out would have one really good consequence—it would get him out of a dinner date at the Brewsters' house. He and Fred Brewster were friends and business associates, and he enjoyed the time he spent with the older man. Well, except for two members of his family, he amended darkly. He didn't like Fred's sister, Lydia. She was a busybody who had highfalutin ideas. Fortunately, she was hardly ever around and she didn't live with Fred. He had mixed feelings about Fred's daughter, Janie, who was twenty-one and bristling with psychology advice after her graduation from a junior college in that subject. She'd made Cag furious with her analyses of his food preferences, and Leo was becoming adept at avoiding invitations that would put him in her line of fire.

Not that she was bad looking. She had long, thick, light brown hair and a neat little figure. But she also had a crush on Leo, which was very visible. He considered her totally unacceptable as a playmate for a man his age, and he knocked back her attempts at flirting with lazy skill. He'd known her since she was ten and wearing braces on her teeth. It was hard to get that image out of his mind.

Besides, she couldn't cook. Her rubber chicken dinners were infamous locally, and her biscuits could be classified as lethal weapons.

Thinking about those biscuits made him pick up the phone and dial Marilee.

She was curt when she picked up the phone, but the minute he spoke, her voice softened.

"Well, hello, Leo," she said huskily.

"What time do you want me to pick you up Saturday night?"

There was a faint hesitation. "You won't, uh, mention this to Janie?"

"I have as little contact with Janie as I can. You know that," he said impatiently.

"Just checking," she teased, but she sounded worried. "I'll be ready to leave about six."

"Suppose I pick you up at five and we'll have supper in Houston before the ballet?"

"Wonderful! I'll look forward to it. See you then."

"See you."

He hung up, but picked up the receiver again and dialed the Brewsters' number.

As luck would have it, Janie answered.

"Hi, Janie," he said pleasantly.

"Hi, Leo," she replied breathlessly. "Want to talk to Dad?"

"You'll do," he replied. "I have to cancel for dinner Saturday. I've got a date."

There was the faintest pause. It was almost imperceptible. "I see."

"Sorry, but it's a long-standing one," he lied. "I can't get out of it. I forgot when I accepted your dad's invitation. Can you give him my apologies?"

"Of course," she told him. "Have a good time."

She sounded strange. He hesitated. "Something wrong?" he asked.

"Nothing at all! Nice talking to you, Leo. Bye."

Janie Brewster hung up and closed her eyes, sick with disappointment. She'd planned a perfect menu. She'd practiced all week on a special chicken dish that was tender and succulent. She'd practiced an exquisite crème brûlée, as well, which was Leo's favorite dessert. She could even use the little tool to caramelize the sugar topping, which had taken a while to perfect. All that work, and for nothing. She'd have been willing to bet that Leo hadn't had a date for that night already. He'd made one deliberately, to get out of the engagement.

She sat down beside the hall table, her apron almost stiff with flour, her face white with dustings of it, her hair disheveled. She was anything but the picture of a perfect date. And wasn't it just her luck? For the past year, she'd mounted a real campaign to get Leo to notice her.

She'd flirted with him shamelessly at Micah Steele's wedding to Callie Kirby, until a stabbing scowl had turned her shy. It had angered him that she'd caught the bouquet Callie had thrown. It had embarrassed her that he glared so angrily at her. Months later, she'd tried, shyly, every wile she had on him, with no success. She couldn't cook and she was not much more than a fashion plate, according to her best friend, Marilee, who was trying to help her catch Leo. Marilee had plenty of advice, things Leo had mentioned that he didn't like about Janie, and Janie was trying her best to improve in the areas he'd mentioned. She was even out on the ranch for the first time in her life, trying to get used to horses and cattle and dust and dirt. But if she couldn't get Leo to the house to show him her new skills, she didn't have a lot of hope.

"Who was that on the phone?" Hettie, their housekeeper, called from the staircase. "Was it Mr. Fred?"

"No. It was Leo. He can't come Saturday night. He's got a date."

"Oh." Hettie smiled sympathetically. "There will be other dinners, darlin'."

"Of course there will," Janie said and smiled back. She got out of the chair. "Well, I'll just make it for you and me and Dad," she said, with disappointment plain in her voice.

"It isn't as if Leo has any obligation to spend his weekends with us, just because he does a lot of business with Mr. Fred," Hettie reminded her gently. "He's a good man. A little old for you, though," she added hesitantly.

Janie didn't answer her. She just smiled and walked back into the kitchen.

Leo showered, shaved, dressed to the hilt and got into the new black Lincoln sports car he'd just bought. Next year's model, and fast as lightning. He was due for a night on the town. And missing Janie's famous rubber chicken wasn't going to disappoint him one bit.

His conscience did nag him, though, oddly. Maybe it was just hearing Janie's friend, Marilee, harp on the girl all the time. In the past week, she'd started telling him some disturbing things that Janie had said about him. He was going to have to be more careful around Janie. He didn't want her to get the wrong idea. He had no interest in her at all. She was just a kid.

He glanced in the lighted mirror over the steering wheel before he left the sprawling Hart Ranch. He had thick blond-streaked brown hair, a broad forehead, a slightly crooked nose and high cheekbones. But his teeth were good and strong, and he had a square jaw and a nice wide mouth. He wasn't all that handsome, but compared to most of his brothers, he was a hunk. He chuckled at that rare conceit and closed the mirror. He was rich enough that his looks didn't matter.

He didn't fool himself that Marilee would have found him all that attractive without his bankroll. But she was pretty and he didn't mind taking her to Houston and showing her off, like the fishing trophies he displayed on the walls of his study. A man had to have his little vanities, he told himself. But he thought about Janie's disappointment when he didn't show up for supper, her pain if she ever found out her best friend was stabbing her in the back, and he hated the guilt he felt.

He put on his seat belt, put the car in gear and took off down the long driveway. He didn't have any reason to feel guilty, he told himself firmly. He was a bachelor, and he'd never done one single thing to give Janie Brewster the impression that he wanted to be the man in her life. Besides, he'd been on his own too long. A cultural evening in Houston was just the thing to cure the blues.

❖ 1 ❖

Leo Hart was half out of humor. It had been a long week as it was, and now he was faced with trying to comfort his neighbor Fred Brewster who'd just lost the prize young Salers bull that Leo had wanted to buy. The bull was the offspring of a grand champion whose purchase had figured largely in Leo's improved cross-breeding program. He felt as sad as Fred seemed to.

"He was fine yesterday," Fred said heavily, wiping sweat off his narrow brow as the two men surveyed the bull in the pasture. The huge creature was lying dead on its side, not a mark on it. "I'm not the only rancher who's ever lost a prize bull, but these are damned suspicious circumstances."

"They are," Leo agreed grimly, his dark eyes surveying the bull. "It's just a thought, but you haven't had a problem with an employee, have you? Christabel Gaines said they just had a bull die of unknown causes. This happened after they fired a man named Jack Clark a couple of weeks ago. He's working for Duke Wright now, driving a cattle truck."

"Judd Dunn said it wasn't unknown causes that killed the bull, it was bloat. Judd's a Texas Ranger," Fred reminded him. "If there was sabotage on the ranch he co-owns with Christabel, I think he'd know it. No, Christabel had that young bull in a pasture with a lot of clover and she hadn't primed him on hay or tannin-containing forage beforehand. She won't use antibiotics, either, which would have helped prevent trouble. Even so, you can treat bloat if you catch it in time. It was bad luck that they didn't check that pasture, but Christabel's shorthanded and she's back at the vocational school full-time, too. Not much time to check on livestock."

"They had four other bulls that were still alive," Leo pointed out, scowling.

Fred shrugged. "Maybe they didn't like clover, or weren't in the same pasture." He shook his head. "I'm fairly sure their bull died of bloat. That's what Judd thinks, anyway. He says Christabel's unsettled by having those movie people coming next month to work out a shooting schedule on the ranch and she's the only one who thinks there was foul play." Fred rubbed a hand through his silver hair. "But to answer your question— yes, I did wonder about a disgruntled ex-employee, but I haven't fired anybody in over two years. So you can count out vengeance. And it wasn't bloat. My stock gets antibiotics."

"Don't say that out loud," Leo chuckled. "If the Tremaynes hear you, there'll be a fight."

"It's my ranch. I run it my way." Fred looked sadly toward the bull again. He was having financial woes the likes of which he'd never faced. He was too proud to tell Leo the extent of it. "This bull is a hell of a loss right now, too, with my breeding program under way. He wasn't insured, so I can't afford to replace him. Well, not just yet," he amended, because he didn't want Leo to think he was nearly broke.

"That's one problem we can solve," Leo replied. "I've got that beautiful Salers bull I bought two years ago, but it's time I replaced him. I'd have loved to have had yours, but while I'm looking for a replacement, you can borrow mine for your breeding season."

"Leo, I can't let you do that," Fred began, overwhelmed by the offer. He knew very well what that bull's services cost.

Leo held up a big hand and grinned. "Sure you can. I've got an angle. I get first pick of your young bulls next spring."

"You devil, you," Fred said, chuckling. "All right, all right. On that condition, I'll take him and be much obliged. But I'd feel better if there was a man sitting up with him at night to guard him."

Leo stretched sore muscles, pushing his Stetson back over his blond-streaked brown hair. It was late September, but still very hot in Jacobsville, which was in southeastern Texas. He'd been helping move bulls all morning, and he was tired. "We can take care of security for him," Leo said easily. "I've got two cowboys banged up in accidents who can't work cattle. They're still on my payroll, so they can sit over here and guard my bull while they recuperate."

"And we'll feed them," Fred said.

Leo chuckled. "Now that's what I call a real nice solution. One of them," he confided, "eats for three men."

"I won't mind." His eyes went back to the still bull one more time. "He was the best bull, Leo. I had so many hopes for him."

"I know. But there are other champion-sired Salers bulls," Leo said.

"Sure. But not one like that one." He gestured toward the animal. "He had such beautiful conformation—" He broke off as a movement to one side caught his attention. He turned, leaned forward and then gaped at his approaching daughter. "Janie?" he asked, as if he wasn't sure of her identity.

Janie Brewster had light brown hair and green eyes. She'd tried going blond once, but these days her hair was its natural color. Straight, thick and sleek, it hung to her waist. She had a nice figure, a little on the slender side, and pretty little pert breasts. She even had nice legs. But anyone looking at her right now could be forgiven for mistaking her for a young bull rider.

She was covered with mud from head to toe. Even her hair was caked with it. She had a saddle over one thin shoulder, leaning forward to take its weight. The separation between her boots and jeans was imperceptible. Her blouse and arms were likewise. Only her eyes were visible, her eyebrows streaked where the mud had been haphazardly wiped away.

"Hi, Daddy," she muttered as she walked past them with a forced smile. "Hi, Leo. Nice day."

Leo's dark eyes were wide-open, like Fred's. He couldn't even manage words. He nodded, and kept gaping at the mud doll walking past.

"What have you been doing?" Fred shouted after his only child.

"Just riding around," she said gaily.

"Riding around," Fred murmured to himself as she trailed mud onto the porch and stopped there, calling for their housekeeper. "I can't remember the last time I saw her on a horse," he added.

"Neither can I," Leo was forced to admit.

Fred shook his head. "She has these spells lately," he said absently. "First it was baling hay. She went out with four of the hands and came home covered in dust and thorns. Then she took up dipping cattle." He cleared his throat. "Better to forget that altogether. Now it's riding. I don't know what the hell's got into her. She was all geared up to transfer to a four-year college and get on with her psychology degree. Then all of a sudden, she announces that she's going to learn ranching." He threw up his hands. "I'll never understand children. Will you?" he asked Leo.

Leo chuckled. "Don't ask me. Fatherhood is one role in life I have no desire to play. Listen, about my bull," he continued. "I'll have him trucked right over, and the men will come with him. If you have any more problems, you just let me know."

Fred was relieved. The Harts owned five ranches. Nobody had more clout than they did, politically and financially. The loan of that bull would help him re-coup his losses and get back on his feet. Leo was a gentleman. "I'm damned grateful, Leo. We've been having hard times lately."

Leo only smiled. He knew that the Brewsters were having a bad time financially. He and Fred had swapped and traded bulls for years—although less expensive ones than Fred's dead Salers bull—and they frequently did business together. He was glad he could help.

He did wonder about Janie's odd behavior. She'd spent weeks trying to vamp him with low-cut blouses and dresses. She was always around when he came to see Fred on business, waiting in the living room in a seductive pose. Not that Janie even knew how to be seductive, he told himself amusedly. She was twenty-one, but hardly in the class with her friend Marilee Morgan, who was only four years older than Janie but could give Mata Hari lessons in seduction.

He wondered if Marilee had been coaching her in tomboyish antics. That would be amusing, because lately Marilee had been using Janie's tactics on him. The former tomboy-turned-debutante had even finagled him into taking her out to eat in Houston. He wondered if Janie knew. Sometimes friends could become your worst enemy, he thought. Luckily Janie only had a crush on him, which would wear itself out all the faster once she knew he had gone out with her best friend. Janie was far too young for him, and not only in age. The sooner she realized it, the better. Besides, he didn't like her new competitive spirit. Why was she trying to compete with her father in ranch management all of a sudden? Was it a liberation thing? She'd never shown any such inclination before, and her new appearance was appalling. The one thing Leo had admired about her was the elegance and sophistication with which she dressed. Janie in muddy jeans was a complete turnoff.

He left Fred at the pasture and drove back to the ranch, his mind already on ways and means to find out what had caused that healthy bull's sudden demise.

Janie was listening to their housekeeper's tirade through the bathroom door.

"I'll clean it all up, Hettie," she promised. "It's just dirt. It will come out."

"It's red mud! It will never come out!" Hettie was grumbling. "You'll be red from head to toe forever! People will mistake you for that nineteenth-century Kiowa, Satanta, who painted everything he owned red, even his horse!"

Janie laughed as she stripped off the rest of her clothes and stepped into the shower. Besides being a keen student of Western history, Hettie was all fire and wind, and she'd blow out soon. She was such a sweetheart. Janie's mother had died years ago, leaving behind Janie and her father and Hettie—and Aunt Lydia who lived in Jacobsville. Fortunately, Aunt Lydia only visited infrequently. She was so very house-proud, so clothes-conscious, so debutante! She was just like Janie's late mother, in fact, who had raised Janie to be a little flower blossom in a world of independent, strong women. She spared a thought for her mother's horror if she could have lived long enough to see what her daughter had worn at college. There, where she could be herself, Janie didn't wear designer dresses and hang out with the right social group. Janie studied anthropology, as well as the psychology her aunt Lydia had insisted on—and felt free to insist, since she helped pay Janie's tuition. But Janie spent most of her weekends and afternoons buried in mud, learning how to dig out fragile pieces of ancient pottery and projectile points.

But she'd gone on with the pretense when she was home—when Aunt Lydia was visiting, of course—proving her worth at psychology. Sadly, it had gone awry when she psychoanalyzed Leo's brother Callaghan last year over the asparagus. She'd gone to her room howling with laughter after Aunt Lydia had hung on every word approvingly. She was sorry she'd embarrassed Cag, but the impulse had been irresistible. Her aunt was *so* gullible. She'd felt guilty afterward, though, for not telling Aunt Lydia her true interests.

She finished her shower, dried off and changed into new clothes so that she could start cleaning up the floors where she'd tracked mud. Despite her complaints, Hettie would help. She didn't really mind housework. Neither did Janie, although her late mother would be horrified if she could see her only child on the floor with a scrub brush alongside Hettie's ample figure.

Janie helped with everything, except cooking. Her expertise in the kitchen was, to put it mildly, nonexistent. But, she thought, brightening, that was the next thing on her list of projects. She was undergoing a major self-improvement. First she was going to learn ranching—even if it killed her—and then she was going to learn to cook.

She wished this transformation had been her idea, but actually, it had been Marilee's. The other girl had told her, in confidence, that she'd been talking to Leo and Leo had told her flatly that the reason he didn't notice Janie was that she didn't know anything about ranching. She was too well-dressed, too chic, too sophisticated. And the worst thing was that she didn't know anything about cooking, either, Marilee claimed. So if Janie wanted to land that big, hunky fish, she was going to have to make some major changes.

It sounded like a good plan, and Marilee had been her

friend since grammar school, when the Morgan family had moved next door. So Janie accepted Marilee's advice with great pleasure, knowing that her best friend would never steer her wrong. She was going to stay home—not go back to college—and she was going to show Leo Hart that she could be the sort of woman who appealed to him. She'd work so hard at it, she'd have to succeed!

Not that her attempts at riding a horse were anything to write home about, she had to admit as she mopped her way down the long wooden floor of the hall. But she was a rancher's daughter. She'd get better with practice.

She did keep trying. A week later, she was making biscuits in the kitchen—or trying to learn how—when she dropped the paper flour bag hard on the counter and was dusted from head to toe with the white substance.

It would have to be just that minute that her father came in the back door with Leo in tow.

"Janie?" her father exclaimed, wide-eyed.

"Hi, Dad!" she said with a big grin. "Hi, Leo."

"What in blazes are you doing?" her father demanded.

"Putting the flour in a canister," she lied, still smiling.

"Where's Hettie?" he asked.

Their housekeeper was hiding in the bedroom, supposedly making beds, and trying not to howl at Janie's pitiful efforts. "Cleaning, I believe," she said.

"Aunt Lydia not around?"

"Playing bridge with the Harrisons," she said.

"Bridge!" her father scoffed. "If it isn't bridge, it's golf. If it isn't golf, it's tennis… Is she coming over today to go over those stocks with me or not?" he persisted, because they jointly owned some of his late wife's shares and couldn't sell them without Lydia's permission. If he could ever find the blasted woman!

"She said she wasn't coming over until Saturday, Dad," Janie reminded him.

He let out an angry sigh. "Well, come on, Leo, I'll show you the ones I want to sell and let you advise me. They're in my desk… Damn bridge! I can't do a thing until Lydia makes up her mind."

Leo gave Janie a curious glance but he kept walking and didn't say another word to her. Minutes later, he left—out the front door, not the back.

Janie's self-improvement campaign continued into the following week with calf roping, which old John was teaching her out in the corral. Since she could now loop the rope around a practice wooden cow with horns, she was progressing to livestock.

She followed John's careful instruction and tossed her loop over the head of the calf, but she'd forgotten to dig her heels in. The calf hadn't. He jerked her off her feet and proceeded to run around the ring like a wild thing, trying to get away from the human slithering after him at a breakneck pace.

Of course, Leo would drive up next to the corral in time to see John catch and throw the calf, leaving Janie covered in mud. She looked like a road disaster.

This time Leo didn't speak. He was too busy laughing. Janie couldn't speak, either, her mouth was full of mud. She gave both men a glare and stomped off toward the back door of the house, trailing mud and unspeakable stuff, fuming the whole while.

A bath and change of clothes improved her looks and her smell. She was resigned to finding Leo gone when she got out, so she didn't bother to dress up or put on makeup. She wandered out to the kitchen in jeans and a loose long-sleeved denim shirt, with her hair in a lopsided ponytail and her feet bare.

"You'll step on something sharp and cripple yourself," Hettie warned, turning from the counter where she was making rolls, her ample arms up to the elbows in flour.

"I have tough feet," Janie protested with a warm smile. She went up and hugged Hettie hard from behind, loving the familiar smells of freshly washed cotton and flour that seemed to cling to her. Hettie had been around since Janie was six. She couldn't imagine life without the gray-haired, blue-eyed treasure with her constantly disheveled hair and worried expression. "Oh, Hettie, what would we do without you?" she asked on a sigh, and closed her eyes.

"Get away, you pest," Hettie muttered, "I know what you're up to...Janie Brewster, I'll whack you!"

But Janie was already out of reach, dangling Hettie's apron from one hand, her green eyes dancing with mischief.

"You put that back on me or you'll get no rolls tonight!" Hettie raged at her.

"All right, all right, I was only kidding," Janie chuckled. She replaced the apron around Hettie's girth and was fastening it when she heard the door open behind her.

"You stop teaching her these tricks!" Hettie growled at the newcomer.

"Who, me?" Leo exclaimed with total innocence.

Janie's hands fumbled with the apron. Her heart ran wild. He hadn't left. She'd thought he was gone, and she hadn't bothered with her appearance. He was still here, and she looked like last year's roast!

"You'll drop that apron, Janie," Leo scolded playfully.

Janie glanced at him as she retied the apron. "You can talk," she chided. "I hear your housekeepers keep quitting because you untie aprons constantly! One kept a broom handle!"

"She broke it on my hard head," he said smugly. "What are you making, Hettie?"

"Rolls," she said. She glanced warily at Leo. "I can't make biscuits. Sorry."

He gave her a hard glare. "Just because I did something a little offbeat..."

"Carried that little chef right out of his restaurant, with him kicking and screaming all the way, I heard," Hettie mused, eyes twinkling.

"He said he could bake biscuits. I was only taking him home with me to let him prove it," Leo said belligerently.

"That's not what he thought," Hettie chuckled. "I hear he dropped the charges...?"

"Nervous little guy," Leo said, shaking his head. "He'd never have worked out, anyway." He gave her a long look. "You sure you can't bake a biscuit? Have you ever tried?"

"No, and I won't. I like working here," she said firmly.

He sighed. "Just checking." He peered over her shoulder fondly. "Rolls, huh? I can't remember when I've had a homemade roll."

"Tell Fred to invite you to supper," Hettie suggested.

He glanced at Janie. "Why can't she do it?"

Janie was tongue-tied. She couldn't think at all.

The lack of response from her dumbfounded Leo. To have Janie hesitate about inviting him for a meal was shocking. Leo scowled and just stared at her openly, which only made her more nervous and uncertain. She knew she looked terrible. Leo wanted a woman who could do ranch work and cook, but surely he wanted one who looked pretty, too. Right now, Janie could have qualified for the Frump of the Year award.

She bit her lower lip, hard, and looked as if she were about to cry.

"Hey," he said softly, in a tone he'd never used with her before, "what's wrong?"

"Have to let this rise," Hettie was murmuring after she'd covered the dough and washed her hands, oblivious to what was happening behind her. "Meanwhile I'm going to put another load of clothes in the washer, darlin'," she called to Janie over her shoulder.

The door into the dining room closed, but they didn't notice.

Leo moved closer to Janie, and suddenly his big, lean hands were on her thin shoulders, resting heavily over the soft denim. They were warm and very strong.

Her breath caught in the back of her throat while she looked up into black eyes that weren't teasing or playful. They were intent, narrow, faintly glittering. There was no expression on his handsome face at all. He looked into her eyes as if he'd never seen them, or her, before—and she looked terrible!

"Come on," he coaxed. "Tell me what's wrong. If it's something I can fix, I will."

Her lips trembled. Surely, she could make up something, quick, before he moved away!

"I got hurt," she whispered in a shameful lie. "When the calf dragged me around the corral."

"Did you?" He was only half listening. His eyes were on her mouth. It was the prettiest little mouth, like a pink bow, full and soft, just barely parted over perfect, white teeth. He wondered if she'd been kissed, and how often. She never seemed to date, or at least, he didn't know about her boyfriends. He shouldn't be curious, either, but Marilee had hinted that Janie had more boyfriends than other local girls, that she was a real rounder.

Janie was melting. Her knees were weak. Any minute, she was going to be a little puddle of love looking up at his knees.

He felt her quiver under his hands, and his scowl grew darker. If she was as sophisticated as Marilee said she was, why was she trembling now? An experienced woman would be winding her arms around his neck already, offering her mouth, curving her body into his…

His fingers tightened involuntarily on her soft arms. "Come here," he said huskily, and tugged her right up against his tall, muscular body. Of all the Harts, he was the tallest, and the most powerfully built. Janie's breasts pressed into his diaphragm. She felt him tauten at the contact, felt his curiosity as he looked down into her wide, soft, dazed eyes. Her hands lightly touched his shirtfront, but hesitantly, as if it embarrassed her to touch him at all.

He let out a soft breath. His head was spinning with forbidden longings. Janie was barely twenty-one. She was the daughter of a man he did business with. She was off-limits. So why was he looking at her mouth and feeling his body swell sensuously at just the brush of her small breasts against him?

"Don't pick at my shirt," he said quietly. His voice was unusually deep and soft, its tone unfamiliar. "Flatten your hands on my chest."

She did that, slowly, as if she were just learning how to walk. Her hands were cold and nervous, but they warmed on his body. She stood very still, hoping against hope that he wasn't going to regain the senses she was certain he'd momentarily lost. She didn't even want to breathe, to do anything that would distract him. He seemed to be in a trance, and she was feeling dreams come true in the most unexpected and delightful way.

He smiled quizzically. "Don't you know how?"

Her lips were dry. She moistened them with just the tip of her tongue. He seemed to find that little movement fascinating. He watched her mouth almost hungrily. "How...to...do what?" she choked.

His hand went to her cheek and his thumb suddenly ran roughly over her lips, parting them in a whip of urgent, shocking emotion. "How to do this," he murmured as his head bent.

She saw the faint smile on his hard mouth as his lips parted. They brushed against hers in tiny little whispers of contact that weren't nearly enough to feed the hunger he was coaxing out of her.

Her nails curled into his shirt and he tensed. She felt thick hair over the warm, hard muscles of his chest. Closer, she felt the hard, heavy thunder of his pulse there, under her searching hands.

"Nice," he whispered. His voice was taut now, like his body against her.

She felt his big hands slide down her waist to her hips while he was playing with her mouth in the most arousing way. She couldn't breathe. Did he know? Could he tell that she was shaking with desire?

Her lips parted more with every sensuous brush of his mouth against them. At the same time, his hands moved to her narrow hips and teased against her lower spine. She'd never felt such strange sensations. She felt her body swell, as if it had been stung all over by bees, but the sensation produced pleasure instead of pain.

He nibbled at her upper lip, feeling it quiver tentatively as his tongue slid under it and began to explore. One lean hand slid around to the base of her hips and slowly gathered them into his, in a lazy movement that made her suddenly aware of the changing contours of his body.

She gasped and pulled against his hand.

He lifted his head and searched her wide, shocked green eyes. "Plenty of boyfriends, hmm?" he murmured sarcastically, almost to himself.

"Boy…friends?" Her voice sounded as if she were being strangled.

His hand moved back to her waist, the other one moved to her round chin and his thumb tugged gently at her lower lip. "Leave it like this," he whispered. His mouth hovered over hers just as it parted, and she found herself going on tiptoe, leaning toward him, almost begging for his mouth to come down and cover hers.

But he was still nibbling at her upper lip, gently toying with it, until he tilted her chin and his teeth tugged softly at the lower lip. His mouth brushed roughly over hers, teaching it to follow, to plead, then to demand something more urgent, more thorough than this slow torment.

Her nails bit into his chest and she moaned.

As if he'd been waiting patiently for that tiny little sound, his arms swallowed her up whole and his eyes, when they met hers, glittered like candlelight from deep in a cave.

His hand was in her ponytail, ripping away the rubber band so that he could catch strands of it in his strong fingers and angle her face just where he wanted it.

"Maybe you are old enough…" he breathed just before his mouth plunged deeply into hers.

She tautened all over with heated pleasure. Her body arched against him, no longer protesting the sudden hardness of him against her. She reached up to hold him, to keep that tormenting, hungry mouth against her lips. It was every dream she'd ever dreamed, coming true. She could hardly believe it was happening here, in broad daylight, in the kitchen where she'd been trying so hard to learn to make things that would please him. But he seemed to be pleased, just the same. He groaned against her lips, and his arms were bruising now, as if he wasn't quite in control. That was exciting. She threw caution to the winds and opened her mouth deliberately under the crush of his, inviting him in.

She felt his tongue go deep into the soft darkness, and she shivered as his mouth devoured hers.

Only the sound of a door slamming penetrated the thick sensual fog that held them both in thrall.

Leo lifted his head, slowly, and looked down into a face he didn't recognize. Janie's green eyes were like wet emeralds in her flushed face. Her lips were swollen, soft, sensual. Her body was clinging to his. He had her off the floor in his hungry embrace, and his body was throbbing with desire.

He knew that she could feel him, that she knew he was aroused. It was a secret thing, that only the two of them knew. It had to stay that way. He had to stop. This was wrong…!

He let go of her slowly, easing her back, while he sucked in a long, hard breath and shivered with a hunger he couldn't satisfy. He became aware of the rough grip he had on her upper arms and he relaxed it at once. He'd never meant to hurt her.

He fought for control, reciting multiplication tables silently in his mind until he felt his body unclench and relax.

It troubled him that he'd lost control so abruptly, and with a woman he should never have touched. He hadn't meant to touch her in the first place. He couldn't understand why he'd gone headfirst at her like that. He was usually cool with women, especially with Janie.

The way she was looking at him was disturbing. He was going to have a lot of explaining to do, and he didn't know how to begin. Janie was years too young for him, only his body didn't think so. Now he had to make his mind get himself out of this predicament.

"That shouldn't have happened," he said through his teeth.

She was hanging on every word, deaf to meanings, deaf to denials. Her body throbbed. "It's like the flu," she said, dazed, staring up at him. "It makes you...ache."

He shook her gently. "You're too young to have aches," he said flatly. "And I'm old enough to know better than to do something this stupid. Are you listening to me? This shouldn't have happened. I'm sorry."

Belatedly, she realized that he was backtracking. Of course he hadn't meant to kiss her. He'd made his opinion of her clear for years, and even if he liked kissing her, it didn't mean that he was ready to rush out and buy a ring. Quite the opposite.

She stepped away from him, her face still flushed, her eyes full of dreams she had to hide from him.

"I...I'm sorry, too," she stammered.

"Hell," he growled, ramming his hands into his pockets. "It was my fault. I started it."

She moved one shoulder. "No harm done." She cleared her throat and fought for inspiration. It came unexpectedly. Her eyes began to twinkle wickedly. "I have to take lessons when they're offered."

His eyebrows shot up. Had he heard her say that, or was he delusional?

"I'm not the prom queen," she pointed out. "Men

aren't thick on the ground around here, except old bachelors who chew tobacco and don't bathe."

"I call that prejudice," he said, relaxing into humor.

"I'll bet you don't hang out with women who smell like dirty horses," she said.

He pursed his lips. Like hers, they were faintly swollen. "I don't know about that. The last time I saw you, I recall, you were neck-deep in mud and sh—"

"You can stop right there!" she interrupted, flushing.

His dark eyes studied her long hair, liking its thick waves and its light brown color. "Pity your name isn't Jeanie," he murmured. "Stephen Foster wrote a song about her hair."

She smiled. He liked her hair, at least. Maybe he liked her a little, too.

She was pretty when she smiled like that, he thought, observing her. "Do I get invited to supper?" he drawled, lost in that soft, hungry look she was giving him. "If you say yes, I might consider giving you a few more lessons. Beginner class only, of course," he added with a grin.

2

Janie was sure she hadn't heard him say that, but he was still smiling. She smiled back. She felt pretty. No makeup, no shoes, disheveled—and Leo had kissed her, anyway. She beamed. At least, she beamed until she remembered the Hart bread mania. Any of them would do anything for a biscuit. Did that extend to homemade rolls?

"You're looking suspicious," he pointed out.

"A man who would kidnap a poor little pastry chef might do anything for a homemade roll," she reminded him.

He sighed. "Hettie makes wonderful rolls," he had to admit.

"Oh, you!" She hit him gently and then laughed. He was impossible. "Okay, you can come to supper."

He beamed. "You're a nice girl."

Nice. Well, at least he liked her. It was a start. It didn't occur to her, then, that a man who was seriously interested in her wouldn't think of her as just "nice."

Hettie came back into the room, still oblivious to the undercurrents, and got out a plastic bowl. She filled it with English peas from the crisper. "All right, my girl, sit down here and shell these. You staying?" she asked Leo.

"She said I could," he told Hettie.

"Then you can go away while we get it cooked."

"I'll visit my bull. Fred's got him in the pasture."

Leo didn't say another word. But the look he gave Janie before he left the kitchen was positively wicked.

But if she thought the little interlude had made any permanent difference in her relationship with Leo, Janie was doomed to disappointment. He came to supper, but he spent the whole time talking genetic breeding with Fred, and although he was polite to Janie, she might as well have been on the moon.

He didn't stay long after supper, either, making his excuses and praising Hettie for her wonderful cooking. He smiled at Janie, but not the way he had when they were alone in the kitchen. It was as if he'd put the kisses out of his mind forever, and expected her to act as if he'd never touched her. It was disheartening. It was heart-breaking. It was just like old times, except that now Leo had kissed her and she wanted him to do it again. Judging by his attitude over supper, she had a better chance of landing a movie role.

She spent the next few weeks remembering Leo's hungry kisses and aching for more of them. When she wasn't daydreaming, she was practicing biscuit-making. Hettie muttered about the amount of flour she was going through.

"Janie, you're going to bankrupt us in the kitchen!" the older woman moaned when Janie's fifth batch of biscuits came out looking like skeet pigeons. "That's your second bag of flour today!"

Janie was glowering at her latest effort on the baking sheet. "Something's wrong, and I can't decide what. I mean, I put in salt and baking powder, just like the recipe said…"

Hettie picked up the empty flour bag and read the label. Her eyes twinkled. "Janie, darlin', you bought self-rising flour."

"Yes. So?" she asked obliviously.

"If it's self-rising, it already has the salt and baking powder in it, doesn't it?"

Janie burst out laughing. "So that's what I'm doing wrong! Hand me another bag of flour, could you?"

"This is the last one," Hettie said mournfully.

"No problem. I'll just drive to the store and get some more. Need anything?"

"Milk and eggs," Hettie said at once.

"We've got four chickens," Janie exclaimed, turning, "and you have to buy eggs?"

"The chickens are molting."

Janie smiled. "And when they molt, they don't lay. Sorry. I forgot. I'll be back in a jiffy," she added, peeling off her apron.

She paused just long enough to brush her hair out, leaving it long, and put on a little makeup. She thrust her arms into her nice fringed leather jacket, because it was seasonably cool outside as well as raining, and popped into her red sports car. You never could tell when you might run into Leo, because he frequently dashed into the supermarket for frozen biscuits and butter when he was between cooks.

Sure enough, as she started for the checkout counter with her milk, eggs and flour, she spotted Leo, head and shoulders above most of the men present. He was wearing that long brown Australian drover's coat he favored in wet weather, and he was smiling in a funny sort of way.

That was when Janie noticed his companion. He was bending down toward a pretty little brunette who was chattering away at his side. Janie frowned, because that dark wavy hair was familiar. And then she realized who it was. Leo was talking to Marilee Morgan!

She relaxed. Marilee was her friend. Surely, she was talking her up to Leo. She almost rushed forward to say hello, but what if she interrupted at a crucial moment? There was, after all, the annual Jacobsville Cattleman's Ball in two weeks, the Saturday before Thanksgiving. It was very likely that Marilee was dropping hints right and left that Janie would love Leo to escort her.

She chuckled to herself. She was lucky to have a friend like Marilee.

If Janie had known what Marilee was actually saying to Leo, she might have changed her mind about the other woman's friendship and a lot of other things.

"It was so nice of you to drive me to the store, Leo," Marilee was cooing at Leo as they walked out. "My wrist is really sore from that fall I took."

"No problem," he murmured with a smile.

"The Cattleman's Ball is week after next," Marilee

added coyly. "I would really love to go, but nobody's asked me. I won't be able to drive by then, either, I'm sure. It was a bad sprain. They take almost as long as a broken bone to heal." She glanced up at him, weighing her chances. "Of course, Janie's told everybody that you're taking her. She said you're over there all the time now, that it's just a matter of time before you buy her a ring. Everybody knows."

He scowled fiercely. He'd only kissed Janie, he hadn't proposed marriage, for God's sake! Surely the girl wasn't going to get possessive because of a kiss? He hated gossip, especially about himself. Well, Janie could forget any invitations of that sort. He didn't like aggressive women who told lies around town. Not one bit!

"You can go with me," he told Marilee nonchalantly. "Despite what Janie told you, I am no woman's property, and I'm damned sure not booked for the dance!"

Marilee beamed. "Thanks, Leo!"

He shrugged. She was pretty and he liked her company. She wasn't one of those women who felt the need to constantly compete with men. He'd made his opinion about that pretty clear to Marilee in recent weeks. It occurred to him that Janie was suddenly trying to do just that, what with calf roping and ranch work and hard riding. Odd, when she'd never shown any such inclination before. But her self-assured talk about being his date for the ball set him off and stopped his mind from further reasoning about her sudden change of attitude.

He smiled down at Marilee. "Thanks for telling me about the gossip," he added. "Best way to curb it is to disprove it publicly."

"Of course it is. You mustn't blame Janie too much," she added with just the right amount of affection. "She's very young. Compared to me, I mean. If we hadn't been neighbors, we probably wouldn't be friends at all. She seems so…well, so juvenile at times, doesn't she?"

Leo frowned. He'd forgotten that Marilee was older than Janie. He thought back to those hard, hungry kisses he'd shared with Janie and could have cursed himself for his weakness. She was immature. She was building a whole affair on a kiss or two. Then he remembered something unexpectedly.

He glanced down at Marilee. "You said she had more boyfriends than anybody else in town."

Marilee cleared her throat. "Well, yes, *boy*friends. Not men friends, though," she added, covering her bases. It was hard to make Janie look juvenile if she was also a heartbreaking rounder.

Leo felt placated, God knew why. "There's a difference."

Marilee agreed. A tiny voice in her mind chided her for being so mean to her best friend, but Leo was a real hunk, and she was as infatuated with him as Janie was. All was fair in love and war, didn't they say? Besides, it was highly unlikely that Leo would ever ask Janie out—but, just in case, Marilee had planted a nice little suspicion in his mind to prevent that. She smiled as she walked beside him to his truck, dreaming of the first of many dances and being in Leo's arms. One day, she thought ecstatically, he might even want to marry her!

Janie went through two more bags of flour with attempts at biscuits that became better with each failed try. Finally, after several days' work, she had produced an edible batch that impressed even Hettie.

In between cooking, she was getting much better on horseback. Now, mounted on her black-and-white quarter horse, Blackie, she could cut out a calf and drive it into the makeshift corral used for doctoring sick animals. She could throw a calf, too, with something like professionalism, despite sore muscles and frequent bruises. She could rope, after a fashion, and she was riding better all the time. At least the chafing of her thighs against the saddle had stopped, and the muscles had acclimatized to the new stress being placed on them.

Saturday night loomed. It was only four days until the Cattleman's Ball, and she had a beautiful spaghetti-strapped lacy oyster-white dress to wear. It came to her ankles and was low-cut in front, leaving the creamy skin of her shoulders bare. There was a side-slit that went up her thigh, exposing her beautiful long legs. She paired the dress with white spiked high heels sporting ankle straps which she thought were extremely sexy, and she had a black velvet coat with a white silk lining to defend against the cold evening air. Now all she lacked was a date.

She'd expected Leo to ask her to the ball after those hungry kisses, despite his coolness later that day. But he hadn't been near the ranch since he'd had supper with her and her father. What made it even more peculiar was that he'd talked with her father out on the ranch several times. He just didn't come to the house. Janie assumed that he was regretting those hard kisses, and was afraid that she was taking him too seriously. He was avoiding her. He couldn't have made it plainer.

That made it a pretty good bet that he wasn't planning to take her to any Cattleman's Ball. She phoned Marilee in desperation.

The other woman sounded uneasy when she heard Janie's voice, and she was quick to ask why Janie had phoned.

"I saw you with Leo in the grocery store week before last," Janie began, "and I didn't interfere, because I was sure you were trying to talk him into taking me to the ball. But he didn't want to, did he?" she added sadly.

There was a sound like someone swallowing, on the other end of the phone. "Well, actually, no. I'm sorry." Marilee sounded as if she were strangling on the words.

"Don't feel bad," Janie said gently. "It's not your fault. You're my best friend in the whole world. I know you tried."

"Janie…"

"I had this beautiful white dress that I bought specially," Janie added on a sigh. "Well, that's that. Are you going?"

There was a tense pause. "Yes."

"Good! Anybody I know?"

"N…no," Marilee stammered.

"You have fun," Janie said.

"You…uh…aren't going, are you?" Marilee added.

Her friend certainly was acting funny, Janie thought. "No, I don't have a date," Janie chuckled. "There'll be other dances, I guess. Maybe Leo will ask me another time." *After he's got over being afraid of me,* she added silently. "If you see him," she said quickly, "you might mention that I can now cut out cattle and throw a calf. And I can make a biscuit that doesn't go through the floor when dropped!"

She was laughing, but Marilee didn't.

"I have to get to the hairdresser, Janie," Marilee said. "I'm really sorry...about the ball."

"Not your fault," Janie repeated. "Just have enough fun for both of us, okay?"

"Okay. See you."

The line went dead and Janie frowned. Something must be very wrong with Marilee. She wished she'd been more persistent and asked what was the matter. Well, she'd go over to Marilee's house after the dance to pump her for all the latest gossip, and then she could find out what was troubling her friend.

She put the ball to the back of her mind, despite the disappointment, and went out to greet her father as he rode in from the pasture with two of his men.

He swung out of the saddle at the barn and grinned at her. "Just the girl I wanted to see," he said at once. He pulled out his wallet. "I've got to have some more work gloves, just tore the last pair I had apart on barbed wire. How about going by the hardware store and get me another pair of those suede-palmed ones, extra large?"

"My pleasure," Janie said at once. Leo often went to the hardware store, and she might accidentally run into him there. "Be back in a jiffy!"

"Don't speed!" her father called to her.

She only chuckled, diving into her sports car. She remembered belatedly that she didn't have either her purse or car keys, or her face fixed, and jumped right back out again to rectify those omissions.

Ten minutes later, she was parking her car in front of the Jacobsville Hardware Store. With a wildly beating heart, she noticed one of the black double-cabbed Hart Ranch trucks parked nearby. Leo! She was certain it was Leo!

With her heart pounding, she checked her makeup in the rearview mirror and tugged her hair gently away from her cheeks. She'd left it down today deliberately, remembering that Leo had something of a weakness for long hair. It was thick and clean, shining like a soft brown curtain. She was wearing a long beige skirt with riding boots, and a gold satin blouse. She looked pretty good, even if she did say so herself! Now if Leo would just notice her...

She walked into the hardware store with her breath catching in her throat as she anticipated Leo's big smile at her approach. He was the handsomest of the Hart brothers, and really, the most personable. He was kindness itself. She remembered his soft voice in her kitchen, asking what was wrong. Oh, to have that soft voice in her ear forever!

There was nobody at the counter. That wasn't unusual, the clerks were probably waiting on customers. She walked back to where the gloves were kept and suddenly heard Leo's deep voice on the other side of the high aisle, unseen.

"Don't forget to add that roll of hog wire to the order," he was telling one of the clerks.

"I won't forget," Joe Howland's pleasant voice replied. "Are you going to the Cattleman's Ball?" Joe added just as Janie was about to raise her voice and call to Leo over the aisle.

"I guess I am," Leo replied. "I didn't plan to, but a pretty friend needed a ride and I'm obliging."

Janie's heart skipped and fell flat. Leo already had a date? Who? She moved around the aisle and in sight of Leo and Joe. Leo had his back to her, but Joe noticed her and smiled.

"That friend wouldn't be Janie Brewster, by any chance?" Joe teased loudly.

The question made Leo unreasonably angry. "Listen, just because she caught the bouquet at Micah Steele's wedding is no reason to start linking her with me," he said shortly. "She may have a good family background, she may be easy on the eyes, she may even learn to cook someday—miracles still happen. But no matter what she does, or how well, she is never going to appeal to me as a woman!" he added. "Having her spreading ludicrous gossip about our relationship all over town isn't making her any more attractive to me, either. It's a dead turnoff!"

Janie felt a shock like an electric jolt go through her. She couldn't even move for the pain.

Joe, horrified, opened his mouth to speak.

Leo made a rough gesture with one lean hand, burning with pent-up anger. "She looks like the rough side of a corncob lately, anyway," Leo continued, warming to his subject. "The only thing she ever had going for her were her looks, and she's spent the last few weeks covered in mud or dust or bread flour. She's out all hours proving she can compete with any man on the place and she can't stop bragging about what a great catch she's made with me. She's already told half the town that I'm a kiss short of buying her an engagement ring. That is, when she isn't putting it around that I'm taking her to the Cattleman's Ball, when I haven't even damned well asked her! Well, she's got her eye on the wrong man. I don't want some half-baked kid with a figure like a boy and an ego the size of my boots! I wouldn't have Janie Brewster for a wife if she came complete with a stable of purebred Salers bulls, and that's saying something. She makes me sick to my stomach!"

Joe had gone pale and he was grimacing. Curious, Leo turned…and there was Janie Brewster, staring at him down the aisle with a face as tragic as if he'd just taken a whittling knife to her heart.

"Janie," he said slowly.

She took a deep, steadying breath and managed to drag her eyes away from his face. "Hi, Joe," she said with a wan little smile. Her voice sounded choked. She couldn't possibly look for gloves, she had to get away! "Just wanted to check and see if you'd gotten in that tack Dad ordered last week," she improvised.

"Not just yet, Janie," Joe told her in a gentle tone. "I'm real sorry."

"No problem. No problem at all. Thanks, Joe. Hello, Mr. Hart," she said, without really meeting Leo's eyes, and she even managed a smile through her tattered dignity. "Nice day out, isn't it? Looks like we might even get that rain we need so badly. See you."

She went out the door with her head high, as proudly as a conquering army, leaving Leo sick to his stomach for real.

"Why the hell didn't you say something?" Leo asked Joe furiously.

"Didn't know how," Joe replied miserably.

"How long had she been standing there?" Leo persisted.

"The whole time, Leo," came the dreaded reply. "She heard every word."

As if to punctuate the statement, from outside came the sudden raucous squeal of tires on pavement as Janie took off toward the highway in a burst of speed. She was driving her little sports car, and Leo's heart stopped as he realized how upset she was.

He jerked his cell phone out of his pocket and dialed the police department. "Is that Grier?" he said at once when the call was answered, recognizing Jacobsville's new assistant police chief's deep voice. "Listen, Janie Brewster just lit out of town like a scalded cat in her sports car. She's upset and it's my fault, but she could kill herself. Have you got somebody out on the Victoria road who could pull her over and give her a warning? Yeah. Thanks, Grier. I owe you one."

He hung up, cursing harshly under his breath. "She'll be spitting fire if anybody tells her I sent the police after her, but I can't let her get hurt."

"Thought she looked just a mite too calm when she walked out the door," Joe admitted. He glanced at Leo and grimaced. "No secret around town that she's been sweet on you for the past year or so."

"If she was, I've just cured her," Leo said, and felt his heart sink. "Call me when that order comes in, will you?"

"Sure thing."

Leo climbed into his truck and just sat there for a minute, getting his bearings. He could only imagine how Janie felt right now. What he'd said was cruel. He'd let his other irritations burst out as if Janie were to blame for them all. What Marilee had been telling him about Janie had finally bubbled over, that was all. She'd never done anything to hurt him before. Her only crime, if there was one, was thinking the moon rose and set on Leo Hart and taking too much for granted on the basis of one long kiss.

He laughed hollowly. Chances were good that she wouldn't be thinking it after this. Part of him couldn't help blaming her, because she'd gone around bragging about how he was going to marry her, and how lucky he was to have a girl like her in his life. Not to mention telling everybody he was taking her to the Cattleman's Ball.

But Janie had never been one to brag about her accomplishments, or chase men. The only time she'd tried to vamp Leo, in fact, had been in her own home, when her father was present. She'd never come on to him when they were alone, or away from her home. She'd been old-fashioned in her attitudes, probably due to the strict way she'd been raised. So why should she suddenly depart from a lifetime's habits and start spreading gossip about Leo all over Jacobsville? He remembered at least once when she'd stopped another woman from talking about a girl in trouble, adding that she hated gossip because it was like spreading poison.

He wiped his sweaty brow with the sleeve of his shirt and put his hat on the seat beside him. He hated what he'd said. Maybe he didn't want Janie to get any ideas about him in a serious way, but there would have been kinder methods of accomplishing it. He didn't think he was ever going to forget the look on her face when she heard what he was saying to Joe. It would haunt him forever.

Meanwhile, Janie was setting new speed records out on the Victoria road. She'd already missed the turnoff that led back toward Jacobsville and her father's ranch. She was seething, hurting, miserable and confused. How could Leo think such things about her? She'd never told anybody how she felt about him, except Marilee, and she hadn't been spreading gossip. She hated gossip. Why did he know so little about her, when they'd known each other for years? What hurt the most was that he obviously believed those lies about her.

She wondered who could have told him such a thing. Her thoughts went at once to Marilee, but she chided herself for thinking ill of her only friend, her best friend. Certainly it had to be an enemy who'd been filling Leo's head full of lies. But…she didn't have any enemies that she knew of.

Tears were blurring her eyes. She knew she was going too fast. She should slow down before she wrecked the car or ran it into a fence. She was just thinking about that when she heard sirens and saw blue lights in her rearview mirror.

Great, she thought. *Just what I need. I'm going to be arrested and I'll spend the night in the local jail....*

She stopped and rolled down her window, trying unobtrusively to wipe away the tears while waiting for the uniformed officer to bend down and speak to her.

He came as a surprise. It wasn't a patrolman she knew, and she knew most of them by sight at least. This one had black eyes and thick black hair, which he wore in a ponytail. He had a no-nonsense look about him, and he was wearing a badge that denoted him as the assistant chief.

"Miss Brewster?" he asked quietly.

"Y...yes."

"I'm Cash Grier," he introduced himself. "I'm the new assistant police chief here."

"Nice to meet you," she said with a watery smile. "Sorry it has to be under these circumstances." She held out both wrists with a sigh. "Want to handcuff me?"

He pursed his lips and his black eyes twinkled unexpectedly. He didn't look like a man who knew what humor was. "Isn't that a little kinky for a conversation? What sort of men *are* you used to?"

She hesitated for just a second before she burst out laughing. He wasn't at all the man he appeared to be. She put her hands down.

"I was speeding," she reminded him.

"Yes, you were. But since you don't have a rap sheet, you can have a warning, just this once," he added firmly. "The speed limit is posted. It's fifty on all county roads."

She peered up at him. "This is a *county* road?" she emphasized, which meant that he was out of his enforcement area.

Nodding, he grinned. "And you're right, I don't have any jurisdiction out here, so that's why you're getting a warning and a smile." The smile faded. "In town, you'll get a ticket and a heavy scowl. Remember that."

"I will. Honest." She wiped at her eyes again. "I got a little upset, but I shouldn't have taken it out on the road. I'm sorry. I won't do it again."

"See that you don't." His dark eyes narrowed as if in memory. "Accidents are messy. Very messy."

"Thanks for being so nice."

He shrugged. "Everybody slips once in a while."

"That's exactly what I did…"

"I didn't mean you," he interrupted. His lean face took on a faintly dangerous cast. "I'm not nice. Not ever."

She was intimidated by that expression. "Oh."

He wagged a finger at her nose. "Don't speed."

She put a hand over her heart. "Never again. I promise."

He nodded, walked elegantly to his squad car and drove toward town. Janie sat quietly for a minute, getting herself back together. Then she started the car and went home, making up an apology for her father about his gloves without telling him the real reason she'd come home without them. He said he'd get a new pair the next day himself, no problem.

Janie cried herself to sleep in a miserable cocoon of shattered dreams.

As luck would have it, Harley Fowler, Cy Parks's foreman, came by in one of the ranch pickup trucks the very next morning and pulled up to the back door when he saw Janie walk out dressed for riding and wearing a broad-brimmed hat. Harley's boss, Cy, did business with Fred Brewster, and Harley was a frequent visitor to the ranch. He and Janie were friendly. They teased and played like two kids when they were together.

"I've been looking for you," Harley said with a grin as he paused just in front of her. "The Cattleman's Ball is Saturday night and I want to go, but I don't have a date. I know it's late to be asking, but how about going with me? Unless you've got a date or you're going with your dad…?" he added.

She grinned back. "I haven't got a date, and Dad's away on business and has to miss the ball this year. But I do have a pretty new dress that I'm dying to wear! I'd love to go with you, Harley!"

"Really?" His lean face lit up. He knew Janie was sweet on Leo Hart, but it was rumored that he was avoiding her like measles these days. Harley wasn't in love with Janie, but he genuinely liked her.

"Really," Janie replied. "What time will you pick me up?"

"About six-thirty," he said. "It doesn't start until seven, but I like to be on time."

"That makes two of us. I'll be ready. Thanks, Harley!"

"Thank you!" he said. "See you Saturday."

He was off in a cloud of dust, waving his hand out the window as he pulled out of the yard. Janie sighed with relief. She wanted nothing more in the world than to go to that dance and show Leo Hart how wrong he was about her chasing him. Harley was young and nice looking. She liked him. She would go and have a good time. Leo would be able to see for himself that he was off the endangered list, and he could make a safe bet that Janie would never go near him again without a weapon! As she considered it, she smiled coldly. Revenge was petty, but after the hurt she'd endured at Leo's hands, she felt entitled to a little of it. He was never going to forget this party. Never, as long as he lived.

✤ 3 ✤

The annual Jacobsville Cattleman's Ball was one of the newer social events of the year. It took place the Saturday before Thanksgiving like clockwork. Every cattleman for miles around made it a point to attend, even if he avoided all other social events for the year. The Ballenger brothers, Calhoun and Justin, had just added another facility to their growing feedlot enterprise, and they looked prosperous with their wives in gala attire beside them. The Tremayne brothers, Connal, Evan, Harden and Donald, and their wives, were also in attendance, as were the Hart boys; well, Corrigan, Callaghan, Rey and Leo at least, and their wives. Simon and Tira didn't attend many local events except the brothers' annual Christmas party on the ranch.

Also at the ball were Micah Steele, Eb Scott, J. D. Langley, Emmett Deverell, Luke Craig, Guy Fenton, Ted Regan, Jobe Dodd, Tom Walker and their wives. The guest list read like a who's who of Jacobsville, and there were so many people that the organizers had rented the community center for it. There was a live country-western band, a buffet table that could have fed a platoon of starving men, and enough liquor to drown a herd of horses.

Leo had a highball. Since he hadn't done much drinking in recent years, his four brothers were giving him strange looks. He didn't notice. He was feeling so miserable that even a hangover would have been an improvement.

Beside him, Marilee was staring around the room with wide, wary eyes.

"Looking for somebody?" Leo asked absently.

"Yes," she replied. "Janie said she wasn't coming, but that isn't what your sister-in-law Tess just told me."

"What did she say?"

Marilee looked worried. "Harley Fowler told her he was bringing Janie."

"Harley?" Leo scowled. Harley Fowler was a courageous young man who'd actually backed up the town's infamous mercenaries—Eb Scott, Cy Parks and Micah Steele—when they helped law enforcement face down a gang of drug dealers the year before. Harley's name hadn't been coupled with any of the local belles, and he was only a working-class cowboy. Janie's father might be financially pressed at the moment, but his was a founding family of Jacobsville, and the family had plenty of prestige. Fred and his sister-in-law Lydia would be picky about who Janie married. Not, he thought firmly, that Janie was going to be marrying Harley....

"Harley's nice," Marilee murmured. "He's Cy Parks's head foreman now, and everybody says he's got what it takes to run a business of his own." What Marilee didn't add was that Harley had asked her out several times before his raid on the drug lord with the local mercenaries, and she'd turned him down flat. She'd thought he bragged and strutted a little too much, that he was too immature for her. She'd even told him so. It had made her a bitter enemy of his.

Now she was rather sorry that she hadn't given him a chance. He really was different these days, much more mature and very attractive. Not that Leo wasn't a dish. But she felt so guilty about Janie that she couldn't even enjoy his company, much less the party. If Janie showed up and saw her with Leo, she was going to know everything. It wasn't conducive to a happy evening at all.

"What's wrong?" Leo asked when he saw her expression.

"Janie's never going to get over it if she shows up and sees me with you," she replied honestly. "I didn't think how it would look…"

"I don't belong to anybody," Leo said angrily. "It's just as well to let Janie know that. So what if she does show up? Who cares?"

"I do." Marilee sighed.

Just as she spoke, Janie came in the door with a tall, good-looking, dark-haired man in a dark suit with a ruffled white shirt and black bow tie. Janie had just taken off her black velvet coat and hung it on the rack near the door. Under it, she was wearing a sexy white silk gown that fell softly down her slender figure to her shapely ankles. The spaghetti straps left her soft shoulders almost completely bare, and dipped low enough to draw any man's eyes. She was wearing her thick, light brown hair down. It reached almost to her waist in back in a beautiful, glossy display. She wore just enough makeup to enhance her face, and she was clinging to Harley's arm with obvious pleasure as they greeted the Ballengers and their wives.

Leo had forgotten how pretty Janie could look when

she worked at it. Lately, he'd only seen her covered in mud and flour. Tonight, her figure drew eyes in that dress. He remembered the feel of her in his arms, the eager innocence of her mouth under his, and he suddenly felt uneasy at the way she was clinging to Harley's arm.

If he was uncomfortable, Marilee was even more so. She stood beside Leo and looked as if she hated herself. He took another long sip of his drink before he guided her toward Harley and Janie.

"No sense hiding, is there?" he asked belligerently.

Marilee sighed miserably. "No sense at all, I guess."

They moved forward together. Janie noticed them and her eyes widened and darkened with pain for an instant. Leo's harsh monologue at the hardware store had been enough to wound her, but now she was seeing that she'd been shafted by her best friend, as well. Marilee said Janie didn't know her date, but all along, apparently, she'd planned to come with Leo. No wonder she'd been so curious about whether or not Janie was going to show up.

Everything suddenly made perfect sense. Marilee had filled Leo up with lies about Janie gossiping about him, so that she could get him herself. Janie felt like an utter fool. Her chin lifted, but she didn't smile. Her green eyes were like emerald shards as they met Marilee's.

"H–hi, Janie," Marilee stammered, forcing a smile. "You said you weren't coming tonight."

"I wasn't," Janie replied curtly. "But Harley was at a loose end and didn't have a date, so he asked me." She looked up at the tall, lean man beside her, who was some years younger than Leo, and she smiled at him with genuine affection even through her misery. "I haven't danced in years."

"You'll dance tonight, darlin'," Harley drawled, smiling warmly as he gripped her long fingers in his. He looked elegant in his dinner jacket, and there was a faint arrogance in his manner now that hadn't been apparent before. He glanced at Marilee and there was barely veiled contempt in the look.

Marilee swallowed hard and avoided his piercing gaze.

"I didn't know you could dance, Harley," Marilee murmured, embarrassed.

He actually ignored her, his narrow gaze going to Leo. "Nice turnout, isn't it?" he asked the older man.

"Nice," Leo said, but he didn't smile. "I haven't seen your boss tonight."

"The baby had a cold," Harley said. "He and Lisa don't leave him when he's sick." He looked down at Janie deliberately. "Considering how happy the two of them are, I guess marriage isn't such a bad vocation, after all," he mused.

"For some, maybe," Leo said coldly. He was openly glaring at Harley.

"Let's get on the dance floor," Harley told Janie with a grin. "I'm anxious to try out that waltz pattern I've been learning."

"You'll excuse us, I'm sure," Janie told the woman who was supposed to be her best friend. Her eyes were icy as she realized how she'd been betrayed by Marilee's supposed "help" with Leo.

Marilee grimaced. "Oh, Janie," she groaned. "Let me explain...."

But Janie wasn't staying to listen to any halfhearted explanations. "Nice to see you, Marilee. You, too, Mr. Hart," she added with coldly formal emphasis, not quite meeting Leo's eyes. But she noted the quick firming of his chiseled lips with some satisfaction at the way she'd addressed him.

"Why do you call him Mr. Hart?" Harley asked as they moved away.

"He's much older than we are, Harley," she replied, just loudly enough for Leo to hear her and stiffen with irritation. "Almost another generation."

"I guess he is."

Leo took a big swallow of his drink and glared after them.

"She'll never speak to me again," Marilee said in a subdued tone.

He glared at her. "I'm not her personal property," he said flatly. "I never was. It isn't your fault that she's been gossiping and spreading lies all over town."

Marilee winced.

He turned his attention back to Janie, who was headed onto the dance floor with damned Harley. "I don't want her. What the hell do I care if she likes Harley?"

The music changed to a quick, throbbing Latin beat. Matt Caldwell and his wife, Leslie, were out on the dance floor already, making everybody else look like rank beginners. Everybody clapped to the rhythm until the very end, when the couple left the dance floor. Leo thought nobody could top that display until Harley walked to the bandleader, and the band suddenly broke into a Strauss waltz. That was when Harley and Janie took the floor. Then, even Matt and Leslie stood watching with admiration.

Leo stared at the couple as if he didn't recognize them. Involuntarily, he moved closer to the dance floor to watch. He'd never seen two people move like that to music besides Matt and Leslie.

The rhythm was sweet, and the music had a sweeping beauty that Janie mirrored with such grace that it was like watching ballet. Harley turned and Janie followed every nuance of movement, her steps matching his exactly. Her eyes were laughing, like her pretty mouth, as they whirled around the dance floor in perfect unison.

Harley was laughing, too, enjoying her skill as much as she enjoyed his. They looked breathless, happy—young.

Leo finished his drink, wishing he'd added more whiskey and less soda. His dark eyes narrowed as they followed the couple around the dance floor as they kept time to the music.

"Aren't they wonderful?" Marilee asked wistfully. "I don't guess you dance?"

He did. But he wasn't getting on that floor and making a fool of himself with Marilee, who had two left feet and the sense of rhythm of a possum.

"I don't dance much," Leo replied tersely.

She sighed. "It's just as well, I suppose. That would be a hard act to follow."

"Yes."

The music wound to a peak and suddenly ended, with Janie draped down Harley's side like a bolt of satin. His mouth was almost touching hers, and Leo had to fight not to go onto the floor and throw a punch at the younger man.

He blinked, surprised by his unexpected reaction. Janie was nothing to him. Why should he care what she did? Hadn't she bragged to everyone that he was taking her to this very dance? Hadn't she made it sound as if they were involved?

Janie and Harley left the dance floor to furious, genuine applause. Even Matt Caldwell and Leslie congratulated them on the exquisite piece of dancing. Apparently, Harley had been taking lessons, but Janie seemed to be a natural.

But the evening was still young, as the Latin music started up again and another unexpected couple took the floor. It was Cash Grier, the new assistant police chief, with young Christabel Gaines in his arms. Only a few people knew that Christabel had been married to Texas Ranger Judd Dunn since she was sixteen—a marriage on paper, only, to keep herself and her invalid mother from losing their family ranch. But she was twenty-one now, and the marriage must have been annulled, because there she was with Cash Grier, like a blond flame in his arms as he spun her around to the throbbing rhythm and she matched her steps to his expert ones.

Unexpectedly, as the crowd clapped and kept time for them, handsome dark-eyed Judd Dunn himself turned up in evening dress with a spectacular redhead on his arm. Men's heads turned. The woman was a supermodel, internationally famous, who was involved at a film shoot out at Judd and Christabel's ranch. Gossip flew. Judd watched Christabel with Grier and glowered. The redhead said something to him, but he didn't appear to be listening. He watched the two dancers with a rigid posture and an expression more appropriate for a duel than a dance. Christabel ignored him.

"Who is that man with Christabel Gaines?" Marilee asked Leo.

"Cash Grier. He used to be a Texas Ranger some years ago. They say he was in government service, as well."

Leo recalled that Grier had been working in San Antonio with the district attorney's office before he took the position of assistant police chief in Jacobsville. There was a lot of talk about Grier's mysterious past. The man was an enigma, and people walked wide around him in Jacobsville.

"He's dishy, isn't he? He dances a *paso doble* even better than Matt, imagine that!" Marilee said aloud. "Of course, Harley does a magnificent waltz. Who would ever have thought he'd turn out to be such a sexy, mature man…"

Leo turned on his heel and left Marilee standing by herself, stunned. He walked back to the drinks table with eyes that didn't really see. The dance floor had filled up again, this time with a slow dance. Harley was holding Janie far too close, and she was letting him. Leo remembered what he'd said about her in the hardware store, and her wounded expression, and he filled another glass with whiskey. This time he didn't add soda. He shouldn't have felt bad, of course. Janie shouldn't have been so possessive. She shouldn't have gossiped about him…

"Hi, Leo," his sister-in-law Tess said with a smile as she joined him, reaching for a clear soft drink.

"No booze, huh?" he asked with a grin, noting her choice.

"I don't want to set a bad example for my son," she teased, because she and Cag had a little boy now. "Actually, I can't hold liquor. But don't tell anybody," she added. "I'm the wife of a tough ex-Special Forces guy. I'm supposed to be a real hell-raiser."

He smiled genuinely. "You are," he teased. "A lesser woman could never have managed my big brother and an albino python all at once."

"Herman the python's living with his own mate these days," she reminded him with a grin, "and just between us, I don't really miss him!" She glanced toward her husband and sighed. "I'm one lucky woman."

"He's one lucky man." He took a sip of his drink and she frowned.

"Didn't you bring Marilee?" she asked.

He nodded. "Her wrist was still bothering her too much to drive, so I let her come with me. I've been chauffeuring her around ever since she sprained it."

Boy, men are dense, Tess was thinking. *As if a woman*

couldn't drive with only one hand. She glanced past him at Marilee, who was standing by herself watching as a new rhythm began and Janie moved onto the floor with Harley Fowler. "I thought she was Janie's best friend," she mentioned absently. "You can never tell about people."

"What do you mean?"

She shrugged. "I overheard her telling someone that Janie had been spreading gossip about you and her all over town." She shook her head. "That's not true. Janie's so shy, it's hard for her to even talk to most men. I've never heard her gossip about anyone, even people she dislikes. I can't imagine why Marilee would tell lies about her."

"Janie told everybody I was bringing her to the ball," he insisted with a scowl.

"Marilee told people that Janie said that," Tess corrected. "You really don't know, do you? Marilee's crazy about you. She had to cut Janie out of the picture before she could get close to you. I guess she found the perfect way to do it."

Leo started to speak, but he hesitated. That couldn't be true.

Tess read his disbelief and just smiled. "You don't believe me, do you? It doesn't matter. You'll find out the truth sooner or later, whether you want to or not. I've got to find Cag. See you later!"

Leo watched her walk away with conflicting emotions. He didn't want to believe—he *wouldn't* believe—that he'd been played for a sucker. He'd seen Janie trying to become a cattleman with his own eyes, trying to compete with him. He knew that she wanted him because she'd tried continually to tempt him when he went to visit her father. She flirted shamelessly with him. She'd melted in his arms, melted under the heat of his kisses. She hadn't made a single protest at the intimate way he'd held her. She felt possessive of him, and he couldn't really blame her, because it was his own lapse of self-control that had given her the idea that he wanted her. Maybe he did, physically, but Janie was a novice and he didn't seduce innocents. Her father was a business associate. It certainly wouldn't be good business to cut his own throat with Fred by making a casual lover of Janie.

He finished the whiskey and put the glass down. He felt light-headed. That was what came of drinking when he hadn't done it in a long time. This was stupid. He had to stop behaving like an idiot just because Fred Brewster's little girl had cut him dead in the receiving line and treated him like an old man. He forced himself to walk normally, but he almost tripped over Cag on the way.

His brother caught him by the shoulders. "Whoa, there," he said with a grin. "You're wobbling."

Leo pulled himself up. "That whiskey must be 200 proof," he said defensively.

"No. You're just not used to it. Leave your car here when it's time to go," he added firmly. "Tess and I will drop Marilee off and take you home. You're in no fit state to drive."

Leo sighed heavily. "I guess not. Stupid thing to do."

"What, drinking or helping Marilee stab Janie in the back?"

Leo's eyes narrowed on his older brother's lean, hard face. "Does Tess tell you everything?"

He shrugged. "We're married."

"If I ever get married," Leo told him, "my wife isn't going to tell anybody anything. She's going to keep her mouth shut."

"Not much danger of your getting married, with that attitude," Cag mused.

Leo squared his shoulders. "Marilee looks really great tonight," he pointed out.

"She looks pretty sick to me," Cag countered, eyeing the object of their conversation, who was standing alone against the opposite wall, trying to look invisible. "She should, too, after spreading that gossip around town about Janie chasing you."

"Janie did that, not Marilee," Leo said belligerently.

"She didn't have any reason to make it sound like we were engaged, just because I kissed her."

Cag's eyebrows lifted. "You kissed her?"

"It wasn't much of a kiss," Leo muttered gruffly. "She's so green, it's pathetic!"

"She won't stay that way long around Harley," Cag chuckled. "He's no playboy, but women love him since he helped our local mercs take on that drug lord Manuel Lopez and won. I imagine he'll educate Janie."

Leo's dark eyes narrowed angrily. He hated the thought of Harley kissing her. He really should do something about that. He blinked, trying to focus his mind on the problem.

"Don't trip over the punch bowl," Cag cautioned dryly. "And for God's sake, don't try to dance. The gossips would have a field day for sure!"

"I could dance if I wanted to," Leo informed him.

Cag leaned down close to his brother's ear. "Don't 'want to.' Trust me." He turned and went back to Tess, smiling as he led her onto the dance floor.

Leo joined Marilee against the wall.

She glanced at him and grimaced. "I've just become the Bubonic Plague," she said with a miserable sigh. "Joe Howland from the hardware store is here with his wife," she added uncomfortably. "He's telling people what you said to Janie and that I was responsible for her getting the rough side of your tongue."

He glanced down at her. "How is it your fault?"

She looked at her shoes instead of at him. She felt guilty and hurt and ashamed. "I sort of told Janie that you said you'd like her better if she could ride and rope and make biscuits, and stop dressing up all the time."

He stiffened. He felt the jolt all the way to his toes. "You told her that?"

"I did." She folded her arms over her breasts and stared toward Janie, who was dancing with Harley and apparently having a great time. "There's more," she added, steeling herself to admit it. "It wasn't exactly true that she was telling people you were taking her to this dance."

"Marilee, for God's sake! Why did you lie?" he demanded.

"She's just a kid, Leo," she murmured uneasily. "She doesn't know beans about men or real life, she's been protected and pampered, she's got money, she's pretty...." She moved restlessly. "I like you a lot. I'm older, more mature. I thought, if she was just out of the picture for a little bit, you...you might start to like me."

Now he understood the look on Janie's face when he'd made those accusations. Tess was right. Marilee had lied. She'd stabbed her best friend in the back, and he'd helped her do it. He felt terrible.

"You don't have to tell me what a rat I am," she continued, without looking up at him. "I must have been crazy to think Janie wouldn't eventually find out that I was lying about her." She managed to meet his angry eyes. "She never gossiped about you, Leo. She wanted you to take her to this party so much that it was all she talked about for weeks. But she never told anybody you were going to. She thought I was helping her by hinting that she'd like you to ask her." She laughed coldly. "She was the best friend I ever had, and I've stabbed her in the back. She'll never speak to me again after tonight, and I deserve whatever I get. For what it's worth, I'm really sorry."

Leo was still trying to adjust to the truth. He could talk himself blue in the face, but Janie would never listen to him now. He was going to be about as welcome as a fly at her house from now on, especially if Fred found out what Leo had said to and about her. It would damage their friendship. It had already killed whatever feeling Janie had for him. He knew that without the wounded, angry glances she sent his way from time to time.

"You said you didn't want her chasing you," Marilee reminded him weakly, trying to find one good thing to say.

"No danger of that from now on, is there?" he agreed, biting off the words.

"None at all. So a little good came out of it."

He looked down at her with barely contained anger. "How could you do that to her?"

"I don't even know." She sighed raggedly. "I must have been temporarily out of my mind." She moved away from the wall. "I wonder if you'd mind driving me home? I...I really don't want to stay any longer."

"I can't drive. Cag's taking us home."

"You can't drive? Why?" she exclaimed.

"I think the polite way of saying it is that I'm stinking drunk," he said with glittery eyes blazing down at her.

She grimaced. No need to ask why he'd gotten that way. "Sorry," she said inadequately.

"You're sorry. I'm sorry. It doesn't change anything." He looked toward Janie, conscious of new and painful regrets. It all made sense now, her self-improvement campaign. She'd been dragged through mud, thrown from horses, bruised and battered in a valiant effort to become what she thought Leo wanted her to be.

He winced. "She could have killed herself," he said huskily. "She hadn't been on a horse in ages or worked around cattle." He looked down at Marilee with a black scowl. "Didn't you realize that?"

"I wasn't thinking at the time," Marilee replied. "I've always worked around the ranch, because I had to. I never thought of Janie being in any danger. But I guess she was, at that. At least she didn't get hurt."

"That's what you think," Leo muttered, remembering how she'd looked at the hardware store.

Marilee shrugged and suddenly burst into tears. She dashed toward the ladies' room to hide them.

At the same time, Harley left Janie at the buffet table and went toward the rest rooms himself.

Leo didn't even think. He walked straight up to Janie and caught her by the hand, pulling her along with him.

"What do you think you're doing?" she raged. "Let go of me!"

He ignored her. He led her right out the side door and onto the stone patio surrounded by towering plants that, in spring, were glorious in blossom. He pulled the glass door closed behind him and moved Janie off behind one of the plants.

"I want to talk to you," he began, trying to get his muddled mind to work.

She pulled against his hands. "I don't want to talk to you!" she snapped. "You go right back in there to your date, Leo Hart! You brought Marilee, not me!"

"I want to tell you..." he tried again.

She aimed a kick at his shin that almost connected.

He sidestepped, overbalancing her so that she fell heavily against him. She felt good in his arms, warm, delicate and sweetly scented. His breath caught at the feel of her soft skin under his hands where the dress was low-cut in back.

"Harley will...be missing me!" she choked.

"Damn Harley," he murmured huskily and the words went into her mouth as he bent and took it hungrily.

His arms swallowed her, warm under the dark evening suit, where her hands rested just at his rib cage. His mouth was ardent, insistent, on her parted lips.

He forced them apart, nipping the upper one with his teeth while his hands explored the softness of her skin. He was getting drunk on her perfume. He felt himself going taut as he registered the hunger he was feeling to get her even closer. It wasn't enough....

His hands went to her hips and jerked them hard into the thrust of his big body, so that she could feel how aroused he was.

She stiffened and then tried to twist away, frantic at the weakness he was making her feel. He couldn't do this. She couldn't let him do it. He was only making a point, showing her that she couldn't resist him. He didn't even like her anymore. He'd brought her best friend to the most talked-about event in town!

"You...let me go!" she sobbed, tearing her mouth from his. "I hate you, Leo Hart!"

He was barely able to breathe, much less think, but he

wasn't letting go. His eyes glittered down at her. "You don't hate me," he denied. "You want me. You tremble every time I get within a foot of you. It's so noticeable a blind man couldn't mistake it." He pulled her close, watching her face as her thighs touched his. "A woman's passion arouses a man's," he whispered roughly. "You made me want you."

"You said I made you sick," she replied, her voice choking on the word.

"You do." His lips touched her ear. "When a man is this aroused, and can't satisfy the hunger, it makes him sick," he said huskily, with faint insolence. He dragged her hips against his roughly. "Feel that? You've got me so hot I can't even think…!" Leo broke off abruptly as Janie stomped on his foot.

"Does that help?" she asked while he was hobbling on the foot her spiked heel hadn't gone into.

She moved back from him, shaking with desire and anger, while he cursed roundly and without inhibition.

"That's what you get for making nasty remarks to women!" she said furiously. "You don't want me! You said so! You want Marilee. That's why you're taking her around with you. Remember me? I'm that gossiping pest who runs after you everywhere. Except that I'll never do it again, you can bet your life on that! I wouldn't have you on ice cream!"

He stood uneasily on both feet, glaring at her. "Sure you would," he said with a venomous smile. His eyes glittered like a diamondback uncoiling. "Just now, I could have had you in the rosebushes. You'd have done anything I wanted."

He was right. That was what hurt the most. She pushed back her disheveled hair with a trembling hand. "Not anymore," she said, feeling sick. "Not when I know what you really think of me."

"Harley brought you," he said coldly. "He's a boy playing at being a man."

"He's closer to my age than you are, Mr. Hart!" she shot back.

His face hardened and he took a quick step toward her.

"That's what you've said from the start," she reminded him, near tears. "I'm just a kid, you said. I'm just a kid with a crush, just your business associate's pesky daughter."

He'd said that. He must have been out of his mind. Looking at her now, with that painful maturity in her face, he couldn't believe he'd said any such thing. She was all woman. And she was with Harley. Damn Harley!

"Don't worry, I won't tell Dad that you tried to seduce me on the patio with your new girlfriend standing right inside the room," she assured him. "But if you ever touch me again, I'll cripple you, so help me God!"

298 ❧ DIANA PALMER

She whirled and jerked open the patio door, slamming it behind her as she moved through the crowd toward the buffet table.

Leo stood alone in the cold darkness with a sore foot, wondering why he hadn't kept his mouth shut. If a bad situation could get worse, it just had.

✤ 4 ✤

Janie and Harley were back on the dance floor by the time Leo made his way inside, favoring his sore foot.

Marilee was standing at the buffet table, looking as miserable as he felt.

"Harley just gave me hell," she murmured tightly as he joined her. "He said I was lower than a snake's belly, and it would serve me right if Janie never spoke to me again." She looked up at him with red-rimmed eyes. "Do you think your brother would mind dropping us off now? He could come right back…"

"I'll ask him," Leo said, sounding absolutely fed up.

He found Cag talking to Corrigan and Rey at the buffet table. Their wives were in another circle, talking to each other.

"Could you run Marilee home now and drop me off on the way back?" he asked Cag in a subdued tone.

Corrigan gaped at him. "You've never left a dance until the band packed up."

Leo sighed. "There's a first time for everything."

The women joined them. Cag tugged Tess close. "I have to run Leo and Marilee home."

Tess's eyebrows went up. "Now? Why so early?"

Leo glared. His brothers cleared their throats.

"Never mind," Cag said quickly. "I won't be a minute…"

"Rey and I would be glad to do it…" Meredith volunteered, with a nod from her husband.

"No need," Dorie said with a smile, cuddling close to her husband. "Corrigan can run Leo and Marilee home and come right back. Can't you, sweetheart?" she added.

"Sure I can," he agreed, lost in her pretty eyes.

"But you two don't usually leave until the band does, either," Leo pointed out. "You'll miss most of the rest of the dance if you drive us."

Corrigan pursed his lips. "Oh, we've done our dancing for the night. Haven't we, sweetheart?" he prompted.

Dorie's eyes twinkled. She nodded. "Indeed we have!

I'll just catch up on talk until he comes back. We can have the last dance together. Don't give it a thought, Leo."

Leo was feeling the liquor more with every passing minute, but he was feeling all sorts of undercurrents. The women looked positively gleeful. His brothers were exchanging strange looks.

Corrigan looked past Leo to Cag and Rey. "You can all come by our house after the dance," he promised.

"What for?" Leo wanted to know, frowning suspiciously.

Corrigan hesitated and Cag scowled.

Rey cleared his throat. "Bull problems," he said finally, with a straight face. "Corrigan's advising me."

"He's advising me, too," Cag said with a grin. "He's advising both of us."

All three of them looked guilty as hell. "I know more about bulls than Corrigan does," Leo pointed out. "Why don't you ask me?"

"Because you're in a hurry to go home," Corrigan improvised. "Let's go."

Leo went to get Marilee. She said a subdued, hurried goodbye to Cag and Rey and then their wives. Leo waited patiently, vaguely aware that Cag and Rey were standing apart, talking in hushed whispers. They were both staring at Leo.

As Marilee joined him, Leo began to get the idea. Corrigan had sacrificed dancing so that he could pump Leo for gossip and report back to the others. They knew he was drinking, which he never did, and they'd probably seen him hobble back into the room. Then he'd wanted to leave early. It didn't take a mind reader to put all that together. Something had happened, and his brothers—not to mention their wives—couldn't wait to find out what. He glared at Corrigan, but his brother only grinned.

"Let's go, Marilee," Leo said, catching her by the arm.

She gave one last, hopeful glance at Janie, but was pointedly ignored. She followed along with Leo until the music muted to a whisper behind them.

When Marilee had been dropped off, and they were alone in the car, Corrigan glanced toward his brother with mischievous silvery eyes and pursed his lips.

"You're limping."

Leo huffed. "You try walking normally when some crazy woman's tried to put her heel through your damned boot!"

"Marilee stepped on you?" Corrigan said much too carelessly.

"Janie stepped on me, on purpose!"

"What were you doing to her at the time?"

Leo actually flushed. It was visible in the streetlight they stopped under waiting for a red light to change on the highway.

"Well!" Corrigan exclaimed with a knowing expression.

"She started it," he defended himself angrily. "All these months, she's been dressing to the hilt and waylaying me every time I went to see her father. She damned near seduced me on the cooking table in her kitchen last month, and then she goes and gets on her high horse because I said a few little things I shouldn't have when she was eavesdropping!"

"You said a lot of little things," his brother corrected. "And from what I hear, she left town in a dangerous rush and had to be slowed down by our new assistant chief. In fact, you called and asked him to do it. Good thinking."

"Who told you that?" Leo demanded.

Corrigan grinned. "Our new assistant chief."

"Grier can keep his nose out of my business or I'll punch it for him!"

"He's got problems of his own, or didn't you notice him step outside with Judd Dunn just before we left?" Corrigan whistled softly. "Christabel may think she's her own woman, but Judd doesn't act like any disinterested husband I ever saw."

"He's got a world-famous model on his arm," Leo pointed out.

"It didn't make a speck of difference once he saw Christabel on that dance floor with Grier. He was ready to make a scene right there." He glanced at Leo. "And *he* wasn't drinking," he emphasized.

"I am not jealous of Janie Brewster," Leo told him firmly.

"Tell that to Harley. He had to be persuaded not to go after you when Janie came back inside in tears," Corrigan added, letting slip what he'd overheard.

That made it worse. "Harley can mind his own damned business, too!"

"He is. He likes Janie."

"Janie's not going to fall for some wet-behind-the-ears would-be world-saver," Leo raged.

"He's kind to her. He teases her and picks at her. He treats her like a princess." He gave his brother a wry glance. "I'll bet he wouldn't try to seduce her in the rosebushes."

"I didn't! Anyway, there weren't any damned rose-bushes out there."

"How do you know that?"

Leo sighed heavily. "Because if there had been, I'd be wearing them."

Corrigan chuckled. Having had his own problems

with the course of true love, he could sympathize with his brother. Sadly, Leo had never been in love. He'd had crushes, he'd had brief liaisons, but there had never been a woman who could stand him on his ear. Corrigan was as fascinated as their brothers with the sudden turn of events. Leo had tolerated Janie Brewster, been amused by her, but he'd never been involved enough to start a fight with her, much less sink two large whiskeys when he'd hardly even touched beer.

"She's got a temper, fancy that?" Corrigan drawled.

Leo sighed. "Marilee was telling lies," he murmured. "She said Janie had started all sorts of gossip about us. I'd kissed her, and liked it, and I was feeling trapped. I thought the kiss gave her ideas. And all the time... Damn!" he ground out. "Tess knew. She told me that Marilee had made up the stories, and I wouldn't listen."

"Tess is sharp as a tack," his older brother remarked.

"I'm as dull as a used nail," Leo replied. "I don't even know when a woman is chasing me. I thought Janie was. And all the time, it was her best friend, Marilee." He shook his head. "Janie said I was the most conceited man she ever met. Maybe I am." He glanced out the window at the silhouettes of buildings they passed in the dark. "She likes Harley. That would have been funny a few months ago, but he keeps impressive company these days."

"Harley's matured. Janie has, too. I thought she handled herself with dignity tonight, when she saw you with Marilee." He chuckled. "Tira would have emptied the punch bowl over her head," he mused, remembering his redheaded sister-in-law's temper.

"Simon would have been outraged," he added. "He hates scenes. You're a lot like him," he said unexpectedly, glancing at the younger man. "You can cut up, but you're as somber as a judge when you're not around us. Especially since we've all married."

"I'm lonely," Leo said simply. "I've had the house to myself since Rey married Meredith and moved out, almost a year ago. Mrs. Lewis retired. I've got no biscuits, no company…"

"You've got Marilee," he was reminded.

"Marilee sprained her wrist. She's needed me to drive her places," Leo said drowsily.

"Marilee could drive with one hand. I drove with a broken arm once."

Leo didn't respond. They were driving up to the main ranch house, into the driveway that made a semicircle around the front steps. The security lights were on, so was the porch light. But even with lights on in the front rooms of the sprawling brick house, it looked empty.

"You could come and stay with any of us, whenever

you wanted to," Corrigan reminded him. "We only live a few miles apart."

"You've all got families. Children. Well, except Meredith and Rey."

"They're not in a hurry. Rey's the youngest. The rest of us are feeling our ages a bit more."

"Hell," Leo growled, "you're only two years older than me."

"You're thirty-five," he was reminded. "I'll be thirty-eight in a couple of months."

"You don't look it."

"Dorie and the babies keep me young," Corrigan admitted with a warm smile. "Marriage isn't as bad as you think it is. You have someone to cook for you, a companion to share your sorrows when the world hits you in the head, and your triumphs when you punch back. Not to mention having a warm bed at night."

Leo opened the door but hesitated. "I don't want to get married."

Corrigan's pale eyes narrowed. "Dorie was just a little younger than Janie when I said the same thing to her. I mistook her for an experienced woman, made a very heavy pass, and then said some insulting things to her when she pulled back at the last minute. I sent her running for the nearest bus, and my pride stopped me from carrying her right back off it again. She went away. It was eight long years before she came home, before I was able to start over with her." His face hardened. "You know what those years were like for me."

Leo did. It was painful even to recall them. "You never told me why she left."

Corrigan rested his arm over the steering wheel. "She left because I behaved like an idiot." He glanced at his brother. "I don't give a damn what Marilee's told you about Janie, she isn't any more experienced than Dorie was. Don't follow in my footsteps."

Leo wouldn't meet the older man's eyes. "Janie's a kid."

"She'll grow up. She's making a nice start, already."

Leo brushed back his thick, unruly hair. "I was way out of line with her tonight. She said she never wanted to see me again."

"Give her time."

"I don't care if she doesn't want to see me," Leo said belligerently. "What the hell do I want with a mud-covered little tomboy, anyway? She can't even cook!"

"Neither can Tira," Corrigan pointed out. "But she's a knockout in an evening gown. So is our Janie, even if she isn't as pretty as Marilee."

Leo shrugged. "Marilee's lost a good friend."

"She has. Janie won't ever trust her again, even if she can forgive her someday."

Leo glanced back at his older brother. "Isn't it amazing how easy it is to screw up your whole life in a few unguarded minutes?"

"That's life, *compadre*. I've got to go. You going to be okay?"

Leo nodded. "Thanks for the ride." He glowered at Corrigan. "I guess you're in a hurry to get back, right?"

Corrigan's eyes twinkled. "I don't want to miss the last dance!"

Or the chance to tell his brothers everything that had happened. But, what the hell, they were family.

"Drive safely," Leo told Corrigan as he closed the car door.

"I always do." Corrigan threw up his hand and drove away.

Leo disarmed the alarm system and unlocked the front door, pausing to relock it and rearm the system. He'd been the victim of a mugging last October in Houston, and it had been Rey's new wife, Meredith, who had saved him from no worse than a concussion. But now he knew what it was to be a victim of violent crime, and he was much more cautious than he'd ever been before.

He tossed his keys on his chest of drawers and took off his jacket and shoes. Before he could manage the rest, he passed out on his own bed.

★ ★ ★

Janie Brewster was very quiet on the way home. Harley understood why. He and Janie weren't an item, but he hated seeing a woman cry. He'd wanted, very badly, to punch Leo Hart for that.

"You should have let me hit him, Janie," he remarked thoughtfully.

She gave him a sad little smile. "There's been enough gossip already, although I appreciate the thought."

"He was drinking pretty heavily," Harley added. "I noticed that one of his brothers took him and Marilee home early. Nice of him to find a designated driver, in that condition. He looked as if he was barely able to walk without staggering."

Janie had seen them leave, with mixed emotions. She turned her small evening bag in her lap. "I didn't know he drank hard liquor at all."

"He doesn't," Harley replied. "Eb Scott said that he'd never known Leo to take anything harder than a beer in company." He glanced at her. "That must have been some mixer you had with him."

"He'd been drinking before we argued," she replied. She looked out the darkened window. "Odd that Marilee left with him."

"You didn't see the women snub her, I guess," he murmured. "Served her right, I thought." His eyes narrowed angrily as he made the turn that led to her father's ranch. "It's low to stab a friend in the back like that. Whatever her feelings for Hart, she should have put your feelings first."

"I thought you liked her, Harley."

He stiffened. "I asked her out once, and she laughed."

"What?"

He stared straight ahead at the road, the center of which was lit by the powerful headlights of the truck he was driving. "She thought it was hilarious that I had the nerve to ask her to go on a date. She said I was too immature."

Ouch, she thought. A man like Harley would have too much pride to ever go near a woman who'd dented his ego that badly.

He let out a breath. "The hell of it is, she was right," he conceded with a wry smile. "I had my head in the clouds, bragging about my mercenary training. Then I went up against Lopez with Eb and Cy and Micah." He grimaced. "I didn't have a clue."

"We heard that it was a firefight."

He nodded. His eyes were haunted. "My only experience of combat was movies and television." His lean hands gripped the wheel hard. "The real thing is less... comfortable. And that's all I'll say."

"Thank you for taking me to the ball," she said, changing the subject because he'd looked so tormented.

His face relaxing, he glanced at her. "It was my pleasure. I'm not ready to settle down, but I like you. Anytime you're at a loose end, we can see a movie or get a burger."

She chuckled. "I feel the same way. Thanks."

He pursed his lips and gave her a teasing glance. "We could even go dancing."

"I liked waltzing."

"I want to learn those Latin dances, like Caldwell and Grier." He whistled. "Imagine Grier doing Latin dances! Even Caldwell stood back and stared."

"Mr. Grier is a conundrum," she murmured. "Not the man he seems, on the surface."

"How would you know?" he asked.

She cleared her throat. "He stopped me for speeding out on the Victoria road."

"Good for him. You drive too fast."

"Don't you start!"

He frowned. "What was he doing out there? He doesn't have jurisdiction outside Jacobsville."

"I don't know. But he's very pleasant."

He hesitated. "There's some, shall we say, unsavory gossip about him around town," he told her.

"Unsavory, how?" she asked, curious.

"It's probably just talk."

"Harley!"

He slowed for a turn. "They say he was a government assassin at one point in his life."

She whistled softly. "You're kidding!"

He glanced at her. "When I was in the Rangers, I flew overseas with a guy who was dressed all in black, armed to the teeth. He didn't say a word to the rest of us. I learned later that he was brought over for a very select assignment with the British commandos."

"What has that got to do with Grier?"

"That's just the thing. I think it *was* Grier."

She felt cold chills running up her arms.

"It was several years ago," he reiterated, "and I didn't get a close look, but sometimes you can tell a man just by the way he walks, the way he carries himself."

"You shouldn't tell anybody," she murmured, uneasy, because she liked Grier.

"I never would," Harley assured her. "I told my boss, but nobody else. Grier isn't the sort of man you'd ever gossip about, even if half the things they tell are true."

"There's more?" she exclaimed.

He chuckled. "He was in the Middle East helping pinpoint the laser-guided bombs, he broke up a spy ring in Manhattan as a company agent, he fought with the freedom fighters in Afghanistan, he foiled an assassination attempt against one of our own leaders under the nose of the agency assigned to protect them...you name it, he's done it. Including a stint with the Texas Rangers and a long career in law enforcement between overseas work."

"A very interesting man," she mused.

"And intimidating to our local law enforcement guys. Interesting that Judd Dunn isn't afraid of him."

"He's protective of Christabel," Janie told him. "She's sweet. She was in my high school graduating class."

"Judd's too old for her," Harley drawled. "He's about Leo Hart's age, isn't he, and she's just a few months older than you."

He was insinuating that Leo was too old for her. He was probably right, but it hurt to hear someone say it. Nor was she going to admit something else she knew about Christabel, that Judd had married the girl when she was just sixteen so that she wouldn't lose her home. Christabel was twenty-one and Judd had become her worst enemy.

"Sorry," Harley said when he noticed her brooding expression.

"About what?" she asked, diverted.

"I guess you think I meant Leo Hart's too old for you."

"He is," she said flatly.

He looked as if he meant to say more, but the sad expression on her face stopped him. He pulled into her driveway and didn't say another word until he stopped the truck at her front door.

"I know how you feel about the guy, Janie," he said then. "But you can want something too much. Hart isn't a marrying man, even if his brothers were. He's a bad risk."

She turned to face him, her eyes wide and eloquent. "I've told myself that a hundred times. Maybe it will sink in."

He grimaced. He traced a pattern on her cheek with a lean forefinger. "For what it's worth, I'm no stranger to unreturned feelings." He grimaced. "Maybe some of us just don't have the knack for romance."

"Speak for yourself," she said haughtily. "I have the makings of a Don Juanette, as Leo Hart is about to discover!"

He tapped her cheek gently. "Stop that. Running wild won't change anything, except to make you more miserable than you are."

She drew in a long breath. "You're right, of course. Oh, Harley, why can't we make people love us back?"

"Wish I knew," he said. He leaned forward and kissed her lightly on the lips. "I had fun. I'm sorry you didn't."

She smiled. "I did have fun. At least I didn't end up at the ball by myself, or with Dad, to face Leo and Marilee."

He nodded, understanding. "Where is your dad?"

"Denver," she replied on a sigh. "He's trying to interest a combine in investing in the ranch, but you can't tell anybody."

He scowled. "I didn't realize things were that bad."

She nodded. "They're pretty bad. Losing his prize bull was a huge financial blow. If Leo hadn't loaned him that breeding bull, I don't know what we'd have done. At least he likes Dad," she added softly.

It was Harley's opinion that he liked Fred Brewster's daughter, too, or he wouldn't have been putting away whiskey like that tonight. But he didn't say it.

"Can I help?" he asked instead.

She smiled at him. "You're so sweet, Harley. Thanks. But there's not much we can do without a huge grubstake. So," she added heavily, "I'm going to give up school and get a job."

"Janie!"

"College is expensive," she said simply. "Dad can't really afford it right now, and I'm not going to ask him to try. There's a job going at Shea's…"

"You can't work at Shea's!" Harley exclaimed. "Janie, it's a roadhouse! They serve liquor, and most nights there's a fight."

"They serve pizza and sandwiches, as well, and that's what the job entails," she replied. "I can handle it."

It disturbed Harley to think of an innocent, sweet girl like Janie in that environment. "There are openings at fast-food joints in town," he said.

"You don't get good tips at fast-food joints. Stop while you're ahead, Harley, you won't change my mind," she said gently.

"If you take the job, I'll stop in and check on you from time to time," he promised.

"You're a sweetheart, Harley," she said, and meant it. She kissed him on the cheek, smiled and got out of the cab. "Thanks for taking me to the ball!"

"No sweat, Cinderella," he said with a grin. "I enjoyed it, too. Good night!"

"Good night," she called back.

She went inside slowly, locking the door behind her. Her steps dragging, she felt ten years older. It had been a real bust of an evening all around. She thought about Leo Hart and she hoped he had the king of hangovers the next morning!

The next day, Janie approached the manager of Shea's, a nice, personable man named Jed Duncan, about the job.

He read over her résumé while she sat in a leather chair across from his desk and bit her fingernails.

"Two years of college," he mused. "Impressive." His

dark eyes met hers over the pages. "And you want to work in a bar?"

"Let me level with you," she said earnestly. "We're in financial trouble. My father can't afford to send me back to school, and I won't stand by and let him sink without trying to help. This job doesn't pay much, but the tips are great, from what Debbie Connor told me."

Debbie was her predecessor, and had told her about the job in the first place. Be honest with Jed, she'd advised, and lay it on the line about money. So Janie did.

He nodded slowly, studying her. "The tips are great," he agreed. "But the customers can get rowdy. Forgive me for being blunt, Miss Brewster, but you've had a sheltered upbringing. I have to keep a bouncer here now, ever since Calhoun Ballenger had it out with a customer over his ward—now his wife—and busted up the place. Not that Calhoun wasn't in the right," he added quickly. "But it became obvious that hot tempers and liquor don't mix, and you can't run a roadhouse on good intentions."

She swallowed. "I can get used to anything, Mr. Duncan. I would really like this job."

"Can you cook?"

She grinned. "Two months ago, I couldn't. But I can now. I can even make biscuits!"

He chuckled. "Okay, then, you should be able to make a pizza. We'll agree that you can work for two weeks and we'll see how it goes. You'll waitress and do some cooking. If you can cope, I'll let you stay. If not, or if you don't like the work, we'll call it quits. That suit you?"

She nodded. "It suits me very well. Thank you!"

"Does your father know about this?" he added.

She flushed. "He will, when he gets home from Denver. I don't hide things from him."

"It's not likely that you'll be able to hide this job from him," he mused with a chuckle. "A lot of our patrons do business with him. I wouldn't like to make more enemies than I already have."

"He won't mind," she assured him with a smile. She crossed her fingers silently.

"Then come along and I'll acquaint you with the job," Jed said, moving around the desk. "Welcome aboard, Miss Brewster."

She smiled. "Thanks!"

✦ 5 ✦

Fred Brewster came home from Denver discouraged. "I couldn't get anybody interested," he told Janie as he flopped down in his favorite easy chair in the living room. "Everybody's got money problems, and the market is down. It's a bad time to fish for partners."

Janie sat down on the sofa across from him. "I got a job."

He just stared at her for a minute, as if he didn't hear her. "You what?"

"I got a job," she said, and smiled at him. "I'll make good money in tips. I start tonight."

"Where?" he asked.

"A restaurant," she lied. "You can even come and eat there, and I'll serve you. You won't have to tip me, either!"

"Janie," he groaned. "I wanted you to go back and finish your degree."

She leaned forward. "Dad, let's be honest. You can't afford college right now, and if I went, it would have to be on work-study. Let me do this," she implored. "I'm young and strong and I don't mind working. You'll pull out of this, Dad, I know you will!" she added gently. "Everybody has bad times. This is ours."

He scowled. "It hurts my pride…"

She knelt at his feet and leaned her arms over his thin, bony knees. "You're my dad," she said. "I love you. Your problems are my problems. You'll come up with an angle that will get us out of this. I don't have a single doubt."

Those beautiful eyes that were so like his late wife's weakened his resolve. He smiled and touched her hair gently. "You're like your mother."

"Thanks!"

He chuckled. "Okay. Do your waitress bit for a few weeks and I'll double my efforts on getting us out of hock. But no late hours," he emphasized. "I want you home by midnight, period."

That might be a problem. But why bother him with complications right now?

"We'll see how it goes," she said easily, getting to her feet. She planted a kiss on his forehead. "I'd better get you some lunch!"

She dashed into the kitchen before he could ask any more questions about her new employment.

But she wasn't so lucky with Hettie. "I don't like the idea of you working in a bar," she told Janie firmly.

"Shhhh!" Janie cautioned, glancing toward the open kitchen door. "Don't let Dad hear you!"

Hettie grimaced. "Child, you'll end up in a brawl, sure as God made little green apples!"

"I will not. I'm going to waitress and make pizzas and sandwiches, not get in fights."

Hettie wasn't convinced. "Put men and liquor together, and you get a fight every time."

"Mr. Duncan has a bouncer," she confided. "I'll be fine."

"Mr. Hart won't like it," she replied.

"Nothing I do is any of Leo Hart's business anymore," Janie said with a glare. "After the things he's said about me, his opinion wouldn't get him a cup of coffee around here!"

"What sort of things?" Hettie wanted to know.

She rubbed her hands over the sudden chill of her

arms. "That I'm a lying, gossiping, man-chaser who can't leave him alone," she said miserably. "He was talking about me to Joe Howland in the hardware store last week. I heard every horrible word."

Hettie winced. She knew how Janie felt about the last of the unmarried Hart brothers. "Oh, baby. I'm so sorry!"

"Marilee lied," she added sadly. "My best friend! She was telling me what to do to make Leo notice me, and all the time she was finding ways to cut me out of his life. She was actually at the ball with Leo. He took her…" She swallowed hard and turned to the task at hand. Brooding was not going to help her situation. "Want a sandwich, Hettie?"

"No, darlin', I'm fine," the older woman told her. She hugged Janie warmly. "Life's tangles work themselves out if you just give them enough time," she said, and went away to let that bit of homespun philosophy sink in.

Janie was unconvinced. Her tangles were bad ones. Maybe her new job would keep Leo out of her thoughts. At least she'd never have to worry about running into him at Shea's, she told herself. After Saturday night, he was probably off hard liquor for life.

By Saturday night, Janie had four days of work under her belt and she was getting used to the routine. Shea's opened at lunchtime and closed at eleven. Shea's served pizza and sandwiches and chips, as well as any sort of liquor a customer could ask for. Janie often had to serve drinks in between cooking chores. She got to recognize some of the customers on sight, but she didn't make a habit of speaking to them. She didn't want any trouble.

Her father had, inevitably, found out about her nocturnal activities. Saturday morning, he'd been raging at her for lying to him.

"I do work in a restaurant," she'd defended herself. "It's just sort of in a bar."

"You work in a bar, period!" he returned, furious. "I want you to quit, right now!"

It was now or never, she told herself, as she faced him bravely. "No," she replied quietly. "I'm not giving notice. Mr. Duncan said I could work two weeks and see if I could handle it, and that's just what I'm going to do. And don't you dare talk to him behind my back, Dad," she told him.

He looked tormented. "Girl, this isn't necessary!"

"It is, and not only because we need the money," she'd replied. "I need to feel independent."

He hadn't considered that angle. She was determined, and Duncan did have a good bouncer, a huge man called, predictably, Tiny. "We'll see," he'd said finally.

Janie had won her first adult argument with her parent. She felt good about it.

Harley showed up two of her five nights on the job, just to check things out. He was back again tonight. She grinned at him as she served him pizza and beer.

"How's it going?" he asked.

She looked around at the bare wood floors, the no-frills surroundings, the simple wooden tables and chairs and the long counter at which most of the customers—male customers—sat. There were two game machines and a jukebox. There were ceiling fans to circulate the heat, and to cool the place in summer. There was a huge dance floor, where people could dance to live music on Friday and Saturday night. The band was playing now, lazy Western tunes, and a couple was circling the dance floor alone.

"I really like it here," she told Harley with a smile. "I feel as if I'm standing on my own two feet for the first time in my life." She leaned closer. "And the tips are really nice!"

He chuckled. "Okay. No more arguments from me." He glanced toward Tiny, a huge man with tattoos on both arms and a bald head, who'd taken an immediate liking to Janie. He was reassuringly close whenever she spoke to customers or served food and drinks.

"Isn't he a doll?" Janie asked, smiling toward Tiny,

who smiled back a little hesitantly, as if he were afraid his face might crack.

"That's not a question you should ask a man, Janie," he teased.

Grinning, she flipped her bar cloth at him, and went back to work.

Leo went looking for Fred Brewster after lunch on Monday. He'd been out of town at a convention, and he'd lost touch with his friend.

Fred was in his study, balancing figures that didn't want to be balanced. He looked up as Hettie showed Leo in.

"Hello, stranger," Fred said with a grin. "Sit down. Want some coffee? Hettie, how about…!"

"No need to shout, Mr. Fred, it's already dripping," she interrupted him with a chuckle. "I'll bring it in when it's done."

"Cake, too!" he called.

There was a grumble.

"She thinks I eat too many sweets," Fred told Leo. "Maybe I do. How was the convention?"

"It was pretty good," Leo told him. "There's a lot of talk about beef exports to Japan and improved labeling of beef to show country of origin. Some discussion of artificial additives," he confided with a chuckle. "You can guess where that came from."

"J. D. Langley and the Tremayne brothers."

"Got it in one guess." Leo tossed his white Stetson into a nearby chair and sat down in the one beside it. He ran a hand through his thick gold-streaked brown hair and his dark eyes pinned Fred. "But aside from the convention, I've heard some rumors that bother me," he said, feeling his way.

"Oh?" Fred put aside his keyboard mouse and sat back. He'd heard about Janie's job, he thought, groaning inwardly. He drew in a long breath. "What rumors?" he asked innocently.

Leo leaned forward, his crossed arms on his knees. "That you're looking for partners here."

"Oh. That." Fred cleared his throat and looked past Leo. "Just a few little setbacks…"

"Why didn't you come to me?" Leo persisted, scowling. "I'd loan you anything you needed on the strength of your signature. You know that."

Fred swallowed. "I do…know that. But I wouldn't dare. Under the circumstances." He avoided Leo's piercing stare.

"What circumstances?" Leo asked with resignation, when he realized that he was going to have to pry every scrap of information out of his friend.

"Janie."

Leo's breath expelled in a rush. He'd wondered if Fred knew about the friction between the two of them. It was apparent that he did. "I see."

Fred glanced at him and winced. "She won't hear your name mentioned," he said apologetically. "I couldn't go to you behind her back, and she'd find out, anyway, sooner or later. Jacobsville is a small town."

"She wouldn't be likely to find out when she's away at college," Leo assured him. "She has gone back, hasn't she?"

There was going to be an explosion. Fred knew it without saying a word. "Uh, Leo, she hasn't gone back, exactly."

His eyebrows lifted. "She's not here. I asked Hettie. She flushed and almost dragged me in here without saying anything except Janie wasn't around. I assumed she'd gone back to school."

"No. She's, uh, got a job, Leo. A good job," he added, trying to reassure himself. "She likes it very much."

"Doing what, for God's sake?" Leo demanded. "She has no skills to speak of!"

"She's cooking. At a restaurant."

Leo felt his forehead. "No fever," he murmured to himself. It was a well-known fact that Janie could burn water in a pan. He pinned Fred with his eyes. "Would you like to repeat that?"

"She's cooking. She can cook," he added belligerently at Leo's frank astonishment. "Hettie spent two months with her in the kitchen. She can even make—" he started to say "biscuits" and thought better of it "—pizza."

Leo whistled softly. "Fred, I didn't know things were that bad. I'm sorry."

"The bull dying was nobody's fault," Fred said heavily. "But I used money I hoped to recoup to buy him, and there was no insurance. Very few small ranchers could take a loss like that and remain standing. He was a champion's offspring."

"I know that. I'd help, if you'd let me," Leo said earnestly.

"I appreciate it. But I can't."

There was a long, pregnant pause. "Janie told you about what happened at the ball, I suppose," Leo added curtly.

"No. She hasn't said a single word about that," Fred replied. He frowned. "Why?" He understood, belatedly, Leo's concerned stare. "She did tell me about what happened in the hardware store," he added slowly. "There's more?"

Leo glanced away. "There was some unpleasantness at the ball, as well. We had a major fight." He studied his big hands. "I've made some serious mistakes lately. I believed some gossip about Janie that I should never have credited. I know better now, but it's too late. She won't let me close enough to apologize."

That was news. "When did you see her?" Fred asked, playing for time.

"In town at the bank Friday," he said. "She snubbed me." He smiled faintly. It had actually hurt when she'd given him a harsh glare, followed by complete oblivion to his presence. "First time that's happened to me in my life."

"Janie isn't usually rude," Fred tried to justify her behavior. "Maybe it's just the new job…"

"It's what I said to her, Fred," the younger man replied heavily. "I really hurt her. Looking back, I don't know why I ever believed what I was told."

Fred was reading between the lines. "Marilee can be very convincing, Janie said. And she had a case on you."

"It wasn't mutual," Leo said surprisingly. "I didn't realize what was going on. Then she told me all these things Janie was telling people…" He stopped and cursed harshly. "I thought I could see through lies. I guess I'm more naive than I thought I was."

"Any man can be taken in," Fred reassured him. "It was just bad luck. Janie never said a word about you in public. She's shy, although you might not realize it. She'd never throw herself at a man. Well, not for real," he amended with a faint smile. "She did dress up and flirt with you. She told Hettie it was the hardest thing she'd ever done in her life, and she agonized over it for days afterward. Not the mark of a sophisticated woman, is it?"

Leo understood then how far he'd fallen. No wonder she'd been so upset when she overheard him running down her aggressive behavior. "No," he replied. "I wish I'd seen through it." He smiled wryly. "I don't like aggressive, sophisticated women," he confessed. "Call it a fatal flaw. I liked Janie the way she was."

"Harmless?" Fred mused.

Leo flushed. "I wouldn't say that."

"Wouldn't you?" Fred leaned back in his chair, smiling at the younger man's confusion. "I've sheltered Janie too much. I wanted her to have a smooth, easy path through life. But I did her no favors. She's not a dress-up doll, Leo, she's a woman. She needs to learn independence, self-sufficiency. She has a temper, and she's learning to use that, too. Last week, she stood up to me for the first time and told me what she was going to do." He chuckled. "I must confess, it was pretty shocking to realize that my daughter was a woman."

"She's going around with Harley," Leo said curtly.

"Why shouldn't she? Harley's a good man—young,

but steady and dependable. He, uh, did go up against armed men and held his own, you know."

Leo did know. It made him furious to know. He didn't hang out with professional soldiers. He'd been in the service, and briefly in combat, but he'd never fought drug dealers and been written up in newspapers as a local hero.

Fred deduced all that from the look on Leo's lean face. "It's not like you think," he added. "She and Harley are friends. Just friends."

"Do I care?" came the impassioned reply. He grabbed up his Stetson and got to his feet. He hesitated, turning back to Fred. "I won't insist, but Janie would never have to know if I took an interest in the ranch," he added firmly.

Fred was tempted. He sighed and stood up, too. "I've worked double shifts for years, trying to keep it solvent. I've survived bad markets, drought, unseasonable cold. But this is the worst it's ever been. I could lose the property so easily."

"Then don't take the risk," Leo insisted. "I can loan you what it takes to get you back in the black. And I promise you, Janie will never know. It will be between the two of us. Don't lose the ranch out of pride, Fred. It's been in your family for generations."

Fred grimaced. "Leo…"

The younger man leaned both hands on the desk and impaled Fred with dark eyes. "Let me help!"

Fred studied the determination, the genuine concern in that piercing stare. "It would have to be a secret," he said, weakening.

Leo's eyes softened. "It will be. You have my word. Blake Kemp's our family attorney. I'll make an appointment. We can sit down with him and work out the details."

Fred had to bite down hard on his lower lip to keep the brightness in his eyes in check. "You can't possibly know how much…" He choked.

Leo held up a hand, embarrassed by his friend's emotion. "I'm filthy rich," he said curtly. "What good is money if you can't use it to help out friends? You'd do the same for me in a heartbeat if our positions were reversed."

Fred swallowed noticeably. "That goes without saying." He drew in a shaky breath. "Thanks," he bit off.

"You're welcome." Leo slanted his hat across his eyes. "I'll phone you. By the way, which restaurant is Janie working at?" he added. "I might stop by for lunch one day."

"That wouldn't be a good idea just yet," Fred said, feeling guilty because Leo still didn't know what was going on.

Leo considered that. "You could be right," he had to agree. "I'll let it ride for a few days, then. Until she cools down a little, at least." He grinned. "She's got a hell of a temper, Fred. Who'd have guessed?"

Fred chuckled. "She's full of surprises lately."

"That she is. I'll be in touch."

Leo was gone and Fred let the emotion out. He hadn't realized how much his family ranch meant to him until he was faced with the horrible prospect of losing it. Now, it would pass to Janie and her family, her children. God bless Leo Hart for being a friend when he needed one so desperately. He grabbed at a tissue and wiped his eyes. Life was good. Life was very good!

Fred was still up when Janie got home from work. She was tired. It had been a long night. She stopped in the kitchen to say good-night to Hettie before she joined her father in his study.

"Hettie said Leo came by," she said without her usual greeting. She looked worried. "Why?"

"He wanted to check on his bull," he lied without meeting her eyes.

She hesitated. "Did he...ask about me?"

"Yes," he said. "I told him you had a job working in a restaurant."

She stared at her feet. "Did you tell him which one?"

He looked anxious. "No."

She met his eyes. "You don't have to worry, Dad. It's none of Leo Hart's business where I work, or whatever else I do."

"You're still angry," he noted. "I understand. But he wants to make peace."

She swallowed, hearing all over again his voice taunting her, baiting her. She clenched both hands at her sides. "He wants to bury the hatchet? Good. I know exactly where to bury it."

"Now, daughter, he's not a bad man."

"Of course he's not. He just doesn't like me," she bit off. "You can't blame him, not when he's got Marilee."

He winced. "I didn't think. You lost your only friend."

"Some friend," she scoffed. "She's gone to spend the holidays in Colorado," she added smugly. "A rushed trip, I heard."

"I imagine she's too ashamed to walk down the main street right now," her father replied. "People have been talking about her, and that's no lie. But she's not really a bad woman, Janie. She just made a mistake. People do."

"You don't," she said unexpectedly, and smiled at him. "You're the only person in the world who wouldn't stab me in the back."

He flushed. Guilt overwhelmed him. What would she say when she knew that he was going to let Leo Hart buy into the ranch, and behind her back? It was for a good cause, so that she could eventually inherit her birthright, but he felt suddenly like a traitor. He could only imagine how she'd look at him if she ever found out....

"Why are you brooding?" she teased. "You need to put away those books and go to bed."

He stared at the columns that wouldn't balance and thought about having enough money to fix fences, repair the barn, buy extra feed for the winter, buy replacement heifers, afford medicine for his sick cattle and veterinarian's fees. The temptation was just too much for him. He couldn't let the ranch go to strangers.

"Do you ever think about down the road," Fred murmured, "when your children grow up and take over the ranch?"

She blinked. "Well, yes, sometimes," she confessed. "It's a wonderful legacy," she added with a soft smile. "We go back such a long way in Jacobsville. It was one of your great-uncles who was the first foreman of the Jacobs ranch properties when the founder of our town came here and bought cattle, after the Civil War. This ranch was really an offshoot of that one," she added. "There's so much history here!"

Fred swallowed. "Too much to let the ranch go down the tube, or end up in the hands of strangers, like the Jacobs place did." He shook his head. "That was sad, to see Shelby and Ty thrown off their own property. That ranch had been in their family over a hundred years."

"It wasn't much of a ranch anymore," she reminded him. "More of a horse farm. But I understand what you mean. I'm glad we'll have the ranch to hand down to our descendants." She gave him a long look. "You aren't thinking of giving it up without a fight?"

"Heavens, no!"

She relaxed. "Sorry. But the way you were talking…"

"I'd do almost anything to keep it in the family," Fred assured her. "You, uh, wouldn't have a problem with me taking on a partner or an investor?"

"Of course not," she assured him. "So you found someone in Colorado, after all?" she added excitedly. "Somebody who's willing to back us?"

"Yes," he lied, "but I didn't hear until today."

"That's just great!" she exclaimed.

He gave her a narrow look. "I'm glad you think so. Then you can give up that job and go back to college…"

"No."

His eyebrows went up. "But, Janie…"

"Dad, even with an investor, we still have the day-to-day operation of the ranch to maintain," she reminded him gently. "How about groceries? Utilities? How about cattle feed and horse feed and salt blocks and fencing?"

He sighed. "You're right, of course. I'll need the investment for the big things."

"I like my job," she added. "I really do."

"It's a bad place on the weekends," he worried.

"Tiny likes me," she assured him. "And Harley comes in at least two or three times a week, mostly on Fridays and Saturdays, to make sure I'm doing all right. I feel as safe at Shea's as I do right here with you."

"It's not that I mind you working," he said, trying to explain.

"I know that. You're just worried that I might get in over my head. Tiny doesn't let anybody have too much to drink before he makes them leave. Mr. Duncan is emphatic about not having drunks on the place."

Fred sighed. "I know when I'm licked. I may show up for pizza one Saturday night, though."

She grinned. "You'd be welcome! I could show you off to my customers."

"Leo wanted to know where you were working," he said abruptly. "He wanted to come by and see you."

Her face tautened. "I don't want to see him."

"So I heard. He was, uh, pretty vocal about the way you snubbed him."

She tossed back her hair. "He deserved it. I'm nobody's doormat. He isn't going to walk all over me and get away with it!"

"He won't like you working at Shea's, no matter what you think."

"Why do you care?" she asked suspiciously.

He couldn't tell her that Leo might renege on the loan if he knew Fred was letting her work in such a dive. He felt guilty as sin for not coming clean. But he was so afraid of losing the ranch. It was Janie's inheritance. He had to do everything he could to keep it solvent.

"He's my friend," he said finally.

"I used to think he was mine, too," she replied. "But friends don't talk about each other the way he was talking about me. As if I'd ever gossip about him!"

"I think he knows that now, Janie."

She forced the anger to the back of her mind. "I guess if he knew what I was doing, he'd faint. He doesn't think I can cook at all."

"I did tell him you had a cooking job," he confided.

Her eyes lit up. "You did? What did he say?"

"He was...surprised."

"He was astonished," she translated.

"It bothered him that you snubbed him. He said he felt really bad about the things he said, that you overheard. He, uh, told me about the fight you had at the ball, too."

Her face colored. "What did he tell you?"

"That you'd had a bad argument. Seemed to tickle him that you had a temper," he added with a chuckle.

"He'll find out I have a temper if he comes near me again." She turned. "I'm going to bed, Dad. You sleep good."

"You, too, sweetheart. Good night."

He watched her walk away with a silent sigh of relief. So far, he thought, so good.

6

The following Wednesday, Leo met with Blake Kemp and Fred Brewster in Kemp's office, to draw up the instrument of partnership.

"I'll never be able to thank you enough for this, Leo," Fred said as they finished a rough draft of the agreement.

"You'd have done it for me," Leo said simply. "How long will it take until those papers are ready to sign?" he asked Kemp.

"We'll have them by Monday," Kemp assured him.

"I'll make an appointment with your receptionist on the way out," Leo said, rising. "Thanks, Blake."

The attorney shook his outstretched hand, and then Fred's. "All in a day's work. I wish most of my business was concluded this easily, and amiably," he added wryly.

Leo checked his watch. "Why don't we go out to Shea's and have a beer and some pizza, Fred?" he asked the other man, who, curiously, seemed paler.

Fred was scrambling for a reason that Leo couldn't go to Shea's. "Well, because, uh, because Hettie made chili!" he remembered suddenly. "So why don't you come home and eat with me? We've got Mexican corn bread to go with it!"

Leo hesitated. "That does sound pretty good," he had to admit. Then he remembered. Janie would be there. He was uncomfortable with the idea of rushing in on her unexpectedly, especially in light of recent circumstances. He was still a little embarrassed about his own behavior. He searched for a reason to refuse, and found one. "Oh, for Pete's sake, I almost forgot!" he added, slapping his forehead. "I'm supposed to have supper with Cag and Tess tonight. We're going in together on two new Santa Gertrudis bulls. How could I have forgotten... Got to run, Fred, or I'll never make it on time!"

"Sure, of course," Fred said, and looked relieved. "Have a good time!"

Leo chuckled. "I get to play with my nephew. That's fun, all right. I like kids."

"You never seemed the type," Fred had to admit.

"I'm not talking about having any of my own right away," Leo assured him. "I don't want to get married. But I like all my nephews, not to mention my niece."

Fred only smiled.

"Thanks for the offer of supper, anyway," he told the older man with a smile. "Sorry I can't come."

Fred relaxed. "That's okay, Leo. More for me," he teased. "Well, I'll go home and have my chili. Thanks again. If I can ever do anything for you, anything at all, you only have to ask."

Leo smiled. "I know that, Fred. See you."

They parted in the parking lot. Leo got in his double-cabbed pickup and gunned the engine.

Fred got into his own truck and relaxed. At least, he thought, he didn't have to face Leo's indignation today. With luck, Leo might never realize what was going on.

Leo, honest to the core, phoned Cag and caged an invitation to supper to discuss the two new bulls the brothers were buying. But he had some time before he was due at his brother's house. He brooded over Fred's dead bull, and Christabel's, and he began to wonder. He had a bull from that same lot, a new lineage of Salers bulls that came from a Victoria breeder. Two related bulls dying in a month's time seemed just a bit too much for coincidence. He picked up the phone and called information.

★ ★ ★

Cag and Tess were still like newlyweds, Leo noted as he carried their toddler around the living room after supper, grinning from ear to ear as the little boy, barely a year old, smiled up at him and tried to grab his nose. They sat close together on the sofa and seemed to radiate love. They were watching him with equal interest.

"You do that like a natural," Cag teased.

Leo shifted the little boy. "Lots of practice," he chuckled. "Simon's two boys, then Corrigan's boy and their new girl, and now your son." He lifted an eyebrow. "Rey and Meredith are finally expecting, too, I hear."

"They are," Cag said with a sigh. He eyed his brother mischievously. "When are you planning to throw in the towel and join up?"

"Me? Never," Leo said confidently. "I've got a big house to myself, all the women I can attract, no responsibilities and plenty of little kids to spoil as they grow." He gave them an innocent glance. "Why should I want to tie myself down?"

"Just a thought," Cag replied. "You'll soon get tired of going all the way to town every morning for a fresh biscuit." Cag handed the baby back to Tess.

"I'm thinking of taking a cooking course," Leo remarked.

Cag roared.

"I could cook if I wanted to!" Leo said indignantly.

Tess didn't speak, but her eyes did.

Leo stuffed his hands in his pockets. "Well, I don't really want to," he conceded. "And it is a long way to town. But I can manage." He sprawled in an easy chair. "There's something I want to talk to you about—besides our new bulls."

"What?" Cag asked, sensing concern.

"Fred's big Salers bull that died mysteriously," Leo said. "Christabel and Judd Dunn lost one, too, a young bull."

"Judd says it died of bloat."

"I saw the carcass, he didn't. He thinks Christabel made it up, God knows why. He wouldn't even come down from Victoria to take a look at it. It wasn't bloat. But she didn't call a vet out, and they didn't find any marks on Fred's bull." He sighed. "Cag, I've done a little checking. The bulls are related. The young herd sire of these bulls died recently, as well, and the only champion Salers bull left that's still walking is our two-year-old bull that I loaned to Fred, although it's not related to the dead ones."

Cag sat up straight, scowling. "You're kidding."

Leo shook his head. "It's suspicious, isn't it?"

"You might talk to Jack Handley in Victoria, the rancher we bought our bull from."

"I did." He leaned forward intently. "Handley said he fired two men earlier this year for stealing from him. They're brothers, John and Jack Clark. One of them is a thief, the other has a reputation for vengeance that boggles the mind. When one former employer fired Jack Clark, he lost his prize bull and all four young bulls he'd got from it. No apparent cause of death. Handley checked and found a pattern of theft and retribution with those brothers going back two years. At least four employers reported similar problems with theft and firing. There's a pattern of bull deaths, too. The brothers were suspects in a recent case in Victoria, but there was never enough evidence to convict anyone. Until now, I don't imagine anyone's connected the dots."

"How the hell do they keep getting away with it?" Cag wanted to know.

"There's no proof. And they're brawlers," Leo said. "They intimidate people."

"They wouldn't intimidate us," Cag remarked.

"They wouldn't. But do you see the common thread here? Handley crossed the brothers. He had a new, expensive Salers bull that he bred to some heifers, and he sold all the young bulls this year, except for his seed bull. His seed bull, and all its offspring, which isn't many, have died. Christabel Gaines's young bull was one of Hand-

ley's, like Fred's. And Jack Clark was fired by Judd Dunn
for stealing, too."

Cag was scowling. "Where are the brothers now?"

"I asked Handley. He says John Clark is working on
a ranch near Victoria. We know that Jack, the one with
a reputation for getting even, is right here in Jacobsville,
driving a cattle truck for Duke Wright," Leo said. "I
called Wright and told him what I know. He's going to
keep an eye on the man. I called Judd Dunn, too, but
he was too preoccupied to listen. He's smitten with that
redheaded supermodel who's in the movie they're making on Christabel's ranch—Tippy Moore, the 'Georgia
Firefly.'"

"He'll land hard, if I make my guess," Cag said. "She's
playing. He isn't."

"He's married, too," Leo said curtly. "Something he
doesn't seem to remember."

"He only married Christabel because she was going
to lose the ranch after her father beat her nearly to death
in a drunken rage. Her mother was an invalid. No way
could the two of them have kept it solvent," Cag added.
"That's not a real marriage. I'm sure he's already looked
into annulling it when she turns twenty-one."

"She was twenty-one this month," Leo said. "Poor
kid. She's got a real case on him, and she's fairly plain

except for those soulful brown eyes and a nice figure. She couldn't compete with the Georgia Firefly."

"So ask yourself what does a supermodel worth millions want with a little bitty Texas Ranger?" Cag grinned.

Tess gave him a speaking look. "As a happily married woman, I can tell you that if I wasn't hung up on you, Judd Dunn would make my mouth water."

Cag whistled.

Leo shrugged. "Whatever. But I think we should keep a close eye on our Salers bull, as well as Wright's new cattle-truck driver. Handley says Clark likes to drink, so it wouldn't hurt to keep an eye out at Shea's, as well."

Cag frowned thoughtfully. "You might have a word with Janie…"

"Janie?"

"Janie Brewster," his brother said impatiently. "Tell her what the man looks like and have her watch him if he ever shows up out there."

Leo stared at his brother. "Will you make sense? Why would Janie be at Shea's roadhouse in the first place?"

Realization dawned. Cag looked stunned, and then uncomfortable.

Tess grimaced. "He doesn't know. I guess you'd better tell him."

"Tell me what?" Leo grumbled.

"Well, it's like this," Cag said. "Janie's been working at Shea's for a couple of weeks…"

"She's working in a bar?" Leo exploded violently.

Cag winced. "Now, Leo, she's a grown woman," he began calmly.

"She's barely twenty-one!" he continued, unabashed. "She's got no business working around drunks! What the hell is Fred thinking, to let her get a job in a place like that?"

Cag sighed. "Talk is that Fred's in the hole and can hardly make ends meet," he told Leo. "I guess Janie insisted on helping out."

Leo got to his feet and grabbed up his white Stetson, his lips in a thin line, his dark eyes sparking.

"Don't go over there and start trouble," Cag warned. "Don't embarrass the girl with her boss!"

Leo didn't answer him. He kept walking. His footsteps, quick and hard, described the temper he was in. He even slammed the door on the way out, without realizing he had.

Cag looked at Tess worriedly as Leo's car careened down the driveway. "Should I warn her?" he asked Tess.

She nodded. "At least she'll be prepared."

Cag thought privately that it was unlikely that anybody could prepare for Leo in a temper, but he picked up the phone just the same.

★ ★ ★

Shea's wasn't crowded when Leo jerked to a stop in the parking lot. He walked into the roadhouse with blood in his eye. Three men at a table near the door stopped talking when they saw him enter. Apparently they thought he looked dangerous.

Janie was thinking the same thing. She'd assured Cag that she wasn't afraid of Leo, but it was a little different when the man was walking toward her with his eyes narrow and his lips compressed like that.

He stopped at the counter. He noted her long apron, her hands with a dusting of flour, a pencil behind her ear. She looked busy. There were three cowboys at the counter drinking beers and apparently waiting for pizzas. A teenage boy was pulling a pizza on a long paddle out of a big oven behind her.

"Get your things," he told Janie in a tone he hadn't used with her since she was ten and had gotten into a truck with a cowboy who offered her a trip to the visiting carnival. He'd busted up that cowboy pretty bad, and for reasons Janie only learned later. She'd had a very close call. Leo had saved her. But she didn't need saving right now.

She lifted her chin and glared at him, The night of the ball came back to her vividly. "How's your foot?" she asked with sarcasm.

"My foot is fine. Get your things," he repeated curtly.

"I work here."

"Not anymore."

She crossed her arms. "You planning to carry me out kicking and screaming? Because that's the only way I'm leaving."

"Suits me." He started around the counter.

She picked up a pitcher of beer and dumped the contents on him. "Now you listen to me...Leo!"

The beer didn't even slow him down. He had her up in his arms and he turned, carrying her toward the door. She was kicking and screaming for all she was worth.

That attracted Tiny, the bouncer. He was usually on the job by six, but he'd arrived late today. To give him credit, the minute he saw Janie, he turned and went toward the big man bullying her.

He stepped in front of Leo. "Put her down, Leo," he drawled.

"You tell him, Tiny!" Janie sputtered.

"I'm taking her home where she'll be safe," Leo replied. He knew Tiny. The man was sweet-natured, but about a beer short of a six-pack on intelligence. He was also as big as a house. It didn't hurt to be polite. "She shouldn't be working in a bar."

"It isn't a bar," Tiny said reasonably. "It's a roadhouse.

It's a nice roadhouse. Mr. Duncan don't allow no drunks. You put Miss Janie down, Leo, or I'll have to hit you."

"He'll do it," Janie warned. "I've seen him do it. He's hit men even bigger than you. Haven't you, Tiny?" she encouraged.

"I sure have, Miss Janie."

Leo wasn't backing down. He glared at Tiny. "I said," he replied, his voice dangerously soft, "I'm taking her home."

"I don't think she wants to go, Mr. Hart," came a new source of interference from the doorway behind him.

He swung around with Janie in his big arms. It was Harley Fowler, leaning against the doorjamb, looking intimidating. It would have been a joke a year ago. The new Harley made it look good.

"You tell him, Harley!" Janie said enthusiastically.

"You keep still," Leo told her angrily. "You've got no business working in a rough joint like this!"

"You have no right to tell me where I can work," Janie shot right back, red-faced and furious. "Won't Marilee mind that you're here pestering me?" she added viciously.

His cheeks went red. "I haven't seen Marilee in two weeks. I don't give a damn if I never see her again, either."

That was news. Janie looked as interested as Harley seemed to.

Tiny was still hovering. "I said, put her down," he persisted.

"Do you really think you can take on Tiny and me both?" Harley asked softly.

Leo was getting mad. His face tautened. "I don't know about Tiny," he said honestly, putting Janie back on her feet without taking his eyes off Harley. "But you're a piece of cake, son."

As he said it, he stepped forward and threw a quick punch that Harley wasn't expecting. With his mouth open, Harley tumbled backward over a table. Leo glared at Janie.

"You want this job, keep it," he said, ice-cold except for the glitter in those dark eyes. "But if you get slugged during a brawl or hassled by amorous drunks, don't come crying to me!"

"As…as if I ever…would!" she stammered, shocked by his behavior.

He turned around and stalked out the door without giving Harley a single glance.

Janie rushed to Harley and helped him back to his feet. "Oh, Harley, are you hurt?" she asked miserably.

He rubbed his jaw. "Only my pride, darlin'," he murmured with a rough chuckle. "Damn, that man can throw a punch! I wasn't really expecting him to do it."

His eyes twinkled. "I guess you're a little more important to him than any of us realized."

She flushed. "He's just trying to run my life."

Tiny came over and inspected Harley's jaw. "Gonna have a bruise, Mr. Fowler," he said politely.

Harley grinned. He was a good sport, and he knew a jealous man when he saw one. Leo had wanted to deck him at the ball over Janie, but he'd restrained himself. Now, maybe, he felt vindicated. But Harley wished there had been a gentler way of doing it. His jaw was really sore.

"The beast," Janie muttered. "Come on, Harley, I'll clean you up in the bathroom before it gets crowded. Okay, guys, fun's over. Drink your beer and eat your pizzas."

"Yes, mother," one of the men drawled.

She gave him a wicked grin and led Harley to the back. She was not going to admit the thrill it had given her that Leo was worried about her job, or that people thought he was jealous of Harley. But she felt it all the way to her bones.

Leo was lucky not to get arrested for speeding on his way to Fred's house. He had the sports car flat-out on the four lane that turned onto the Victoria road, and he burned rubber when he left the tarmac and turned into Fred's graveled driveway.

Fred heard him coming and knew without a doubt what was wrong.

He stood on the porch with his hands in his jean pockets as he studied the darkening sky behind Leo, who was already out of the car and headed for the porch. His Stetson was pulled down right over his eyes, cocked as they said in cowboy vernacular, and Fred had never seen Leo look so much like a Hart. The brothers had a reputation for being tough customers. Leo looked it right now.

"I want her out of that damned bar," Leo told Fred flatly, without even a conventional greeting. "You can consider it a term of the loan, if you like, but you get her home."

Fred grimaced. "I did try to talk her out of it, when I found out where she was working," he said in his own defense. "Leo, she stood right up to me and said she was old enough to make her own decisions. What do I say to that? She's twenty-one and she told me she wasn't giving up her job."

Leo cursed furiously.

"What happened to your shirt?" Fred asked suddenly. He leaned closer and made a face. "Man, you reek of beer!"

"Of course I do! Your daughter baptized me in front of

a crowd of cowboys with a whole pitcher of the damned stuff!" Leo said indignantly.

Fred's eyes opened wide. "Janie? My Janie?"

Leo looked disgusted. "She flung the pitcher at me. And then she set the bouncer on me and appealed to Harley Fowler for aid."

"Why did she need aid?" Fred asked hesitantly.

"Oh, she was kicking and screaming, and they thought she was in trouble, I guess."

"Kicking…?"

Leo's lips compressed. "All right, if you have to know, I tried to carry her out of the bar and bring her home. She resisted."

Fred whistled. "I'd say she resisted." He was trying very hard not to laugh. He looked at Leo's clenched fists. One, the right one, was bleeding. "Hit somebody, did you?"

"Harley," he returned uncomfortably. "Well, he shouldn't have interfered! He doesn't own Janie, she's not his private stock. If he were any sort of a man, he'd have insisted that she go home right then. Instead, he stands there calmly ordering me to put her down. Ordering me. Hell! He's lucky it was only one punch!"

"Oh, boy," Fred said, burying his face in his hand. Gossip was going to run for a month on this mixer.

"It wasn't my fault," Leo argued, waving his hands.

"I went in there to save her from being insulted and harassed by drunk men, and look at the thanks I get? Drenched in beer, threatened by ogres, giggled at…"

"Who giggled?"

Leo shifted. "This little brunette who was sitting with one of the Tremayne brothers' cowboys."

Fred cleared his throat. He didn't dare laugh. "I guess it was a sight to see."

Grimacing, Leo flexed his hand. "Damned near broke my fingers on Harley's jaw. He needs to learn to keep his mouth shut. Just because he's not afraid of drug lords, he shouldn't think he can take me on and win."

"I'm sure he knows that now, Leo."

Leo took a deep breath. "You tell her I said she's going to give up that job, one way or the other!"

"I'll tell her." *It won't matter, though,* he thought privately. Janie was more than likely to dig her heels in big time after Leo's visit to Shea's.

Leo gave him a long, hard stare. "I'm not mean with money, I don't begrudge you that loan. But I'm not kidding around with you, Fred. Janie's got no business in Shea's, even with a bouncer on duty. It's a rough place. I've been there on nights when the bouncer didn't have time for a cup of coffee, and there's been at least one shooting. It's dangerous. Even more dangerous right now."

Something in the younger man's tone made Fred uneasy. "Why?"

"Fred, you don't breathe a word of this, even to Janie, understand?"

Fred nodded, curious.

Leo told him what he'd learned from Handley about the Clark brothers, and the loss of the related Salers bulls.

Fred's jaw flew open. "You think my bull was killed deliberately?"

"Yes, I do," Leo admitted solemnly. "I'm sorry to tell you that, because I can't prove it and neither can you. Clark is shrewd. He's never been caught in the act. If you can't prove it, you can't prosecute."

Fred let out an angry breath. "Of all the damned mean, low things to do!"

"I agree, and it's why I'm putting two men over here to watch my bull," he added firmly. "No sorry cattle-killer is going to murder my bull and get away with it. I'm having video cameras installed, too. If he comes near that bull, I'll have his hide in jail!"

Fred chuckled. "Don't I wish he'd try," he said thoughtfully.

"So do I, but I don't hold out a lot of hope," Leo returned. He moved his shoulders restlessly. The muscles were stretched, probably from Janie's violent squirming. He remembered without wanting to the feel of her soft breasts pressed hard against his chest, and he ached.

"Uh, about Janie," Fred continued worriedly.

Leo stared at him without speaking.

"Okay," the older man said wearily. "I'll try to talk some sense into her." He pursed his lips and peered up at Leo. "Of course, she could be a lot of help where she is right now," he murmured thoughtfully. "With the Clark man roaming around loose, that is. She could keep an eye on him if he comes into Shea's. If he's a drinking man, that's the only joint around that sells liquor by the drink."

"She doesn't know what he looks like," Leo said.

"Can't you find out and tell her?"

Leo sighed. "I don't like her being in the line of fire."

"Neither do I." Fred gave the other man a curious scrutiny. "You and Harley and I could arrange to drop in from time to time, just to keep an eye on her."

"She'll have to ask Harley. I won't."

"You're thinking about it, aren't you?" Fred persisted.

Leo was. His eyes narrowed. "My brothers could drop in occasionally, and so could our ranch hands. The Tremaynes would help us out. I know Harden. I'll talk to him. And most of our cowhands go into Shea's on the weekend. I'll talk to our cattle foreman."

"I know Cy Parks and Eb Scott," Fred told him. "They'd help, too."

Leo perked up. With so many willing spies, Janie would be looked after constantly, and she'd never know it. He smiled.

"It's a good idea, isn't it?"

Leo glared at him. "You just don't want to have to make Janie quit that job. You're scared of her, aren't you? What's the matter, think she'd try to drown you in cheap beer, too?"

Fred burst out laughing. "You have to admit, it's a shock to think of Janie throwing beer at anybody."

"I guess it is, at that," Leo seconded, remembering how shy Janie had been. It was only after Marilee had caused so much trouble with her lies that Leo had considered Janie's lack of aggression.

In the past, that was, he amended, because he'd never seen such aggression as he'd encountered in little Janie Brewster just an hour ago.

He shook his head. "It was all I could do not to get thrown on the floor. She's a handful when she's mad. I don't think I've ever seen her lose her temper before."

"There's a lot about her you don't know," Fred said enigmatically.

"Okay, she can stay," Leo said at once. "But I'll find out what Clark looks like. I'll get a picture if I can manage it. Maybe Grier at the police station would have an idea. He's sweet on Christabel Gaines, and she lost a bull to this dude, so he might be willing to assist."

"Don't get Judd Dunn mad," Fred warned.

Leo shrugged. "He's too stuck on his pretty model to care much about Christabel right now, or Grier, either. I don't want any more bulls killed, and I want that man out of the way before he really hurts somebody."

"Have you talked to his boss?"

"Duke Wright didn't have a clue that his new truck driver was such an unsavory character," Leo said, "and he was keen to fire him on the spot. I persuaded him not to. He needs to be where we can watch him. If he puts a foot wrong, we can put him away. I love animals," Leo said in an uncharacteristically tender mood. "Especially bulls. The kind we keep are gentle creatures. They follow us around like big dogs and eat out of our hands." His face hardened visibly. "A man who could cold-bloodedly kill an animal like that could kill a man just as easily. I want Clark out of here. Whatever it takes. But Janie's going to be watched, all the time she's working," Leo added firmly. "Nobody's going to hurt her."

Fred looked at the other man, sensing emotions under the surface that Leo might not even realize were there.

"Thanks, Leo," he said.

The younger man squared his shoulders and shrugged.

"I've got to go home and change my shirt." He looked down at himself and smiled ruefully. "Damn. I may never drink another beer."

"It tastes better than it wears," Fred said, deadpan.

Leo gave him a haughty look and went home.

✦ 7 ✦

Leo stopped by Cash Grier's office at the police station in Jacobsville, catching the new assistant chief of police on his lunch hour.

"Come on in," Grier invited. He indicated his big desk, which contained a scattering of white boxes with metal handles. "Like Chinese food? That's moo goo gai pan, that's sweet-and-sour pork and that's fried rice. Help yourself to a plate."

"Thanks, but I had barbecue at Barbara's Café," Leo replied, sitting down. He noted with little surprise that the man was adept with chopsticks. "I saw Toshiro Mifune catch flies with those things in one of the *Samurai Trilogy* films," he commented.

Grier chuckled. "Don't believe everything you see, and only half of what you hear," he replied. He gave Leo a dark-eyed appraisal over his paper plate. "You're here about Clark, I guess."

Leo's eyebrows jumped.

"Oh, I'm psychic," Grier told him straight-faced. "I learned that when I was in the CIA knocking off enemy government agents from black helicopters with a sniper kit."

Leo didn't say a word.

Grier just shook his head. "You wouldn't believe the stuff I've done, to hear people talk."

"You're mysterious," Leo commented. "You keep to yourself."

Grier shrugged. "I have to. I don't want people to notice the aliens spying on me." He leaned forward confidentially. "You see them, too, don't you?" he asked in a hushed tone.

Leo began to get it. He started laughing and was secretly relieved when Grier joined him. The other man leaned back in his chair, with his booted feet propped on his desk. He was as fit as Leo, probably in even better condition, if the muscles outlined under that uniform shirt were any indication. Grier was said to move like lightning, although Leo had never seen him fight. The man was an enigma, with his black hair in a rawhide ponytail and his scarred face giving away nothing—unless he wanted it to.

"That's more like it," Grier said as he finished his lunch. "I thought I'd move to a small town and fit in." He smiled wryly. "But people are all the same. Only the scenery changes."

"It was the same for Cy Parks when he first moved here," Leo commented.

Grier gave him a narrow look. "Are you asking a question?"

"Making a comment," Leo told him. "One of our local guys was in the military during a conflict a few years back, in a special forces unit," he added deliberately, recounting something Cy Parks had told him about Harley Fowler. "He saw you on a plane, out of uniform and armed to the teeth."

Grier began to nod. "It's a small world, isn't it?" he asked pleasantly. He put down his plate and the chopsticks with deliberate preciseness. "I did a stint with military intelligence. And with a few...government agencies." He met Leo's curious eyes. "How far has that gossip traveled?"

"It got to Cy Parks and stopped abruptly," Leo replied, recalling what Cy had said to Harley about loose lips.

"Jacobsville is a small town. We consider people who live here family, whether or not we're related to them. Gossip isn't encouraged."

Grier was surprised. He actually smiled. "If you asked Parks, or Steele, or Scott why they moved here," he said after a minute, "I imagine you'd learn that what they wanted most was an end to sitting with their backs to the wall and sleeping armed."

"Isn't that why you're here?" Leo wanted to know.

Grier met his eyes levelly. "I don't really know why I'm here, or if I can stay here," he said honestly. "I think I might eventually fit in. I'm going to give it a good try for six months," he added, "no matter how many rubber-necked yahoos stand outside my office trying to hear every damned word I say!" he raised his voice.

There were sudden, sharp footfalls and the sound of scurrying.

Leo chuckled. Grier hadn't even looked at the door when he raised his voice. He shrugged and smiled sheepishly. "I don't have eyes in the back of my head, but I love to keep people guessing about what I know."

"I think that may be part of the problem," Leo advised.

"Well, it doesn't hurt to keep your senses honed. Now. What do you want to know about Clark?"

"I'd like some way to get a photo of him," Leo confessed. "A friend of mine is working at Shea's. I'm going to ask her if she'll keep an eye on who he talks to, what he does, if he comes in there. She'll need to know what he looks like."

Grier sobered at once. "That's dangerous," he said. "Clark's brother almost killed a man he suspected of spying on him, up in Victoria. He made some threats, too."

Leo frowned. "Why are guys like that on the streets?"

"You can't shoot people or even lock them up without due process here in the States," Grier said with a wistful smile. "Pity."

"Listen, do they give you real bullets to go with that gun?" Leo asked, indicating the .45 caliber automatic in a shoulder holster that the man was wearing.

"I haven't shot anybody in months," Grier assured him. "I was a cyber crime specialist in the D.A.'s office San Antonio. I didn't really beat up that guy I was accused of harassing, I just told him I'd keep flies off him if he didn't level with me about his boss's illegal money laundering. I had access to his computerized financial records," he added with a twinkle in his dark eyes.

"I heard about that," Leo chuckled. "Apparently you used some access codes that weren't in the book."

"They let me off with a warning. When they checked my ID, I still had my old 'company' card."

Leo just shook his head. He couldn't imagine Grier

being in trouble for very long. He knew too much. "All that specialized background, and you're handing out speeding tickets in Jacobsville, Texas."

"Don't knock it. Nobody's shot at me since I've been here." He got up and opened his filing cabinet with a key. "I have to keep it locked," he explained. "I have copies of documents about alien technology in here." He glanced at Leo to see if he was buying it and grinned. "Did you read that book by the Air Force guy who discovered night vision at a flying saucer crash?" He turned back to the files. "Hell, I should write a book. With what I know, governments might topple." He hesitated, frowned, with a file folder in his hand. "Our government might topple!"

"Clark?" Leo prompted.

"Clark. Right." He took a paper from the file, replaced it, closed the cabinet and locked it again. "Here. You don't have a clue where this photo came from, and I never saw you."

Leo was looking at a photograph of two men, obviously brothers, in, of all things, a newspaper clipping. Incredibly, they'd been honored with a good citizen award in another Texas town for getting a herd of escaped cattle out of the path of traffic and back into a fenced pasture with broken electric fencing.

"Neat trick," Grier said. "They cut the wire to steal

the cattle, and then were seen rounding them up. Everybody thought they were saving the cattle. They had a tractor trailer truck just down the road and told people they were truck drivers who saw the cattle out and stopped to help." He laughed wholeheartedly. "Can you believe it?"

"Can you copy this for me?"

"That's a copy of the original. You can have it," Grier told him. "I've got two more."

"You were expecting trouble, I gather," Leo continued.

"Two expensive bulls in less than a month, both from the same herd sire, is a little too much coincidence even for me," Grier said as he sat back down. "When I heard Clark was working for Duke Wright, I put two and two together."

"There's no proof," Leo said.

"Not yet. We'll give him a little time and see if he'll oblige us by hanging himself." He laced his lean, strong hands together on the desk in front of him. "But you warn your friend not to be obvious. These are dangerous men."

"I'll tell her."

"And stop knocking men over tables in Shea's. It's outside the city limits, so I can't arrest you. But I can have the sheriff pick you up for brawling," Grier said abruptly, and he was serious. "You can't abduct women in plain sight of the public."

"I wasn't abducting her, I was trying to save her!"

"From what?"

"Fistfights!"

Grier lost it. He got up from his desk. "Get out," he invited through helpless laughter. "I have real work to do here."

"If Harley Fowler said I hit him without provocation, he's lying," Leo continued doggedly. "He never should have ordered me to put her down, and leave my hands free to hit him!"

"You should just tell the woman how you feel," Grier advised. "It's simpler." He glanced at Leo's swollen hand. "And less painful."

Leo didn't really know how he felt. That was the problem. He gave Grier a sardonic look and left.

He worried about letting Janie get involved, even from the sidelines, with Clark. Of course, the man might not even come near Shea's. He might buy a bottle and drink on the ranch, in the bunkhouse. But it wasn't a long shot to think he might frequent Shea's if he wanted company while he drank.

He disliked anything that might threaten Janie, and he didn't understand why he hated Harley all of a sudden.

But she was in a great position to notice a man without being obvious, and for everyone's sake, Clark had to be watched. A man who would kill helpless animals was capable of worse.

He went looking for her Sunday afternoon, in a misting rain. She wasn't at home. Fred said that she was out, in the cold rain no less, wandering around the pecan trees in her raincoat. Brooding, was how Fred put it. Leo climbed back into his pickup and went after her.

Janie was oblivious to the sound of an approaching truck. She had her hands in her pockets, her eyes on the ground ahead of her, lost in thought.

It had been a revelation that Leo was concerned about her working at Shea's, and it had secretly thrilled her that he'd tried to make her quit. But he'd washed his hands of her when she wouldn't leave willingly, and he'd hurt her feelings with his comment that she shouldn't complain if she got in trouble. She didn't know what to make of his odd behavior. He'd given her a hard time, thanks to Marilee. But she hadn't been chasing him lately, so she couldn't understand why he was so bossy about her life. And she did feel guilty that he'd slugged poor Harley, who was only trying to help her.

The truck was almost on top of her before she finally heard the engine and jumped to the side of the ranch trail.

Leo pulled up and leaned over to open the passenger door. "Get in before you drown out there," he said.

She hesitated. She wasn't sure if it was safe to get that close to him.

He grimaced. "I'm not armed and dangerous," he drawled. "I just want to talk."

She moved closer to the open door. "You're in a very strange mood lately," she commented. "Maybe the lack of biscuits in your life has affected your mind."

Both eyebrows went up under his hat.

She flushed, thinking she'd been too forward. But she got into the truck and closed the door, removing the hood of her raincoat from her long, damp hair.

"You'll catch cold," he murmured, turning up the heat.

"It's not that wet, and I've got a lined raincoat."

He drove down the road without speaking, made a turn, and ended up in a field on the Hart ranch, a place where they could be completely alone. He put the truck in Park, cut off the engine and leaned back against his door to study her from under the wide brim of his Stetson. "Your father says you won't give up the job."

"He's right," she replied, ready to do battle.

His fingers tapped rhythmically on the steering wheel. "I've been talking to Grier," he began.

"Now listen here, you can't have me arrested because I won't quit my job!" she interrupted.

He held up a big, lean hand. "Not about that," he corrected. "We've got a man in town who may be involved in some cattle losses. I want you to look at this picture and tell me if you've ever seen him in Shea's."

He took the newspaper clipping out of his shirt pocket, unfolded it, and handed it to her.

She took it gingerly and studied the two faces surrounded by columns of newsprint. "I don't know the man on the left," she replied. "But the one on the right comes in Saturday nights and drinks straight whiskey," she said uneasily. "He's loud and foul-mouthed, and Tiny had to ask him to leave last night."

Leo's face tightened. "He's vindictive," he told her.

"I'll say he is," she agreed at once. "When Tiny went out to get into his car, all his tires were slashed."

That was disturbing. "Did he report it to the sheriff?"

"He did," she replied. "They're going to look into it, but I don't know how they'll prove anything."

Leo traced an absent pattern on the seat behind her head. They were silent while the rain slowly increased, the sound of it loud on the hood and cab of the truck. "The man we're watching is Jack Clark," he told her, "the man you recognize in that photo." He took it back from her, refolded it and replaced it in his pocket. "If he comes back in, we'd like you to see who he talks to. Don't be obvious about it. Tell Tiny to let it slide about his tires, I'll see that they're replaced."

"That's nice of you," she replied.

He shrugged. "He's protective of you. I like that."

His eyes were narrow and dark and very intent on her face. She felt nervous with him all at once and folded her hands in her lap to try and keep him from noticing. It was like another world, closed up with him in a truck in a rainstorm. It outmatched her most fervent dreams of close contact.

"What sort of cattle deaths do you suspect him of?" she asked curiously.

"Your father's bull, for one."

Her intake of breath was audible. "Why would he kill Dad's bull?" she wanted to know.

"It was one of the offspring of a bull he killed in Victoria. He worked for the owner, who fired him. Apparently his idea of proper revenge is far-reaching."

"He's nuts!" she exclaimed.

He nodded. "That's why you have to be careful if he comes back in. Don't antagonize him. Don't stare at him. Don't be obvious when you look at him." He sighed angrily. "I hate the whole idea of having you that close to a lunatic. I should have decked Tiny as well as Fowler and carried you out of there, anyway."

His level, penetrating gaze made her heart race. "I'm not your responsibility," she challenged.

"Aren't you?" His dark eyes slid over her from head to toe. His head tilted back at a faintly arrogant angle.

She swallowed. He looked much more formidable now than he had at Shea's. "I should go," she began.

He leaned forward abruptly, caught her under the arms, and pulled her on top of him. He was sprawled over the front seat, with one long, powerful leg braced against the passenger floorboard and the other on the seat. Janie landed squarely between his denim-clad legs, pressed intimately to him.

"Leo!" she exclaimed, horribly embarrassed at the intimate proximity and trying to get up.

He looped an arm around her waist and held her there, studying her flushed face with almost clinical scrutiny. "If you keep moving like that, you're going to discover the major difference between men and women in a vivid way, any minute."

She stilled at once. She knew what he meant. She'd felt that difference with appalling starkness at the ball. In fact, she was already feeling it again. She looked at him and her face colored violently.

"I told you," he replied, pursing his lips as he surveyed the damage. "My, my, didn't we know that men are easily aroused when we're lying full length on top of them?" he drawled. "We do now, don't we?"

She hit his shoulder, trying to hold on to her dignity as well as her temper. "You let go of me!"

"Spoilsport," he chided. He shifted her so that her head fell onto his shoulder and he could look down into her wide, startled eyes. "Relax," he coaxed. "What are you so afraid of?"

She swallowed. The closeness was like a drug. She felt swollen. Her legs trembled inside the powerful cage his legs made for them. Her breasts were hard against his chest, and they felt uncomfortably tight, as well.

He looked down at them with keen insight, even moving her back slightly so that he could see the hard tips pressing against his shirt.

"You stop…looking at that!" she exclaimed without thinking.

He lifted an eyebrow and his smile was worldly. "A man likes to know that he's making an impression," he said outrageously.

She bit her lower lip, still blushing. "You're making too much of an impression already," she choked.

He leaned close and brushed his mouth lazily over her parted lips. "My body likes you," he whispered huskily. "It's making very emphatic statements about what it wants to do."

"You need…to speak…firmly to it," she said. She was trying to sound adult and firm, but her voice shook. It was hard to think, with his mouth hovering like that.

"It doesn't listen to reason," he murmured. He nibbled tenderly at her upper lip, parting it insistently from its companion. His free hand came up to tease around the corners of her mouth and down her chin to the opening her v-necked blouse made inside her raincoat.

His mouth worked on her lips while his hands freed her from the raincoat and slowly, absently, from her blouse, as well. She was hardly aware of it. His mouth was doing impossibly erotic things to her lips, and one of his lean, strong hands was inside her blouse, teasing around the lacy edges of her brassiere.

The whole time, one long, powerful leg was sliding against the inside of her thigh, in a way so arousing that she didn't care what he did to her, as long as he didn't try to get up.

Her hands had worked their way into his thick, soft hair, and she was lifting up, trying to get closer to those slow, maddening fingers that were brushing against the soft flesh inside her bra. She'd never dreamed that a man could arouse her so quickly with nothing more invasive than a light brushing stroke of his hand. But she was on fire with hunger, need, aching need, to have him thrust those fingers down inside her frilly bra and close on her breast. It was torture to have him tease her like this. He was watching her face, too, watching the hunger grow with a dark arrogance that was going to make her squirm later in memory.

Right now, of course, she didn't care how he looked at her. If he would just slide that hand…down a…couple of…inches!

She was squirming in another way now, twisting her body ardently, pushing up against his stroking fingers while his mouth nibbled and nipped at her parted lips and his warm breath went into her mouth.

The rain was falling harder. It banged on the hood, and on top of the cab, with tempestuous fury. Inside, Janie could hear the tormented sound of her own breathing, feel her heartbeat shaking her madly, while Leo's practiced caresses grew slower and lazier on her taut body.

"Will you…please…!" she sputtered, gripping his arms.

"Will I please, what?" he whispered into her mouth.

"T-t-touch me!" she cried.

He nipped her upper lip ardently. "Touch you where?" he tormented.

Tears of frustration stung her eyes as they opened, meeting his. "You…know…where!"

He lifted his head. His face was taut, his eyes dark and

glittery. He watched her eyes as his hand slowly moved down to where she ached to have it. She ground her teeth together to keep from crying out when she felt that big, warm, strong hand curl around her breast.

She actually shuddered, hiding her face in his throat as the tiny culmination racked her slender body and made it helpless.

"You are," he breathed, "the most surprising little treasure..."

His mouth searched for hers and suddenly ravished it while his hand moved on her soft flesh, molding it, tracing it, exploring it, in a hot, explosive silence. He kissed her until her mouth felt bruised and then she felt his hand move again, lifting free of her blouse, around to her back, unhooking the bra.

She didn't mind. She lifted up to help him free the catch. She looked up at him with wild, unsatisfied longing, shivering with reaction to the force of the desire he was teaching her.

"It will change everything," he whispered as he began to move the fabric away from her body. "You know that."

"Yes." She shivered.

Both hands slid against her rib cage, carrying the fabric up with them until he uncovered her firm, tip-tilted little breasts. He looked at them with pure pleasure and delight. His thumbs edged out and traced the wide, soft nipples until they drew into hard, dusky peaks. His mouth ached to taste them.

She shifted urgently in his arms, feeling him turn toward her, feeling his leg insinuate itself even more intimately against her. He looked into her dazed eyes as his hand pressed hard against the lowest part of her spine and moved her right in against the fierce arousal she'd only sensed before.

She gasped, but he didn't relent. If anything, he brought her even closer, so that he was pressed intimately to her and the sensations exploded like sensual fire in her limbs.

"Leo!" she cried out, shivering.

"You turn me on so hard that I can't even think," he ground out as he bent to her open mouth. "I didn't mean for this to happen, Janie," he groaned into her mouth as he turned her under him on the seat and pressed his hips down roughly against hers. "Feel me," he whispered. "Feel me wanting you!"

She was lost, helpless, utterly without hope. She clung to him with no thought for her virtue or the future. She was drowning in the most delicious erotic pleasure she'd ever dreamed of experiencing. She could feel him, feel the rough, thrusting rhythm of his big body as he buffeted her against the seat. Something hit her arm. She was twisted in his embrace, and one leg was almost bent backward as he crushed her under him. Any minute, limbs were going to start breaking, she thought, and even that didn't matter. She wanted him…! She didn't realize she'd said it aloud until she heard his voice, deep and strained.

"I want you, too," he whispered back.

She felt his hand between them, working at her jeans. His hand was unfastening them. She felt it, warm and strong, against her belly. It was sliding down. She moved to make it easier for him, her mouth savage under the devouring pressure of his lips…

Leo heard the loud roar of an approaching engine in his last lucid second before he went in over his head. He froze against Janie's warm, welcoming body. His head lifted. He could barely breathe.

He looked down into her wide, misty eyes. It only then occurred to him that they were cramped together on the seat, his body completely covering hers, her bra and blouse crumpled at her collarbone, her jeans halfway down over her hips.

"What the hell are we doing!" he burst out, shocked.

"You mean you don't know?" she gasped with unconscious humor.

He looked at the windows, so fogged up that nothing

was visible outside them. He looked down at Janie, lying drowsy and submissive under the heavy crush of him.

He drew his hand away from her jeans and whipped onto his back so that he could help her sit up. He slid back into his own seat, watching her fumble her clothes back on while he listened, shell-shocked, to the loud tone of a horn from the other vehicle.

Janie was a mess. Her lips were swollen. Her cheeks were flushed. Her clothes were wrinkled beyond belief. Her hair stood out all around from the pressure of his hands in it.

He was rumpled, too, his hair as much as hers. His hat was on the floorboard somewhere, streaked with water from her raincoat and dirt from the floor mats. His shirt had obvious finger marks and lipstick stains on it.

He just stared at her for a long moment while the other vehicle came to a stop beside his truck. He couldn't see anything. All the windows were thickly fogged. Absently, he dug in the side pocket of the door for the red rag he always carried. He wiped the fog from the driver's window and scowled as he saw his brother Cag sitting in another ranch truck, with Tess beside him. They were trying not to stare and failing miserably!

8

Belatedly, Leo rolled the window down and glared at his brother and sister-in-law. "Well?" he asked belligerently.

"We just wondered if you were all right," Cag said, clearing his throat and trying very hard not to look at Janie. "The truck was sitting out here in the middle of nowhere, but we didn't see anybody inside."

"That's right," Tess said at once. "We didn't see anybody. At all. Or anything."

"Not anything." Cag nodded vigorously.

"I was showing Janie a photo of the Clark man," Leo said curtly. He pulled it out of his pocket. It was crumpled and slightly torn. He glared at it, trying to straighten it. "See?"

Cag cleared his throat and averted his eyes. "You, uh, should have taken it out of your pocket before you showed it to her… I'm going!"

Cag powered his window up with a knowing grin and gunned the engine, taking off in a spray of mud. Leo let his own window back up with flattened lips.

Janie was turned away from him, her shoulders shaking. Odd little noises that she was trying to smother kept slipping out. She was about to burst trying not to laugh.

He leaned back against the seat and threw the clipping at her.

"It's not my fault," she protested. "I was sitting here minding my own business when you got amorous."

He pursed his swollen lips and gave her a look that would have melted butter. "*Amorous*. That's a good word for it."

She was coming down from the heights and feeling self-conscious. She picked up the clipping and handed it back to him, belatedly noticing his white Stetson at her feet. She picked it up, too, and grimaced. "Your poor hat."

He took it from her and tossed it into the small back seat of the double cab. "It will clean," he said impatiently.

She folded her hands in her lap, toying with the streaked raincoat that she'd propped over her legs.

"Marilee caused a lot of trouble between us," he said after a minute, surprising her into meeting his somber gaze. "I'm sorry about that."

"You mean I don't really make you sick?" she asked in a thin voice.

He winced. "I was furious about what I thought you'd done," he confessed. "It was a lie, Janie, like all the other terrible things I said. I'm sorry for every one of them, if it does any good."

She toyed with a button on her raincoat and stared out the window at the rain. It did help, but she couldn't stop wondering if he hadn't meant it. Maybe guilt brought the apology out of him, rather than any real remorse. She knew he didn't like hurting people.

A long sigh came from the other side of the pickup. "I'll drive you back home," he said after a minute, and put the truck in gear. "Fasten your seat belt, honey."

The endearment made her feel warm all over, but she didn't let it show. She didn't really trust Leo Hart.

He turned back onto the main road. "Fred and I are going to mob you with company at Shea's," he said conversationally. "Between us, we know most of the ranchers around Jacobsville. You can ask Harley to keep dropping in from time to time, and Fred and I will talk to the others."

She gave him a quick glance. "Harley's jaw was really bruised."

His eyes darkened. "He had no business interfering. You don't belong to damned Harley!"

She didn't know what to say. That sounded very much like jealousy. It couldn't be, of course.

His dark eyes glanced off hers. "Do you sit around in parked trucks with him and let him take your blouse off?" he asked suddenly, furiously.

"I do *not!*" she exploded.

He calmed down at once. He shifted in the seat, still uncomfortable from the keen hunger she'd kindled in his powerful body. "Okay."

Her long fingers clenched on the fabric of the coat. "You have no right to be jealous of me!" she accused angrily.

"After what we just did?" he asked pleasantly. "In your dreams, Janie."

"I don't belong to you, either," she persisted.

"You almost did," he replied, chuckling softly. "You have no idea what a close call that was. Cag and Tess saved you."

"Excuse me?"

He gave her a rueful glance. "Janie, I had your jeans half off, or have you forgotten already?"

"Leo!"

"I'm not sure I could have stopped," he continued, slowing to make a turn. "And you were no damned help at all," he added with affectionate irony, "twisting your hips against me and begging me not to stop."

She gasped. Her face went scarlet. "Of all the blatant…!"

"That's how it was, all right," he agreed. "Blatant. For the record, when a man gets that hard, it's time to call a halt any way you can, before you get in over your head. I can tell you haven't had much practice at it, but now is a good time to listen to advice."

"I don't need advice!"

"Like hell you don't. Once I got my mouth on your soft belly, you'd never have been able to make me stop."

She stared at him with slowly dawning realization. She remembered the hot, exquisite pleasure of his mouth on her breasts. She could only imagine how it would feel to let him kiss her there, on her hips, on her long legs….

"You know far too much about women," she gritted.

"You know absolutely nothing about men," he countered. He smiled helplessly. "I love it. You were in over your head the minute I touched you with intent. You'd have let me do anything I wanted." He whistled softly.

"You can't imagine how I felt, knowing that. You were the sweetest candy I've ever had."

He was confounding her. She didn't know what to make of the remarks. He'd been standoffish, insulting, offensive and furious with her. Now he'd done a complete about-face. He was acting more like a lover than a big brother.

His dark eyes cut around sideways and sized up her expression. "Do you think things can just go back to the way they were before?" he asked softly. "I remember telling you that it was going to change everything."

She swallowed. "I remember."

"It already has. I look at you and get aroused, all over again," he said bluntly. "It will only get worse."

Her face flamed. "I will not have an affair with you."

"Great. I'm glad to know you have that much self-control. You can teach it to me."

"I won't get in a truck with you again," she muttered.

"I'll bring the car next time," he said agreeably. "Of course, we'll have to open both doors. I'll never be able to stretch out in the front seat the way I did in the cab of this truck."

Her fingers clenched on the raincoat. "That won't happen again."

"It will if I touch you."

She glared at him. "You listen here…!"

He pulled the truck onto a dirt road that led through one of Fred's pastures, threw it out of gear, switched off the engine and reached for Janie with an economy of motion that left her gasping.

He had her over his lap, and his mouth hit hers with the force of a gust of wind. He burrowed into her parted lips while one lean hand went to her spine, grinding her into the fierce arousal that just the touch of her had provoked.

"Feel that?" he muttered against her lips. "Now try to stop me."

She went under in a daze of pleasure. She couldn't even pretend to protest, not even when his big hand found her breast and caressed it hungrily right through the cloth of her blouse.

Her arms went around his neck. She lifted closer, shivering, as she felt the aching hunger of his body echo in her own. She moaned helplessly.

"Of all the stupid things I've done lately..." He groaned, too, his big arms wrapping her up tight as the kiss went on and on and on.

He moved out from under the steering wheel and shifted her until she was straddling his hips, her belly lying against his aroused body so blatantly that she should have been shocked. She wasn't. He felt familiar to her, beloved to her. She wanted him. Her body yielded submissively to the insistent pressure of both his hands on her hips, dragging them against his in a fever of desire.

The approaching roar of a truck engine for the second time in less than an hour brought his head up. He looked down into Janie's heated face, at the position they were in. His dazed eyes went out the windshield in time to see Fred's old pickup coming down the long pasture road about a quarter mile ahead of them.

He let out a word Janie had only heard Tiny use during heated arguments with patrons, and abruptly put her back in her own seat, pausing to forcefully strap her into her seat belt.

She felt shaky all over. Her eyes met his and then went involuntarily to what she'd felt so starkly against her hungry body. She flushed.

"Next time you'll get a better look," he said harshly. "I wish I could explain to you how it feels."

She wrapped her arms around her body. "I know… how it feels," she whispered unsteadily. "I ache all over."

The bad temper left him at once. He scowled as he watched her, half-oblivious to Fred's rapid approach. He couldn't take his eyes off her. She was delicious.

She managed to meet his wide, shocked eyes. "I'm sorry."

"For what?" he asked huskily. "You went in head-first, just like I did."

She searched his eyes hungrily. Her body was on fire for him. "If you used something…" she said absently.

He actually flushed. He got back under the steering wheel and avoided looking at her. He couldn't believe what she was saying.

Fred roared up beside them and pulled onto the hard ground to let his window down.

"Rain's stopped," he told Leo. "I thought I'd run over to Eb Scott's place and have a talk with him about getting his cowboys to frequent Shea's at night."

"Good idea," Leo said, still flushed and disheveled.

Fred wisely didn't look too closely at either of them, but he had a pretty good idea of what he'd interrupted. "I won't be long, sweetheart," he told Janie.

"Okay, Dad. Be careful," she said in a husky voice.

He nodded, grinned and took off.

Leo started the engine. He was still trying to get his breath. He stared at the dirt path ahead instead of at Janie. "I could use something," he said after a minute. "But lovemaking is addictive, Janie. One time would be a beginning, not a cure, do you understand?"

She shook her head, embarrassed now that her blood was cooling.

He reached out and caught one of her cold hands in his, intertwining their fingers. "You can't imagine how flattered I am," he said quietly. "You're a virgin, and you'd give yourself to me…"

She swallowed hard. "Please. Don't."

His hand contracted. "I'll drive you home. If you weren't working next Saturday, we could take in a movie and have dinner somewhere."

Her heart jumped up into her throat. "M-me?"

He looked down at her with the beginnings of possession. "You could wear that lacy white thing you wore to the ball," he added softly. "I like your shoulders bare. You have beautiful skin." His eyes fell to her bodice and darkened. "Beautiful breasts, too, with nice nipples…"

"Leo Hart!" she exclaimed, horrified.

He leaned over and kissed her hungrily. "I'll let you look at me next time," he whispered passionately. "Then you won't be so embarrassed when we compare notes."

She thought of seeing him without clothes and her whole face colored.

"I know what I said, but…" she protested.

He stopped the truck, bent, and kissed her again with breathless tenderness. "You've known me half your life, Janie," he said, and he was serious. He searched her worried eyes. "Am I the kind of man who takes advantage of a green girl?"

She was worried, too. "No," she had to admit.

His breathing was uneven as he studied her flushed

face. "I never would," he agreed. "You were special to me even before I kissed you the first time, in your own kitchen." His head bent again. His mouth trailed across hers in soft, biting little kisses that made her moan. "But now, after the taste of you I've just had, I'm going to be your shadow. You don't even realize what's happened, do you?"

"You want me," she said huskily.

His teeth nibbled her upper lip. "It's a little more complicated than sex." He kissed her again, hard, and lifted his head with flattering reluctance. "Look up addiction in the dictionary," he mused. "It's an eye-opener."

"Addiction?"

His nose brushed hers. "Do you remember how you moaned when I put my hands inside your blouse?"

She swallowed. "Yes."

"Now think how it would feel if I'd put my mouth on your breast, right over the nipple."

She shivered.

He nodded slowly. "Next time," he promised, his voice taut and hungry. "You have that to look forward to. Meanwhile, you keep your eyes and ears open, and don't do anything at work that gives Clark a hint that you're watching him," he added firmly.

"I'll be careful," she promised unsteadily.

His eyes were possessive on her soft face. "If he touches you, I'll kill him."

It sounded like a joke. It wasn't. She'd never seen that look in a man's eyes before. In fact, the way he was watching her was a little scary.

His big hand slid under her nape and brought her mouth just under his. "You belong to me, Janie," he whispered as his head moved down. "Your first man is going to be me. Believe it!"

The kiss was as arousing as it was tender, but it didn't last long. He forced himself to let her go, to move away. He started the truck again, put it in gear and went back down the farm road. But his hand reached for hers involuntarily, his fingers curling into hers, as if he couldn't bear to lose contact with her. She didn't know it, but he'd reached a decision in those few seconds. There was no going back now.

Jack Clark did show up in the bar, on the following Friday night.

Janie hadn't told any of the people she worked with about him, feeling that any mention of what she knew about him might jeopardize her safety.

But she did keep a close eye on him. The man was rangy and uncouth. He sat alone at a corner table, look-

ing around as if he expected trouble and was impatient
for it to arrive.

A cowboy from Cy Parks's spread, one of Harley
Fowler's men, walked to the counter and sat down, ordering a beer and a pizza.

"Hey, Miss Janie," he said with a grin that showed a
missing front tooth. "Harley said to tell you he'd be in
soon to see you."

"That's sweet of him," she said with a grin. "I'll just
put your order in, Ned."

She scribbled the order on a slip of green paper and
put it up on the long string for Nick, the teenage cook,
with a clothespin.

"Where's my damned whiskey?" Clark shouted. "I
been sitting here five minutes waiting for it!"

Janie winced as Nick glanced at her and shrugged, indicating the pizza list he was far behind on. He'd taken
the order and got busy all of a sudden. Tiny was nowhere in sight. He was probably out back having a cigarette. Nick was up to his elbows in dough and pizza
sauce. Janie had to get Clark's order, there was nobody
else to do it.

She got down a shot glass, poured whiskey into it and
put it on one of the small serving trays.

She took it to Clark's table and forced a smile to her

lips. "Here you are, sir," she said, placing the shot glass in front of him. "I'm sorry it took so long."

Clark glared up at her from watery blue eyes. "Don't let that happen again. I don't like to be kept waiting."

"Yes, sir," she agreed.

She turned away, but he caught her apron strings and jerked her back. She caught her breath as his hand slid to the ones tied at her waist.

"You're kind of cute. Why don't you sit on my lap and help me drink this?" he drawled.

He was already half-lit, she surmised. She would have refused him the whiskey, if Tiny had been close by, despite the trouble he'd already caused. But now she was caught and she didn't know how to get away. All her worst fears were coming to haunt her.

"I have to get that man's drink," she pointed to Harley's cowboy. "I'll come right back, okay?"

"That boy can get his drink."

"He's making pizza," she protested. "Please."

That was a mistake. He liked it when women begged. He smiled at her. It wasn't a pleasant smile. "I said, come here!"

He jerked her down on his thin, bony legs and she screamed.

In a flash, two cowboys were on their feet and heading toward Clark, both of them dangerous-looking.

"Well, looky, looky, you've got guardian angels in cowboy boots!" Clark chuckled. He stood up, dragging Janie with him. "Stay back," he warned, catching her hair in its braid. "Or else." He slapped her, hard, across the face, making her cry out, and his hand went into his pocket and came out with a knife. He flicked it and a blade appeared. He caught her around the shoulders from behind and brandished the knife. "Stay back, boys," he said again. "Or I'll cut her!"

The knife pressed against her throat. She was shaking. She remembered all the nice self-defense moves she'd ever learned in her life from watching television or listening to her father talk. Now, she knew how useless they were. Clark would cut her throat if those men tried to help her. She had visions of him dragging her outside and assaulting her. He could do anything. There was nobody around to stop him. These cowboys weren't going to rush him and risk her life. If only Leo were here!

She was vaguely aware of Nick sliding out of sight toward the telephones. If he could just call the sheriff, the police, anybody!

Her hands went to Clark's wrist, trying to get him to release the press of the blade.

"You're hurting," she choked.

"Really?" He pressed harder.

Janie felt his arm cutting off the blood to her head.

Then she remembered something she'd heard of a female victim doing during an attack. If she fainted, he might turn her loose.

"Can't…breathe…" she gasped, and closed her eyes. He might drop her if she sagged, he might cut her throat. She could die. But they'd get him. That would almost be worth it….

She let her body sag just as she heard a shout from the doorway. She pretended to lose consciousness. In the next few hectic seconds, Clark threw her to the floor so hard that she hit right on her elbow and her head, and groaned aloud with the pain of impact.

At the same moment, Leo Hart and Harley Fowler exploded into the room from the front door and went right for Clark, knife and all. They'd been in the parking lot, talking about Janie's situation, and had come running when they heard the commotion.

Harley aimed a kick at the knife and knocked it out of Clark's hands, but Clark was good with his feet, too. He landed a roundhouse kick in Harley's stomach and put him over a table. Leo slugged him, but he twisted around, got Leo's arm behind him and sent him over a table, too.

The two cowboys held back, aware of Leo's size and Harley's capability, and the fact that Clark had easily put both of them down.

There was a sudden silence. Janie dragged herself into a sitting position in time to watch Cash Grier come through the doorway and approach Clark.

Clark dived for the knife, rolled, and got to his feet. He lunged at Grier with the blade. The assistant police chief waited patiently for the attack, and he smiled. It was the coldest, most dangerous smile Janie had ever seen in her life.

Clark lunged confidently. Grier moved so fast that he was like a blur.

Seconds later, the knife was in Grier's hand. He threw it, slamming it into the wall next to the counter so deep that it would take Tiny quite some time, after the brawl, to pull it out again. He turned back to Clark even as the knife hit, fell into a relaxed stance and waited.

Clark rushed him, tipsy and furious at the way the older man had taken his knife away. Grier easily side-stepped the intended punch, did a spinning heel kick that would have made Chuck Norris proud and proceeded to beat the living hell out of the man with lightning punches and kicks that quickly put him on the floor, breathless and drained of will. It was over in less than three minutes. Clark held his ribs and groaned. Grier stood over him, not even breathing hard, his hand going to the handcuffs on his belt. He didn't even look winded.

Leo had picked himself up and rushed to Janie, propping her against his chest while she nursed her elbow.

"Is it broken?" he asked worriedly.

She shook her head. "Just bruised. Is my mouth bleeding?" she asked, still dazed from the confrontation.

He nodded. His face was white. He cursed his own helplessness. Between them, he and Harley should have been able to wipe the floor with Clark. He pulled out a white linen handkerchief and mopped up the bleeding lip and the cut on her cheek from Clark's nails. A big bad bruise was already coming out on the left side of her face.

By now, Grier had Clark against a wall with a minimum of fuss. He spread the man's legs with a quick movement of his booted feet and nimbly cuffed him.

"I'll need a willing volunteer to see the magistrate and file a complaint," Grier asked.

"Right here," Harley said, wiping his mouth with a handkerchief. "I expect Mr. Hart will do the same."

"You bet," Leo agreed. "But I've got to get Janie home first."

"No rush," Grier said, with Clark by the neck. "Harley, you know where magistrate Burr Wiley lives, don't you? I'm taking Clark by there now."

"Yes, sir, I do, I'll drive right over there and swear out a complaint so you can hold that…gentleman," Harley agreed, substituting for the word he really meant to use. "Janie, you going to be okay?" he added worriedly.

She was wobbly, but she got to her feet, with Leo's support. "Sure," she said. She managed a smile. "I'll be fine."

"I'll get you!" Clark raged at Janie and Leo. "I'll get both of you!"

"Not right away," Grier said comfortably. "I'll have the judge set bail as high as it's possible to put it, and we'll see how many assault charges we can press."

"Count on me for two of them!" Janie volunteered fearlessly, wincing as her jaw protested.

"But not tonight," Leo said, curling his arm around her. "Come on, honey," he said gently. "I'll take you home."

They followed Grier with his prisoner and Harley out the door and over to Leo's big double-cabbed pickup truck.

He put her inside gently and moved around to the driver's seat. She noticed then, for the first time, that he was in working clothes.

"You must have come right from work," she commented.

"We were moving livestock to a new pasture," he replied. "One of the bulls got out and we had to chase him through the brush. Doesn't it show?" he added with a nod toward his scarred batwing chaps and his muddy boots. "I meant to be here an hour ago. Harley and I arrived together. Just in the nick of time, too."

"Two of Cy Parks's guys were at the counter," she said, "but when Clark threatened to cut me, they were afraid to rush him."

He caught her hand in his and held it tight, his eyes going to the blood on her face, her blouse, her forearm. She was going to have a bruise on her pretty face. The sight of those marks made him furious.

"I'll be all right, thanks to all of you," she managed to say.

"We weren't a hell of a lot of help," he said with a rueful smile. "Even Harley didn't fare well. Clark must have a military background of some sort. But he was no match for Grier." He shook his head. "It was like watching a martial arts movie. I never even saw Grier move."

She studied him while he started the truck and put their seat belts on. "Did he hurt you?"

"Hurt my pride," he replied, smiling gently. "I've never been put across a table so fast."

"At least you tried," she pointed out. "Thank you."

"I should never have let you stay in there," he said. "It's my fault."

"It was my choice."

He kissed her eyelids shut. "My poor baby," he said

softly. "I'm not taking you to your father in this condition," he added firmly, noting the blood on her blouse and face. "I'll take you home with me and clean you up, first. We'll phone him and tell him there was a little trouble and you'll be late."

"Okay," she said. "But he's no wimp."

"I know that." He put the truck in gear. "Humor me. I want to make sure you're all right."

"I'm fine," she argued, but then she smiled. "You can clean me up, anyway."

He pursed his lips and smiled wickedly. "Best offer I've had all night," he replied as he pulled out of the parking lot.

9

The house was quiet, deserted. The only light was the one in the living room. Leo led Janie down the hall to his own big bedroom, closed the door firmly and led her into his spacious blue-tiled bathroom.

The towels were luxurious, sea-blue and white-striped blue towels, facecloths and hand towels. There were soaps of all sorts, a huge heated towel rack, and a whirlpool bath.

He tugged her to the medicine cabinet and turned her so that he could see her face. "You've got a bad scratch here," he remarked. He tilted her chin up, and found another smaller cut on the side of her throat, thankfully not close enough to an artery to have done much damage.

His hands went to her blouse. She caught them.

"It's all right," he said gently.

She let go.

He unfastened the blouse and tossed it onto the floor, looking her over for other marks. He found a nasty bruise on her shoulder that was just coming out. He unfastened the bra and let it fall, too, ignoring her efforts to catch it. There was a bruise right on her breast, where Clark had held her in front of him.

"The bastard," he exclaimed, furious, as he touched the bruise.

"He got a few bruises, too, from Grier," she said, trying to comfort him. He looked devastated.

"He'd have gotten more from me, if I hadn't walked right into that punch," he said with self-contempt. "I can't remember the last time I took a stupid hit like that."

She reached up and touched his lean face gently. "It's all right, Leo."

He looked down at her bare breasts and his eyes narrowed hotly. "I don't like that bruise."

"I got a worse one when my horse threw me last month," she told him. "It will heal."

"It's in a bad place."

She smiled. "So was the other one."

He unzipped her jeans and she panicked.

He didn't take any notice. He bent and removed her shoes and socks and then stripped the jeans off her. She was wearing little lacy white briefs and his hands lingered on them.

"Leo!" she screeched.

He grimaced. "I knew it was going to be a fight all the way, and you're in no condition for another one." He unbraided her hair and let it tangle down her shoulders. He turned and started the shower.

"I can do this!" she began.

His hands were already stripping off the briefs. He stopped with his hands on her waist and looked at her with barely contained passion. "I thought you'd be in a class of your own," he said huskily. "You're a knockout, baby." He lifted her and stood her up in the shower, putting a washcloth in her hand before he closed the sliding glass door. "I'll get your things in the wash."

She was too shell-shocked to ask if he knew how to use a washing machine. *Well, you fool,* she told herself, *you stood there like a statue and let him take your clothes off and stare at you! What are you complaining about?*

She bathed and used the shampoo on the shelf in the shower stall, scrubbing until she felt less tainted by Clark's filthy touch.

She turned off the shower and climbed out, wrapping

herself in one of the sea-blue towels. It was soft and huge, big enough for Leo, who was a giant of a man. It swallowed her up whole.

Before she could wonder what she was going to do about something to wear, he opened the door and walked right in with a black velvet robe.

"Here," he said, jerking the towel away from her and holding out the robe.

She scurried into it, red-faced and embarrassed.

He drew her back against him and she realized that she wasn't the only one who'd just had a shower. He was wearing a robe, too. But his was open, and the only thing under it was a pair of black silk boxer shorts that left his powerful legs bare. His chest was broad and covered with thick curling hair. He turned her until she was facing him, and his eyes were slow and curious.

"You'll have bruises. Right now, I want to treat those cuts with antibiotic cream. Then we'll dry your hair and brush it out." He smiled. "It's long and thick and glossy. I love your hair."

She smiled shyly. "It takes a lot of drying."

"I'm not in a hurry. Neither are you. I phoned your dad and told him as little as I could get away with."

"Was he worried?"

He lifted an eyebrow as he dug in the cabinet for the

antibiotic cream. "About your virtue, maybe," he teased. "He thinks I've got you here so I can make love to you."

She felt breathless. "Have you?" she asked daringly.

He turned back to her with the cream in one big hand. His eyes went over her like hands. "If you want it, yes. But it's up to you."

That was a little surprising. She stood docilely while he applied the cream to her cuts and then put it away. He hooked a hair dryer to a plug on the wall and linked his fingers through her thick light brown hair while he blew it dry. There was something very intimate about standing so close to him while he dried her hair. She thought she'd never get over the delight of it, as long as she lived. Every time she washed her hair from now on, she'd feel Leo's big hands against her scalp. She smiled, her head back, her eyes closed blissfully.

"Don't go to sleep," he teased as he put the hair dryer down.

"I'm not."

She felt his lips in her hair at the same moment she felt his hands go down over her shoulders and into the gap left by the robe.

If she'd been able to protest, that would have been the time to do it. But she hesitated, entranced by the feel of his hands so blatantly invading the robe, smoothing down over her high, taut breasts as if he had every right to touch her intimately whenever he felt like it.

Seconds later, the robe was gone, she was turned against him, his robe was on the floor and she was experiencing her first adult embrace without clothing.

She whimpered at the fierce pleasure of feeling his bare, hair-roughened chest against her naked breasts. Her nails bit into the huge muscles of his upper arms as she sucked in a harsh breath and tried to stay on her feet.

"You like that, do you?" he whispered at her lips. "I know something that's even more exciting."

He picked her up in his arms and started kissing her hungrily. She responded with no thought of denying him whatever he wanted.

He carried her to the bed, paused to whip the covers and the pillows out of the way, and placed her at the center of it. His hands went to the waistband of his boxer shorts, but he hesitated, grinding his teeth together as he looked at her nudity with aching need.

He managed to control his first impulse, which was to strip and bury himself in her. He eased onto the bed beside her, his chest pressing her down into the mattress while his mouth opened on her soft lips and pressed them wide apart.

"I've ached for this," he ground out, moving his hands

from her breasts down her hips to the softness inside of her thighs. "I've never wanted anything so much!"

She tried to speak, but one of his hands invaded her in the most intimate touch she'd ever experienced. Her eyes flew open and she gaped up at him.

"You're old enough, Janie," he whispered, moving his hand just enough to make her tense. "And I've waited as long as I can."

As he spoke, he touched her delicately and when she protested, he eased down to cover her mouth with his. His fingers traced her, probed, explored her until she began to whimper and move with him. It was incredible. She was lying here, naked, in his bed, letting him explore her body as if it belonged to him. And she was... enjoying it. Glorying in it. Her back arched and she moaned as he found a pressure and a rhythm that lifted her off the bed on a wave of pleasure.

One of his long, powerful legs hooked over one of hers. She felt him at her hip, aroused and not hiding it. Through the thin silk, she was as aware of him as if he'd been naked.

"Touch me," he groaned. "Don't make me do it all. Help me."

She didn't understand what he wanted. Her hands went to his chest and began to draw through the thick hair there.

"No, baby," he whispered into her mouth. He caught one of her hands and tugged it down to the shorts he was wearing. "Don't be afraid. It's all right."

He coaxed her hand onto that part of him that was blatantly male. She gasped. He lifted his head and looked into her eyes, but he wouldn't let her hand withdraw. He spread her fingers against him, grimacing as the waves of pleasure hit him and closed his eyes on a shudder.

His reaction fascinated her. She knew so little. "Does it…hurt?"

"What?" he asked huskily. "Your hand, or what it's doing?"

"Both. Either."

He pressed her hand closer, looking down. "Look," he whispered, coaxing her eyes to follow his. It was intimate. But not intimate enough for him.

"Don't panic, baby," he whispered, levering onto his back. He ripped off the shorts and tossed them onto the carpet. He rolled onto his side and caught one of her hands, insistent now, drawing it to him.

She made a sound as she looked, for the first time, at an aroused male without a thing to conceal him except her hand.

"Don't be embarrassed," he whispered roughly. "I wouldn't want any other woman to see me like this."

"You wouldn't?"

He shook his head. It was difficult not to lose control. But he eased her fingers back to him and held them there. "I'm vulnerable."

Her eyes brightened. "Oh." She hadn't considered that he was as helpless as she was to resist the pleasure of what they were doing.

His own hand went back to her body. He touched her, as she was touching him, and he smiled at her fascination.

She couldn't believe it was happening at all. She stared up at him with all her untried longings in her eyes, on her rapt face. She belonged to him. He belonged to her. It was incredible.

"Are you going to?" she whispered.

He kissed her eyelids lazily. "Going to what?"

"Take me," she whispered back.

He chuckled, deep in his throat. "What a primitive description. It's a mutual thing, you know. Wouldn't you take me, as well?"

Her eyes widened. "I suppose I would," she conceded. She stiffened and shivered. "Oh!"

His eyes darkened. There was no more humor on his face as his touch became slowly invasive. "Will you let me satisfy you?" he asked.

"I don't...understand."

"I know. That's what makes it so delicious." He bent slowly, but not to her mouth. His lips hovered just above her wide nipple. "This is the most beautiful thing I've ever done with a woman," he whispered. His lips parted. "I want nothing, except to please you."

His mouth went down over the taut nipple in a slow, exquisite motion that eventually all but swallowed her breast. She felt his tongue moving against the nipple, felt the faint suction of his mouth. All the while, his hand was becoming more insistent, and far more intimate, on her body. He felt her acceptance, even as she opened her legs for him and began to moan rhythmically with every movement of his hands.

"Yes," he whispered against her breast when he felt the pulsing of her body. "Let me, baby." He lifted his head and looked down into her eyes as she moaned piteously.

She was pulsating. She felt her body clench. She was slowly drifting up into a glorious, rhythmic heat that filled her veins, her arteries, the very cells of her body with exquisite pleasure. She'd never dreamed there was such pleasure.

"Janie, touch me, here," he whispered unsteadily.

She felt his hand curling around her fingers, teaching her, insistent, his breath jerky and violent as he twisted against her.

"Baby," he choked, kissing her hungrily. "Baby, baby!"

He moved, his big body levering slowly between her long legs. He knelt over her, his eyes wild, his body shuddering, powerfully male, and she looked up at him with total submission, still shivering from the taste of pleasure he'd already given her. It would be explosive, ecstatic. She could barely breathe for the anticipation. She was lost. He was going to have her now. She loved him. She was going to give herself. There was nothing that could stop them, nothing in all the world!

"Mr. Hart! Oh, Mr. Hart! Are you in here?"

Leo stiffened, his body kneeling between her thighs, his powerful hands clenching on them. He looked blindly down into her wide, dazed eyes. He shuddered violently and his eyes closed on a harsh muffled curse.

He threw himself onto the bed beside her, on his belly. He couldn't stop shaking. He gasped at a jerky breath and clutched the sheet beside his head as he fought for control.

"Mr. Hart!" the voice came again.

He suddenly remembered that he hadn't locked the bedroom door, and the cowboy didn't know that he wasn't alone. Even as he thought it, he heard the door-knob turn. "Open that door...and you're fired!" he shouted hoarsely. Beside him, Janie actually gasped as she belatedly realized what was about to happen.

The doorknob was released at once. "Sorry, sir, but I need you to come out here and look at this bull. I think there's something wrong with him, Mr. Hart! We got him loaded into one of the trailers and put him in the barn, but…"

"Call the vet!" he shouted. "I'll be there directly!"

"Yes, sir!"

Footsteps went back down the carpeted hall. Leo lifted his head. Beside him, Janie looked as shattered as he felt. Tears were swimming in her eyes.

He groaned softly, and pulled her to him, gently. "It's all right," he whispered, kissing her eyelids shut. "Don't cry, baby. Nothing happened."

"Nothing!" she choked.

His hands smoothed down the long line of her back. "Almost nothing," he murmured dryly.

She was horrified, not only at her own behavior, but at what had almost happened. "If he hadn't called to you," she began in a high-pitched whisper.

His hands tangled in her long hair and he brought her mouth under his, tenderly. He nibbled her upper lip. "Yes, I know," he replied gently. "But he did." He pulled away from her and got to his feet, stretching hugely, facing her. He watched her try not to look at him with amused indulgence. But eventually, she couldn't resist it. Her eyes were huge, shocked…delighted.

"Now, when we compare notes, you'll have ammunition," he teased.

She flushed and averted her eyes, belatedly noticing

that she wasn't wearing clothes, either. She tugged the sheet up over her breasts, but it was difficult to feel regrets when she looked at him.

He was smiling. His eyes were soft, tender. He looked down at what he could see of her body above the sheet with pride, loving the faint love marks on her breasts that his mouth had made.

"Greenhorn," he chided at her scarlet blush. "Well, you know a lot more about men now than you did this morning, don't you?"

She swallowed hard. Her eyes slid down him. She didn't look away, but she was very flushed, and not only because of what she was seeing. Her body throbbed in the most delicious way.

"I think I'd better take you home. Now," he added with a rueful chuckle. "From this point on, it only gets worse."

He was still passionately aroused. He wondered if she realized what it meant. He chuckled at her lack of comprehension. "I could have you three times and I'd still be like this," he said huskily. "I'm not easily satisfied."

She shivered as she looked at him, her body yielded, submissive.

"You want to, don't you?" he asked quietly, reading her expression. "So do I. More than you know. But we're not going that far together tonight. You've had enough trauma for a Friday night."

He caught her hand and pulled her up, free of the sheet and open to his eyes as he led her back into the bathroom. He turned on the shower and climbed in with her, bathing both of them quickly and efficiently, to her raging embarrassment.

He dried her and then himself before he put his shorts back on and left her to get her things. He'd washed them while she was in the shower the first time and put them in the dryer. They were clean and sweet-smelling, and the bloodstains were gone.

But when she went to take them from him, he shook his head. "One of the perks," he said softly. "I get to dress you."

And he did, completely. Then he led her to the dresser, and ran his own brush through her long, soft hair, easing it back from her face. The look in his eyes was new, fascinating, incomprehensible. She looked back at him with awe.

"Now you know something about what sex feels like, even though you're still very much a virgin," he said matter-of-factly. "And you won't be afraid of the real thing anymore, when it happens, will you?"

She shook her head, dazed.

He put the brush down and framed her face in his

big, lean hands. He wasn't smiling. "You belong to me now," he said huskily. "I belong to you. Don't agonize over what you let me do to you tonight. It's as natural as breathing. Don't lie awake feeling shame or embarrassment. You saw me as helpless as I saw you. There won't be any jokes about it, any gossiping about it. I'll never tell another living soul what you let me do."

She relaxed. She hadn't really known what to expect. But he sounded more solemn than he'd ever been. He was looking at her with a strange expression.

"Are you sorry?" she asked in a hushed whisper.

"No," he replied quietly. "It was unavoidable. I was afraid for you tonight. I couldn't stop Clark. Neither could Harley. Until Grier walked in, I thought you'd had it. What happened in here was a symptom of the fear, that's all. I wanted to hold you, make you part of me." He drew in a shaky breath and actually shivered. "I wanted to go right inside you, Janie," he whispered bluntly. "But we'll save that pleasure for the right time and place. This isn't it."

She colored and averted her eyes.

He turned her face back to his. "Meanwhile," he said slowly, searching her eyes, "we'll have no more secrets, of any kind, between us."

She stood quietly against him, watching his face. "Nobody's seen me without my clothes since I was a little kid," she whispered, as if it were a fearful secret.

"Not that many women have seen me without mine," he replied unexpectedly. He smiled tenderly.

Her eyebrows arched.

"Shocked?" he mused, moving away to pull clothes out of his closet and socks out of his drawers. He sat down to pull on the socks, glancing at her wryly. "I'm not a playboy. I'm not without experience, but there was always a limit I wouldn't cross with women I only knew slightly. It gives people power over you when they know intimate things about you."

"Yes," she said, moving to sit beside him on the bed, with her hands folded in her lap. "Thanks."

"For what?"

She smiled. "For making it feel all right. That I...let you touch me that way, I mean."

He finished pulling on his socks and tilted her face up to his. He kissed her softly. "I won't ever touch another woman like that," he whispered into her mouth. "It would be like committing adultery, after what we did on this bed."

Her heart flew up into the clouds. Her wide, fascinated eyes searched his. "Really?"

He chuckled. "Are you anxious to rush out and experiment with another man?"

She shook her head.

"Why?"

She smiled shyly. "It would be like committing adultery," she repeated what he'd said.

He stood up and looked down at her with possession. "It was a near thing," he murmured. "I don't know whether to punch that cowboy or give him a raise for interrupting us. I lost it, in those last few seconds. I couldn't have stopped."

"Neither could I." She lifted her mouth for his soft kiss. She searched his eyes, remembering what he'd told her. "But the books say a man can only do it once," she blurted out, "and then he has to rest."

He laughed softly. "I know. But a handful of men can go all night. I'm one of them."

"Oh!"

He pulled up his slacks and fastened them before he shouldered into a knit shirt. He turned back to her, smoothing his disheveled hair. "I was contemplating even much more explosive pleasures when someone started shouting my name."

This was interesting. "More explosive pleasures?" she prompted.

He drew her up against him and held her close. "What we did and what we didn't do, is the difference between licking an ice-cream cone and eating a banana split," he teased. "What you had was only a small taste of what we can have together."

"Wow," she said softly.

"Wow," he echoed, bending to kiss her hungrily. He sighed into her mouth. "I was almost willing to risk getting you pregnant, I was so far gone." He lifted his head and looked at her. "How do you feel about kids, Janie?"

"I love children," she said honestly. "How about you?"

"Me, too. I'm beginning to rethink my position on having them." His lean hand touched her belly. "You've got nice wide hips," he commented, testing them.

She felt odd. Her body seemed to contract. She searched his eyes because she didn't understand what was happening to her.

"You can tell Shea's you're through," he said abruptly. "I'm not risking you again. If we can't keep Clark in jail for the foreseeable future, we have to make plans to keep you safe."

Her lips parted. She'd all but forgotten her horrible experience. She touched her throat and felt again the prick of the knife. "You said he was vindictive."

"He'll have to get through me," he said. "And with a gun, I'm every bit his equal," he added.

She reached up and touched his hard mouth. "I don't want you to get hurt."

"I don't want you to get hurt," he seconded. His face

twisted. "Baby, you are the very breath in my body," he whispered, and reached for her.

She felt boneless as he kissed her with such passion and fire that she trembled.

"I wish I didn't have to take you home," he groaned at her lips. "I want to make love to you completely. I want to lie against you and over you, and inside you!"

She moaned at his mouth as it became deep and insistent, devouring her parted lips.

He was shivering. He had to drag his mouth away from hers. He looked shattered. He touched her long hair with a hand that had a faint tremor. "Amazing," he whispered gruffly. "That I couldn't see it, before it happened."

"See what?" she asked drowsily.

His eyes fell to her swollen, parted lips. "Never mind," he whispered. He bent and kissed her with breathless tenderness. "I'm taking you home. Then I'll see about my bull. Tomorrow morning, I'll come and get you and we'll see about swearing out more warrants against Clark."

"You don't think Clark will get out on bond?" she asked worriedly.

"Not if Grier can prevent it." He reached for his truck keys and took her by the arm. "We'll go out the back," he said. "I don't want anyone to know you were here with me tonight. It wouldn't look good, even under the circumstances."

"Don't worry, nobody will know," she assured him.

The next morning, Fred Brewster came into the dining room looking like a thunderstorm.

"What were you doing in Leo Hart's bedroom last night when you were supposed to be working, Janie?" he asked bluntly.

She gaped at him with her mouth open. He was furious.

"How in the world…?" she exclaimed.

"One of the Harts' cowboys went to get him about a sick bull. He saw Leo sneaking you out the back door!" He scowled and leaned closer. "And what the hell happened to your face? Leo said you had a troublesome customer and he was bringing you home! What the hell's going on, Janie?"

She was scrambling for an answer that wouldn't get her in even more trouble when they heard a pickup truck roar up the driveway and stop at the back door. A minute later there was a hard rap, and the door opened by itself.

Leo came in, wearing dressy boots and slacks, a white shirt with a tie and a sports coat. His white Stetson had been cleaned and looked as if it had never been introduced to a muddy truck mat. He took off the hat and tossed it onto the counter, moving past Fred to look at Janie's face.

"Damn!" he muttered, turning her cheek so that the violet bruise was very noticeable. "I didn't realize he hit you that hard, baby!"

"Hit her?" Fred burst out. "Who hit her, and what was she doing in your bedroom last night?!"

Leo turned toward him, his face contemplative, his dark eyes quiet and somber. "Did she tell you?" he asked.

"I never!" Janie burst out, flushing.

"One of your cowboys mentioned it to one of my cowboys," Fred began.

Leo's eyes flashed fire. "He'll be drawing his pay at the end of the day. Nobody, but nobody, tells tales about Janie!"

Father and daughter exchanged puzzled glances.

"Why are you so shocked?" he asked her when he saw her face. "Do you think I take women to my house, ever?"

She hadn't considered that. Her lips parted on a shocked breath.

He glanced at Fred, who was still unconvinced. "All right, you might as well know it all. Jack Clark made a pass at her in Shea's and when she protested, he pulled a knife on her." He waited for that to sink in, and for Fred to sit down, hard, before he continued. "Harley and I got there about the same time and heard yelling. We went inside to find Janie with a knife at her throat. We rushed Clark, but he put both of us over a table. Janie's co-worker had phoned the sheriff, but none of the deputies were within quick reach, so they radioed Grier and he took Clark down and put him in jail." He grimaced, looking at Janie's face. "She was covered with blood and so upset that she could hardly stand. I couldn't bring myself to take her home in that condition, so I took her home with me and cleaned her up and calmed her down first."

Fred caught Janie's hand in his and held it hard. "Oh, daughter, I'm sorry!"

"It's okay. We were trying to spare you, that's all," she faltered.

Leo pulled a cell phone from his pocket, dialed a number, and got his foreman. "You tell Carl Turley that he's fired. You get him the hell out of there before I get home, or he'll need first aid to get off the ranch. Yes. Yes." His face was frightening. "It was true. Clark's in jail now, on assault charges. Of course nothing was going on, and you can repeat that, with my blessing! Just get Turley out of there! Right."

He hung up and put the phone away. He was vibrating with suppressed fury, that one of his own men would gossip about him and Janie, under the circumstances. "So much for gossip," he gritted.

"Thanks, Leo," Fred said tersely. "And I'm sorry I jumped to the wrong conclusion. It's just that, normally, a man wouldn't take a woman home with him late at night unless he was...well..."

"Planning to seduce her?" Leo said for him. He looked at Janie and his eyes darkened.

She flushed.

"Yes," Fred admitted uncomfortably.

Leo's dark eyes began to twinkle as they wandered over Janie like loving hands. "Would this be a bad time to tell you that I have every intention of seducing her at some future time?"

✴ 10 ✴

Fred looked as if he'd swallowed a chicken, whole. He flushed, trying to forget that Leo had loaned him the money to save his ranch, thinking only of his daughter's welfare. "Now, look here, Leo…" he began.

Leo chuckled. "I was teasing. She's perfectly safe with me, Fred," he replied. He caught Janie's hand and tugged her to her feet. "We have to go see the magistrate about warrants," he said, sobering. "I want him to see these bruises on her face," he added coldly. "I don't think we'll have any problem with assault charges."

Janie moved closer to Leo. He made her feel safe, protected. He bent toward her, his whole expression one of utter tenderness. Belatedly, Fred began to understand what he was seeing. Leo's face, to him, was an open book. He was shocked. At the same time, he realized that Janie didn't understand what was going on. Probably she thought he was being brotherly.

"Don't you want breakfast first?" Fred offered, trying to get his bearings again.

For the first time, Leo seemed to notice the table. His hand, holding Janie's, contracted involuntarily. Bacon, scrambled eggs and...biscuits? Biscuits! He scowled, letting go of Janie's fingers to approach the bread basket. He reached down, expecting a concretelike substance, remembering that he and Rey had secretly sailed some of Janie's earlier efforts at biscuit-making over the target range for each other and used them for skeet targets. But these weren't hard. They were flaky, delicate. He opened one. It was soft inside. It smelled delicious.

He was barely aware of sitting down, dragging Janie's plate under his hands. He buttered a biscuit and put strawberry jam on it. He bit into it and sighed with pure ecstasy.

"I forgot about the biscuits," Janie told her father worriedly.

Fred glanced at their guest and grimaced. "Maybe we should have saved it for a surprise."

Leo was sighing, his eyes closed as he chewed.

"We'll never get to the magistrate's now," Janie thought aloud.

"He'll run out of biscuits in about ten minutes, at that rate," Fred said with a grin.

"I'll get another plate. We can split the eggs and bacon," Janie told her father, inwardly beaming with pride at Leo's obvious enjoyment of her efforts. Now, finally, the difficulty of learning to cook seemed worth every minute.

Leo went right on chewing, oblivious to movement around him.

The last biscuit was gone with a wistful sigh when he became aware of his two companions again.

"Who made the biscuits?" Leo asked Janie.

She grimaced. "I did."

"But you can't cook, honey," he said gently, trying to soften the accusation.

"Marilee said you didn't like me because I couldn't make biscuits or cook anything edible," she confessed without looking at him. "So I learned how."

He caught her fingers tightly in his. "She lied. But those were wonderful biscuits," he said. "Flaky and soft inside, delicately browned. Absolutely delicious."

She smiled shyly. "I can make them anytime you like."

He was looking at her with pure possession. "Every morning," he coaxed. "I'll stop by for coffee. If Fred doesn't mind," he added belatedly.

Fred chuckled. "Fred doesn't mind," he murmured dryly.

Leo scowled. "You look like a cat with a mouse."

Fred shrugged. "Just a stray thought. Nothing to worry about."

Leo held the older man's reluctant gaze and understood the odd statement. He nodded slowly. He smiled sheepishly as he realized that Fred wasn't blind at all.

Fred got up. "Well, I've got cattle to move. How's your bull, by the way?" he added abruptly, worried.

"Colic," Leo said with a cool smile. "Easily treated and nothing to get upset over."

"I'm glad. I had visions of you losing yours to Clark, as well."

"He isn't from the same herd as yours was, Fred," Leo told him. "But even so, I think we'll manage to keep Clark penned up for a while. Which reminds me," he added, glancing at Janie. "We'd better get going."

"Okay. I'll just get the breakfast things cleared away first."

Leo sat and watched her work with a smitten expression on his face. Fred didn't linger. He knew a hooked fish when he saw one.

LIONHEARTED ❧ 431

They swore out warrants and presented them to the sheriff. Clark had already been transferred to the county lockup, after a trip to the hospital emergency room the night before, and Leo and Janie stopped in to see Grier at the police station.

Grier had just finished talking to the mayor, a pleasant older man named Tarleton Connor, newly elected to his position. Connor and Grier had a mutual cousin, as did Grier and Chet Blake, the police chief. Chet was out of town on police business, so Grier was nominally in charge of things.

"Have a seat," Grier invited, his eyes narrow and angry on Janie's bruised face. "If it's any consolation, Miss Brewster, Clark's got bruised ribs and a black eye."

She smiled. It was uncomfortable, because it irritated the bruise. "Thanks, Mr. Grier," she said with genuine appreciation.

"That goes double for me," Leo told him. "He put Harley and me over a table so fast it's embarrassing to admit it."

"Why?" Grier asked, sitting down behind his desk. "The man was a martial artist," he elaborated. "He had a studio up in Victoria for a while, until the authorities realized that he was teaching killing techniques to ex-cons."

Leo's jaw fell.

Grier shrugged. "He was the equivalent of a black belt, too. Harley's not bad, but he needs a lot more training from Eb Scott before he could take on Clark." He pursed his lips and his eyes twinkled as he studied Leo's expression. "Feel better now?"

Leo chuckled. "Yes. Thanks."

Grier glanced at Janie's curious expression. "Men don't like to be overpowered by other men. It's a guy thing," he explained.

"Anybody ever overpower you?" Leo asked curiously.

"Judd Dunn almost did, once. But then, I taught him everything he knows."

"You know a lot," Janie said. "I never saw anybody move that fast."

"I was taught by a guy up in Tarrant County," Grier told her with a smile. "He's on television every week. Plays a Texas Ranger."

Janie gasped.

"Nice guy," Grier added. "And a hell of a martial artist."

Leo was watching him with a twinkle in his own eyes. "I did think the spinning heel kick looked familiar."

Grier smiled. He sat up. "About Clark," he added. "His brother came to see him at the county lockup this morning and got the bad news. With only one charge so far, Harley's, he's only got a misdemeanor..."

"We took out a warrant for aggravated assault and battery," Leo interrupted. "Janie had a knife at her throat just before you walked in."

"So I was told." Grier's dark eyes narrowed on Janie's throat. The nick was red and noticeable this morning. "An inch deeper and we'd be visiting you at the funeral home this morning."

"I know," Janie replied.

"You kept your head," he said with a smile. "It probably saved your life."

"Can you keep Clark in jail?" she asked worriedly.

"I'll ask Judge Barnett to set bail as high as he can. But Clark's brother isn't going to settle for a public defender. He said he'd get Jack the best attorney he could find, and he'd pay for it." He shrugged. "God knows what he'll pay for it with," he added coldly. "John Clark owes everybody, up to and including his boss. So does our local Clark brother."

"He may have to have a public defender."

"We'll see. But meanwhile, he's out of everybody's way, and he'll stay put."

"What about his brother?" Leo wanted to know. "Is Janie in any danger?"

Grier shook his head. "John Clark went back to Victoria after he saw his brother. I had him followed, by one of my off-duty guys, just to make sure he really left. But I'd keep my eyes open, if I were you, just the same. These boys are bad news."

"We'll do that," Leo said.

He drove Janie back to his own ranch and took her around with him while he checked on the various projects he'd initiated. He pulled up at the barn and told her to stay in the truck.

She was curious until she remembered that he'd fired the man who'd interrupted them the night before. She was glad about the interruption, in retrospect, but uneasy about the gossip that man had started about her and Leo.

He was back in less than five minutes, his face hard, his eyes blazing. He got into the truck and glanced at her, forcibly wiping the anger out of his expression.

"He's gone," he told her gently. "Quit without his check," he added with a rueful smile. "I guess Charles told him what I said." He shrugged. "He wasn't much of a cowboy, at that, if he couldn't tell colic from bloat."

She reached out and put her nervous fingers over his big hand on the steering wheel. He flinched and she jerked her hand back.

"No!" He caught her fingers in his and held them tight. "I'm sorry," he said at once, scowling. "You've never touched me voluntarily before. It surprised me. I like it," he added, smiling.

She was flushed and nervous. "Oh. Okay." She smiled shyly.

He searched her eyes with his for so long that her heart began to race. His face tautened. "This won't do," he said in a husky, deep tone. He started the truck with a violent motion and drove back the way they'd come, turning onto a rutted path that led into the woods and, far beyond, to a pasture. But he stopped the truck halfway to the pasture, threw it out of gear and cut off the engine.

He had Janie out of her seat belt and into his big arms in seconds, and his hungry mouth was on her lips before she could react.

She didn't have any instincts for self-preservation left. She melted into his aroused body, not even protesting the intimate way he was pressing her hips against his. Her arms curled around his neck and she kissed him back with enthusiasm.

She felt his hands going under her blouse, against her breasts. That felt wonderful. It was perfectly all right, because she belonged to him.

He lifted his mouth from hers, breathing hard, and watched her eyes while his hands caressed her. She winced and he caught his breath.

"I'm sorry!" he said at once, soothing the bruise he'd

forgotten about. "I didn't mean to hurt you," he whispered.

She reached up to kiss his eyelids shut, feeling the shock that ran through him at the soft caress. His hands moved to her waist and rested there while he held his breath, waiting. She felt the hunger in him, like a living thing. Delighted by his unexpected submission to her mouth, she kissed his face softly, tenderly, drawing her lips over his thick eyebrows, his eyelids, his cheeks and nose and chin. They moved to his strong throat and lingered in the pulsating hollow.

One lean hand went between them to the buttons of his cotton shirt. He unfastened them quickly, jerking the fabric out of her way, inviting her mouth inside.

Her hands spread on the thick mat of hair that covered the warm, strong muscles of his chest. Her mouth touched it, lightly, and then not lightly. She moved to where his heart beat roughly, and then over the flat male nipple that was a counterpart to her own. But the reaction she got when she put her mouth over it was shocking.

He groaned so harshly that she was sure she'd hurt him. She drew back, surprising a look of anguish on his lean face.

"Leo?" she whispered uneasily.

"It arouses me," he ground out, then he shivered.

She didn't know what to do next. He looked as if he ached to have her repeat the caress, but his body was as taut as a rope against her.

"You'll have to tell me what to do," she faltered. "I don't want to make it worse."

"Whatever I do is going to shock you speechless," he choked out. "But, what the hell...!"

He dragged her face back to his nipple and pressed it there, hard. "You know what I want."

She did, at some level. Her mouth eased down against him with a soft, gentle suction that lifted him back against the seat with a harsh little cry of pleasure. His hands at the back of her head were rough and insistent. She gave in and did what he was silently asking her for. She felt him shudder and gasp, his body vibrating as if it was overwhelmed by pleasure. He bit off a harsh word and trembled violently for a few seconds before he turned her mouth away from him and pressed her unblemished cheek against his chest. His hands in her hair trembled as they caressed her scalp. His heartbeat was raging under her mouth.

He fought to breathe normally. "Wow," he whispered unsteadily.

Her fingers tangled in the thick hair under them. "Did you really like it?" she whispered back.

He actually laughed, a little unsteadily. "Didn't you feel what was happening to me?"

"You were shaking."

"Yes. I was, wasn't I? Just the way you were shaking last night when I touched you…"

Her cheek slid back onto his shoulder so that she could look up into his soft eyes. "I didn't know a man would be sensitive, there, like a woman is."

He bent and drew his lips over her eyelids. "I'm sensitive, all right." His lips moved over her mouth and pressed there hungrily. "It isn't enough, Janie. I've got to have you. All the way."

"Right now?" she stammered.

He lifted his head and looked down at her in his arms. He was solemn, unsmiling, as he met her wide eyes. His body was still vibrating with unsatisfied desire. Deliberately, he drew her hips closer against his and let her feel him there.

She didn't protest. If anything, her body melted even closer.

One lean hand went to her belly and rested there, between them, while he searched her eyes. "I want…to make you pregnant," he said in a rough whisper.

Her lips fell open. She stared at him, not knowing what to say.

He looked worried. "I've never wanted that with

a woman," he continued, as if he was discussing the weather. His fingers moved lightly on her body. "Not with anyone."

He was saying something profound. She hadn't believed it at first, but the expression on his face was hard to explain away.

"My father would shoot you," she managed to say weakly.

"My brothers would shoot me, too," he agreed, nodding.

She was frowning. She didn't understand.

He bent and kissed her, with an odd tenderness. He laughed to himself. "Just my luck," he breathed against her lips, "to get mixed up with a virgin who can cook."

"We aren't mixed up," she began.

His hand contracted against the base of her spine, grinding her into him, and one eyebrow went up over a worldly smile as she blushed.

She cleared her throat. "We aren't very mixed up," she corrected.

He nibbled at her upper lip. "I look at you and get turned on so hard I can hardly walk around without bending over double. I touch you and I hurt all over. I dream of you every single night of my life and wake up vibrating." He lifted his head and looked down into her misty eyes. He wasn't smiling. He wasn't kidding.

"Never like this, Janie. Either we have each other, or we stop it, right now."

Her fingers touched his face lovingly. "You can do whatever you like to me," she whispered unsteadily.

His jaw tautened. "Anything?"

She nodded. She loved him with all her heart.

His eyes closed. His arms brought her gently against him, and his mouth buried itself in her throat, pressing there hot and hard for a few aching seconds. Then he dragged in a harsh breath and sat up, putting her back in her seat and fastening her seat belt.

He didn't look at her as he fastened his own belt and started the truck. She sat beside him as he pulled out onto the highway, a little surprised that he didn't turn into the road that led to his house. She'd expected him to take her there. She swallowed hard, remembering the way they'd pleasured each other on his big bed the night before, remembering the look of his powerful body without clothes. She flushed with anticipated delight. She was out of her mind. Her father was going to kill her. She looked at Leo with an ache that curled her toes up inside her shoes, and didn't care if he did. Some things were worth dying for.

Leo drove right into town and pulled into a parking spot in front of the drugstore. Right, she thought nervously, he was going inside to buy...protection...for what they were going to do. He wanted a child, though, he'd said. She flushed as he got out of the truck and came around to open her door.

He had to unfasten her seat belt first. She didn't even have the presence of mind to accomplish that.

He helped her out of the truck and looked down at her with an expression she couldn't decipher. He touched her cheek gently, and then her hair, and her soft mouth. His eyes were full of turmoil.

He tugged her away from the truck and closed her door, leading her to the sidewalk with one small hand tightly held in his fingers.

She started toward the drugstore.

"Wrong way, sweetheart," he said tenderly, and led her right into a jewelry store.

The clerk was talking to another clerk, but he came forward, smiling, when they entered the shop.

"May I help you find something?" he asked Leo.

"Yes," Leo said somberly. "We want to look at wedding bands."

Janie felt all the blood draining out of her face. It felt numb. She hoped she wasn't going to pass out.

Leo's hand tightened around her fingers, and slowly linked them together as he positioned her in front of the case that held engagement rings and wedding rings.

The clerk took out the tray that Leo indicated. Leo looked down at Janie with quiet, tender eyes.

"You can have anything you want," he said huskily, and he wasn't talking solely of rings.

She met his searching gaze with tears glistening on her lashes. He bent and kissed the wetness away.

The clerk averted his eyes. It was like peering through a private window. He couldn't remember ever seeing such an expression on a man's face before.

"Look at the rings, Janie," Leo said gently.

She managed to focus on them belatedly. She didn't care about flashy things, like huge diamonds. She was a country girl, for all her sophistication. Her eyes kept coming back to a set of rings that had a grape leaf pattern. The wedding band was wide, yellow gold with a white gold rim, the pattern embossed on the gold surface. The matching engagement ring had a diamond, but not a flashy one, and it contained the same grape leaf pattern on its circumference.

"I like this one," she said finally, touching it.

There was a matching masculine-looking wedding band. She looked up at Leo.

He smiled. "Do you want me to wear one, too?" he teased.

Her eyes were breathless with love. She couldn't manage words. She only nodded.

He turned his attention back to the clerk. "We'll take all three," he said.

"They'll need to be sized. Let me get my measuring rod," the clerk said with a big grin. The rings were expensive, fourteen karat, and that diamond was the highest quality the store sold. The commission was going to be tasty.

"It isn't too expensive?" Janie worried.

Leo bent and kissed the tip of her nose. "They're going to last a long time," he told her. "They're not too expensive."

She couldn't believe what was happening. She wanted to tell him so, but the clerk came back and they were immediately involved in having their fingers sized and the paperwork filled out.

Leo produced a gold card and paid for them while Janie looked on, still shell-shocked.

Leo held her hand tight when they went back to the truck. "Next stop, city hall," he murmured dryly. "Rather, the fire station—they take the license applications when city hall is closed. I forgot it was Saturday." He lifted both eyebrows at her stunned expression. "Might as well get it all done in one day. Which reminds me." He pulled out his cell phone after he'd put her in the truck and phoned the office of the doctors Coltrain. While Janie listened, spellbound, he made an appointment for blood tests for that afternoon. The doctors Coltrain had a Saturday clinic.

He hung up and slipped the phone back into his pocket with a grin. "Marriage license next, blood tests later and about next Wednesday, we'll have a nice and quiet small wedding followed by," he added huskily, "one hell of a long passionate wedding night."

She caught her breath at the passion in his eyes. "Leo, are you sure?" she wanted to know.

He dragged her into his arms and kissed her so hungrily that a familiar couple walking past the truck actually stared amusedly at them for a few seconds before hurrying on past.

"I'm sorry, baby. I can't...wait...any longer," he ground out into her eager mouth. "It's marriage or I'm leaving the state!" He lifted his head, and his eyes were tortured. He could barely breathe. "Oh, God, I want you, Janie!"

She felt the tremor in his big body. She understood what he felt, because it was the same with her. She drew in a slow breath. It was desire. She thought, maybe, there was some affection, as well, but he was dying to have her, and that was what prompted marriage plans. He'd said often enough that he was never going to get married.

He saw all those thoughts in her eyes, even through

the most painful desire he'd ever known. "I'll make you glad you said yes," he told her gruffly. "I won't ever cheat on you, or hurt you. I'll take care of you all my life. All of yours."

It was enough, she thought, to take a chance on. "All right," she said tenderly. She reached up and touched his hard, swollen mouth. "I'll marry you."

It was profound, to hear her say it. He caught his breath at the raging arousal the words produced in his already-tortured body. He groaned as he pressed his mouth hard into the palm of her hand.

She wasn't confident enough to tease him about his desire for her. But it pleased her that he was, at least, fiercely hungry for her in that way, if no other.

He caught her close and fought for control. "We'd better go and get a marriage license," he bit off. "We've already given Evan and Anna Tremayne an eyeful."

"What?" she asked drowsily.

"They were walking past when I kissed you," he said with a rueful smile.

"They've been married for years," she pointed out.

He rubbed his nose against hers. "Wait until we've been married for years," he whispered. "We'll still be fogging up windows in parked trucks."

"Think so?" she asked, smiling.

"Wait and see."

He let go of her, with obvious reluctance, and moved back under the steering wheel. "Here we go."

They applied for the marriage license, had the blood tests, and then went to round up their families to tell them the news.

Janie's aunt Lydia had gone to Europe over the holidays on an impromptu sightseeing trip, Fred Brewster told them when they gave him the news. "She'll be livid if she misses the wedding," he said worriedly.

"She can be here for the first christening," Leo said with a grin at Janie's blush. "You can bring Hettie with you, and come over to the ranch for supper tomorrow night," he added, amused at Fred's lack of surprise at the announcement. "I've invited my brothers to supper and phoned Barbara to have it catered. I wanted to break the news to all of them at once."

"Hettie won't be surprised," Fred told them, tongue-in-cheek. "But she'll enjoy a night out. We'll be along about six."

"Fine," Leo said, and didn't offer to leave Janie at home. He waited until she changed into a royal-blue pantsuit with a beige top, and carried her with him to the ranch.

He did chores and paperwork with Janie right beside him, although he didn't touch her.

"A man only has so much self-control," he told her with a wistful sigh. "So we'll keep our hands off each other, until the wedding. Fair enough?"

She grinned at him. "Fair enough!"

He took her home after they had supper at a local restaurant. "I'd love to have taken you up to Houston for a night on the town," he said when he walked her to her door. "But not with your face like that." He touched it somberly. "Here in Jacobsville, everybody already knows what happened out at Shea's last night. In Houston, people might think I did this, or allowed it to happen." He bent and kissed the painful bruise. "Nobody will ever hurt you again as long as I live," he swore huskily.

She closed her eyes, savoring the soft touch of his mouth. "Are you sure you want to marry me?" she asked.

"I'm sure. I'll be along about ten-thirty," he added.

She looked up at him, puzzled. "Ten-thirty?"

He nodded. "Church," he said with a wicked grin. "We have to set a good example for the kids."

She laughed, delighted. "Okay."

"See you in the morning, pretty girl," he said, and brushed his mouth lightly over hers before he bounded back down the steps to his car and drove off with a wave of his hand.

★ ★ ★

Fred was amazed that Leo did take her to church, and then came back to the house with her for a lunch of cold cuts. He and Fred talked cattle while Janie lounged at Leo's side, still astounded at the unexpected turn of events. Fred couldn't be happier about the upcoming nuptials. He was amused that Hettie had the weekend off and didn't know what had happened. She had a shock coming when she arrived later in the day.

Leo took Janie with him when he went home, approving her choice of a silky beige dress and matching high heels, pearls in her ears and around her throat, and her hair long and luxurious down her back.

"Your brothers will be surprised," Janie said worriedly on the way there.

Leo lifted an eyebrow. "After the Cattleman's Ball? Probably not," he said. Then he told her about Corrigan offering to drive him home so that he could pump him for information to report back to the others.

"You were very intoxicated," she recalled, embarrassed when she recalled the fierce argument they'd had.

"I'd just found out that Marilee had lied about you," he confided. "And seeing you with damned Harley didn't help."

"You were jealous," she realized.

"Murderously jealous," he confessed at once. "That

only got worse, when you took the job at Shea's." He glanced at her. "I'm not having you work there any longer. I don't care what compromises I have to make to get you to agree."

She smiled to herself. "Oh, I don't mind quitting," she confessed. "I'll have enough to do at the ranch, after we're married, getting settled in."

"Let's try not to talk about that right now, okay?"

She stared at him, worriedly. "Are you getting cold feet?" she asked.

"I'll tell you what I'm getting," he said, turning dark eyes to hers. And he did tell her, bluntly, and starkly. He nodded curtly at her scarlet flush and directed his attention back at the road. "Just for the record, the word *marriage* reminds me of the words *wedding night,* and I go nuts."

She whistled softly.

"So let's think about food and coffee and my brothers and try not to start something noticeable," he added in a deep tone. "Because all three of them are going to be looking for obvious signs and they'll laugh the place down if they see any."

"We can recite multiplication tables together," she agreed.

He glanced at her with narrow eyes. "Great idea," he

replied sarcastically. "That reminds me of rabbits, and guess what rabbits remind me of?"

"I know the Gettysburg Address by heart," she countered. "I'll teach it to you."

"That will put me to sleep."

"I'll make biscuits for supper."

He sat up straight. "Biscuits? For supper? To go with Barbara's nice barbecue, potato salad and apple pie. Now that's an idea that just makes my mouth water! And here I am poking along!" He pushed down on the accelerator. "Honey, you just said the magic word!"

She chuckled to herself. Marriage, she thought, was going to be a real adventure.

✤ 11 ✤

Not only did Corrigan, Rey, and Cag show up for supper with their wives, Dorie, Meredith and Tess, but Simon and Tira came all the way from Austin on a chartered jet. Janie had just taken off her apron after producing a large pan of biscuits, adding them to the deliciously spread table that Barbara and her assistant had arranged before they left.

All four couples arrived together, the others having picked up Simon and Tira at the Jacobsville airport on the way.

Leo and Janie met them at the door. Leo looked unprepared.

"All of you?" he exclaimed.

Simon shrugged. "I didn't believe them," he said, pointing at the other three brothers. "I had to come see for myself."

"We didn't believe him, either," Rey agreed, pointing at Leo.

They all looked at Janie, who moved closer to Leo and blushed.

"If she's pregnant, you're dead," Cag told Leo pointedly when he saw the look on Janie's face. He leaned closer before Leo could recover enough to protest. "Have you been beating her?"

"She is most certainly not pregnant!" Leo said, offended. "And you four ought to know that I have never hit a woman in my life!"

"But he hit the guy who did this to me," Janie said with pride, smiling up at him as she curled her fingers into his big ones.

"Not very effectively, I'm afraid," Leo confessed.

"That's just because the guy had a black belt," Janie said, defending Leo. "Nobody but our assistant police chief had the experience to bring him down."

"Yes, I know Grier," Simon said solemnly. "He's something of a legend in law enforcement circles, even in Austin."

"He has alien artifacts in his filing cabinet, and he

was a government assassin," Janie volunteered with a straight face.

Everybody stared at her.

"He was kidding!" Leo chuckled.

She grinned at him. He wrinkled his nose at her. They exchanged looks that made the others suddenly observant. All at once, they became serious.

"We can do wedding invitations if we email them tonight," Cag said offhand. He pulled a list from his pocket. "This is a list of the people we need to invite."

"I can get the symphony orchestra to play," Rey said, nodding. "I've got their conductor's home phone number in my pocket computer." He pulled it out.

"We can buy the gown online and have it overnighted here from Neiman-Marcus in Dallas," Corrigan volunteered. "All we need is her dress size. What are you, a size ten?"

Janie balked visibly, but nodded. "Here comes her father," Dorie said enthusiastically, noting the new arrival.

"I'll email the announcement to the newspaper," Tess said. "They have a Tuesday edition, we can just make it. We'll need a photo."

There was a flash. Tira changed the setting on her digital camera. "How's this?" she asked, showing it to Tess and Meredith.

"Great!" Meredith said. "We can use Leo's computer

to download it and email it straight to the paper, so they'll have it first thing tomorrow. We can email it to the local television station, as well. Come on!"

"Wait for me! I'll write the announcement," Dorie called to Corrigan, following along behind the women.

"Hey!" Janie exclaimed.

"What?" Tira asked, hesitating. "Oh, yes, the reception. It can be held here. But the cake! We need a caterer!"

"Cag can call the caterer," Simon volunteered his brother.

"It's my wedding!" Janie protested.

"Of course it is, dear," Tira said soothingly. "Let's go, girls."

The women vanished into Leo's study. The men went into a huddle. Janie's father and Hettie came in the open door, looking shell-shocked.

"Never mind them," Leo said, drawing Janie to meet her parent and her housekeeper. "They're taking care of the arrangements," he added, waving his hand in the general direction of his brothers and sisters-in-law. "Apparently, it's going to be a big wedding, with a formal gown and caterers and newspaper coverage." He grinned. "You can come, of course."

Janie hit him. "We were going to have a nice, quiet little wedding!"

"You go tell them what you want, honey," he told Janie. "Just don't expect them to listen."

Hettie started giggling. Janie glared at her.

"You don't remember, do you?" the housekeeper asked Janie. "Leo helped them do the same thing to Dorie, and Tira, and Tess, and even Meredith. It's payback time. They're getting even."

"I'm afraid so," Leo told Janie with a smug grin. "But look at the bright side, you can just sit back and relax and not have to worry about a single detail."

"But, my dress…" she protested.

He patted her on the shoulder. "They have wonderful taste," he assured her.

Fred was grinning from ear to ear. He never would have believed one man could move so fast, but he'd seen the way Leo looked at Janie just the morning before. It was no surprise to him that a wedding was forthcoming. He knew a man who was head over heels when he saw one.

By the end of the evening, Janie had approved the wedding gown, provided the statistics and details of her family background and education, and climbed into the car with Leo to let him take her home.

"The rings will be ready Tuesday, they promised," he

told her at her father's door. He smiled tenderly. "You'll be a beautiful bride."

"I can't believe it," she said softly, searching his lean face.

He drew her close. "Wednesday night, you'll believe it," he said huskily, and bent to kiss her with obvious restraint. "Now, good night!"

He walked to the car. She drifted inside, wrapped in dreams.

It was a honey of a society wedding. For something so hastily concocted, especially with Christmas approaching, it went off perfectly. Even the rings were ready on time, the dress arrived by special overnight delivery, the blood tests and marriage license were promptly produced, the minister engaged, press coverage assured, the caterer on time—nothing, absolutely nothing, went wrong.

Janie stood beside Leo at the Hart ranch at a makeshift arch latticed with pink and white roses while they spoke their vows. Janie had a veil, because Leo had insisted. And after the last words of the marriage ceremony were spoken, he lifted the veil from Janie's soft eyes and looked at her with smoldering possession. He bent and kissed her tenderly, his lips barely brushing hers. She had a yellowing bruise on one cheek and she was careful to keep that side away from the camera, but Leo didn't seem to notice the blemish.

"You are the most beautiful bride who ever spoke her vows," he whispered as he kissed her. "And I will cherish you until they lay me down in the dark!"

She reached up and kissed him back, triggering a burst of enthusiastic ardor that he was only able to curb belatedly. He drew away from her, smiling sheepishly at their audience, caught her hand, and led her back to the house through a shower of rice.

The brothers were on the job even then. The press was delicately prompted to leave after the cake and punch were consumed, the symphony orchestra was coaxed to load their instruments. The guests were delicately led to the door and thanked. Then the brothers carried their wives away in a flurry of good wishes and, at last, the newlyweds were alone, in their own home.

Leo looked at Janie with eyes that made her heart race. "Alone," he whispered, approaching her slowly, "at last."

He bent and lifted her, tenderly, and carried her down the hall to the bedroom. He locked the door. He took the phone off the hook. He closed the curtains. He came back to her, where she stood, a little apprehensive, just inside the closed door.

"I'm not going to hurt you," he said softly. "You're a priceless treasure. I'm going to be slow, and tender, and

I'm going to give you all the time you need. Don't be afraid of me."

"I'm not, really," she said huskily, watching him divest her of the veil and the hairpins that held her elaborate coiffure in place with sprigs of lily of the valley. "But you want me so much," she tried to explain. "What if I can't satisfy you?"

He laughed. "You underestimate yourself."

"Are you sure?"

He turned her around so that he could undo the delicate hooks and snaps of her gown. "I'm sure."

She let him strip her down to her lacy camisole, white stockings and lacy white garter belt, her eyes feeding on the delighted expression that claimed his lean face.

"Beautiful," he said huskily. "I love you in white lace."

"You're not bad in a morning coat," she teased, liking the vested gray ceremonial rig he was wearing.

"How am I without it?" he teased.

"Let's find out." She unbuttoned his coat and then the vest under it. He obligingly stripped them off for her, along with his tie, and left the shirt buttons to her hands. "You've got cuff links," she murmured, trying to release them.

"I'll do it." He moved to the chest of drawers and put his cuff links in a small box, along with his pocket change and keys. He paused to remove his shirt and slacks, shoes and socks before he came back to her, in silky gray boxer shorts like the ones he'd worn the night they were almost intimate.

"You are…magnificent," she whispered, running her hands over his chest.

"You have no idea how magnificent, yet." He unsnapped the shorts and let them fall, coaxing her eyes to him. He shivered at the expression on her face, because he was far more potent than he'd been the one time she'd looked at him like this.

While she was gaping, he unfastened the camisole with a delicate flick of his fingers and unhooked the garter belt. He stripped the whole of it down her slender body and tipped her back onto the bed while he pulled the stockings off with the remainder of her clothing.

He pulled back the cover and tossed the pillows off to the side before he arranged her on the crisp white sheets and stood over her, vibrating with desire, his eyes eating her nude body, from her taut nipples to the visible trembling of her long, parted legs.

She watched him come down to her with faint apprehension that suddenly vanished when he pressed his open mouth down, hard, right on her soft belly.

He'd never touched her like that, and in the next few feverish minutes, she went from shock to greater shock as he displayed his knowledge of women.

"No, you can't, you can't!" she sobbed, but he was, he did, he had!

She arched up toward his mouth with tears of tortured ecstasy raining down her cheeks in a firestorm of sensation, sobbing as the pleasure stretched her tight as a rope under the warm, expert motions of his lips.

She gasped as the wave began to hit her. Her eyes opened, and his face was there, his body suddenly right over hers, his hips thrusting down. She felt him, and then looked and saw him, even as she felt the small stabbing pain of his invasion. The sight of what was happening numbed the pain, and then it was gone altogether as he shifted roughly, dragging his hips against hers as he enforced his possession of her innocence.

Her nails bit into his long back as he moved on her, insisting, demanding. His face, above her, was strained, intent.

"Am I hurting you?" he ground out.

"N-no!" she gasped, lifting toward him, her eyes wide, shocked, fascinated.

He looked down, lifting himself so that he could watch her body absorb him. "Look," he coaxed through his teeth. "Look, Janie. Look at us."

She glanced down and her breath caught at the intimate sight that met her eyes. She gasped.

"And we've barely begun," he breathed, shifting suddenly, fiercely, against her.

She sobbed, shivering.

He did it again, watching her face, assessing her reaction. "I can feel you, all around me, like a soft, warm glove," he whispered, his lips compressing as pleasure shot through him with every deepening motion of his hips. "Take me, baby. Take me inside you. Take all of me. Make me scream, baby," he murmured.

She was out of her mind with the pleasure he was giving her. She writhed under him, arching her hips, pushing against him, watching his face. She shifted and he groaned harshly. She laughed, through her own torment, and suddenly cried out as the pleasure became more and more unbearable. Her hands went between them, in a fever of desire.

"Yes," he moaned as he felt her trembling touch. "Yes. Oh...God...baby...do it, do it! Do it!"

She was going to die. She opened her eyes and looked at him, feeling her body pulse as he shortened and deepened his movements, watching her with his mouth compressed, his eyes feverish.

"Do it...harder," she choked.

He groaned in anguish and his hips ground into hers suddenly, his hands catching her wrists and slamming them over her head as he moved fiercely above her, his eyes holding hers prisoner as his body enforced its possession violently.

She felt her body strain to accommodate him and in the last few mad seconds, she wondered if she would be able to…

He blurred in her sight. She was shaking. Her whole body rippled in a shuddering parody of convulsions, whipping against his while her mouth opened, gasping at air, and her voice uttered sounds she'd never heard from it in her entire life.

"Get it," he groaned. "Yes. Get it…!"

He cried out and then his body, too, began to shudder rhythmically. A sound like a harsh sob tore from his throat. He groaned endlessly as his body shivered into completion. Seconds, minutes, hours, an eternity of pleasure later, he collapsed on her.

They both shivered in the aftermath. She felt tears on her face, in her mouth. She couldn't breathe. Her body ached, even inside, and when she moved, she felt pleasure stab her in the most secret places, where she could still feel him.

She sobbed, her nails biting into the hands pinning her wrists.

He lifted his head. "Look at me," he whispered, and when she did, he began to move again.

She sobbed harder, her legs parting, her hips lifting

for him, her whole body shivering in a maelstrom of unbelievable delight.

"I can go again, right now," he whispered huskily, holding her eyes. "Can you? Or will it hurt?"

"I can't…feel pain," she whimpered. Her eyes closed on a shiver and then opened again, right into his. "Oh, please," she whispered brokenly. "Please, please…!"

He began to move, very slowly. "I love watching you," he whispered breathlessly. "Your face is beautiful, like this. Your body…" He looked down at it, watching its sensuous movements in response to his own. "I could eat you with a spoon right now, Mrs. Hart," he added shakily. "You are every dream of perfection that I've ever had."

"And you…are mine," she whispered. She lifted up to him, initiating the rhythm, whimpering softly as the pleasure began to climb all over again. "I love you…so much," she sobbed.

His body clenched. He groaned, arched, his face going into her throat as his body took over from his mind and buffeted her violently.

She went over the edge almost at once, holding on for dear life while he took what he wanted from her. It was feverish, ardent, overwhelming. She thought she might faint from the ecstasy when it throbbed into endless satiation. He went with her, every second of the way. She felt him when his body gave up the pleasure he sought, felt the rigor, heard the helpless throb of his voice at her ear when he shuddered and then relaxed completely.

She held him close, drinking in the intimate sound and feel and scent of his big body over hers in the damp bed. It had been a long, wild loving. She'd never imagined, even in their most passionate encounters, that lovemaking would be like this.

She told him so, in shy whispers.

He didn't answer her. He was still, and quiet, for such a long time that she became worried.

"Are you all right?" she whispered at his ear. Over her, she could hear and feel the beat of his heart as it slowly calmed.

His head lifted, very slowly. He looked into her wide eyes. "I lost consciousness for a few seconds," he said quietly. He touched her lower lip, swollen from the fierce pressure of his mouth just at the last. "I thought...I might die, trying to get deep enough to satisfy us both."

She flushed.

He put his finger over her lips. He wasn't smiling. He moved deliberately, letting her feel him. "You aren't on the Pill," he said. "And I was too hot to even think of any sort of birth control. Janie," he added, hesitantly, "I think I made you pregnant."

Her eyes searched his. "You said you wanted to," she reminded him in a whisper.

"I do. But it should have been your choice, too," he continued, sounding worried.

She traced his long, elegant nose and smiled with delicious exhaustion. "Did you hear me shouting, 'Leo, stop and run to the pharmacy to buy protection!'"

He laughed despite the gravity of the situation. "Was that about the time I was yelling, 'get it, baby'?"

She hit his chest, flushed, and then laughed.

"You did, too, didn't you?" he asked with a smug grin. "So did I. Repeatedly." He groaned as he moved slowly away from her and flopped onto his back, stretching his sore muscles. "Damn, I'm sore! And I told you I could go all night, didn't I?"

She sat up, torn between shock and amusement as she met his playful eyes. "Sore? Men get sore?"

"When they go at it like that, they do," he replied sardonically. "What a wedding night," he said, whistling through his lips as he studied her nude body appreciatively. "If they gave medals, you could have two."

Her eyebrows arched. "Really? I was...I was all right?"

He tugged her down to him. "Women have egos, too, don't they?" he asked tenderly. He pushed her damp hair away from her cheeks and mouth. "You were delicious. I've never enjoyed a woman so much."

"I didn't know anything at all."

He brought her head down and kissed her eyelids. "It isn't a matter of knowledge."

She searched his eyes. "You had enough of that for both of us," she murmured.

"Bodies in the dark," he said, making it sound unimportant. "I wanted to have you in the light, Janie," he said solemnly. "I wanted to look at you while I was taking you."

"That's a sexist remark," she teased.

"You took me, as well," he conceded. He touched her mouth with a long forefinger. "I've never seen anything so beautiful," he whispered, and sounded breathless. "Your face, your body..." His face clenched. "And the pleasure." His eyes closed and he shivered. "I've never known anything like it." His eyes opened again. "It was love," he whispered to her, scowling. "Making love. Really making love."

Her breath caught in her throat. She traced his sideburn to his ear. "Yes."

"Do you know what I'm trying to tell you?" he asked quietly.

She looked down into his eyes and saw it there. Her heart jumped into her throat. "You're telling me that you love me," she said.

He nodded. "I love you. I knew it when Clark assaulted you, and I went at him. It hurt my pride that I couldn't make him beg for forgiveness. I cleaned you up and dried your hair, and knew that I loved you, all at once. It was a very small step from there to a wedding ring." He brought hers to his lips and kissed it tenderly. "I couldn't bear the thought of losing you. Not after that."

She smiled dreamily. "I loved you two years ago, when you brought me a wilted old daisy you'd picked out in the meadow, and teased me about it being a bouquet. You didn't know it, but to me, it was."

"I've given you a hard time," he told her, with obvious regret. "I'm sorry."

She leaned down and kissed him tenderly. "You made up for it." She moved her breasts gently against his chest. "I really can go all night," she whispered. "When you've recovered, I'll show you."

He chuckled under the soft press of her mouth, and his big arms swallowed her. "When *you're* recovered, I'll let you. I love you, Mrs. Hart. I love you with all my heart."

"I love you with all mine." She kissed him again, and thought how dreams did, sometimes, actually come true.

A week later, they celebrated their first Christmas together at a family party, to which Janie's father, Aunt Lydia and Hettie were also invited. After kissing her with exquisite tenderness beneath the mistletoe, Leo gave Janie an emerald necklace, to match her eyes, he said, and she gave him an expensive pocket watch, with his name and hers engraved inside the case.

On New Year's Eve, the family gathered with other families at the Jacobsville Civic Center for the first annual celebration. A live band played favorites and couples danced on the polished wood floor. Calhoun Ballenger had mused aloud that since Jacobsville's economy was based on cattle and agriculture, they should drop a pair of horns instead of a ball to mark the new year. He was red-faced at the celebration, when the city fathers took him seriously and did that very thing.

While Leo and Janie stood close together on the patio of the second floor ballroom to watch the neon set of longhorns go down to the count, a surprising flurry of snow came tumbling from the sky to dust the heads of the crowd.

"It's snowing!" Janie exclaimed, holding out a hand to catch the fluffy precipitation. "But it never snows in Jacobsville! Well, almost never."

Leo caught her close as the horns went to the bottom of the courthouse tower across the street and bent to her mouth, smiling. "One more wish come true," he teased, because he knew how much she loved snow. "Happy New Year, my darling," he whispered.

"Happy New Year," she whispered back, and met his kiss with loving enthusiasm, to the amused glances of the other guests. They were, after all, newlyweds.

The new year came and soon brought with it unexpected tragedy. John Clark went back to Victoria to get his jailed brother a famous attorney, but he didn't have any money. So he tried to rob a bank to get the money. He was caught in the act by a security guard and a Texas Ranger who was working on a case locally. Judd Dunn was one of the two men who exchanged shots with Clark in front of the Victoria Bank and Trust. Clark missed. Judd and the security guard didn't. Ballistics tests were required to pinpoint who fired the fatal bullet.

Jack Clark, still in jail in Victoria, was let out long enough to attend his brother's funeral in Victoria. He escaped from the kindly sheriff's deputy who was bringing him back in only handcuffs instead of handcuffs and leg chains. After all, Jack Clark had been so docile and polite, and even cried at his brother's grave. The deputy was rewarded for his compassion by being knocked over the head twice with the butt of his own .38 caliber service revolver and left for dead in a driving rain in the grass next to the Victoria road. Later that day, his squad car was found deserted a few miles outside Victoria.

It was the talk of the town for several days, and Leo and Janie stayed close to home, because they knew Clark had scores to settle all around Jacobsville. They were in their own little world, filled with love. They barely heard all the buzz and gossip. But what they did hear was about Tippy Moore and Cash Grier.

"Tippy's not Grier's sort," Janie murmured sleepily. They didn't do a lot of sleeping at night, even now. She cuddled up in her husband's lap and nuzzled close. "He needs someone who is gentle and sweet. Not a harpy."

He wrapped her up close and kissed the top of her head. "What would you know about harpies?" he teased. "You're the single sweetest human being I've ever known."

She smiled.

"Well, except for me, of course," he added.

"Leo Hart!" she exclaimed, drawing back.

"You said I was sweet," he murmured, bending his head. "You said it at least six times. You were clawing my back raw at the time, and swearing that you were never going to live through what I was doing to you…"

She tugged his head down and kissed him hungrily. "You're sweet, all right," she whispered raggedly. "Do it again…!"

He groaned. They were never going to make it to the bed. But the doors were locked…what the hell.

An hour later, he carried her down the hall to their

bedroom and tucked her up next to him, exhausted and still smiling.

"At least," he said wearily, "hopefully Clark will go to prison for a long, long time when he's caught. He won't be in a position to threaten you again."

"Or you." She curled closer. "Did I tell you that Marilee phoned me yesterday?"

He stiffened. "No."

She smiled. "It's okay. She only wanted to apologize. She's going to Europe to visit her grandmother in London. I told her to have a nice trip."

"London's almost far enough away."

She sighed, wrapping her arms around him. "Be generous. She'll never know what it is to be as happy as we are."

"Who will?" he teased, but the look he gave her was serious. He touched her hair, watching her succumb to sleep.

He lay awake for a long time, his eyes intent on her slender, sleeping body. She made wonderful biscuits, she could shoot a shotgun, she made love like a fairy. He wondered what he'd ever done in his life to deserve her.

"Dreams," she whispered, shocking him.

"What, honey?"

She nuzzled her face into his throat and melted into

him. "Dreams come true," she whispered, falling asleep again.

He touched her lips with his and smoothed back her long hair. "Yes, my darling," he whispered with a long, sweet smile. "Dreams come true."

★ ★ ★ ★ ★